PSYCHO-PATHS

Tor books by Robert Bloch

American Gothic
Fear and Trembling
Firebug
The Kidnapper
The Jekyll Legacy (with Andre Norton)
Lori
Midnight Pleasures
The Night of the Ripper
Night-World
Psycho
Psycho II
Psycho House
Psycho-Paths (editor)

PSYCHO-PATHS

edited by
Robert Bloch

TOR ®
HORROR

A TOM DOHERTY ASSOCIATES BOOK
NEW YORK

PSYCHO-PATHS

Copyright © 1991 by Robert Bloch and Martin Harry Greenberg

A Tor Book
Published by Tom Doherty Associates, Inc.
49 West 24th Street
New York, N.Y. 10010

Library of Congress Cataloging-in-Publication Data

Psycho-paths / edited by Robert Bloch.
    p.   cm.
    "A Tom Doherty Associates book."
   ISBN 0-312-85048-4
    1. Horror tales, American.   I. Bloch, Robert, 1917–
PS648.H6P78   1991
813'.0873808—dc20   90-49031
                                                CIP

Printed in the United States of America

First edition: March 1991

0 9 8 7 6 5 4 3 2 1

Acknowledgments

Contents

Introduction

▲▲▲▲▲▲▲

Let's talk about obscenity.

As all of us know, the vilest terms in the English language are the four-letter words. Words like fear, pain, dead.

We all know what they mean, many of us think about them frequently, but we tend to pretend otherwise.

Scornfully, we equate fear with cowardice. Only the weak and helpless are allowed to admit being afraid. In all others, such an admission is despised.

To an even greater extent, such disdain is bestowed on admissions of pain. The male mode has been that of a stoic Sioux, although there is little actual evidence that ancient Greek philosophers or Plains Indian warriors were all that indifferent to the levels of their pain thresholds.

As for being dead, forget it. That's right—try, and try hard. It isn't easy in this world of natural and unnatural disasters.

But while many of us refuse to contemplate these obscene words as they relate to ourselves, we have in many instances learned how to heroically bear the sufferings and misfortunes of others.

In truth, we have always borne this burden gladly. Even eagerly, as literature and drama attests. There is little need to expatiate upon the fact that fairy tales deal fancifully with the very perils from which adults attempt to shield children in reality. So do today's animated cartoons.

Reality often hurts. That's a lesson many of us learn the hard way and most of us would prefer to forget. Hence, our lifelong reliance upon escape into make-believe. What we view, read, or hear is largely fantasy. Even factual content is determined by editing in print or in film. Graphic art, sculpture, or any other form of representation is also "edited" by the process of selection; an arbitrary choice on the part of its creator which is not necessarily consonant with perceptual reality.

Of course, we all know that artists are crazy, right? The real reason those weirdos write, paint, sculpt, compose, choreograph, or make obscene phone calls collect is because they can't cope the way the rest of us do. Granted, we rely on these freakos to provide us with entertainment, but most of the time we live in the real world and know the difference between fantasy and reality.

Sure we do. Once we forsake imaginary playmates for dolls that can talk and walk, then forsake the dolls for real companions in the "Bang! You're dead!" routines, we begin to approach adulthood and face hard facts.

Adults are capable of dealing with such realities as our dignified and democratically determined political conventions, our demographically selected "World Champion," winners of the World Series, and the choice of Miss America, Mrs. America, and the Ten Best of anything. Genuine grown-ups can also accept the down-to-earth concert dress and activities of rock groups, the boyish dedication to true sportsmanship of football teams, the necessity to wear a special costume in order to take part in a wedding ceremony, the urgent need to identify automobile models with names that suggest a macho quality and christen perfumes to evoke an erotic image. Adults drive freeways that are not free, try to take their sick leaves when they are well, mortgage their futures to live in ranch houses which aren't located within hundreds of miles of the nearest ranch. And if by chance they ever tire of the superpleasures of standing in line at a supermarket checkout counter to hand over a piece of plastic instead of the money they haven't got (and which, by the way, is not backed up by gold, silver, or any equivalent), they can lose themselves in the objectivities of gaming and gambling. Plus, of course, alcohol, prescription drugs, recreational drugs, designer drugs, and just plain good old-fashioned crack.

So much for reality.

Fantasy is another matter. Academics have traced its roots from legend to mythology, superstition to theology, from tales told around tribal campfires to the printed page and the modern miracles of theatrical technology. Over the last two centuries its preoccupation with the ghosts, devils, demons, vampires, werewolves, and myriad monsters of the past gradually gave way to science fiction's fairy tales of the future.

Despite science fiction's inroads, works of supernatural fantasy and horror never entirely vanished from the literary landscape. Towering against that landscape a century and a half ago, Edgar Allan Poe altered it to suit his needs. If he wanted to utilize its castles or the picturesque pageantry of masques and revels, he transported his settings to the past. Tales with more modern backgrounds often made significant use of the latest scientific or pseudoscientific discoveries. In both instances his purpose was to lend verisimilitude. After all, what proof have we that a story handed down over the centuries isn't true? And if stories of today's world deal with today's advances in science, what more validation do you need?

A turn-of-the-century master of horror, Arthur Machen, didn't alter the supernatural landscape; his method of avoidance was to burrow under it.

More precisely, he burrowed under the British Isles and carved out a subterranean realm wherein lurked a race of dwarfish troglodytes. These were the original inhabitants of the land who sought refuge underground after the Celtic and Roman invasions, but still survived below. Their magic too survived, as did their rituals, and both retained the power to menace chance trespassers upon their domain or wanderers who might roam above it upon the dark and lonely hills. Those who later settled in the Isles knew and feared the stunted creatures, whispered of thievish habits and worse; of infants stolen from cradles and changelings left in their place. But aloud they alluded to the evildoers guardedly, creating a mythology in which these monsters were rechristened as gnomes, elves, fairies, sprites. Ignoring the true nature of their threat to kith, kin and kine, the denizens of darkness were praised for their "good deeds" and the "gifts and treasures" they bestowed upon mere mortals who sought their aid. In actuality the mere and miserable mortals were the ones who took pains to leave gifts of food, drink and material offerings in appropriate spots, hoping to appease the other horrid hungers of the prehuman race which ruled below.

Machen did not make extensive use of this concept, and it was not his only contribution to the lasting literature of the fantastic. But unquestionably his pseudoanthropological hypothesis proved popular with many of the writers who followed him. As with Poe, his influence is still felt today.

Early science fiction writers traveled through time, spanned space and sought out horror in the stars. Poe found his horrors upon the face of earth, past and present. Machen's dreads dwelt in the depth beneath.

But it remained for H. P. Lovecraft to create a new cosmology encompassing the horrors of time, space, dimensions and all that is above, upon or within earth itself. For Lovecraft, horror was everywhere, omnipresent in what we, in our ignorance, call life, death, consciousness and dreams.

Not all of Lovecraft's work dealt directly with his cosmological concept. Its range extended from fantasy to science fiction, yet with few exceptions the emphasis was upon horror, supernatural or mundane.

Some of the tales emerging from this diversified output have attained widespread recognition, but the immensity and enormity of his cosmogenesis exerted a lasting impact upon readers and writers alike. His so-called Cthulhu Mythos postulated the existence of entities evolving and existing from time immemorial throughout the known and unknown reaches of the universe. These huge, almost indescribable monstrosities were served by alien beings, some of which were equally fearsome. All shared the same hunger for control of the cosmos, and their interstellar warfare eventually resulted in a waning of power. Though eternal, many existed in states of comatose slumber on distant planets.

Several still remained here on earth far beneath the surface of land or sea. Memories of their mastery and magic survived, preserved by secret cults throughout the world. And their human followers made contact with other servitors from the stars. Matings with mankind produced hideous mutations; men and monsters mingling in dedication to the resurrection and/or return of the beings they worshiped. In Lovecraft's world, Lovecraft's universe, paranoia reigned supreme.

Most writers' early work is influenced by other writers, predecessors or contemporaries, both in style and content.

Poe's madmen, Machen's prehuman presences, Lovecraft's Elder Gods and Great Old Ones—all had their effect upon me, first as a reader and then as an auctorial aspirant. Perhaps I'm more conscious of that effect than most, for while I never had any contact with Arthur Machen, it was H. P. Lovecraft who suggested I try writing horror fiction, then encouraged me in my teenage efforts. And it was some years later that I, in effect, collaborated with Edgar Allan Poe by completing his final, unfinished tale, *The Light-House*.

By then, however, I had developed a hit-or-miss style of my own. And my notions of what constituted the content of fantasy, horror and science fiction had drastically changed.

Speaking at the then-equivalent World Science Fiction Convention in 1948, I suggested that the time had come to forsake literary voyages through outer space in favor of exploring "inner space"—the mysterious realm of the human mind.

In so doing, I was far from the originator of such a concept. Many members of the literary establishment had employed it in a variety of ways. James Joyce offered stream-of-consciousness stylization, Dostoevsky examined the workings of the mind in what then amounted to clinical detail, and the characters of Shakespeare, Jonson and Marlowe did a lot of thinking out loud.

But with few exceptions science fiction had not followed the example of Robert Louis Stevenson's 1886 masterwork, *The Strange Case of Dr. Jekyll and Mr. Hyde*.

Having turned much of my own efforts to the more

mundane fields of mystery and suspense fiction, I was increasingly aware of a similar neglect therein. Though the plots of such genre novels often revolved around the machinations of what were then called "madmen," we seldom were given a glimpse of the world through their eyes.

Nor did we hear their voices. It was the eloquence of the detective which most frequently found favor, or the admiring accounts of a narrator obviously prejudiced in his or her favor. Reading the words of Dr. Watson was all very well, but speaking for myself, I would dearly have loved to see how the same story might flow from the pen of Professor Moriarty.

Incompetent to assume the persona of "The Napoleon of Crime," at times I elected to enter into the minds of less masterly criminals, including a number who suffered from various forms of mental illness. It became increasingly apparent to me that if even something like Lovecraft's concept of cosmic dread actually existed, there was no necessity to track down terrors from beyond the stars; horror might just happen to live next door. It can whisper to you over the phone, it can knock on your door, it can crawl into your bed.

Properly presented amidst commonplace but convincing everyday surroundings, real horrors can be far more frightening than the fantastic. The credible is always a greater menace than the incredible, merely because we know it *can* happen and—even worse—it can happen to *us.*

That's one of the secrets shared in common by every writer whose work appears in this anthology. I reveal it only because it is the sole secret which I myself can understand. Other secrets, the deeper and darker ones pertaining to their sources of inspiration, their ability to create destruction, their talent for terror—well, there are some things man is not meant to know.

But I do know this; our deepest fears lie buried in our imaginations, and our best summoned forth by whispers rather than screams. Nothing exceeds like excess.

Many years ago, when considering the future of film, I asked an obvious question—"What's going to come out of those people who think that *Night of the Living Dead* isn't enough?"

Time has offered answers, and what has come out of those people is plain to see onscreen in all its gory glory. Blood splatters, brains burst, bodies burn, blow to bits, are ripped apart, even turned inside out. Rivers of red spurt from the stumps of amputated limbs, eyes torn from their sockets dangle loosely in exaggerated presbyopia. And the cannibalism, of course, continues. Entrails trail while the eat goes on. People have become munchies for monsters.

But the people are—as befits their cardboard characterizations—quite tasteless, and the monsters have false teeth.

Despite vivisections made vivid by Technicolor and shrieks of agony enhanced by stereophonic sound, despite on-camera atrocity and cruelty in close-up, all that the filmmakers have given us over the years is more ketchup on our people-burgers.

Traditionally, the strength of the so-called horror cinema has always lain in its performers. Conrad Veidt, Paul Wegener and Werner Krauss made lasting reputations in German silent films. Lon Chaney, Boris Karloff, Bela Lugosi, Peter Lorre and Vincent Price gained worldwide fame in American productions; Christopher Lee and Peter Cushing did the same in England. Actors made big reputations in small-budget pictures because audiences came to see the stars. Since then the budgets have become more monstrous than the films they finance, and technology can transform fantasy into seeming reality. But despite these added advantages and despite the huge increase in the number of annual releases, modern horror films have created few memorable monsters, and no true stars whatsoever.

Today's monsters are merely the product of makeup, and today's stars are the special effects.

It must be conceded that with few exceptions, horror pictures are scarcely more credible than *Wuthering Heights* or *Gone With the Wind*. As is the case with these mainstream examples, farfetched plots depend on characterization for credibility. Beneath Lon Chaney's gallery of grotesques he gave us glimpses of humanity; Karloff's creature has a depth and dimension that evokes empathy. Temporarily we suspend our disbelief in filmic fantasies because the actors' artistry compels us to believe in the characters they portray.

This temporary suspension of disbelief is, of course, a classic and much-reiterated requisite of fiction in the genre. Unfortunately the author can bring few artificial aids to his task. His lines have no musical accompaniment to enhance mood, no sound effects for sudden shock; his words appear upon the printed page in a simple arrangement of black and white, without transformation to Technicolor. And while he can use as many players in as many settings as he chooses without regard for budgetary restrictions, the creative responsibilities are his alone. He has no producer to oversee all of the aspects and elements which must be assembled for use in his project. He himself must take on the role of director and decide how he wants his characters to act, how he wishes them to deliver their lines. He is his sole cinematographer; lining up the shots, coming in for a close-up of a character here, pulling back for an action shot there, and making sure that everyone in the scene hits the chalk marks he's drawn for them in his own mind. He is also the makeup artist, the costume designer, sound engineer, set-builder, prop man, stunt advisor, research consultant, supervisor of special effects, and anything or everything else the production demands. All he will have to fall back upon later is an editor, but like the director of a film, he too will share responsibility for the cuts and changes which may be made.

Every contributor to these pages is, accordingly, the exemplar of talent far more protean than that of the most adulated filmmakers. Even an Orson Welles was dependent upon the quite considerable help of a Herman Mankiewicz, a Gregg Toland, a Bernard Herrmann. The writers represented in this anthology had to perform their task without assistance from others, but however variable the results, the task itself was a constant—to tell a story. In this instance, a horror story dealing with the psychopathological rather than the supernatural.

No explicit limitations were placed on content; the very nature of the theme suggests that shock and shudders spring not from the nature of the deed but from the nature of the thought which prompts it.

If there's any pattern to these tales, their purpose is to explore the *rationale* and *irrationale* of violent behavior. This anthology was not meant to demonstrate that if you build a grosser gross-out than your neighbor, the world will beat a path to your door.

Such attempts are already available, enough to warrant a neologistic designation of their own as "splatterpunk." Activists and apologists involved in this area have announced their intention "to go too far" and, eventually, "to go all the way," with the implication that this mystical mission will effect some sort of mental and/or spiritual purgation. These efforts, we are told, will bring about a genre revolution.

Experience suggests otherwise. In the sixties the hippies switched from pot to substances which afforded increasingly stronger effects. The honest majority freely admitted they indulged in search of an increased "high."

But the articulate minority insisted on informing us that they were using LSD and similar drugs in a quest for "heightened consciousness" and "expanding awareness." Some of them continued their search for this holy grail for many years, but we have seen few genuine intellectual revelations forthcoming from the self-proclaimed messiahs of the drug culture.

Today one hears echoes of this apologia from the devisers and devotees of S and M in film and in print, but apart from the change in lyrics it's the same old song. If someone wants to get wired on the weird, that's their privilege, but let them not insult our intelligence by pretending that they're really on some sort of spiritual trip.

More is not a synonym for *better*. It does not necessarily lead either to revelation or revolution.

Over twenty years ago John Waters made a film called *Pink Flamingos*, generously endowed with something to offend everybody. Dramatizing its creator's apocalyptic vision, a poodle defecated on-camera, whereupon a three-hundred-pound transvestite named Divine promptly ingested the results. At the time many believed that this act of cinematic coprophagy went too far, but today everyone knows that *Pink Flamingos* did not revolutionize motion pictures.

The idea that a road through hell is the best route to heaven has both theological and historical antecedents. It's my understanding that one of the precepts of Tantric Buddhism involves seeking salvation through debauchery, a principle also reputedly espoused by Rasputin. Tantric doctrine has not revolutionized Buddhism, nor did Rasputin overturn Greek Orthodoxy.

In the light of such examples I venture to predict that "splatterpunk" will not have much of a metaphysical and/or metamorphic effect on horror fiction. While the Marquis de Sade perpetuated his name in the lexicon of psychotherapy, his work did not effect any radical change in the horror tale per se.

If there is any value in exposure to extreme dosages of graphic violence, then what need is there to filter it through fiction? There are enough factual accounts of cruel behavior and hideous happenings to supply any conceivable requirements. The greatest horror story of all is history.

To return for a moment to our filmic analogy: if the intention is merely to shock and nauseate, why write screenplays when you can run newsreels?

The same holds true for equivalent offerings on the printed page. One of the apparent misconceptions of the writers is that describing the infliction of pain or the throes of death makes their stories realistic. All it does, actually, is demonstrate that they've been seeing too many movies.

The basic flaw of "spatterpunk" fiction lies in the conscious or unconscious imitation of comic books and contemporary slice-and-dice films. Its concept of reality consists of continuous involvement with drugs, sex and violence on the part of people blessed with an ability to communicate with others through a shared vocabulary of vulgarisms. The "real" world in which they live is populated by a superbly versatile group of cops and robbers. Good and bad alike, they can instantly understand and operate any form of computerized device, expertly handle every kind of weapon, pilot all types of aircraft at a moment's notice, and kill without hitch or hesitation. Their macho attitude and image is derived from espionage comics and capers.

Meanwhile, in another world—the one many of us actually live in—most people don't seem to be quite that knowledgeable or sophisticated. Nor do they seem so stolid, with so little reaction to slaughter and its aftermath.

It is this world, and those people, which are dealt with by the writers who have contributed to the content of this anthology. In so doing they have contributed their concepts of horror and where it's at—not in the weapon or the wounds it inflicts, not in the knife itself but in Jack the Ripper. Each and every author has offered an individual insight into the dark recesses of the human mind where true dread dwells.

It is customary, in volumes like these, to summarize the personal backgrounds and achievements of the writers represented therein, very much as if one were providing them with individual résumés and lists of credentials. I tend to doubt that readers are greatly influenced by learning that Mr. Poe won a prize for his poem or short story, that Mr. Machen entered an acting career in middle age, or that Mr. Lovecraft was a closet ichthyophobe. Nor does it matter which of the three enjoyed the greatest popular recognition or critical acclaim.

Many of the contributors here are well-known to readers familiar with the genre. Other names, I predict, will soon become so. If you admire them as much as I do, seek out other works in magazines or books bearing their by-lines. None of them require advocacy; their stories speak for themselves.

Some of these stories are violent, some are gruesome, but none depend upon death for their existence, nor upon a supernatural premise. They depend upon characters and characterization. They afford insight, which is the first step toward understanding. And understanding is the only way to exorcise our fears.

These writers have found the source of many of those daily dreads. Today's bogeyman is the psychopath, and he is all too real. He assumes many guises; the terrorist, the serial killer, the mass-murderer, the sadist, the revenge-seeker.

But whatever mask he wears, he cannot escape recognition by our writers. They have had the courage to confront him in the pages that follow; stay close to them and you will not be harmed.

I hope.

—Robert Bloch

PSYCHO-PATHS

Them Bleaks

Gahan Wilson

Sheriff Olson had no sooner emerged from Mae's Cafe and tilted the big, gold-starred car toward the driver's side by heaving his considerable bulk down behind its wheel than he heard the voice of Wilbur, his chief deputy, fighting its way through the speaker of the two-way radio along with a tangle of static.

"It's them Bleaks, Sheriff." Wilbur's voice was muffled in what seemed to be a fearsome cold. "It's that Mr. Bleak, the writer fellah. He just called in and says you're to hurry over to his place right away on account of what he found."

Olson leaned forward and snatched the microphone from its dashboard hammock as the frown line between his tufty orange eyebrows extended slightly. There had been no frown line on the sheriff's broad, smooth forehead before the Bleaks moved into Commonplace, but now there was, and every week it seemed to grow just a little longer and dig in just a little deeper.

"What's he got to show me, Wilbur?" the sheriff asked, speaking very calmly.

"He says he's gone and found somebody what's been murdered."

The crease in the sheriff's forehead climbed like the red

1

line in a thermometer nearly halfway up to the edge of his close-cropped copper hair. Wilbur's words had struck him like a snake. He turned, quietly and gently like a fragile man, and then suddenly pounded the cushions violently enough to bounce himself in the seat.

"Damn!" he shouted, raising muffled echoes from the car's padded insides. "Damn and double goddamn damn!"

He took three deep breaths in a row, holding the microphone helpless in a strangler's grip before his blotching, swelling face. Now he could no longer even pretend to doubt. Now he knew for certain sure he'd been wrong all along about the Bleaks.

"I'll take care of that call, Wilbur." He growled it out in a soft, confidential whisper through grinding teeth. "Don't you let nobody else take that call, you hear me? Don't you let nobody else get *near* it!"

The second he heard Wilbur's awed "Yezzur," he started up the engine with a roar, gripped the wheel with both his big, freckly hands, and spat gravel as he spun out of Mae's parking lot and down the road with the car's sparklers and sirens on full tilt.

They'd seemed to be so nice, he thought grimly to himself, giving his square head a fierce, bulldog shake as two of Willy Orville's chickens died all unnoticed underneath his wheels. He'd checked the whole family over carefully, or thought he had, and they'd looked to be just as nice and friendly a bunch as you could hope for.

Of course he'd been downright pleased when they'd come house hunting here in Commonplace half a year ago, bringing their two kids and their big, black, toothy old mastiff. He had to admit he was awed by the very idea a famous and successful writer like Robert Bleak, a man who could live wherever he chose, would even consider living in Le Piege County. Most outsiders who had any choice at all steered clear of this whole part of the state and were unkind enough to call it the armpit of America when they didn't call it worse.

It seemed difficult for strangers to get by the endless flatness of the landscape, not to mention the unusual and persistent gloominess of its climate, and he supposed that the grey, twisty scrub growth together with the withered, gnarly trees didn't help too much, nor did those bogs and swamps and hollows full of all that spooky, clammy mist. You had to make the best of things in Le Piege County, truth be told.

Then people would keep on spreading the worst rumors they could get hold of, going all the way back to those foolish tales the early settlers spread about every local Indian they came across being a cannibal down to the last brave and squaw, and if the newspapers or the television anchormen ever spoke of the area, they were always sure to insert some witty reference to those old-time legends about the scruffy, spooky Hawker family and the weird and deadly hotel they operated during the gold rush days where the guests were killed and robbed and then served up as stew dinners to any following pioneers who'd paused to take advantage of the Hawker hospitality.

Of course what really got the place's reputation permanently into trouble was the Worper child, Wendell, who'd killed his bullying mother and then stitched her up and stuffed her because he'd felt guilty about hacking her into small, gory pieces with his ax, and because he didn't like messes. When Wendell saw that she'd come out of the process looking rather well, it seemed to have stirred up some sort of peculiar creative spark in the boy and inspired him to go on to produce further artistic sculptures using the corpses of other ladies he'd acquired from various local graveyards and from killing a variety of old women who'd been unlucky enough to remind him of his mother.

Naturally all that might have gone unnoticed and no one the wiser, but Wendell hadn't been content with confining his new hobby to interior decoration, no, he'd felt the need to continue by suspending a quantity of new dead females from the outside corners of his house like gargoyles and to beautify the roof with others, including rigging up one of them so that she held out a black lace umbrella and then mounting her onto a swivel atop the peak over the widow's walk to serve as a weather vane.

3

Even that wasn't enough for Wendell now he'd hit his full creative stride and he was soon happily absorbed in the process of posing and arranging more than a dozen more stuffed dead women as lawn ornaments on the property overlooking the road. It may be significant that he was working on the thirteenth one, seating her on a planter made from a truck tire painted white, when a gentleman from the Museum of Folk Art in the city who was passing through had to stop his car in the middle of the road at the sight of all that beauty, and in no time at all Wendell found himself having a one-man retrospective show filling two floors of the museum. But when the big-city police read the rave reviews in the papers and started pondering his sources of supply, Wendell soon commenced his long unhappy slide into trouble and the State Asylum for the Criminally Insane.

However none of all that seemed to bother the Bleaks the tiniest little bit. They even surprised Dorry Phipps, the realtor who showed them the place, by falling in love with the Worper place on first sight—which she had to admit to herself was a decidedly gloomy old pile, especially now that it had been cleared of the brightening effect which Wendell's funereally gaudy artworks had lent it—and when she finally got her nerve up enough to tell Mr. Bleak about who had lived there, she was amazed and delighted to find the author was so pleased about the revelation that he clapped his hands and chuckled!

The rest of the family seemed just as nice, Dorry said, and she told about Mrs. Bleak lighting up when she spotted some pumpkins growing in a corner of a field and making a homely little joke about having a jack-o'-lantern patch, and Dorry and old Ned Whalen at the garage had to smile at one another when they saw the Bleak children enthusiastically pretending to bring a plastic toy Frankenstein monster to life in the backseat of the car when the family stopped for a little gas. The sheriff listened to all that along with a good many other encouraging reports, and when he read a few of the horror stories Mr. Bleak wrote for a living on top of that, every doubt fled and it seemed to him that

4

they were just the sort of people who'd blend right into the admittedly eccentric ways of Commonplace without giving the town any problems at all. Now, speeding faster and faster down Route 46 until the fence posts blended, he knew with a sickening certainty that he had aided and abetted the establishment of a viper's nest in the very heart of the community he'd solemnly sworn to protect.

The first hints he might have guessed wrong on the Bleaks came in fairly early, but though they did sound a little odd, he didn't find it all that hard to brush them off, and he never even so much as noticed the first little dent between his eyes which marked the commencement of his brand-new frown line.

The postman Harry Billings started it all by informing the sheriff about the time he came by with his mail truck and found Mrs. Bleak pulling weeds alongside the fence as he drove up. He had barely managed to get in a "good morning" before she stood, wringing her hands, and proceeded to go on about how worried she was about their neighbors on the opposite hill, the Whitbys, and she asked him in a whisper did he know if there'd been some tragedy? When Harry said as how he didn't know of one Mrs. Bleak anxiously told him about the Whitbys' lights going off and on at "odd hours" during the night, and how she and Mr. Bleak had been awakened time after time by "strange noises." Harry asked her what kind of noises and she paused and swallowed and then suddenly blurted out that they were sometimes "like the horrible screams of people being killed!", and when Harry gave her a grin and shrugged and tried to reassure her by pointing out that since it was warm and folks's windows weren't shut like they would be in colder times, you had to expect to hear private doings every now and again, this reassurance did not seem to calm Mrs. Bleak in the least. She silently opened and closed her mouth a couple of times as though she were trying to speak but only succeeded in making a couple of soft little squawks, and Harry said she watched after him as he drove off, and kept doing it till he was all the way out of sight, and he recalled clearly that she had a very odd look on her face.

Then one day Ed Pierce at the hardware store started to chuckle and told the sheriff about the time Mr. Bleak had been in to buy a shotgun because he and Mrs. Bleak were terribly concerned about "all the people" they'd heard lately sneaking about on the grounds outside the house in the dark of night, and how once they thought they'd caught a glimpse of someone dragging someone else wrapped in what looked to be a bloody sheet. Ed said when he tried to calm him down by telling him you "just naturally got to expect folks to take advantage of these nice summer nights," Bleak went still and then, after staring at him very intently and quietly for a moment or two, told him to add on five more boxes of ammo to his order. Sheriff Olson looked in the mirror while he was shaving the very next morning after he heard that and for the first time noticed a tiny frown line had blossomed on his forehead.

But though he didn't like the sound of what he'd heard, the sheriff assumed it was all only a case of city people being understandably jumpy because they were new to the country life-style, to all that quiet at night, to the way the local inhabitants tended to keep their private business private. He would listen to the stories, and then he would smile and scratch his big jaw and try to paper it over by telling anybody who had brought him another depressing story to be patient, that it wouldn't be any time at all before the Bleaks got used to things, that soon you wouldn't hear of any more complaining. He would assure them all the Bleaks would fit in fine.

But the stories kept coming in and they kept adding up. Ben Frazier at the butcher shop said he saw Mrs. Bleak studying the specialty meats in the separate case at the back with extreme care one day when she was waiting for the rain to ease off, when suddenly she gave a little cry and began to peer harder and harder until she started to actually tremble. When Ben walked over to her she pointed at an arm and asked him *"What's that?"* in a kind of a hiss, and there was something in her tone of voice that made him decide not to tell her just then what it was, so he said it was a leg of veal though he knew she didn't believe him.

6

After she left he looked at the meat carefully and was more than a little irritated to realize that the tourist lady's watch had left an easily recognizable indentation on her wrist.

And Doc Huggins at the pharmacy said he cut Mr. Bleak short with a friendly smile once when he'd started going on and on about how he was killing some rats in order to explain why he needed a tin of cyanide he'd come to buy. Doc did his best to assure him that no excuses at all were needed when it came to buying poison in Commonplace; he told him that as a matter of fact the store took special pride in the quality and wide variety of the poisons which they stocked. He was in the process of proving the point by bending down and fishing around in a lower drawer in order to get a jar of the new nerve gas the Ryan boy had brought in on his last leave from the Marines, but when he straightened up with the jar in his hand he realized Mr. Bleak had left and that he'd scuttled right out of the establishment in such a rush that he'd left his package of cyanide behind all wrapped up neatly and tidily as you please on the counter.

There was all of that and a lot more and it just would not stop and the frown line got so deep and long that the sheriff's wife had taken to fretting over it audibly, but somehow he'd managed to fend all these tales away, to keep pushing them off, to make excuses.

Then, just before he'd left the cafe and gotten that call from Wilbur which had proven to be the final straw, Mae had to go and tell him her funny little story.

It would never have seemed anywhere near so ominous by itself since it wasn't more than a tiny thing, but landing as it did atop of all those other accumulated accounts which had been steadily heaping up through the days and weeks and months, it somehow managed to strike Sheriff Olson as being particularly discouraging.

He remembered he'd paused after turning off the engine when he'd parked in Mae's lot to stand and listen to the early morning birds chirping in the soft, fresh air, and it had put him into such a pleasant, peaceful mood that he'd walked into the cafe whistling, something he'd never done before, but he stopped that on a dime when he saw Mae

7

studying him sidewise and slyly with her tiny, cold little eyes and noticed she was wearing that twisty, snaky smile she only let show when she knew she'd snagged onto something that would really hurt.

She didn't say anything much in particular while he worked his way through his chili burger, she just hovered over her grill, picking at little raised bits of carbon with the sharp tip of a long, red fingernail. He ate as quietly as he could, then snuck his money under the side of his plate, and was nearly beginning to believe he'd managed to sneak out of there without her noticing when she was on him with the suddenness of a shark, full of simpers and coy cooings and giving his cup an extra, unwanted pour of coffee.

"You hear about what little Harold Perkins told his maw and paw about the Bleak kids, Sheriff, honey?" she asked in an almost motherly manner.

"Can't say as I have, Mae," he murmured.

"Well, it's quite a shock and that's the truth," she said, shaking her head in a slow, sad, righteous manner. "Particularly seeing as how it all come up in a schoolyard where you wouldn't expect anything of that nature to take place."

"In a schoolyard," he repeated.

"All the poor, dear children was trying to do was teach them Bleak kids an innocent playground game when the girl begun to cry and holler something awful and her brother got so darn-fool mad things almost ended in a fistfight!"

"What game was that, Mae?" Sheriff Olson asked, standing and carefully adjusting his belt so that his belly would pop over it comfortably.

"Why good old Rob the Coffin," said Mae, her eyes widening with astonishment. "The same game as you and I and every boy and girl that's grown up around hereabouts has played since Lord knows when. The sweet little dears explained them all the rules, such as how each member of the one team plays a body part—choosing the head or the heart or the bowels and such—whilst the other team plays the ghouls. That cute little Finley girl was showing them how you draw the blood pump in the funeral parlor diagram with a stick on the playground dirt, and Harold Perkins was

8

explaining how if you shout 'I'm embalmed!' three times before the ghouls grab you they can't eat you, when out of the blue and all of a sudden the Bleak girl began screaming and carrying on fit to beat the band and her brother got all mad and uppity and like to pop poor Harold Perkins right on the nose and maybe broke it if the teacher hadn't heard all the caterwauling and come rushing out to calm things down."

Mae paused in order to give the counter a little swipe with a paper towel before she twisted her knife.

"I hate to mention it because I know you vouched for them Bleaks, Sheriff, honey, and are more responsible than anybody else for them presently living in our little community," she purred. "But I feel it's my civic duty, painful though it may be, and besides, we're all sure you'll put things right again once you've gone and realized your mistake."

When Sheriff Olson saw the shiny new stainless steel mailbox with BLEAK glued on it in bright red, reflective letters he extinguished his car's flashing lights and siren, slowed to a civilian speed, and turned off Route 46 onto a dirt road winding up a craggy hill. He cringed a little when, in the process of doing all this, he caught a peek at his reflection in the rearview mirror and hoped he hadn't looked that dismally gloomy when he'd been leaving Mae's Cafe as it would have pleased her far too much. The frown line, which was now the most noticeable feature of his face, presently traversed the entire length of his forehead and he feared if it cut any deeper it might expose his very skull.

He chewed a corner of his moustache as he bumped up the road, watching the grey spot on the mountain's top grow into a big, old, drearily menacing house with tall, thin, secretive windows peering over and under a quantity of crouching roofs, and he didn't even try to fight off wishing little Wendell Worper still lived there. Peaceful Wendell, with never a complaint from him or about him, content to play shyly and quietly with his mother and all the rest of those stuffed dead women, always careful never to bother a soul, save for his victims.

But that brief, nostalgic reverie was exploded by the sight

of Robert Bleak leaning his scrawny frame over the fence and flapping his long arms at him like an agitated blue jay. Olson sighed, smoothed the frown line from his forehead with a great effort, and arranged his face into what he hoped would seem a relaxed, convincingly official smile as he pulled to the side of the road.

"Well, now, Mr. Bleak," he said, easing his big body out of the car. "What seems to be the trouble?"

"That," said Bleak, waving frantically at the ground, and the sheriff saw a pale object jammed onto the end of a short board stuck into the ground. It was a hand with its index finger pointed in Bleak's general direction and its other fingers and thumb tightly clenched. It was a macabre object, without doubt, but it undeniably had a peculiar kind of charm. It looked very much like an antique direction indicator in some old-fashioned place of business except, perhaps, for its gory stump.

Sheriff Olson studied it for a moment with his eyes narrowed slightly and his head tilted to one side. There seemed to be something oddly familiar about that hand; those chubby, spatulate fingers definitely rang a muffled bell.

"Well, now," said Olson after a pause, "so this here is why you called me? This is what the fuss is all about?"

"All the fuss?" gritted Bleak, leaning even further over his fence and firmly fixing his visitor with an incredulous glare. "All the *fuss*? I should think the discovery of an item as horrible and gruesome as this would be a perfectly appropriate occasion for a fuss! I should indeed!"

"Well, now," Olson said again, visibly disconcerted at the sight of Bleak actually wringing his hands. "I want you please to understand I meant no offense when I said that, Mr. Bleak, sir, none at all. The truth be told, I'd really hoped you'd take it as a kind of compliment!"

Bleak blinked, obviously puzzled. His jaw moved slightly as if he were chewing over what he'd just heard.

"Compliment?" he said at length. "I'm afraid I don't follow you at all on that, Sheriff Olson."

Extending both his palms before him in a double-barreled gesture of peace, Olson made his way to the fence, speaking as he went.

10

"What I was trying to say, sir, is that I wouldn't think a person such as yourself would bother to call the police about some little bitty thing like this," he said, indicating the severed hand with an almost dismissive wave. "I'd expect a lot of folks might be spooked by it, sure, but not you, sir, not *you!*"

Now the sheriff was directly across the fence from Bleak. He was trying to keep his easy, friendly, sheriff's smile in place but it persisted in slipping away whereas his frown line kept treacherously popping into view in spite of all his efforts. The author studied him warily as the sheriff continued speaking more and more in a rush.

"Heck, sir, if anything, I'd have thought you'd be able to manage something like this little old hand, here, a whole lot better than me. Oh, sure, I've seen a bunch of bodies and stuff like that what with one thing and another, but, hell, I'm just a country cop, Mr. Bleak, I'm just a hayseed, and you're worldwide known as a *master of the macabre*, dammit, sir, just like it says on the covers of your books, and I know you really *are*, sir, because I've read those books and what it says is the plain truth, so I just can't see how come a bitty piece of corpse meat has got you so riled up!"

Bleak stared at him with bug-eyed incredulity for a moment, and then pointed back at the pointing hand.

"That thing stuck on that little post in the ground between your feet and mine is real, Sheriff Olson," he said, speaking slowly and grimly. "It is part of a genuine dead body. In my stories amputated hands are only made-up things which I create both because I enjoy doing it and because it makes me a reasonable living. They are works of fiction and therefore they won't slowly turn into green slime or mummify into cracklings or attract worms or do any of the other things a real dead hand such as that one there can do. My dead hands are just pretend dead hands."

Olson took hold of the top rail of the fence as a man will when he clutches something at the edge of a high precipice to keep from falling.

"But those godawful stories you write, sir," he said, an audible desperation creeping into his voice. "Like that *La*

11

Traviata where you dreamt up the dead Italian opera star stuffed full of singing worms, or that yarn of yours which still gives me the jimjams every time I think of it, the one where you show that Jack the Ripper was actually Queen Victoria all along, how can anybody who's thought up such stuff as that be put off by a dinky, no-account, bitty old hand?"

"Since you persist in missing my point, Sheriff Olson," said Bleak, exasperated, "I suggest we abandon it and move on to a far more important aspect of this situation. It is not *only* that hand which concerns me. There is more."

"More?" the sheriff asked in a dazed tone of voice, clearly floundering. "More?"

"More," said Bleak. "See where the hand is pointing."

Sheriff Olson's gape obediently followed the direction indicated by the dead finger as the author had asked him until he saw, lying in the tall grass a little closer to the house, a pale, misshapen lump.

He climbed over the fence without the least awareness he was doing it and followed Bleak as he walked over to the lump. It was the naked left half of a male corpse, minus its hands and head. Its wrist stump was pointing up the slope toward the house as the hand had done. The sheriff peered at the thing thoughtfully for a moment and then jumped and wheeled to his rear at the sound of a soft rustle behind him.

It was Mrs. Bleak, looking pale and distracted. She edged closer to him, wringing her hands almost exactly as Mr. Bleak had done.

"I'm so glad you've come, Sheriff Olson!" she said, speaking with a kind of anxious calm and staring at him with her wide, frightened-looking eyes. "I do so hope you can do something about all these terrible, awful things!"

Olson opened his mouth to reply but Bleak cut him off.

"All he has done so far is to advise me not to take them all that seriously," said the author. "Maybe you can convince him we hold a dim view of this sort of thing. He seems altogether very unimpressed with our corpse so far."

"Then you're just like all the rest of the people here in

Commonplace!" she cried, stepping hurriedly back from the sheriff, a sudden expression of horror on her face.

"Now, please, Mrs. Bleak, just hear me out—" he began, but Bleak cut him off again.

"Being an investigator of crime, you might be at least vaguely interested in looking where this part of the body's pointing," he said.

The sheriff did and there was yet another pale lump in the grass further on ahead, and standing by it, hand in hand, were both of the Bleak children, staring at the lawman accusingly.

"Is he like the others, mommy?" asked the little girl in a tearful voice which made the sheriff wince. "Is he going to tease us about killing people? Is he, mommy?"

The new lump was the right-hand half of the corpse, and now the sheriff knew for certain he'd been acquainted with it in life. Like the left half, it had come from a chubby man, probably somewhere in his mid-thirties. Its wrist, too, pointed ahead and this time Olson needed no prompting to look in the direction specified. There, on the top step of the open storm door leading into the basement, pointing downward, was the other hand, and seated next to it, looking at him in an accusatory fashion, just like every other member of the family, was the Bleaks' big black mastiff.

"I suppose there's more of it down there," said the sheriff.

"There is," said Bleak. "One thing more. Shall we go look at it, or do you think it's not all that important and that we should walk off and forget all about it?"

"Now just hold on," said the sheriff angrily, and then paused to heave a deep sigh. "Let's all just hold on. There's been a misunderstanding here and I admit it's all my fault. I got you folks wrong; it was my business to figure if you would or would not fit in around these parts and I figured wrong. I don't know what I'm going to do about you all, I truly don't, but please understand, no matter what happens, I didn't never mean no harm."

Bleak stared at him for a long moment, then slowly shook his head.

"Perhaps, someday, I'll have at least a vague idea what you meant just then, Sheriff," he said at last. "But for now, just as a matter of form, let's go look at what's down there in the basement."

It was awkward descending the steps in the dark, but the sheriff had gone down them before, on the last occasion to supervise the investigation and photography of the place when it had been Wendell Worper's little embalming room. Here is where the boy had nearly gutted his prey and soaked them in vats of nitron before patting them dry and sewing them up with a stitch he'd learned from studying leather baseball skins. Here is where he dressed them up again in their graveyard clothes which he'd cleaned and pressed for them, or arrayed them in pretty dresses which he'd bought from department stores in the city for just that purpose.

The sheriff paused when he felt the concrete of the basement's floor scuff under his shoes, and at that moment he heard a click behind him as Robert Bleak turned on the lights. There, a yard or two before him, Olson saw a human head sitting on the center of a sterling silver serving platter, resting just where the turkey would ordinarily go. It stared at him openmouthed and stupidly with its round blue eyes as it often had in life, but this time it didn't see him, being dead.

"It's Wilbur," gasped Olson, in astonishment. "It's my deputy, Wilbur! But that can't be because he's the one that called me about this on the damn car radio just a bitty while ago!"

"That wasn't Wilbur," whispered a voice directly behind him which sounded for all the world like Wilbur himself, only with a bad cold, just like he'd had on the radio, "That was me!"

The sheriff turned and his jaw dropped in astonishment both at the sight of the remarkably sinister, bulge-eyed expression playing on Robert Bleak's face and at the enormous chef's knife which he both saw and felt being driven quickly and skillfully through the flesh between his shoulder blades.

The sheriff had only fallen halfway to the ground when

14

Mrs. Bleak, wearing an expression as surprisingly diabolic as her husband's, drove a somewhat smaller, but no less effective, knife firmly into the side of his thick neck as she gave a cachinnating laugh.

The sheriff had barely thumped onto the concrete when he felt simultaneous sharp pains on either side of his torso as his fading vision dimly made out both the Bleak children eagerly and adroitly inserting even smaller knives between his ribs, and just before sight and all other physical sensations departed him altogether, he became aware that the mastiff had enthusiastically begun to tear at his legs.

"I was right, godammit, I was right!" his voice echoed triumphantly, if only in his skull: *"I was right all along about them Bleaks!"*

And the frown line faded completely and entirely and forever from his forehead.

Remains to Be Seen

David Morrell

"On my honor, Your Excellency!" Carlos clicked his heels together and jerked his right arm upward, outward, clenching his fist in salute.

"More than your honor! Your life, Carlos! Swear it on your life!"

"My life, Your Excellency! I swear it!"

The Great Man nodded, his dark eyes burning. His once robust face had shrunk around his cheekbones, giving him a grimace of perpetual sorrow. His pencil-thin mustache, formerly as dark as his eyes, was now gray, his once swarthy skin now sallow. Even if a miracle occurred and His Excellency's forces were able to crush the rebellion, Carlos knew that the strain of the past month's worsening crisis would leave the marks of its ravages upon his leader.

But of course, the miracle would not occur. Already the rattle of machine guns from the outskirts of the city intensified. The echo of explosions rumbled over rooftops. The shimmer of fires reflected off smoky clouds in the night.

A frantic bodyguard approached, his bandolier slapping against his chest, his rifle clutched so rigidly his knuckles were white. "Your Excellency, you have to leave now! The rebels have broken through!"

17

But the Great Man hesitated. "On your life, Carlos. Remember, you swore it."

"I'll never disappoint you."

"I know." The Great Man clasped his shoulders. "You never have. You never will."

Carlos swelled with pride, but sadness squeezed his heart. The gunfire and explosions reminded him of the massive fireworks that had celebrated the Great Man's inauguration to the presidency. Now the golden years were over. Despondent, he followed his leader toward a truck, its rear compartment capped by a tarpaulin.

A crate lay on the cobblestoned courtyard. It was wooden, eight feet long, four feet wide. The Great Man squinted at it. His gaunt cheeks rippling, he clenched his teeth and nodded in command. Six soldiers stepped forward, three on each side, and hastily lifted the crate. It tilted. Something inside thumped.

"Gently!" the Great Man ordered.

Straining with its bulk, glancing fearfully toward the shots that approached the heart of the city, the soldiers slid the crate inside the truck. One yanked down a section of tarpaulin. Another raised the creaky back hatch. The Great Man himself snapped the lockpins into place.

"Your Excellency, please! We have to go!" the bodyguard implored. An explosion shook windows.

The Great Man seemed not to have heard. He continued to stare at the truck.

"Your Excellency!"

The Great Man blinked and turned toward the bodyguard. "Of course." He scanned the flame-haloed outskirts of the city. "We must leave. But one day . . . one day we'll return." He pivoted toward Carlos. "Do your duty. You have the itinerary. When I'm able, I'll contact you." Flanked by bodyguards, he rushed toward his bulletproof limousine.

"But Your Excellency, aren't you coming with me?" Carlos asked.

Racing, the Great Man shouted back, "No! Separately we have a greater chance of confusing the rebels! We have to mislead them! Remember, Carlos! On your life!"

With a final look at the truck, the Great Man surged into his limousine, guards charging after him. As the car roared out of the palace courtyard, speeding southward away from the direction of the rebel attack, Carlos felt suddenly empty. But at once he remembered his vow. "You heard His Excellency! We must go!"

Men snapped to attention. Carlos scrambled into the cabin of the truck. A sergeant slid behind the steering wheel. The truck raced eastward, a jeep before and behind it, each filled with soldiers with automatic weapons.

They'd gone five blocks when a rebel patrol attacked. The front jeep blew apart, fragments of metal and flaming bodies twisting through the air. The truck's driver jerked the steering wheel, skidding around the wreckage. Gunfire shattered the windshield. Glass showered. The driver slammed back, his brains erupting behind his skull. While the truck kept moving, Carlos lunged past the spastic corpse, shoved open the driver's door, and thrust the dead sergeant onto the street. The body bounced. Stomping the accelerator, Carlos rammed through a barricade, gripping the steering wheel with one hand, using his other to fire his pistol through the shattered windshield.

He and the remaining jeep swerved around a gloomy warehouse, raced along the murky waterfront, and screeched to a stop beside the only ship still in port. Its frightened crew flinched from nearby gunfire and scurried down the gangplank toward the truck. They yanked the crate from the back. Again something thumped.

"Gently!" Carlos ordered.

Heeding the nearby gunshots more than his order, they dropped the crate on a sling and shouted obscenities to someone on deck. A motor whined. A crane raised the crate. A rope broke. Carlos felt his heart lurch as the crate dangled halfway out of the sling. The crate kept rising. It swung toward the freighter and landed on deck with a crash.

A deafening explosion followed a moment afterward as, a block from the harbor, a building erupted in a thunderous

19

blaze. The freighter's crew raced up the gangplank, Carlos and his men rushing after them, the gangplank beginning to rise.

Already the freighter was moving. Scraping from the dock, it mustered speed to surge through the night. Ghostly reflections from the fires in the city guided it toward the harbor's exit.

Carlos barked orders to his men—to remove the tarpaulins from the fifty-millimeter cannons at the bow and stern. As they armed the weapons, he tensely watched the freighter's crew repair the sling and lower the crate through an open hatch. Sweating, he waited for the shout from below that would signal the crate's safe arrival in the hold.

Only then did he feel the ache of tension drain from his shoulders. He exhaled. The first stage of his mission had been completed. For now, he had nothing to do except to wait till he reached his next destination and then wait again for further orders from His Excellency.

Behind him, a woman whispered his name.

He spun. "Maria."

Beaming, she hurried toward him: short, with ebony hair and copper skin, handsome more than beautiful. Her pregnancy emphasized her stocky build. Her strong-boned features suggested faithfulness and endurance, the hardy virtues of peasant stock.

They embraced. During the previous hectic week, Carlos hadn't seen his wife at all. Despite his devotion to the Great Man, he'd felt the strain of being separated from her—a strain that must have shown, for a day ago the Great Man had told him to send her a message to meet him on this freighter. Carlos had been overwhelmed by the Great Man's consideration.

"Is it over? Are we safe?" Maria asked.

"For now." He kissed her.

"But His Excellency didn't come with you?"

"No. He plans to meet us later."

"And the crate?"

"What about it, Maria?"

20

"Why is it so important that you had to bring it here under guard?"

"His Excellency never said. I would never have been so bold as to ask. But it must have tremendous value."

"For him to entrust it to you, to ask you to risk your life to protect it? By all the saints, yes, it must have tremendous value!"

She gazed with worship into his eyes.

At three A.M., in a cabin that the Great Man had arranged for them, Carlos made love to his wife. Hearing her moan beneath him, he felt a pang of concern for his benefactor. He prayed that the Great Man had escaped from the city and hoped that His Excellency would contact him soon. His wife thrust against him a final time and went to sleep with a patient sigh as if proud that her marital duty had been accomplished.

Obedience, Carlos thought. Of all the virtues, obedience is the greatest.

At dawn, he was wakened by a soldier pounding on the cabin's door. "Rebel boats!"

Carlos strapped on his pistol. "Maria, stay here!"

In the two-hour battle, he sustained a minor wound to his left arm as he manned the stern's cannon after the soldier at the trigger was sprayed by machine-gun fire.

The freighter too sustained slight damage. But the rebel boats were repelled. The crate was protected. The mission continued.

As the freighter's doctor bandaged his bleeding arm, Carlos peered at a message that the radio operator had given him. The Great Man had escaped from the city and was fleeing through the mountains.

"May God be with him," Carlos said.

But the radio operator looked troubled.

"What is it? What haven't you told me?" Carlos asked.

"The boats that attacked us. I monitored their radio transmissions. They knew His Excellency was in the mountains. They knew *before* they attacked us."

21

Carlos frowned.

The radio operator continued. "Why were they so determined to attack us if they knew His Excellency wasn't on board?"

"I have no idea," Carlos said.

But he lied. He did have an idea.

The crate, he thought.

They wanted whatever's in the crate.

In the hold's fish-smelling darkness, Carlos aimed his flashlight toward the wooden planks that made up the crate. He walked around it, examining every detail. One bottom corner had been splintered—not surprising, given the rough way the crew had brought it aboard. But no bullets had pierced the wooden planks. The contents remained intact. He leaned against a damp bulkhead and stared in puzzlement at the crate.

What was in it? he wondered.

Twenty minutes later, while he continued to stare fascinated at the crate, a crew member found him, bringing a radio message.

Carlos aimed his flashlight at the sheet of paper. *Escape from the mountains accomplished. Avoid first destination. Proceed to checkpoint two. Instructions will follow. Remember, on your life.*

Carlos nodded to the man who'd brought the message. He folded the piece of paper and tucked it into a pocket. Pushing away from the bulkhead, he fully intended to follow the crew member from the hold.

But he couldn't resist the impulse to aim his flashlight at the crate.

What was in it? he thought again. Why was it so important?

"Your arm!" Maria said when Carlos at last emerged on deck. "Does it hurt?"

Carlos shrugged and repressed a wince. "The doctor gave me something for the pain."

"You mustn't strain yourself. You need to rest."

"I'll rest when the Great Man reclaims his property."

"Whatever it is," she said. "Do you think it's gold or jewels? Rare coins? Priceless paintings?"

"Secret documents, most likely. It's none of my business. Tomorrow evening, thank God, my responsibility ends."

But the Great Man wasn't waiting when the freighter docked at the neutral port that was checkpoint two. Instead a nervous messenger raced up the gangplank. Wiping his brow, he blurted out that although the Great Man had reached a neighboring country, the rebels persisted in pursuing him. "He can't risk coming to the freighter. He asks you to proceed to checkpoint three."

"Three days to the north?" Carlos subdued his disappointment. He'd looked forward to showing the Great Man how well he'd done his duty.

"His Excellency said to remind you—you vowed on your honor."

"On my *life!*" Carlos straightened. "I was with him from the beginning. When he and I were frightened peasants, determined to topple the tyrant. I swore allegiance. I'll never disappoint him."

That night while the freighter was still in port, a rebel squad disguised as stevedores snuck on board and nearly succeeded in reaching the hold before a vigilant soldier sounded an alarm. In the furious gun battle, Carlos lost five members of his team. All eight invaders were killed. But not before a grenade was thrown into the hold.

The explosion filled Carlos with panic. He emptied his submachine gun into the rebel who'd thrown the grenade and rushed to the hold, aiming his flashlight, shocked to discover that the grenade had detonated fifteen feet from the crate. Shrapnel had splintered its wooden slats. A large chunk had torn a hole in the side.

Carlos felt smothered, tracing trembling fingers along the damaged wood. If the contents entrusted to him had been destroyed, how could he explain his failure to His Excellency?

23

I swore to protect! Fear made him stiffen. What if the shrapnel had stayed hot enough to smolder inside the crate? What if the contents were secret documents and they burst into flames? Grabbing a crowbar, he jammed it beneath the lid. Nails creaked. Wood snapped. He jerked the lid up, desperate to peer inside, to make sure there wasn't a fire. What he saw made him gasp.

A footstep scraped behind him. Slamming the lid shut, he drew his pistol and spun.

Maria emerged from shadows, frowning, caught by the beam of his flashlight. "Are you all right?"

He exhaled. "I almost . . ." Shaking, he holstered his pistol. "Never creep up behind me."

"But the shooting. I felt so worried."

"Go back to the cabin. Try to sleep."

"Come with me. You need to rest."

"No."

"What did you find?"

"I don't understand."

"When you opened the crate."

"You're mistaken, Maria. I didn't open it."

"But I saw you . . ."

"It's dark down here. My flashlight must have cast shadows and tricked your eyes."

"But I heard you slam down the lid."

"No, you heard me lose my balance and fall against the crate. I didn't open it. Go back to the cabin. Do what I tell you!"

With a plaintive look, she obeyed, the echo of her footsteps dwindling. The flashlight revealed her pregnant silhouette. At the top of the murky metal stairs, a hatch banged shut.

Carlos forced himself to wait. Finally certain she was gone, he turned again toward the crate and slowly lifted the lid. Before he'd been interrupted, he'd had a quick glimpse of the contents, enough to verify that there wasn't a fire, though he didn't dare tell Maria what was in there for fear she'd speak without thinking and reveal the secret.

24

Because what he'd seen had been more startling than a fire. The coffin was made of burnished copper, its gleaming surface marred by pockmarks from shrapnel.

His knees faltered. Fighting dizziness, he leaned down to inspect the desecration. With a sharp breath of satisfaction, he decided the damage was superficial. The coffin had not been penetrated.

But what about the body?

Yes, the body.

Whose?

It was none of his business. The Great Man hadn't seen fit to let him know what he'd pledged his life to protect. No doubt, His Excellency had his reasons.

Carlos subdued his intense curiosity, lowered the lid, and resecured it. He'd exceeded his authority, granted! But for a just motive. To protect what had been entrusted to him. His duty had been honored. The coffin wasn't in danger for the moment. He could have its copper made smooth again. He could replace the crate with one that hadn't been damaged. His Excellency would never know that Carlos had almost failed.

But one container had led to another. The mystery still wasn't solved. The ultimate question remained. Why were the rebels so determined to destroy the crate? Who was in the coffin?

Burdened with responsibility, Carlos climbed from the hold, ordering the freighter's crew, "Bring down a mattress and blankets. A thermos of coffee. Food. A lantern." He told Maria, "I'll be staying in the hold tonight. *Every* night till His Excellency reclaims what's his."

"No! It's damp down there! The air smells foul! You'll get sick!"

"I made a vow! I've ordered my men to triple the guards on the hold! No one but myself is allowed down there! Not even you!"

Three days later, Carlos shuffled from the hold. Unshaven, fetid, and feverish, he squinted through sickening

25

shimmering vision toward the northern neutral port that was checkpoint three.

But again His Excellency wasn't waiting. Another sweating messenger rushed on board. "It's worse than we feared. The rebels are determined to hunt our leader to the ends of the earth. He has to keep running. These are your new instructions."

Shuddering, Carlos studied them. "To *Europe*?"

"Marseilles. That's the only chance to complete the mission."

"Yes." Carlos wavered. "To deliver the crate."

"I know nothing about your purpose. All I know is, it's imperative. His Excellency said to remind you."

"Yes, that I swore . . ."

"On your life."

Carlos trembled. "My promise was solemn. Not just my life. My *soul*."

In the hold, enduring turbulence, nausea, and delirium, Carlos gave in to compulsion. During the seemingly endless route across the Atlantic, the crate and its contents beckoned. The coffin—his only companion—obsessed and drew him. As his lantern hissed and his wounded arm throbbed, he paced before his obligation. The crate. The coffin. The corpse.

But whose?

His deprivation destroyed his resolve. Again he grabbed the crowbar, again pried up the wooden lid. *He had to know.* Leaning down, trembling, he fingered the catches on the coffin's seam, released them, and pushed upward, gradually revealing . . .

The secret.

This time he gasped not from surprise but reverence. His knees wavered. He almost knelt.

Before Her Majesty.

The patroness of her people. The blessed mother of her country. How many days—and far into how many nights— had she made herself available to her loved ones, allowing endless streams of petitioners to come to her, dispensing food, comfort, and hope? How many times had she interceded with His Excellency for the poor and homeless, the disadvantaged she described as her shirtless ones? The Church had called her a saint. The people had called her a God-send.

Her works of mercy had been equaled only by her beauty. Tall, trim, and statuesque, with graceful contours and stunning features, she embodied perfection. Her blond hair—rare among her people—emphasized her uniqueness, her locks so white, so radiant they seemed a halo.

The cancer that destroyed her uterus had been both a real and symbolic abomination. How could someone so giving, so emotionally fertile, have been brought down by rampant corruption at the source of her female essence? God had turned His back on His special creation. The world would not see her likes again.

The people mourned, the Great Man more so. He grieved so hard that he felt compelled to preserve her memory in the flesh, to capture her beauty for as long as science could make possible. No one knew for sure the process involved. Rumor had it that he'd sent for the world's greatest embalmer, the mortician who'd been entrusted with the corpse of the secular god of the Soviets, the leader of their revolution, Lenin himself. It was said that, offering a fortune, the Great Man had instructed the embalmer to use all his skills to preserve Her Majesty forever as she had been in life. Her blood had been replaced with alcohol. Glycerine, at one hundred and forty degrees Fahrenheit, had been pumped through her tissues. Her corpse had been immersed in secret chemicals. Even more secret techniques had preserved her organs. Though her skin had tightened somewhat, it glistened with a radiance greater than she'd had in life. Her blond hair and red lips were resplendent.

Carlos froze with awe. The rumors were true. Her Majesty had been made eternal. He cringed with expectation that she'd open her eyes and speak.

In turmoil, he remembered the rest of the tragedy. Her Majesty's death had begun the Great Man's downfall. He'd tried to maintain his power without her, but the people—always demanding, always ungrateful—had turned against him. It didn't matter that His Excellency had legislated impending social reforms while his wife had soothed social woes merely from day to day. From the people's point of view, the good of now was greater than that of soon. When a charismatic rabble-rouser had promised immediate paradise, a new revolution toppled the Great Man's government.

Now Carlos understood why the rebels were so determined to destroy the crate. To eradicate all vestiges of the Great Man's rule, they had to destroy not only His Excellency but the immortalized remains of the Great Man's love and source of his power, the goddess of her country.

Burdened with greater responsibility, Carlos bowed his head in worship. An hour having seemed like a minute, he lowered the coffin's lid and resecured the top of the crate. He trembled with reverence. During the turbulent voyage across the Atlantic, he twice gave in to temptation, raised the lids from the crate and the coffin, and studied the treasure entrusted to him. The miracle continued. Her Majesty remained as lifelike as ever.

Soon the Great Man will have you back, Carlos thought, smiling.

But His Excellency wasn't waiting when the freighter docked at Marseilles. Yet another frantic messenger hurried on board, reporting that the Great Man was still being chased, delivering new instructions. He frowned at Carlos's beard-stubbled cheeks, flushed skin, and hollow eyes. "But are you well enough to—? Perhaps someone else should—"

"I vowed to His Excellency! He depends on me! My honor's at stake! I *must* complete the mission!"

When Maria objected privately that he *wasn't* well, he told her, "Leave me alone! You don't understand what's involved!"

Distraught, he arranged for the crate to be unloaded from the freighter and placed in a truck. Under guard, it was driven to a secret airstrip, from where the crate was flown to Italy and placed on a waiting train that would take it to Rome. Three times, rebel teams attempted to intercept it, but Carlos took every precaution. The teams were destroyed—though so were several of Carlos's men.

He paced in front of the crate in an otherwise empty boxcar. How had the rebels anticipated the itinerary? As the train chugged into Rome, he was forced to conclude that there must be a spy. One of His Excellency's advisers was passing information to the rebels. The itinerary had to be modified.

On schedule, the crate was rushed to a warehouse. But twelve hours later, Carlos had it unexpectedly moved to the basement of a church and two days later to a storage room in a mortuary. After an uneventful week, only then was it taken to its intended destination, an abandoned villa outside Rome. Carlos hoped that his variation of the schedule had confused the rebels into thinking that the entire itinerary had been altered. Further variations tempted him, but he had to insure that His Excellency could get in touch with him and, most important, rejoin Her Majesty.

The villa was in disrepair, decrepit, depressing, gloomy. The windows had holes. The lights didn't work. Cobwebs floated from the great hall's ceiling. In the middle of the immense dusty marble floor, the crate lay surrounded by candles, so Carlos could see to aim if any of the ruin's numerous rats dared to approach the crate and its sacred contents. His men patrolled the grounds, guarding the mansion's entrances, while Maria had orders to remain in an upper-floor bedroom.

Periodically Carlos opened the crate and the coffin to remind herself of the reason for his sacrifice, of his heed for constant vigilance. His vision of the blessed mystery became increasingly profound. Her Majesty seemed ever more lifelike, beatific, radiant. The illusion was overwhelming— she wasn't dead but merely sleeping.

He couldn't remember the last time he'd bathed. His hair and beard were shaggy, his garments wrinkled, mired. As he slumped in a musty chair, unable to fight exhaustion, his chin on his chest, his gunhand drooping, he vaguely recalled a time when his dreams had been restful. But now he had only nightmares, assaulted by shades of ghouls.

A scrape of metal jerked him awake. A footstep on dust made him spin. His skill defeated his sleep-clouded eyes. He shot repeatedly, roared in triumph, and rushed toward the enemy who'd brazenly violated Her Majesty's sanctum. Preparing to deliver a just-to-be-certain shot to the head, he gaped down at Maria unmoving in a pool of blood, every bullet having pierced her pregnancy.

He shrieked till his throat seized shut.

She was buried behind the villa in one of its numerous, disgraceful, untended gardens. He couldn't risk sending for a priest, who in spite of a bribe would no doubt inform the authorities about the killing. What was more, to leave the villa to take his wife to a church, then a graveyard, was totally out of the question. At all extremes, his duty remained. Her Majesty had to be guarded. Weeping, he patted his shovel on the dirt that covered Maria's corpse. He knelt and planted a single flower, a yellow rose, her favorite.

His grief was tinged with anger. "You were told to stay in the upstairs bedroom! You had your orders just as I have mine. Why didn't you listen? How many times did I tell you? Of all the virtues, obedience is the greatest!"

Unable to control his shudders, he returned to the villa's great hall, relieved the guards who'd taken his place, and commanded them to remain outside. He locked the great hall's door and wearily approached the crate to open the coffin, wavering before Her Majesty. Her blond hair glowed. Her red lips glistened. Her sensuous cheeks were translucent.

"Now you understand how solemnly I swore. On my

30

honor, my life, my soul. I sacrificed my wife for you. My unborn child. There's nothing I wouldn't do for you. Sleep in peace. Never fear. No matter the cost, I'll always protect you."

A tear dropped onto her forehead. Her eyelids seemed to flicker. He gasped. But he was only imagining, he told himself. The movement had simply been the shimmer of light through his tear-misted eyes.

He wiped the tear from her forehead. "I'm sorry, Your Majesty." He tried to resist but couldn't, gave in to the impulse and kissed her brow where the tear had fallen.

A messenger at last arrived. After nights of sleeping in turmoil beside the crate, Carlos sighed, anticipating that the Great Man had escaped and intended to reclaim his treasure. At the same time, he surprised himself by feeling regret that his mission had come to an end. He quickly learned that it hadn't. With an odd relief, he learned that the rebels were adamant, the Great Man was still being chased. He studied his new instructions. To take the crate to Madrid.

"His Excellency," the messenger said, "is obliged to you for your loyalty. He told me to tell you he won't forget."

Carlos fought to still his trembling hands, tugged at his unkempt beard, and brushed back his shaggy hair. "It's my privilege to be the Great Man's servant. No sacrifice is too burdensome."

"You're an inspiration." The messenger frowned at the wild look in Carlos's eyes. "His Excellency heard about the unfortunate loss of your wife. He sends his deep condolences."

Carlos gestured, in grief as well as devotion.

But devotion to whom? he wondered. The Great Man or Her Majesty? "As I said, any sacrifice."

In Madrid, he noticed Her Majesty's lips move and knew he had to feed her.

Three months later, having been ordered to move the crate to Lisbon, he knew that Her Majesty would be cold en route and covered her with a blanket.

Six months later, having relocated in Brussels, he ordered his men to bring him an electric drill.

And finally the message he'd dreaded arrived. *Escape accomplished. Sanctuary achieved. Faithful friend, your obligation is about to end. Directions enclosed. With heartfelt thanks and my immense anticipation, I ask you to return what is mine.*

Yours?

Carlos turned to Her Highness and sobbed.

The motorcade fishtailed up the snowy road that approached the château outside Geneva. The Great Man waited anxiously, breathing frost as he paced the porch. Pressing his chilled hands under the crate, he helped his servants lug it through the opened double door. Impatient, he ordered it placed in the steeple-roofed living room and escorted everyone out, except for the genius mortician who for a fortune had used his secret skills to attempt to preserve the Great Man's love and who now had been summoned to validate the guaranteed results of his promise.

Each breathed quickly, hefting crowbars to raise the crate's lid but finding that the lid was not secure. Distressed, they fumbled to open the coffin but discovered that it wasn't locked.

Her Majesty looked exactly incredibly lifelike as the genius had guaranteed.

Although a hole had been drilled in the lid of her coffin. (For air? As if someone had believed she was truly alive?)

With a matching hole in her skull, the drill having gone too deep.

And rotten food bulged from her mouth.

And brains and blood covered her face.

And her dress was raised, Carlos lying obscenely on top of her, a wound in his eye and the back of his skull, a pistol in his hand, a beatific expression on his face.

No Love
Lost

J. N. Williamson

After Dad became too ill to handle Joshua Addams at home, it seemed perfectly natural for Josh's younger brother, Craig, to make arrangements for Josh's continuing care. There was no consideration given to the possibility of the forty-two-year-old mental patient going to live with Craig Addams and there were sound reasons for that.

First, Joshua was a paranoid schizophrenic, and his steadily deteriorating psychosis included hebephrenic symptoms of worsening hallucination. Second, Craig simply had no room for his brother—nor time, if it came down to that. A thirty-nine-year-old bachelor engaged in a fruitful law practice now approaching its next well-planned peak, Craig was buying a small but tasteful condo and lived alone. As Creggie saw it—that was what Josh called him from the start and it was the name Mom and Dad instantly began to use too—their parents had *wanted* to make room and time for Joshua.

Dad understood.

Even Josh did. Both Dad and Craig believed that, when they were through explaining why a nice, long drive in the country with Creggie was a fine idea. That it was also a fine idea for Joshua to stay at the nice place Creggie had found for him, at least until Daddy got better. That Josh would like it a lot because he was going where Doctor Ben used to say he should go, until Mom got real sick. He remembered that, didn't he, Joshie *did* remember Mom, and Doctor Ben? It was back when poor Mommy was dying and begged for both her boys, Joshie and Creggie, to live with Daddy and her, until . . .

Josh, Craig felt certain, had understood. Well enough, anyway. As well as ol' Josh ever grasped any facts that weren't involved with his toys, his red rubber balls.

Creggie had also given no consideration to his older brother moving in with him because he had picked out this private institution they were headed for three years ago, shortly after Mom died. When Craig caught the unmistakable glint in Dad's eye of a man who was consciously opting out of life. Who'd depart it as soon as he learned how to reverse the will to live and then began shutting down his vital organs. As soon as he could coax cancer to gobble those organs up, one after another.

Which was exactly what Dad had done and was doing, merely at a more accelerated pace than anybody had expected. And, however hard it was for Craig to comprehend that, his dad's love for his wife—Craig's and Josh's mother— was literally motivating him to die. Which made Dad, in his second son's private view, an intriguing intellectual exercise. Craig's hobby for years had been psychology, at least since he'd become old enough to perceive how different his big brother was from him.

Thankfully—because of his own customary foresight— Craig had pulled some political strings and called in a few old fraternity favors. No member of his family would be living out his days in any state-run asylums! Instead, he was driving his tall, much bulkier brother to a privately operated institution where the majority of patients were afflicted with Alzheimer's disease, presenile psychosis, or were just too aged and infirm to get around without assistance. The price Craig was obliged to pay was dear, but Joshie would be tucked safely away in a discreet, unused wing of Colindale.

36

Where he'd kill nobody. Not anyone important or conspicuous, at any rate.

There was one other primary reason why Craig had closed his condo to Josh, and it was prudent. There was no way he intended to let himself be strangled or stabbed to death by a psycho whose inner demons might suddenly see Craig as the Enemy. It seemed obvious to Craig that Josh was getting nearer the edge, the springboard, with every week. It might have been all right for their parents to keep him at home despite Dr. Ben Larkin's rueful advice, especially when Joshie's condition hadn't worsened noticeably and when Dad was still watchful and strong enough to cope. Or when Mom was alive, and there were two people who truly did not want Josh climbing out on that mental springboard.

But if either of the two Addams brothers was destined to jump deeper into any shining seas of life and celebrity, it was not going to be the human anchor who had been hung around Craig's neck since before kindergarten!

There were limits. Virtually any price was worth it to avoid incidents that put blemishes on the Craig Addams's career—and dying was definitely one of them!

Besides, there was nothing wrong with how Colindale looked, its reputation, or its location. Deceptive of size, lacking any hint of spiraling staircases leading to Inquisitional attics or cells studded with glittering manacles, the institution was a well-kept one-story structure located in a once-fashionable suburb of the city. It was still a middle-class neighborhood in excellent repair. Though Josh would not be among them, elderly residents whose attention spans and vision were up to it could squint through neatly draped windows at children on the sidewalks, headed to or from grade school. And even in the new wing where Craig intended to deposit his brother, prying visitors would never discover any surgical theaters where lobotomies were performed or electroconvulsive therapy—shock treatment—was covertly performed during the dead of night. Colindale was *respectable*. It would tarnish no one's reputation.

Allowing Josh to lean much of his ungainly bulk on him—God, he smelled like he hadn't bathed in a week!—

37

Craig guided the slightly taller man up the lane to the entrance. There was only one conceivable hitch: Daniel Florry, the man who'd "agreed" to admit Joshua, was a highly curious bird who had never had any experience in dealing with severe mental illness. Florry was neither a psychiatrist nor a psychologist, and he liked to pry. He'd agreed to hire a guard for the wing, but the man wouldn't begin work at once. Most of Colindale's employees were nurses, women, and no GP was scheduled to come by for days. If Craig's estimate of Joshua's deterioration since Mom and ol' Doctor Ben died was accurate—if Josh was hearing his "voices" more than in the past and on the verge of experiencing violent urges—he was big enough to wreak a hell of a lot of havoc. Josh's one pastime was squeezing two rubber balls he toted everywhere, and his hands were hams.

But Craig had explained those things more than once and they were Dan Florry's concern after this afternoon, not his. He had paid the son of a bitch enough to do the worrying for ten men anyway!

"Could you hold the door for me?"

Craig, startled, glanced down. Just as the heavy door slammed shut behind him and Joshua, a sweet-faced old woman so thin she could not have weighed over ninety pounds wheeled her chair up to the two men. She fixed eyes as clear as a newly man-made lake upon their faces and waited.

"I'm trying to get out of here," she explained as if neither Craig nor Josh had seen an aged, wheelchair-bound person. She was humoring them, obviously. "That door is just too much for me."

Josh's walnut eyes widened behind the opaque lenses of his glasses. Bobbing his big head in enormous assent, he promptly hurled his bulk against the door, pressed it back, and finished with a Halloween pumpkin's smile. His periodic frailty had left him once more. "There you go!" he said in his customary friendly tones—the same bright accents he'd once used to tell Craig that he had destroyed all of Craig's notes for a term paper. The identically amiable voice in which he'd notified Craig that their mother wasn't alive anymore.

But by then Craig knew that his older brother adopted the accents of a mildly retarded person whenever he wished to escape correction for some senseless deed one of his damned voices commanded him to perform. Or simply to hide himself behind a dolt's image while he strove to figure something out—frequently with the exacting planning that was Craig's own. The difference was that Joshua based his reasoning on absolute fantasy, not on facts. Whatever he was planning might very well cause irreparable harm. He'd gotten by with that smile-faced, little-boy act all of their mother's life and it was a sound bet that Josh would wind up their father's life in the same fashion. Which galled Craig Addams badly, because brother dear was a psycho—not an idiot. And he was cunning as a trapped bear.

Maybe he hadn't managed to graduate even from grade school, but Josh Addams's IQ was as normal as their dead mother's apple pie. Not spectacular, but normal.

"Thank you, dear," the old lady with the watery eyes said as she started past the beaming Josh and through the carefully opened door.

"Hold it," a man's voice called. "Don't let Mrs. Lockerbee out—please!"

Craig saw administrator Dan Florry, the frat friend who'd agreed to his brother coming to live at Colindale, rushing toward them, wigwagging his arms above his head.

Promptly, Josh began shoving Mrs. Lockerbee and her wheelchair out onto the sidewalk. Both of them, Craig noted, were grinning hugely.

It took the concerted efforts of Florry, Craig Addams, and a woman nurse to recapture the old lady and wheel her back inside, Josh doing his shame-faced act for his brother and the benefit of the administrator. Craig glared at Josh once, then ignored him. The elder Addams might "hear" a voice commanding him to do anything at all but he never ran away.

"You sons of *bitches*," Mrs. Lockerbee spat with great clarity. The nurse, a black woman with a name tag that read GLORIA, was wrestling the wheelchair around to face a different way. "Bastards!"

Dan Florry gave her a sidelong glance and added a smile

that was pure public relations. Even when he and Craig were fraternity brothers up East, Dan had borne a proximate resemblance to Senator Ted Kennedy. Now in his forties with distinguished gray at the temples and a paunch even his three-piece suit couldn't conceal, the resemblance was stronger—except that Florry stood several inches under six feet. "Mrs. Lockerbee is one of our perpetual escapees," he said, offering a plump hand. "They prey mercilessly on visitors to open the door, help them make their getaways."

"You mean," Craig said in surprise, "there are more like her here?"

"Oh yes." Florry straightened a natty silk tie. "Mrs. Lockerbee is the ringleader."

"You son of a bitch!" the woman with the blue eyes shouted as Gloria, the picture of nonchalance and cool, pushed her up a long hallway. "Eat shit! *Eat shit!*"

"I'd have thought," Craig said carefully, "that people like Mrs. Lockerbee would be . . . well, confined." He shifted his gaze toward Josh. "It's important for my brother simply to be left alone, undisturbed."

"We keep better track of them than you think," Florry said. He motioned for the brothers to follow. Then he led them into a different corridor. "They start out in what we call Skilled where nurses like Gloria must check regularly on their whereabouts, then collect them before they succeed in breaking out." He showed pearly teeth. "It takes hours for some of them to reach an exit because of their wheelchairs, so we've never yet failed to bring 'em back alive."

"All that way for nothing," Joshua said. "That's sad."

The administrator hesitated in the corridor to size up his new patient as if noticing Josh for the first time. It was an old trick of Dan's, Craig knew. Sane or insane, somebody meeting Florry was first impressed by how busy he was, second by the statesmanlike crinkled eyes and thin-lipped, crooked smile. "You must be Joshua, Craig's brother."

"Yes," Josh agreed with a nod, "I must be." He stared down at Florry's extended hand for a moment before taking just the fingertips with utmost caution.

40

"I guess you'll be staying with us for a while." Dan's smile obstinately spread.

"Yes, I must be," Josh said, squeezing Florry's fingers together with considerable pressure. And that, Craig knew, was an old trick of his brother's. "I must stay forever."

"Josh," Craig said quickly, taking hold of a shoulder that was only an inch higher than his own but twice its size, turning Josh so that he'd release his clutch on Dan Florry's fingers, "that's not what Dad and I said. We explained that you'll have to stay here only until Dad is better."

"I know that's what you and Dad told me." Josh continued at his somewhat limping stride up the hallway, unaided. "But that isn't what *they* say."

Craig saw Florry's brows raise. He looked around inquisitively, then hurried after Josh. "What are 'they,' Mr. Addams? Can we discuss them?"

"Dan," Craig hissed, "that's not necessary." The arrangements he had made with Florry and Colindale were for his brother to be housed and fed, to get his standard medication and all the attention needed for his personal care.

Since Dr. Larkin's accidental death around the time of Mom's passing, Josh had received no additional counseling. There had been no change in his medication. Dan Florry didn't know the history, and he didn't need to know it. Doctor Ben had explained decades ago that Joshua was incurable. After Dad's terminal illness began, Craig had convinced him that nothing was to be gained by constantly plaguing Josh with tests or by running up more bills. Aunt Dorothy had imagined that Craig was trying to save Dad's money for himself, but there wasn't a word of truth in it.

Because Craig was a success and Dad didn't have a dime left. It was merely common sense not to throw good money after bad. Josh was a lost cause. It was that simple.

"I'd like to get some idea of what I'm dealing with," Florry whispered hastily. Josh was still lurching up the hall alone, ignoring Dan's question as if it weren't worth the consideration. "If I'm going to help him—"

"You aren't." Craig drew himself erect, clasping his hands before him in a posture his juries had frequently seen. "Let

41

me be clear: You have nothing to 'deal with' where Josh is concerned, nothing. You're to leave him alone."

"Nothing?" Florry said. "Craig, that's your brother."

"I know," Craig continued, "and I know much more about the human mind than you do." He saw the startled expression on Florry's Kennedyesque face and nodded. "I don't mean that derogatorily, I mean it as a fact. Everything that could be done for Josh was done years in the past. I really don't want you going near him."

"How dare you!" Florry flounced from foot to foot. "This is an institution for people who need help—"

"It's a standard old folks' home, Daniel, and you're not a doctor. You're an administrator." Craig patted his forearm. "I know the law. It's illegal for you to 'deal with' your residents remedially. Josh is here to live out his life; nothing more."

The color in Florry's face deepened. "It was I who permitted your brother to be admitted." He spoke tightly. "And just because we pledged together in college. Let me remind you that you have no medical credentials either." His pudgy jaw tightened. "I could arrange for your brother's instant release. Are you aware of that?"

"I'm sure you could," Craig said. Outwardly detached, he trailed after his brother's dwindling figure. "But that wouldn't erase the evidence of our transaction—which I keep in the safe in my office. There's a bit more to it than old school ties." Jogging lightly, he saw that Dan was keeping pace. "There are the Colindale forms we both signed, my canceled check . . . with your signature."

"I don't see why you're taking this tack." Florry peered narrowly at his old acquaintance. "You know, Addams, I'm damned if I see any sign on your part of strong feelings for Josh. Now that I think about it, you were always a cold bastard."

A tic appeared at Craig's temple. He rarely lost his temper but the son of a bitch was practically asking Craig why he'd brought Josh there or what he hoped to get out of it. Not that that would matter once Josh was actually in his rooms; not after tonight. "Dan, Dr. Larkin signed my brother's commitment papers years ago. Just last week our father also signed them." Joshua looked tired, drained, as they caught up. "Now that Dad is dying, I have Josh's power of attorney. I've done nothing remotely illegal."

Abruptly, Florry stopped walking. "What sort of man are you?" he asked softly.

"The rare kind," Craig answered, taking Josh's arm. "Who lives life without wasting sentiment, knows what he wants and goes after it—legally. Dan, don't try to dope out my motives. You don't have a good enough background in psychology for that."

Pleased with his own performance while he longed to slaughter this interfering poseur of a man where he stood, gaping, Craig smiled coolly and helped his brother locate his suite in the plain but immaculate new wing of the institution.

Nobody had ever understood his views on Josh, apart from Josh himself. Those views, that honesty, were the only things they shared in common except for their terminally ill father. It was all they had between them. It had been enough until tonight. It would be for another few hours.

Joshua's quarters—a small front room partitioned from a bedroom with a bed, chest of drawers and a TV, plus a miniature bathroom with a wash basin and shower facilities— were in readiness. Spartan but adequate, new and livable. Remembering the handful of good times he'd shared with the older man, Craig elected to spend a few minutes in private with Josh. He even gave thought to telling Joshie what he meant to do after leaving Colindale.

But the tall and muscular Josh was feeling wan. His periods of animation inevitably fled without warning, just as all his other phases began suddenly, electrically. Leaving on the topcoat Mom had bought for him some years back, Josh was clambering up on the neatly made bed, lying flat on his back and working two red rubber balls between his strong, startlingly nimble fingers. Noiselessly, turning, turning. With the coat and a new pair of brown shoes Craig

43

had brought him just that day, Josh resembled a mammoth child who'd been sent to his room. Or a construct, the batteries for which had run down.

More than a decade ago Craig had wondered if Josh's condition might not be further complicated by manic-depressive tendencies or, if not that, something like catatonia. He was sometimes cheerful and cooperative in doing something but he was often dejected. He ranged from excitability and madness to extended periods when he was almost as inactive, as inert, as a person sunk deep into a catatonic state.

Craig had broached his curiosity to Larkin, Josh had been in earshot and sighed, "Wouldn't you guys get blue if you were crazy and sort of knew it? Wouldn't you get extra-special happy when things were okay a while and you didn't think anyone was going to kill you?"

Ben, a fool all his life, had agreed, sided with the psycho. He had sworn that Joshua sometimes exhibited greater perception or clarity of thought, more "uncluttered penetration" than others. And yet Josh went on lapsing into his phases, listening to his damned voices reminding him that "some folks aren't nice, and they *kill* people, they really do." When he had looked so much older than Craig during their teens, that had bothered the younger brother more than he'd ever let on. But Ben-the-incompetent went on promising them, "We'll get a handle on all this someday."

Wrong again. No one had ever attached a handle to Josh or Craig Addams. It occurred to the latter as he waited for Joshua to say something that Doctor Ben's death hadn't occurred too soon for any of his patients.

"I'm leaving now." He rose, deciding things were okay. Fine. "Do what the fools in this place say to do and you'll be . . . just fine."

"That's true, yes." Joshua wasn't looking at him.

"Just ignore Florry. He'd never understand."

"I will." Then Josh fell silent for a time. His stare, Craig observed, was centered on the drawn curtains. "Did you know there are bars behind those drapes? Isn't that a fine idea, Creggie? 'Cause no one can come get me, with bars there—except people already *inside* this place."

44

"That's true too, Josh," Craig said, lifting a brow. He tried not to ask the question leaping to mind but hesitated near the door, unable to prevent himself from posing it. "You got into bed almost immediately after we entered this room," he said. "You haven't looked behind the drapes."

"There you go," Josh said noncommittally.

"Then," Craig continued, "how do you know bars are behind the curtains?"

Josh didn't reply at once. His expression, if anything, went momentarily more blank. "You don't want to know, Creggie," he murmured finally.

Do I? Craig wondered. "Yes, I *do*," he said aloud.

"No, not really." Josh closed his eyes, turned them into slits. He held his long arms over his prone body and the rubber balls in his fingers looked squeezed flat.

"Damn it, Joshua," Craig swore, his own hands working, "I *do* want to know."

"They," said Josh. His big head bobbed ponderously. Then he centered his gaze on the acoustical tile ceiling as though other information might be divulged from that source if he concentrated hard enough. "*They* said." At last, he turned his head to peer at Craig. "And I know I'll be real fine here because it's quiet. I can hear what the voices say better when it's really quiet." There was spittle clinging just under his lower lip but he was smiling. "They'll tell me lots of secrets now, Creggie."

"Goodbye, Josh," his brother said, and left.

He can't hear shit *from them! And there isn't any* 'them' *anyway*, Craig thought as he headed back down the long hallway. His feet informed him when he had moved onto different, older carpeting that he was back in the older part of Colindale. All anybody like Josh imagined he heard at first was a deep, thunderlike rumble. That was what all the literature claimed. *It's what every psycho hears*, Craig reminded himself. Then it got louder, happened with greater frequency until the psychos themselves filled in insane, often murderous messages. *There's nothing for him to discover, to learn*, Craig thought, walking more rapidly. There were no secrets he was going to find out; none.

An old woman—another dotty old lady—was perched in

a wheelchair at the front door of the institution. It was almost night now and her hands were folded in her lap in a waiting posture and there was no sound coming from the residential street. The chair fitted her perfectly, like aluminum clothing. It seemed molded to the contours of her thin form.

"Sir," she beckoned Craig, haltingly. "Would you mind terribly holding the door for me? I just can't get through that heavy door in my wheelchair."

Craig glanced down. She had no shoes on her twig-like feet and her veins ran blue like streams that were drying up. Outside Colindale it was autumn, drizzling rain. He would have adored to help her but it was too risky.

"Eat shit," he said and barged through the door.

Pop dwelt in the same frame house he'd occupied when Mom died. It was a shell over a pea but nobody was playing a game, making a gamble, except Craig.

Driving along Winthrop was like slipping into a distantly remembered hallway, half expecting to find oneself at the end. It was like narrowing down into a world that both continued to exist in some inexplicable, rudimentary way, as corpses in graves existed and might periodically twitch without notice, and did not exist at all. *Memory lane, but it's straight down*, Craig thought, spotting the familiar house.

The ghost inside, however, wouldn't be his. The ghost Craig saw every time he entered the house was that of Josh Addams.

He'd haunted it long before Craig picked him out of the shell and put him into the nuthouse.

Trotting up the front steps to the porch, Craig noticed for the first time, six weeks after summer's death, a remnant of Mom's flower bed. It was bickering with untrimmed grass and weeds as if she'd been reincarnated among the dismal stems. To be close to Josh and their father. She'd loved them both, Craig realized, with the inex-

46

pressible fury of frustration at Dad giving her such sons— but God knew she had *tried* expressing it, tried harder than he'd ever seen anybody else try anything. To transfer her disappointment, transform it into real feeling for Joshua, and Dad.

He'd sensed that she knew shortly after his own infancy that it was fruitless to waste her emotions on him.

Now he yearned to dig Dad's unpowered ancient mower from his cluttered garage and mow down everything on Winthrop Avenue. Climbing the crumbling steps, he could almost imagine that the half-dead growths were fawning in apology against his ankles, waiting for him to pause so they might inject their needling poisons. But he couldn't really imagine it because he was virtually incapable of imagining anything—unless it was a soundly workable plan for a wholly reachable, pragmatic goal. Even psychology books did not tell him whether that was just a fault of his DNA— his special genetic makeup—or if it was logical to place part of the blame on Mom.

"Don't leave the door open," Dad said when he'd squinted up at Craig, recognized him. He turned and withdrew into the slowly splitting shell of a house on the brown paper slippers he'd always preferred. He was much shorter than Craig this evening. "It's done, isn't it?"

Craig, just inside the door, held back. He hadn't closed the door. "Josh is ensconced safely. It's taken care of." He realized that the tic that began when he was leaving Josh, and Colindale, hadn't subsided and it was working away hectically in one temple, adding a sense of agitation. Craig loathed being agitated. It made him doubt himself. It might cause mistakes of judgment. "You'd like it there. It's quiet, like here; Joshua mentioned that himself." *Don't thank me, then, for doing what you've lacked the guts to do for thirty-five years.*

"Oh?" The old man was about to lower himself into his chair, the one he'd sat in as long as Craig was able to remember. He was staring across the tiny front room with a belated expression of relief. Dad had never been quick, but his brain was sodden now—with memories an honest fool would have been glad to leave behind. He certainly wasn't going to leave anything else. "That's good."

"Better!" Craig inched forward, pulling the door partway to. He smiled. "It's a *fine* idea I had, Dad. Fine!"

Josh's phrase. The old man shoved tears into his eyes from some forgotten well, apparently touched. Then he dropped with a plop into the chair, his chair, and cleared his throat. Momentarily devoid of expression, he made Craig picture Joshua's blank face and reminded him of how near death Dad was. "If you say so, Craig." Almost inaudibly. They were the same words he'd uttered with such mindless monotony to Mom and Aunt Dorothy and Doctor Ben. Now, though, Dad was reaching a finite point with each of his dreary recollections dragged from his senseless existence. With every neurotic tear, every banal remark, it could be the last. This was the one time Craig had found his father a subject of interest, and it was amusing to perceive that it was because he saw Dad as a kind of cistern. One that had contained only so much murky liquid, after all; and now it was finally being emptied.

"I do say so," Craig responded with a nod. "And I said so many years back when you and my mother were wasting your time and money on Larkin—on behalf of a psychotic who was always in everyone's way, even his own. Did you know, my father, that I began to study psychology not to find ways of coping with Joshua but because I hoped to learn why you and my mother found him so much more interesting than I? Can you recall the good grades I brought home to you—how I eschewed all friendship, required nothing but my studies and my hobby of psychology?"

Dad struggled forward in his chair. "I'd rather you wouldn't talk about your big brother that way, Creggie."

"Did you know, Daddy, that I chose a career in law after discovering certain facts about myself—facts that were beyond wonderful Doctor Ben?" He kept his laugh level. "Why, neither you nor Mom even *asked* why a boy who was fascinated by psychology would enter the law instead!"

"Do close the door all the way, son," Dad said. He gestured feebly, soothingly, for Craig to sit beside him. Craig

48

remained standing. "We were always proud of you, Creggie. I—"

"No."

"We *were*," Dad nodded firmly. "But surely you understood that—"

"Oh, *yes!*"

Startled, the elder Addams looked up fast. His son was leaning over him, the axe-blade nose pressed close. Craig's long fingers supported his thin frame on the chair arms.

"Yes, Dad, I *understood*—that you and my mother discussed *both* your sons behind closed doors, at night. That Mom sensed something might be wrong with me, too, and you always *agreed* with anything she said. Josh and I were *listening* at that door, our father, kneeling on the floor outside your room while I held my hand over his mouth so he wouldn't hear his damn voices and spoil it—spill his guts about the fact that *both* Josh and I wanted to kill you and Mom but just didn't know where we'd *live* after that!" Abruptly, he clutched his father by the jaw, lifted it to make sure Dad was staring straight into his clear, dry eyes. "*You* said maybe I *was* crazy, too, but *differently*—that since I had control of myself, I might turn out all right!"

"But Mom and I found out we were wrong, son," Dad argued,—"about you being crazy. Doctor Ben kept seein' both of you boys and he said you definitely weren't a psycho." He swallowed with difficulty. "Only reason I ever wondered about you was 'cause you didn't have no playmates 'cept Joshie, and you never laughed or cried . . . you didn't want to be picked up and hugged, you didn't *need* us." His eyelids batted. "But you were always awful good t'your brother. Always, Creggie."

"I certainly was. Yes." Nodding, Craig released Dad, straightened. "Always." He smiled. "He was so convenient . . ."

The old man had relaxed minimally but that remark kept him leaning forward. Craig saw the imprint of his fingertips in the sallow cheeks. "What does that mean, Craig? 'Convenient'?"

He gave a shrug, half turned toward an array of family

49

photographs on the mantel. Three with Josh and he together, young. Four shots of Joshie, alone. One of Craig on graduation day from college. He wasn't counting the pictures. He had known how many of each of them had been placed there for years.

"Remember that cat ol' Josh got the blame for when he was nine and I was six?" He kept his inflections casual. "Our dog—remember Shadow, Dad? I was nine, Joshie was twelve." He saw an expression take shape in Dad's face that he liked. In the past, it had been there only when his older brother's latest act of minor savagery was reported. "I had the idea for those. Not Josh, our father." It was really sinking in to Dad now. "Actually, I didn't kill anything that personally affected you or Mom for a long while. There was no reason. Josh enjoyed it so much, and I liked watching him do it. It made us close." Craig chuckled. "When Doctor Ben got around to talking with Josh about those things, he always said his 'voices' commanded him to kill. And he really believed it, Dad." Craig rested his doubled fists on his hips, grinning. "For a long time it was a giggle. Being one of Joshua's voices."

"You *suggested* he do those awful things . . . that your poor brother should *kill*?"

Craig, bobbing his head hugely, gave him a perfect imitation of Josh.

Dad pointed. "Your mother's parakeet, Happy. It got strangled, left on the bottom of its cage." He was leading up to a question, finally got it out: "You?"

Craig bowed. *"Moi."*

The old man was a piece of chalk with moving lips. "Our second Sh-Shadow . . . old Shad—he died last year, run over by a car." He twisted his head in a horror of disbelief. "You loved him too, I thought. Surely, you didn't . . . ?"

Craig felt his grin slip away. "I didn't love the mutt but I didn't kill him either." He forced his lips to turn up at the corners. "I was giving Josh a ride so I let him take the wheel. For Shad."

Then Craig *leaped* at Dad. The weight of his body thrust the old man and his chair back, almost over. Craig caught, supported both, kept them from going the rest of the way. There was no carpeting in front of the mantel. Conspiratorial of manner, he leaned toward his father's frightened face. "Ask me about *more* of them," he urged. His voice would not have been audible even as far away as the front door.

"But there aren't any more," Dad whispered. He shrank away from the hot breath, his eyes wide. "We didn't have no other pets."

"Well, then," Craig pressed, "ask me about more deaths . . . in the family."

Momentarily, Dad ceased to breathe.

"No, wait." Craig let go of the tilting chair with his left hand, allowed it to tip itself, shaking, onto the remaining leg. "Why not start *outside* the family? But not with pets; with people."

Dad gasped. "Are you sayin' you just talked Joshie into those things? And he's not really . . . crazy? But *you are*, after all?"

Fireworks—for an instant—exploded before Craig's vision. He said tensely, "*No*, Daddy," and made himself return his hand to the chair, bring it forward until it was almost righted. A sigh. "You don't win the dream of a lifetime. Your Joshie is mad as a hatter, and I—I am certainly *not* a psycho. That's one of the few facts in this world that Ben Larkin got right." A skyrocket soared in front of his eyes and he let himself go as if he had been detonated. Craig pushed the chair, hard. Watched. Liked. "I *killed* Doctor Ben, our father! He didn't make a mistake in the number of pills he took, like everybody thought—Daddy, he had *help!*"

The chair, spinning as if Dad had given it life over the years, threw him from it. He was stunned by much more than the fall when he did not try to sit, or rise. Physically, he might have. He just looked at his second son, appalled. Terror began.

Craig watched him with a solid start on an erection, on full arousal. He wasn't shocked by it. Seeing Josh take life and then taking it directly, himself, had been a regular charge. Just about the only thing that had ever excited Craig. But this was Dad, father-the-authority-figure—even if it was hard to believe, seeing the skinny wreck sprawled on his own living room floor—and Craig had never felt so charged. Splotches of red warred with liver spots up and down Dad's limbs—he was a checkerboard! Anytime now he'd beg for Craig to hold the door for him, and the answer to that was obvious!

"Larkin told you you shouldn't keep Josh at home, but he felt sorry for him. Like you, like my mother." Between two fingers Craig raised the framed photo depicting his own young face. He wore a mortar board in the picture and clearly remembered how that moment should have established for everyone who the superior Addams was, that it was the fully functioning son who deserved attention, praise. And never got it. Raising the photograph to shoulder level, he let it drop.

There was a tinkling sound as the glass shattered. Then Craig peered back at Dad, who had followed the procedure with his eyes and understood. "Josh was going to be committed—and then my mother fell ill. Remember? So good Doctor Ben asked you to wait, even talked *me* into coming back to stay until she died. So"—he emitted a consciously pitiable sigh—"I came."

Dad stared at him, hard. "Why?"

"Well, hell, it would have really looked bad if I hadn't, right?" Craig picked up his brother's earliest framed picture, carefully. "I stayed here like a good boy, watching Mom get sicker and sicker, making sure Joshie went to the toilet and washed up afterward." Stooping, he rested the photograph of Josh on the rug, an arm's length from Dad, as though it had slipped from his hand. *Identification*, he thought. "But you didn't give a damn about anything but that frustrated tyrant, that hypocritical old bitch who talked behind our backs. You never even *thanked* me for being here."

"Don't you talk like that about my wife," Dad said and groped for Craig's ankles.

And he was like the weeded remnant of flowers rising

from the ground around the front steps to cling and infect Craig with toxins from a past he hadn't understood—despite the times he'd tried, wanted to feel the same things others felt. Now it was too late. His cancer-riddled father was there to be mowed down. Fertile land had to be cleared for Craig to have a chance.

"Listen, Daddy." He stared down with his heart thumping but did nothing to make the old man release his legs. "Are you listening?" He saw a tear-filled eye glance up the length of his body. "*I* returned home because Larkin signed the papers for Josh. It was a deal, a trade. Then it became obvious that I couldn't let my career simply go down the tubes, and that's when I made him take those extra pills."

"We both knew there was something wrong with you," Dad said accusingly.

"Dad, I killed him for all the crazies like Josh who were being held back by stupid family feelings, by useless sentiment. It made sense!"

Dad relinquished his hold on Craig's ankles, tried to get to his knees. It was clear that he was eager to move away from his younger son. "You disgusting psycho," he said.

"*No!*" Putting his smile in place, shaking his head sadly, Craig thrust out a hand to his father. "How many times must I explain, Dad? A psychopath can't tell the difference between reality and fantasy." Dad crawled one foot from the down-thrust arm. "I always know the difference, I'm *always* on the side of what's *real*—solid and true! I *know* it when I lie. I *know* it when I have to hurt someone—and when I kill, Daddy, I *explain* why I'm doing it. If there's time." He caught up with the old man. Smiling crookedly, he reached out to assist Dad to his knees. "Of course, sometimes I murder someone because it's fun, but not usually."

"Is *that* why you killed that nice old doctor?" Dad asked, peering into his face.

"No . . ." Craig replied. He shook his head thoughtfully. It was nice, fine, finally having a chat with his father. "I wanted to kill him for years. But I did it for entirely sound reasons. Once you signed the papers, too, I planned to prevent Josh from being a nuisance any longer. To put him

53

where no one would believe him if he discussed our good times. But Mom got ill, Larkin interfered. Dad, he was starting to learn about—people like me. So that was a rational murder, believe me."

"You're heartless." Shuddering, Dad's gaze scanned the room. The front door remained ajar but this wasn't a nice neighborhood any more and mostly shouts and screams were ignored. Both of them knew that. He looked back at Craig, steadily. "I'm afraid you have no soul, Creggie."

That surprised Craig, intrigued him as did all things pertaining to him. "I don't know, Dad. Maybe not." He was steadying the kneeling father by the arms. "Perhaps I *had* one, or a part of a soul, until I took Doctor Ben's life. After that even, maybe." He put his head forward to search for his father's eyes. "Obviously, I came here to kill you tonight and put the blame on Josh. You're a nuisance now, too—that's a *fact*, don't try to deny it! And I'm too busy to wait until you die. Now, murdering one's own dad would definitely cost anyone his soul." He gave his father a blazing smile. "In reality, though, I doubt that I've had a soul to lose since the night when I put a pillow over my mother's face and killed her."

The old mouth shaped a circle that could have been the start of a gasp or a shriek or even an anticipation of the perpetual pain it represented.

Having said all he meant to say, Craig turned the face's circle into a jagged line. The exacting arc of his swinging leg ended with his heel striking Dad's chin with immense precision and power. It lifted Dad almost to his full height, then shot him back against the mantel.

When the body sagged limply to the floor, Craig was there. He stomped the sick face with the same foot, over and over. As if giving vent to a madman's tantrum. When stickiness coated the sole of Joshua Addams's shoe and the whole exercise was becoming exhausting, Craig leapt up and down on the dead face with both feet till it could not have been recognized—not that that was part of the plan.

Autumn silence seeped through the house like last breaths escaping. Winded but openly enjoying the unique

54

relief that the enactment of each step of a plan provided, Craig removed his brother's shoes, left them where they lay. It took a few seconds to get a pair of his own from the closet in the room where he'd stayed during Mom's final illness, another few to put them on.

He hoped Josh somehow knew about it. Almost laughing, he went to their father's phone to dial Daniel Florry at his home. This would be the last time in any way that he and Josh participated in anything. The relationship was the only one that had brought Craig Addams fulfillment of any kind. It had seemed honest, devoid of social pretense. Purposeful. With no love lost.

Getting the Colindale administrator to meet him there immediately was no more than a question of bluff, lie, and threat—valuable and easily wielded tools throughout Craig's life. More than a few pretty women had caved in before them, if not exactly lived to rue the day. Lightly suggesting that Florry let him into Colindale through a fire exit close to the new wing was a nice touch that enhanced the likelihood of nobody important seeing him there. If they did, he'd take their lives.

Phone back in cradle and car gloves back in pocket, Craig went to the front door, stood in the doorway to appraise matters. Josh's undamaged snapshot rested just out of their father's reach while Craig's own photo, the frame bent, lay in broken glass. Very fine. A psychotic clearly had heard he was to be removed from the house the next day, imagining his father was siding with his younger brother (of all things!) and he'd felt resistive, vengeful. Neighbors might say it was a good thing Craig hadn't been there too, a *fine* thing.

Grinning, Craig pieced it together. A senile old lady, a preoccupied and busy nurse, Dad, and Daniel Florry—they were those who'd known Josh came to Colindale that day. No one else. Tomorrow, two bodies would draw gasps of horror. If Aunt Dorothy or a neighbor happened upon Dad, Joshua would be missing and the only suspect. If a Colindale employee found Florry first, they'd either assume an Alzheimer's patient had flipped out or, if anyone recalled noticing Joshie there, that he had killed Dan during a "phase"—then gone home to revenge himself upon Dad for committing him! Craig would reluctantly have to seek police protection from a psycho who might be wandering around anywhere, out to kill him too!

It was perfection. Except that Dan Florry wasn't yet dead. Craig vaulted the porch steps to evade the rising weeds. Invisible by night, he slid into his BMW, started the quiet engine. The *last* time for him and Josh. Too bad. Not wrenching, not heartbreaking, not anything he couldn't cope with easily, but too bad.

Well, he would just have to go on alone the best he could.

Florid, irate, a brisk Dan Florry led the way to his office. No one else was in sight just on the fringes of the new wing; Florry was divorced, lived alone. Stepping into his office, he wondered what conceivably could not wait until morning.

At the moment Dan turned toward the light switch, Craig showed him: dying. A mallet from the trunk of the BMW squished with a melon sound against his head. Before Florry collapsed to the office floor, Craig had decided not to remove the car gloves he had again donned. A brand-new idea was just taking shape . . .

If he left the gloves on and took the mallet to Josh's rooms, he could get his brother's fingerprints on it. Then he'd steal one of ol' Joshie's rubber balls, take it back to the office, too, and let it roll into a corner—to be discovered, along with the mallet! It made the double-screen better, established a can't-fail setup!

He flipped off the lights and closed Daniel's door without locking it, then passed without haste, humming, into the new wing. Pad-pad on the fine new rug. Dan had died second, after Dad, but that wasn't important. A mere thirty-six minutes separated them and few coroners were able to determine the moment of death that closely. And if one did, so what? It would merely mean that Josh killed Dad before Craig—who would say he'd been waiting in the car to drive his brother to Colindale! He grinned. He was ready to swear to that with ... well, with all his heart and his soul. The owners of the institution would be happy to refund all the money he had paid for poor Joshie's care, but Craig might sue anyway—just because he could!

The short distance to where he'd left Joshua was covered without a sign of interference, and then he was letting himself into his big brother's room, noiselessly.

Surprisingly, the lights were on, Josh was awake and he was reclining on his still-made bed, naked except for the topcoat his mother once gave him. Unselfconscious, he did not close the coat over him. He'd put one of his rubber balls into his mouth and tucked it thoughtfully into one cheek. It gave his face a grotesque deformed look. He glanced at Craig with no more startlement than if the younger brother had stepped out into the hall seconds ago.

The other small red ball was cupped by Joshua's concave navel. He had thrust his immense hands into his shoes— one each—and he was walking them restlessly in the air above him. The hands stopped moving when Josh recognized Craig. "Hi, Creggie," he mumbled, then spat out the ball. "Where you been?"

Craig smiled, approached the bed. "You knew I was going home almost two hours ago. You can drop the little-boy-retardo act, Josh."

"Okay." The pleasant expression vanished. With it went the sole impression of near sanity he was able to convey to Craig. It wasn't so much that Joshua appeared mad. He was simply the only human being Craig had seen anywhere but in a mirror who was capable of allowing any emotions whatever to cross his long-jawed face unhindered by guile. The expression showing on his face now was a free-floating mixture of mild hope, irritability, overt cunning, and secret-keeping. It was as if Josh could make his flesh dissolve into a watercolor wash. "There you go." He paused. "It's been quiet in my room. Very, very, very quiet."

Craig looked down with mild curiosity. "Does that mean you've decided you like it here?"

"I hate the son-of-a-bitching place," Josh said. There was a flicker of passion, no more. He kept staring at the air-walking shoes but turned red to his shoulders. "I hate the sons of a bitches who made me go here and the son of a bitch who wouldn't let the old lady leave."

Craig gave him a genuine chuckle. "Well, that son of a bitch is dead."

"Good." No surprise, nothing there but an instant's exposed satisfaction.

"I thought this would be a fine place after you said you'd be able to hear your voices better." Heel marks, muddy ones, were on the blanket and part of the top sheet from where Joshie had marched the shoes. "Were you wrong about that?"

"I was not, I was not wrong!" A hot glance. His glasses were crooked on his nose and the lenses were fogging up. "They told me things, all right."

"Okay." As casually as he could, Craig stooped to pick up the ball Josh had kept in his mouth, examined it as if he planned to return it. Holding it made him think of toys belonging to Shadow and Shad, their dogs. It was revolting to the touch. "Anything I should know about?"

"Nothing you don't know about *already*, man, man, man!" The hurt, hot stare was back and it held.

All psychos "hear" are rumblings, nothing else, Craig told himself. He *can't* know about Dad and he never found out about Larkin or our mother. "Well, I'll tell you something your voices don't know, Joshie," Craig said when he could do so without his own voice quavering.

"What's that?" The paranoid suspicion was nude, bare-ass, hostile.

Craig waved his hand. "Put your shoes on. I'm taking you home."

The ever-moist long lashes behind the fogged lenses blinked. The eyes themselves went blank. Craig sighed, reached in his hip pocket for the mallet. Josh was "listening" now to someone else, or believed he was. For the first time it occurred to Craig to wonder if his brother's brain invented faces to go with the voices.

Josh squeezed his eyelids shut. "I don't think so . . ."

Craig gasped. How literal was Joshua's doubt? "Well, why

58

not?" he demanded. To no comment. "Did a voice tell you not to go with me?" The eyelids popped back; he bobbed his big head. "Well, who then? *Who* told you not to go with your brother, your only buddy?" It was getting hot in the damned place. "Does he have a name?"

Josh nodded again. "Doctor Ben told me," he said.

Craig's jaw fell open. "Ben Larkin is dead, dammit, Joshie."

"Maybe," Josh said. "But you can't be sure of that." He threw out his hand, dropping one shoe, and snatched the rubber ball from his younger brother's fingers. The ball in his navel rolled under the covers. "You don't know for sure, man, man, man."

"Yes, I can, I *do*," Craig argued, his own gloved fingers working.

"Well, how?" Josh demanded. "How can you be so son-of-a-bitching sure?"

Craig shouted, "Because *I killed him*, Josh!"

Then he held his breath, wishing it was the words he'd just spoken.

A timeless instant passed. "Oh," Josh said at length and pointed. "Why are you wearing your gloves?"

Just then, Craig couldn't remember. He shook his head, removed the shoe from Josh's right hand and gave both of them to him. "Put these on, we're getting out of here."

"But they're not *my* shoes." Joshua took off his glasses, scrubbed at a lens with a corner of his sheet. He was near tears. "Not my nice brown ones, Creggie." He squinted at Craig. "Where did these come from?"

"Don't you remember? I bought them this morning for you." Drenched in sweat, he fell to one knee at the side of the bed and began trying to cram the new shoes on his brother's feet. The mallet in his pocket fell out, rolled under the bed unnoticed. "Since you know now that Doctor Ben is dead—for a fact—and you're not superstitious, you can go with me. Right?"

"No." Josh doubled up his toes, replaced his glasses. The lenses and Joshua's eyes were fairly clear now. "Mom says I shouldn't."

Craig's heart skipped two beats. "Mom . . . Mom is dead too." Perspiration was running down his large nose and into his eyes. Winking, his hands trembling, he pressed the toes of Josh's right foot down and strove to wedge them into a shoe. The toes popped up, the foot wouldn't go, Josh was too strong for him. Joshie was his older, bigger bro, he was stronger than anybody else when he got like this, and he was driving Craig crazy. He bit his lower lip. "You know Mom's dead, Joshie—like that son of a bitch Larkin. Dead, buried, sending no messages to anyone." In his mind's eye he saw himself jumping porch steps and weed-strewn flowers. "Your mother is six feet under, pushing up daisies, and she will never *ever* look at me again the way she did when—" He bit his lower lip through. "She isn't talking, Joshie, Josh. No way."

"That's true," big brother countered swiftly. "But *Daddy* is!"

One foot went all the way into the shoe! "He's dead too, Joshie. Neither of them can be a voice in your head, because they're both—"

Joshua Addams was peering intently into his eyes when Craig glanced up to see if he had been heard and understood.

He had. "Did you take life out of them both, Creggie?" The brother's voice was low-pitched and level, soft and gentle. "Mom back then and Daddy today?"

"*Don't* come with me then!" Craig said, slipping his kneeling foot out in preparation for leaving. Fast. "Just stay here and—"

Huge hands and arms made powerful because of a single-minded preoccupation with two rubber balls embraced Craig and pulled him forward until he was close enough to experience the pain of a dislocated shoulder and to see Joshie was crying. Freely, the tears flooding his glasses and spattering on Craig's frightened face. "I didn't really hear any voices just now, Creggie," he confessed, sobbing. "I haven't heard a single one since you brought me here." He hugged Craig hard. "I just didn't want you t'go *home*, Creggie, I didn't want you to *leave!*"

60

Joshie's emotion was nearly as overpowering to Craig as the uncontrollable hug around his neck. He tried to speak or to break the hold but only succeeded in joining his big brother with his face shoved into a pillow. His mumble could not be heard over Joshie's sobbing convulsion.

"It's fine about Dad and Mom," he said, forgiving Craig as he fumbled under the covers with one hand. "Even if you didn't let me help you like you did before. But see, I get real lonely when I don't have one of my phases, Creggie"—he raised Craig's face briefly from the pillow—" 'cause they're the only friends I got, other than you."

Finding the red rubber ball with his groping free hand, Joshie jammed it between Craig's choking lips. Then he shoved him back into the pillow, and leaned on him for hours.

It was a fine idea Joshie had had even if Creggie didn't say so.

But later in the night, when he was putting on his other new shoe to make Creggie happy, Josh was sure he'd done the right thing.

Doctor Ben, and Mom, and Dad, they all said so.

Before morning, Creggie said so too.

Confession of
a Madman

Chelsea Quinn Yarbro

I n the name of the Father, Son and Holy Spirit, Amen.

I, Brother Luccio, at the behest of the Prior of this monastery, have recorded the Confession of the lunatic known as Brother Rat, though he has said he was once known as Bertoldo Cimoneisi and was an apothecary by trade; the records of the monastery show no such name or calling among the entries, but it may be that this is truly his name and his profession, for he spoke it under the Seal of Confession. Then again, it may be more of his madness.

Brother Rat has been confined here for sixteen years, during which time he has had no visitors; no inquiries have been made for his welfare and no one has attempted to seek him out. Upon his delivery here by the Secular Arm, it was stated that his family and relatives were dead of the Plague that came to Amalfi in the Kingdom of Napoli twenty years ago. He had been given to the Secular Arm before being entrusted to our care, for it was thought that he was filled with heretical notions. When he was given to our care, the Secular Arm had conducted a Process against him. It is written in the records of the monastery that all the fingers of his left hand were broken, that he was blind in his right eye, and that all the lower teeth had been taken from his

63

head. Because of the answers he had given during this Questioning, it was decided that Brother Rat was not a heretic but a madman, and thus was sent to us.

During the last winter, which has lingered well into spring, Brother Rat developed a cough that has not lessened as the weather grows warmer but instead has grown more fierce with each passing day so that it is now acknowledged that there is no medicine but the Hand of God that can deliver him. To that end, so that he may come shriven to the Mercy Seat, I have been entrusted with the task of recording the Confession of Brother Rat for delivery to the Secular Arm and for inclusion in the records of this monastery. May God grant that I perform my mandate without error for His greater Glory.

Because Brother Rat is known to be dangerous, he has been confined to a cell alone. There is a window in the cell, set near the ceiling so that he cannot see out. His legs are shackled and a chain holds him to a cleat in the wall that allows him little more than twice his height in range. He has a pallet for sleep and the rushes are changed twice a year. A single blanket is provided him in the summer, two in the winter. He is fed twice a day, as are all the fifty-four madmen confined within our walls. There is a privy hole in the floor of his cell. He is clothed in a peasant's smock, for it is not fitting that any who are mad should be habited as monks. Brother Rat is very thin, and the cough has taken more flesh from him so that his face is gaunt as a skull. He has some hair left, most of it grey, as is his beard. The nails on his right hand are very long, but on the left they do not grow well since the fingers were broken. His speech is not easily understood because he has so few teeth, nonetheless I have striven to record every word correctly, and if I have not been accurate, I beg forgiveness and offer as my excuse the difficulty of discerning his words.

When Brother Emmerano and I entered the cell, Brother Rat was lying upon his pallet. He blinked many times at the light of the three torches we brought, and shielded his one sighted eye until he was accustomed to the brightness. As he saw who we were, he spoke.

"So I'm dying." He raised himself, spitting copiously as he did. "About time. Perhaps God is more merciful than I thought."

Brother Emmerano blessed the poor madman, and then said, "This is Brother Luccio, who will record everything we say here. He is a scribe and a true monk who will take care to be correct in what he writes. I am come to take your Confession." He spoke slowly and clearly, for he has often maintained that madmen are more sensible when they are addressed in this way. "Two of the lay Brothers wait outside the door."

Brother Rat barked; he might have meant to cough or to laugh. "I cannot attack anyone, Brothers. I am burning with fever and I'm all but starved. You'd better give me some water, out of charity, or I will not be able to speak with you for long." He folded his arms and looked from Brother Emmerano to me with the expression of a man who finds a corpse laid out at his door.

"Be calm." Brother Emmerano signaled to be brought his stool, and for my bench and table. "There is a cask of wine being brought, not sacramental wine for your absolution, which we will provide when your Confession is complete; we will use this to ease your cough. We will be prepared presently." He then nodded toward me. "Remember all of this, Brother Luccio, for you must write it down."

I bowed my head and prayed that God would not take the words from me before my vellum was spread and my ink ground. "I ask that you do not speak too much more until I am prepared," I begged, and was rewarded with silence until the lay Brothers had brought what we needed. Once I was in position, I raised my hood so that my face was shadowed, so that I would be nothing more than a cypher during the Confession. I had four nibs cut and ready in case one should fail. I nodded to Brother Emmerano and put my pen into the ink.

"It is for the salvation of your soul that we seek to hear your Confession, Brother Rat," said Brother Emmerano. "God has blighted your wits, or you were a tool of Satan. Thus you have passed your life here, where you can do no

65

greater harm or call up the forces of Hell to aid you. Either way, you will need to have peace in your life before you depart it, for Grace to be yours."

"What does a madman know of Grace, and a drunken one at that? I haven't tasted wine for more than fifteen years—how many sips will make me senseless, do you think?" Brother Rat asked angrily. "I am addled as it is. God will have mercy on me."

Brother Emmerano nodded slowly. "It is touching to know that faith remains in your heart, Brother Rat. But if you are to be spared more suffering, you must reveal all you can recall in your Confession, and thereby find absolution and redemption."

"So you must take even this," said Brother Rat, as if he shouldered a great burden. He watched as the lay Brother poured out a cupful of wine from the small cask, a bariletto. It was the same wine the Brothers drank at supper, a thin young red that turned sour quickly.

"Do not say disrespectful things, Brother Rat," said Brother Emmerano. "It will not profit your soul to run wild this way. Your madness is beyond you, but try to govern your words." He folded his hands and murmured a prayer before he addressed Brother Rat again. "Can you tell me how you came to be here? Do you recall what is the cause of your madness, or has God hidden that from you?"

Brother Rat coughed and tears ran from his eyes; as soon as he could he took a long draught of the wine. He drew his smock more tightly around him. "Leave me alone."

"Were we tools of Satan, we would," said Brother Emmerano. He touched the Corpus that hung around his neck. "If we were heathen, we would not bring you this comfort. But as Christian monks, we cannot abandon you."

For a short while, Brother Rat continued to cough between sips of wine, then lay back and stared up at the window. "If I don't talk to you, you will only return, won't you?"

"We have our duty to our faith," said Brother Emmerano. He folded his hands again.

"Oh, yes," said Brother Rat, his face taking on a strange light, as if the torches had made another fever in him. He tugged his single blanket higher around his shoulders. "I wish you'd left the second blanket, but since Easter has come and gone, I suppose you . . ." He choked, and turned away.

"Let us hear your Confession, Brother Rat," said Brother Emmerano with admirable persistence. "Let us bring you the joy of Communion before you are too ill to know what is happening to you. Strive to keep God in your heart so that you will not fail."

"Ah." The madman put his taloned hand to his blind eye. "You are not content to have me die, it must be on your terms." His speech seemed to be that of an educated man when you made allowances for his teeth. He addressed Brother Emmerano with curiosity, as if his question were of nothing more than the quality of fruit grown in the orchard. "What is the reason this time?"

"You are corrupted, Brother Rat. You are the tool of Satan when you speak in that way." Brother Emmerano refilled the cup. "Here. Let this good wine calm your body and your soul." He watched while Brother Rat took the wine. "Soon you will stand before God, and the Book will be open before Him. All you have done is written there. In your madness you may forget now, but then there will be no forgetting, and without mercy you will suffer the pains of Hell for eternity." He paused. "I have heard it said that you were in Amalfi at the time of the Plague. Many who did not die of it were touched in their wits because of what God visited on that city."

"It was years and years and years and years ago," said Brother Rat, not bothering to look at Brother Emmerano. "It remains only in my dreams, and they are not sweet. What happened then is between God and me."

"You claimed that to the Secular Arm," said Brother Emmerano gently, "and they feared you were a heretic. You were examined by the Secular Arm; it is in the document that sent you here. Before they discovered your madness, they strove to cleanse you of heresy." He blessed himself, in case the dangerous word would bring contagion to him. "And though you are mad, what you say is heretical."

Brother Rat laughed and then doubled over coughing. His

67

thin, mangled hand shot out and seized the cup. He drank quickly and deeply. "Why not, why not?" he asked of nothing and no one we could see. With that he turned toward Brother Emmerano. "My chest rattles like a tinker's pack and the fever roasts my vitals. Tonight, tomorrow, a day or two at most and I will be gone from here at last. I will escape you, and the Secular Arm." He gestured for more wine before Brother Emmerano could protest so reprehensible a statement. "Go ahead. I'll tell you what you want to know. You can't do anything to me now; you could torture me and it would mean nothing, for I would die at once." He leaned back on his pallet, looking up toward the diffuse light at the window. "Sometimes I can see shadows of things, just there on the wall. Other than that, I have seen nothing but monks and stones for sixteen years. Sixteen years." Another cough rasped out of him. There were two bright places in the hollows of his cheeks and sweat shone on his forehead.

"You know that?" Brother Emmerano asked, a bit surprised.

"I used to count the days, make months and years of them. Now I measure them by Easters." He closed his eyes.

"Resurrection," said Brother Emmerano with satisfaction.

"If you prefer," Brother Rat answered. He rolled to his side and looked directly at Brother Emmerano. "How long have you been here? Not in this cell, a monk in this monastery?"

"I came here eleven years ago, from Benevento." He waited as Brother Rat stared hard at him. He went on when Brother Rat appeared to be satisfied with his response. "It is said you came from Amalfi."

Brother Rat shrugged. "I have been here longer than you have." He regarded Brother Emmerano. "Where is this monastery? They didn't tell me when they brought me here, and"—he indicated his missing lower teeth—"I was not able to ask in any case."

"We are near Anagni, in Campagna. They brought you from Napoli." He considered pouring more wine, then did not.

"From Napoli. That was where the Secular Arm had me," said Brother Rat. "They have prisons in Napoli, such prisons. This is nothing compared to them." He moved his hand to indicate his cell.

"This is not a prison, Brother Rat." Brother Emmerano could not keep his voice even, for it vexed him to hear such things, even from a madman.

"I am shackled and kept in a cell," said Brother Rat. "What difference to me that it is monks and not soldiers who lock the doors?"

Brother Emmerano stiffened. "This monastery cares for the mad. We have none of the Secular Arm here." He leaned forward. "You are nearing the end, but I still may have you beaten if you are taken by a demon. I do not want to bring you more suffering now, but if it is necessary I will do it."

"I am sure you will," said Brother Rat softly. He finished the wine in his cup and set the cup aside. "I would not live through the beating, not now." He made himself sit up, moving slowly as much from the wine he had drunk as from the hold of his sickness. "So I came here to Anagni from Napoli." He put his hand to his chest as if to contain his coughing in his hands. "What did the Secular Arm tell you?"

"That you claim to have been an apothecary and that you were speaking heresy, or so they feared." Brother Emmerano nodded encouragement. "Go on, Brother Rat. Let me hear this Confession. Reveal all that you have hidden for so long so that you will be absolved of your sins before you appear before God." Zeal made Brother Emmerano speak more loudly, and he paused as he realized he had raised his voice.

"It was because of the Black Plague," said Brother Rat after being silent for a time. "The Plague was enough to make heretics of saints and angels. It had more than enough martyrs." He fell silent again.

"Those are dangerous thoughts, Brother Rat." said Brother Emmerano. "It is not strange that the Secular Arm should confine you if you made these accusations when the Plague came."

"I made such statements and many others," said Brother

Rat, as if he were speaking from some distance away. "So you want to know how it was. You were alive when it came—you ought to remember."

"It is not my memories that are important in this Confession," Brother Emmerano reprimanded him. "If we are to record your repentance aright, then you must tell us how it was."

"If you insist," said Brother Rat with a resignation that was touched with despair. "The Plague began as other sicknesses do, but no one feared it then, not twenty years ago in Amalfi. Today I suspect it is different. Today I would think that any minor illness is viewed with alarm, isn't it?" He did not wait for an answer. "I consulted my books, because I hoped that there would be something recorded there that would protect the people of the town. But nothing seemed to help, not the perfumes, not the tea made of rosemary and moss, none of it. So I delved further, into studies in books I was told later were forbidden though they were written by a Franciscan who had been praised for his learning, for it seemed the whole world was afflicted. As my friends and my neighbors died, with black Tokens under their arms and at the groin, I dreaded that the Plague would take my family as well." It was a strange recitation, as if he were thinking of another person, one he had never met. "I had a wife then, and her mother lived with us and our five children. Sometimes, late in the night, I think I hear them speaking again."

"With your family in such danger, did you not appeal to God?" Brother Emmerano demanded.

"Daily," said Brother Rat. "And watched as the priests died with the Host in their hands." He broke off; when he was finished coughing, he held out his cup for more wine. "Is that enough or do you want more?"

"Is that all your Confession?" asked Brother Emmerano, filling the cup with slow deliberation.

"I suppose not," said Brother Rat. He wiped his blanket over his brow. "It ought to be enough, but—" He looked at the wine in the cup. "I need what little wits I have."

"How did you come to heresy? Was it from the forbidden

texts?" Brother Emmerano asked, growing intent to learn the beginning of Brother Rat's madness from whence might come his salvation.

"That is what the Secular Arm said, at first," said Brother Rat. "They were diligent in the Question. They kept me in their charge, and many times brought me to answer them. One of the Inquisitors believed that I was deep in heresy because of what I had read, but most of them were certain what I had found there had turned my wits. For I came to believe what I had read, and I believe it to this day." Until the last Brother Rat had spoken quietly, but now a passion came into his words. "The text was from that Franciscan who had gone to the land of the Great Khan, and it stated—" He stopped, his coughing renewed.

"It stated what? What is this madness you believe?" asked Brother Emmerano, his eyes bright as hot coals.

"What does it matter, after all?" He leaned back and wiped his mouth. "It is all but over. Why not? Why not?"

"Yes," said Brother Emmerano. "It is the Devil who urges you to silence, who makes you question the urgings of your soul to be purged of the evil that brought you to madness. Tell me what transpired and it will be recorded with your Confession. It will show that you have repented the pacts that made you mad. Think, Brother Rat, for the time when you will appear to answer for your sins comes quickly. Be reconciled to God now and—"

"Yes, yes I know," said Brother Rat, waving him to silence. "I have heard it many times. But madness is obdurate, and it has held me too tightly. But now nothing but death holds me."

"The Hand of God holds you, as it holds all the world," said Brother Emmerano. He looked toward me. "Have you taken down all we have said?"

"Yes," I assured him and blessed myself as soon as I had written my response. "It is all here."

"And no matter what Brother Rat says, you are sworn to record it, is that not so?" Brother Emmerano pursued.

"That is the case," I answered, writing as I spoke.

"It will be here, Brother Rat, every word of it, and there

71

will be no doubt of your Confession and the salvation of your soul. No one will be able to question it." He moved his stool a little closer to the pallet. "What was it that caused you to become mad? What thing did you find in those books that reduced you to this?"

It was as if Brother Rat had not heard; for some little time he stared up at the ceiling. "You know," he said after we had all been silent for as long as it would take to recite the Supplication to the Virgin, "I followed what the books suggested. I removed all the rushes from the house and set pots of burning herbs throughout the house, so every room was filled with smoke. I permitted no new rushes to be brought into the house, and I ordered that everyone bathe once a week while the Plague was in the city."

Brother Emmerano was outraged; he could not speak in the soft manner he so often employed for such Confessions. "What blasphemous book taught you that? You said it was a book where you learned this, did you not?"

"A book of things learned by the Franciscan Brother in the great Land of Silk," said Brother Rat. "A Franciscan wrote it, good Brother. A man sworn to God and Christ. He said it was thought by certain of the subjects of the Great Khan that what brought the Plague was vermin—vermin and the vermin of vermin. This book declared that if there were no vermin there would likewise be no Plague."

"God's Wrath brings Plague: God's Wrath and the sins of man," said Brother Emmerano, his voice now very loud.

"Amen." Brother Rat blessed himself. "But the notion took hold of me, in my dread as the corpses were piled in the streets each morning and there were fewer and fewer left alive to see them buried." He had a taste of the wine and set the cup aside. "The priests were in the grave with the rest of them. And you see, only my wife's mother had taken the Plague. My wife lived, and our children were alive. So I kept to what the texts said, and made our house slaves clean each day, scrubbing the floors every morning. They all grumbled, but they lived."

"A ruse of the Devil," said Brother Emmerano.

"Very likely," said Brother Rat with a deep sigh. "It did

not last. My second son began to sweat and became restless, and that was enough to panic our slaves and servants, for they deserted us." He forced himself to sit up properly and then he downed the cup of wine. "I might as well be drunk for this."

"If you can give an honest Confession," warned Brother Emmerano.

"In vino veritas," said Brother Rat. He motioned for more. "My wife nursed the boy, and though she hated all that I did, she did not stop me for she was too worried for the other children to care that I continued to scrub the floors and burn herbs once a day. She would not allow me to have the stuffing of the mattresses changed, for fear of losing the protection of the angels who guard the sick. Then she took the Plague as well." He watched the wine fill the cup. "In the book by that Franciscan there was much about the danger of rats; rats more than mice. So I killed every rat I saw, in the house and anywhere in the town. And as the people died, there were more and more rats, or so it seemed to me." He was agitated now, his cough returning as short, explosive interruptions to what he said. "I thought that the rats were bringing the Plague, because of what the book said. It spoke of the vermin of vermin, and rats, and so I—"

"It is said that you went among the dead, killing rats where you found them. According to the Secular Arm you killed every rat that entered your cell." Brother Emmerano blessed himself. "You kill rats here."

"They are the messengers of the Plague," said Brother Rat with such intense feeling that for once Brother Emmerano shrank back from him. "It is madness to think that, but I have said already I cannot make myself turn my thoughts from that conviction."

Brother Emmerano clasped his hands, but this time he was nervous, and the knuckles stood out white. "But what has brought you to this?"

"The rats," said Brother Rat. "They themselves. I have made a point to look closely at them, and they are alive with vermin of their own. And if their vermin have vermin, might not there be vermin of those, and so into the realms of angels?" He pulled at his blanket, then drank off half the wine, smacking his lips with savor. "I am now never without the conviction that there are vermin so fine and so great in number that they can penetrate anything. The rats bring them."

"But vermin are everywhere," said Brother Emmerano. "Have you lost sight of that? There would have to be these little vermin in all things, and what would be the purpose of that? Where does it say that God brought forth vermin? We know that the Devil brings these tribulations, and it is for us to bear these things without notice so we may the sooner turn our minds from the wiles of the Devil and toward the salvation of Christ."

Brother Rat nodded several times as if his head were not tightly bound to his body. "I know. The Secular Arm reminded me. I know this is madness. But we who are mad cannot set aside our madness because it is what we wish. If it were that, we would be heretics." He finished his wine. "I wish I were a heretic, I wish I did not believe as I do, that I have been corrupted and could be saved from my error. But it is fixed, like the head of an arrow in a healed wound. Broken fingers and teeth could not budge it. This cell has not changed it." He wept suddenly, deeply.

"God will bring you to comfort, Brother Rat," said Brother Emmerano as he clutched his Corpus in a trembling hand.

When the worst of his weeping was over, Brother Rat wiped his face with his blanket once more, and spat several times, as much blood as foam. "I can see it now, or so I tell myself. They ruined this eye trying to make me tell them I could not see these vermin, but . . ."

"It is madness, and they sent you to us," said Brother Emmerano, still trying to quiet himself so that he would be able to sense God's Will.

"Apparently." He considered the cup, then signaled for more. "I suppose the fever burns the wine away. I thought I would be singing by now. There was a time when I might have sung." Now his cough shook him as if he were in the fist of a giant.

74

"Should we send for—" Brother Emmerano began but was cut off by Brother Rat.

"No. What could he do? It is ending for me." He looked away from Brother Emmerano. "And I have been thinking that one of these invisible vermin has brought this cough to me, that it has taken over my body, as the vermin of Plague took my wife and my son, and my wife's mother."

Brother Emmerano hesitated, then asked, "What of your other children? You said you had five children, did you not?"

"Oh, yes," said Brother Rat. "I did. And the neighbors thought I was possessed of a demon, for all that I did in my house. They saw the pots of smoking herbs and they said the Devil was with us. They saw that I had the floors cleaned every morning, and they whispered that I had done atrocious things in the night." He put his hand to his brow. "So the ones who were still alive decided that I had brought the Plague to Amalfi." There were tears on his wrinkled, sunken cheeks yet he made no move to wipe them away. "They gathered together and when next my children went to the church to pray for the soul of their mother, who was dead less than a week, they were met by men and boys with bricks and stones." He closed his eyes.

Brother Emmerano lifted his hand to bless Brother Rat, but faltered. "What became of them? Of your children?"

"I thought that was obvious," said Brother Rat softly, refusing to open his eyes. "They were stoned to death. I found them all broken and in a welter of blood when I came from the burial pit where I had taken flowers in memory of my wife."

As Brother Emmerano lowered his hand, he said, "What was said of that act?"

"I don't know," Brother Rat admitted as he opened his eyes at last. "I was not told." He stared down at his hands as if he had just noticed the fingers of his left hand had been broken. "That night was when I went to the burial pit to kill rats. I had to do something."

"But such a gesture . . . surely you did not think that you could change the death of those poor people by killing rats." Brother Emmerano shifted on his stool again, glancing to-

75

ward the door as if to reassure himself that the lay Brothers were within reach.

"I don't know what I thought," said Brother Rat in bitter amusement. "I was mad. I have been mad since the Plague came. Perhaps I hoped that if I killed the vermin and the vermin of vermin I might find the way to restore those who were dead." He shrugged. "I can't remember what was in my heart then." He coughed, holding his head with his hand. "I am not used to wine. Already my head is throbbing."

Brother Emmerano was not going to permit Brother Rat to turn away from the matter now. "How did you come to be in the hands of the Secular Arm? Surely you did not seek them out, did you? To hear what you say, all of Amalfi died of the Plague."

"Most of it did. Some who could afford it left the city when the disease first struck, and they returned to find a few of us picking our way among the corpses." He slid back on his pallet. "They came with priests and all of us who remained alive were taken to the church to answer the questions of the Bishop, to account for our lack of death. Anyone who gave unsatisfactory answers was sent to the Secular Arm. They burned the tailor as a heretic, and the chimney sweep. Those of us who were still in their keeping had to watch, to see what awaited us if we did not exculpate ourselves."

"A worthy lesson," said Brother Emmerano.

"Yes," Brother Rat said distantly. "Although I hoped then that they would decide I was a heretic, and burn me, for life seemed an impossible burden to me then."

"Such an assertion is close to heresy," Brother Emmerano cautioned.

"My family was dead. I had failed to save them." Brother Rat turned his face to the stones.

"It is not for you to save them, or any man. it is for God to save them, or to move you to find the means to save them. If you usurp that power, you question the divinity of God and Christ. God in His Wisdom called your family to Him, and left you to live on so that you could return again to Christ." Brother Emmerano placed his hand over his heart. "Your soul has been forfeited because you were misled by a Godless book, and for that your family was taken from you, and when that was not sufficient, so were your wits."

"It was vermin that brought Plague, Brother Emmerano. I am mad still, though I pray devoutly that God will pity me and save me from the madness that has claimed the whole of my thoughts for all these years." It was not easy to understand him with his face to the wall. "But suppose it is true? What if my madness is no madness? Suppose that there is truth in those pages, and our efforts have been spent in vain? That is what makes my days' torment: suppose the book is right, and there is vermin and vermin's vermin and vermin's vermin's vermin, and that is what causes Plague when God is displeased with mankind?"

Brother Emmerano sighed. "He should not have drunk so much. The wine has muddled his thoughts. He has had too much, and mad that he is, he is sunk into his madness." He started to rise. "I will have Brother Luccio record all you have said, Brother Rat, and in the morning it will be read to you and you will be absolved, and the priests will anoint you." His habit rustled as he rose, clapping his hands for the lay Brothers at the door.

"There could be other vermin that bring other ills," muttered Brother Rat. "There may be many others. It may not be sufficient only to kill rats." He pulled his blanket close around him and coughed, low and steady, as the writing table and two stools were removed from the cell.

As the lay Brother turned the key in the lock of the cell door, Brother Emmerano blessed him and added a blessing toward the door itself. "You will bring the Confession to me, Brother Luccio. Make sure you include my request to review it."

"As you wish," I told him, lowering my face to show him respect. "As soon as I have presented it to the Prior." I walked behind Brother Emmerano, as was proper. "They say the Plague has returned," I mentioned as we started up the stairs to the refectory.

77

Brother Emmerano nodded. "We have said Masses for the dead already." He paused, his face emotionless. "Poor Brother Rat, if he learns of it. But it is not likely, in God's Mercy."

I bowed my head and protected myself with the Cross. And as we resumed our climb, I could not keep from asking, "Do you suppose there is the least chance he is right? I know he is mad, but some madmen have visions, don't they?"

Brother Emmerano laughed once. "How can that be? Brother Rat has been broken by the wiles of the Devil. Madmen who have visions see angels and the hosts of Heaven and the tribulations of the Martyrs or are offered comfort by Our Lady. They glimpse the world that is beyond the earth, either Heaven or Hell. They do not see the vermin of rats, Brother Luccio."

"Amen," I replied, my faith in Brother Emmerano and God. I resolved not to be led into error, though I had received warning that my sister was ill with a cough and a fever. How simple a thing it would be to blame rats and the vermin of rats instead of God—how simple and how monstrous. I whispered a prayer for her protection as well as my forgiveness and went to my cell to prepare the record of the Confession for the Prior.

Jesse

Steve Rasnic Tem

J esse says he figures it's about time we did another one.

He uses "we" like we're Siamese twins or something, like we both decide what's going to happen and then it happens. Like we just do it, two bodies with one mind like in some weird movie. But it's Jesse that does it, all of it, each and every time. I'm just along for the ride. It's not my fault what Jesse does. I can't stop him—nobody could.

"Why?" I ask, and I feel bad that my voice has to shake, but I can't help it. "Why is it time, Jesse?"

" 'Cause I'm afraid you're forgetting too many things, John. You're forgetting how we do it, and how they look."

We again. Like Jesse doesn't do a thing by himself. But Jesse does everything by himself. "I don't forget," I say.

"Oh, but I think you do. I *know* you do. It's time all right." Then he gets up from his nest in the sour straw and starts toward the barn door. And even though I haven't forgotten how they look, and how we do it, how *he* does it— how could anybody forget something like that?—I get up out of the straw and follow.

* * *

79

When Jesse called me up that day I didn't take him all that seriously. Jesse was always calling me up and saying crazy things.

"Come on over," he said. "I gotta show you something."

I laughed at him. "You're in enough trouble," I said. "Your parents grounded you, remember? Two weeks at least, you told me."

"My parents are dead," he said, in his serious voice. But I had heard his serious voice a thousand times, and I knew what it meant.

I laughed. "Sure, Jesse. Deader than a flat frog on the highway, right?"

"No, deader than your dick, dickhead." He was always saying that. I laughed again. "Come on over. I swear it'll be okay."

"Okay. My mom has to go to the store. She can drop me off and pick me up later."

"No. Don't come with your mom. Take your bike."

"Christ, Jesse. It's *five miles!*"

"You've done it before. Take your bike or don't come at all."

"Okay. Be there when I get there." He made me mad all the time. All he had to do was tell me to do something and I'd do it. When I first knew him I did things he said because I felt sorry for him. His big brother had died when a tractor rolled over on him. I wasn't there but people said it was pretty awful. I heard my dad tell my mom that there must have been a dozen men around but none of them could do a thing. Jesse's brother had been awake the whole time, begging them to get the tractor off, that he could feel his heart getting ready to stop, that he knew it was going to stop any second. Dad said the blood was seeping out from under the tractor, all around his body, and Jesse's brother was looking at it like he just couldn't believe it. And Jesse was there watching the whole thing, Dad said. They couldn't get him to go away.

It gave me the creeps, what Jesse's brother had said. 'Cause I've always been afraid my heart was just going to stop someday, for no good reason. And to *feel* your heart getting ready to stop, that would be horrible.

Because of all that I felt real bad for Jesse, so for a while there he would ask me to do something, anything, and I'd do it for him. I'd steal somebody's lunch or pull down a little kid's pants or walk across the creek on a little skinny board, all kinds of stupid crap. But after a while I just did it because he said. He didn't make you want to feel bad for him. I wasn't even sure that he cared that his brother was dead. Once I asked him if he still felt bad about it and he just said that his brother picked on him all the time. That's all he would say about it. Jesse was always weird like that.

I hadn't ridden my bike in over a year—I wasn't sure I still could. I thought sixteen-year-olds were too old to ride bikes—guys were getting their licenses and were willing to walk or get rides with older friends until that day happened. And I was big for my age, a lot bigger than Jesse. I felt stupid. But I rode my bike the five miles anyway, just because Jesse told me to.

By the time I got to his farm I was so tired and mad I just threw the bike down in the gravel driveway. I didn't care if I broke it—I wasn't going to ride it home no matter what. Jesse came to the screen door with a smirk on his face. "Took you long enough," he said. "I didn't think you were coming."

"I'm here, all right? What'd you want to show me that was so damn important?"

He pulled me down the hall. He was so excited and it was happening so fast I was having a real bad feeling even before I saw them. He stopped in front of the door to his parents' bedroom and knocked it open with his fist. The sound made me jump. Then when I looked inside there were his parents on the floor, sleeping.

A short laugh came out of me like a bark. They looked silly: his mom's dress pulled up above her knees and his dad's mouth hanging open like he was drunk. They had their arms folded over their bellies. I never saw people sleeping that way before. The sheets and blankets and pillows had been pulled off the bed and were arranged around them and underneath them like a nest. His mom had never been a good housekeeper—Jesse told me the place always looked and stank like a garbage dump—but I'd never thought it was this bad, that they had to sleep on the floor.

The room was full of all these big candles, the scented kind. There must have been forty or fifty of them. And big melted patches where there must have been lots more, but they'd burned down and been replaced. There was a box full of them by the dresser, all ready to go. They also had a couple of those weird-looking incense burners going. It made me want to laugh. There were more different smells in that room than I'd smelled my whole life. And all of them so sweet they made my eyes water. But under the sweet there was something else—when a breeze sneaked through and flickered the candles I thought I could smell it—like when we got back from vacation that summer and the freezer broke down while we were away. Mom made Dad move us to a motel for a while. Something like that, but it was having a hard time digging itself out of all that sweetness.

"Candles cost a fortune," Jesse said. "All the money in my dad's wallet plus the coins my mom kept in a fruit jar. She didn't even think I knew about that. But they look pretty neat, huh?"

I took a step into the room and looked at his dad's mouth. Then his mom's mouth. They hung open like they were about to swallow a fly or sing or something. I almost laughed again, but I couldn't. Their mouths looked a little like my dad's mouth, the way he lets it hang open when he falls asleep on the couch watching TV. But different. Their mouths were soft and loose, their lips dark, all dry and cracked, but even though they were holding their mouths open so long no saliva came dripping out. And there was gray and blue under their eyes. There were dark blotches on Jesse's mom's face. They were so still, like they were playing a game on me. Without even thinking about it I pushed on his dad's leg with my foot. It was like pushing against a board. His dad rocked a little, but he was so tight his big arms didn't even wiggle. Jesse always said his old man was "too tight." I really did start to laugh, thinking about that, but it was like my breath exploded instead. I didn't even know I had been holding it. "Jesus . . ." I could feel my chest shake all by itself.

Jesse looked at me almost like he was surprised, like I'd done something wrong. "I told you, didn't I? Don't be a *baby*." He sat down on the floor and started playing with his dad's leg, pushing on it and trying to lift up the knee. "Last night they both started getting stiff. It really happens, you know? It's not just something in the movies. You know *why* it happens, John?" He looked up at me, but he was still poking the leg with his fist, like he was trying to make his dad do something, slap him or something. Any second I figured his dad would reach over and grab Jesse by the hair and pull him down onto the floor beside them.

I shook my head. I was thinking, *No no no*, but I couldn't quite get that out.

Jesse hit his dad on the thigh hard as he could. It sounded like an overstuffed leather chair. It didn't give at all. "Hell, I don't know either. Maybe it's the body fighting off being dead, even after you're dead, you know? It gets all mad and stiff on you." He laughed but it didn't sound much like Jesse's laugh. "I guess it don't know it's dead. It don't know *shit* once the brain is dead. But if I was going to die I guess I'd fight real hard." Jesse looked at his mom and dad and made a twisted face like he was smelling them for the first time. "Bunch of pussies . . ."

He grabbed the arm his dad had folded against his chest and tried to pull it away. His dad held on but then the arm bent a little. The fat shoulders shook when Jesse let go and his dad fell back. The head hit the pillow and left a greasy red smear.

"The old man here started loosening up top a few hours ago, in the same order he got stiff in." Jesse reached over and pinched his dad's left cheek.

"Christ, Jesse!" I ran back into the hall and fell on the floor. I could hardly breathe. Then I started crying, really bawling, and I could breathe again.

After a while I could feel Jesse patting me on the back. "You never saw dead people before, huh, Johnny?"

I just shook my head. "I'm s-sorry, Jesse. I'm s-so sorry."

"They were old," he said. "It's okay. Really."

I looked up at him. I didn't understand. It felt like he wasn't even speaking English. But he just looked at me, then looked back into his parents' bedroom, and didn't say anything more. Finally I knew I had to say something. "How did it happen?"

He looked at me like I was being the one hard to understand. "I told you. They were old."

I thought about the red smear his dad's head made on the pillow, but I couldn't get myself to understand it. "But Jesse ... *at the same time?*"

He shook his head. "What's wrong with you, John? My dad died first. I guess that made my mom so sad she died a few minutes later. You've heard of that. First one old person dies, then the person they're married to dies just a short time after?"

"Yeah ..."

"Their hearts just stopped beating." I looked up at him. I could feel my own heart vibrating in my chest, so hard it hurt my ribs. "I put them together like that. They were my parents. I figured they'd like that."

He had that right, I guess. After all, they were his parents. Maybe he didn't always get along with them, but they were his parents. He could look at them after they were dead.

I made myself look at them. It was a lot easier the second time. A whole lot easier. I felt a little funny about that. Even without his dad's blood on the pillow they were a lot different from sleeping people. There was just no movement at all, and hardly any color but the blue, and they both looked cool, but not a damp kind of cool because they looked so dry, and their eyelids weren't shut all the way, and you could see a little sliver of white where the lids weren't all the way closed. I made myself get as close to their eyes as I could, maybe to make sure one final time they weren't pretending. The sliver of white was dull, like on a fish. Like something thick and milky had grown over their eyes. They looked like dummies some department store had thrown out in the garbage. There wasn't anything alive about them at all.

"When did they die?"

Jesse was looking at them too. Closely, like they were the strangest things anyone had ever seen. "It's been at least a day, I guess. Almost two."

Jesse said we shouldn't call the police just yet. They were his parents, weren't they? Didn't he have the right to be with them for a while? I couldn't argue with that. I guessed Jesse had all kinds of rights when it was *his* parents. But it still felt weird, him being with their dead bodies almost two whole days. I helped him light some more candles when he said the air wasn't sweet enough anymore. I felt a little better helping him do that, like we were having a funeral for them. All those sweet-smelling candles and incense felt real religious. Then I felt bad about thinking he was being weird earlier, like I was being prejudiced or something. But it was there just the same. I quit looking at his mom and dad, except when Jesse told me to. And after a couple of hours of me just standing out in the hallway, or fussing with the candles, trying *not* to look at them, Jesse started insisting.

"You gotta look at them, John."

"I did. You saw me. I looked at them."

"No, I mean *really* look at them. You haven't seen everything there is to see."

I looked at him instead. Real hard. I could hardly believe he was saying this. "Why? I'm sorry they're dead. But why do I have to look a them?"

"Because I want you to."

"Jesse . . ."

". . . And besides, you should know about these things. Your mom and dad don't want you to know about things like this, but I guess it's about the most important thing to know about there is. Everybody gets scared of dying, and just about everybody is scared of the dead. You remember that movie *Zombie* we rented? That's what it was all about. Now we've got two dead bodies here. You're my friend, and I want to help you out. I want to share something with you."

85

"Christ, Jesse. They're your parents."

"What, you think I don't know that? Who else should I learn about this stuff from anyway? If they were still alive, they'd be supposed to teach me. What's wrong with it? And don't just tell me because it's 'weird.' People say something's weird because it makes them nervous. Just because it bothers *them* they don't want you to do it. So what do we care, anyway? Nobody else is gonna know about this."

Jesse could argue better than anybody, and I never knew what to think about anything for sure. Before I knew it he had me back in the bedroom, leaning over the bodies. It was a little better—I guess I was getting used to them. At least I didn't feel ready to throw up like I did a while ago. That surprised me. It surprised me even more when he took my hand and put it on his mom's—his dead mom's—arm, and I didn't jerk it away.

"Jesse . . ." I guess I'd expected it to be still stiff, but it had gotten soft again, as soft as anything I'd ever felt, like I could just dig my fingers into her arm like butter. It was cool, but not what I expected. And dry.

"See the spots?" Jesse said behind me. "Like somebody's been painting her. Like for one of those freak shows. Oh, she'd *hate* it if she knew. She'd think she looked like a whore!"

I saw them all right. Patches of blue-green low down on his dad's belly. Before I could stop him he raised his mom's skirt and showed me that the marks on her were worse: more of the blue-green and little patches of greenish-red, all of it swimming together around her big white panties. I was embarrassed, but I kept staring. That's the way I'd always imagined seeing my first panties on a woman: when she was asleep or—to tell the truth—when she was dead. I used to dream about dead women in their panties and bras, dead women naked with their parts hanging out, and I'd felt ashamed about it, but here it was happening for real and for some reason I was having a hard time feeling too ashamed. I hadn't done it; I hadn't killed her.

"Look," he said. I followed his hand as it moved up his mother's belly. I tensed as he pulled her dress up further, back over her head so that I couldn't see her mouth anymore, her mouth hanging open like she was screaming, but no sound coming out. "I know you always wanted to see one of these up close. Admit it, John." His hand rested on the right cup of her bra. Now I felt real bad, and ashamed, like I had helped him kill her. Her white, loose skin spilled out of the top and bottom of the cup like big gobs of dough. With a jerk of his hand Jesse pulled his mother's bra off. The skin was loose and it all had swollen so much it was beginning to tear. I knew it was going to break like an old fruit any second. "She's gotten bigger since the thing happened," he said. I started to choke. "Come on, John. You always wanted to see this stuff. You wanted to see it, and you wanted to see it dead."

I turned away and walked back into the hall when he started to laugh. His mom was an *it* now. His dad was a thing. But Jesse knew me so well. He knew about the dreams and he knew what would get to me, what I always thought about, even though I'd never told him. It made me wonder if all guys my age think about being dead that way, wanting to see it and touch it, wanting something real like that, even though it was so awful. I used to dream about finding my own parents dead, and what they would look like, but never once did I imagine I would do that to them. Not like Jesse. I knew now what Jesse had done to his parents. No question about that anymore. But I was all mixed up about what I felt about it. Because, even though it was awful, I still wanted to look, and touch. Wasn't that almost as bad?

"Here." Jesse grabbed my arm and turned me around. He led me back over to his mother's body. "You don't have to look. You can close your eyes. Let me just take your hand." But I wanted to look. He took me over to her side. There was a big blister there, full of stuff. Jesse put my hand on it. 'Feels weird, huh?" He didn't look crazy; he looked like some kind of young scientist or something from some dumb TV show. I nodded. "Hey, look at her mouth!" I did. In her big loose mouth I could see pieces of food that had come up. A little dark bug crawled up out of her hair. *This is what it's like, what it's really like,* I thought. I thought about those rock stars I used to like all made up like they were dead, those horror movies I used to watch with Jesse, and all those stoner kids I used to know getting high every chance they had and telling me it don't matter anyway and everything was just a drag with their eyes half shut and their mouths hanging open and their skin getting whiter every day. *All of them, they don't know shit about it,* I thought. *This is what it's really like.*

Jesse left me by his mom and started going to the candles one at a time, snuffing them out. A filmy gray smoke started to fill the bedroom. I could already smell the mix of sweet and sharp smells starting to go away, and underneath that the other truly awful smell creeping in.

Jesse turned to me while the last few candles were still lit. That bad smell was almost all over me now, but I just sat there, holding my breath and waiting for it. He almost grinned but didn't quite make it. "I guess you're ready to take a hit off all this now," he said. I just stared at him. And then I let my clean breath go.

And now Jesse says he figures it's about time we did another one.

We took off from his house with the one bike and Jesse's pack but we had to walk most of the time because Jesse figured we'd better go cross-country, over the fences and through the trees where nobody could see us. He didn't think they'd find the bodies anytime soon but my parents would report me missing after a while. It was hell getting the bike through all that stuff but Jesse said we might need it later so we best take it. The scariest part was when we had to cross a couple of creeks and wading through water up over my belt carrying that bike made me sure I was going to drown. But I thought maybe I even deserved it for what I'd seen, what I'd done, and what I didn't do. I thought about what a body must look like after it drowned—I'd heard they swole up something awful, and I thought about Jesse showing off my body after I'd died, letting people poke it and smell it, and then I didn't want to die anymore.

Once Jesse suggested that maybe we should build a raft and float downriver like Tom Sawyer and Huckleberry Finn. I'd read the two books and he'd seen one of the movies. I thought it was a great idea but then we couldn't figure out how to do it. Jesse bitched about how they don't teach you important stuff like that in school, and they used to, dads taught you stuff like raft-building but they didn't anymore. He said his dad should have taught him stuff like that but he was always too busy.

"Probably," I said, watching Jesse closer all the time because he seemed to be getting frustrated with everything.

I thought a lot about Tom and Huck that first day and how they came back into town just in time to see their own funeral. I wondered if every kid dreamed about doing that. I wondered, if my parents found out what I did in Jesse's house, what they would say about me at my funeral.

We slept the first night under the trees. Or tried to. Jesse walked around a lot in the dark and I couldn't sleep much from watching him. The next morning he was nervous and agitated and first thing he did he found an old dog and beat it over the head with a hammer. I didn't know he had the hammer but it was in his pack and I pretty much guessed what he'd used it for before. He didn't even tell me he was gong to do it, he just saw the dog and as soon as he saw it he did it. We both stood there and looked at the body and touched it and kicked it and I didn't feel a damn thing and I don't think Jesse did, either, because he was still real nervous.

Later that morning the farmer picked us up in his truck.

"Going far?" he asked us from the window and I wanted to tell him to keep driving mister but I didn't. He was old and had a nice face and was probably somebody's father and some kid's grandfather but I couldn't say a thing with Jesse standing there.

"Meadville," Jesse said, smiling. I'd seen that fakey smile on Jesse's face before, when he talked to adults, when he talked to his own parents. "We're gonna help out on my uncle's farm." Jesse smiled and smiled and my throat and my chest and my head started filling up with that awful smell again. The old man looked at me and all I could do was look at him and nod. He let Jesse into the cab of the truck and told me I'd better ride with my bike in the back. The old man smiled at me a real smile, like I was a good boy.

The breeze was cool in the back of the truck and the bed rocked so on the gravelly side road we were on I started falling asleep, but every time I was getting ready to conk out we'd hit a bump or something and my head would snap up. But I still think I must have slept a little because somewhere in there I started to dream. I dreamed that I was riding along in the back of a pickup truck my grandfather was driving. He'd been singing the whole way and I'd been enjoying his singing but then it wasn't singing anymore, it was screaming and a monster was in the front seat with him, Death was in the front seat with him, beating him over the head with a hammer. Then the truck jerked to a stop and I looked through the cab window where Death was hammering the brains out of my grandfather and coating the glass with gray and brown and red. My grandfather scratched at the glass like I should do something but I couldn't because it was just a dream. Then Death turned to me and grinned while he was still swinging the hammer ad fighting with my grandfather and it was my face grinning and speckled with brains and blood.

I turned around to try to get out of the dream, to watch the trees whizz by while the truck was rocking me to sleep, but the land was dark and the trees were tall bodies all swollen in their dying and their heavy heads hanging down and their loose mouths falling open. And the wind through the trees was the breath of the dead—that awful smell I thought we'd left back at Jesse's house.

Later I kissed my grandfather goodbye and helped Jesse bury him under one of those tall trees that smelled so bad.

And now Jesse says he figures it's about time we did another one. He grins and says he's lost the smell. But I can smell it all the time—I smell, taste, and breathe that smell.

Outside Meadville Jesse washed up and stole a shirt and pants off a clothesline. From there we took turns walking and riding the bike to a mall where Jesse did some panhandling. We used the money to buy shakes and burgers. While we were eating Jesse said that panhandling wasn't wrong if you had to do it to get something to eat. I couldn't watch Jesse eat—the food kept coming up out of his mouth. My two burgers smelled so bad I tried to hold my breath while I ate them but that made me choke. But I still ate them. I was hungry.

We walked around the mall for a long time. Other people did the same thing, staring, but never buying anything. It reminded me of one of those zombie pictures. I tried not to touch anybody because they smelled so bad and they held their mouths open so that you could see all their teeth.

Finally Jesse picked out two girls and dragged me over to them. I couldn't get too close because of their smell, but the younger one seemed to like me. She had a nice smile. I looked at Jesse's face. He was grinning at them and then at me. His complexion had gotten real bad since we'd started traveling—there'd been more and more zits on his face every day. Now they were huge. One burst open and a long skinny white worm crawled out. I looked at the girls— they didn't seem to notice.

"His parents are putting him up for adoption so we ran away. I'm trying to hide him until they change their minds." Jesse's breath stank.

The girls looked at me. "Really?" the older one said. Her face had tiny cracks in it. I looked down at my feet.

Both of the girls said "I'm sorry" about the same time, then they got quiet like they were embarrassed. But I still didn't look up. I watched their sandaled feet and the black bugs crawling between their toes.

The older one could drive so they hid us in the backseat of their car and drove to the end of the drive that led to the farmhouse where their family lived. We were supposed to go on to the barn and the girls would bring us out some food later. We never told them about my bike and I kept thinking about it and what people would say when they found it. Even though I never used the bike anymore I was a little sorry about having lost it.

I also thought about those girls and how nice they were

and how the younger one seemed to like me, even though they smelled so bad. I wondered why girls like that were always so nice to guys like us, guys with a story to tell, and I thought about how dumb it was.

After we were in the barn for a couple of hours the girls—they were sisters, if I didn't mention it before—brought us some food. The younger one talked to me a long time while I ate but I don't remember anything she said. The older one talked to Jesse the same way and I heard her say "You're a good person to be helping your friend like this." She leaned over and kissed Jesse on his cheek even though the zits were tearing his face apart. Her skirt rode up on the side and Jesse put his dirty hand there. I saw the blisters rise up out of her skin and break open and the smell was worse than ever in the barn but no one else seemed to notice.

I finished eating and leaned back into the dirty straw. I liked the younger sister but I hoped she wouldn't kiss me the same way. I couldn't stand the idea of her open, loose mouth touching my skin. Underneath the straw I saw that there were hunks of gray flesh, pieces of arms and legs and things inside you I didn't know the name for. But I covered them over with more straw when nobody was looking, and I didn't say anything.

And now Jesse says he figures it's about time we did another one. He thinks I've forgotten. But I haven't.

I've been thinking about the two sisters all night and how much they trust us and how good they've been to us. And I've been thinking how they remind me of the Wilks sisters in *Huckleberry Finn* and how Huck felt so ornery and low-down because he was letting the duke and king rob them of their money after the sisters had been so nice to him. Sometimes I guess you don't know how to behave until you've read it in a book or seen it on TV.

So he gets up from his nest in the sour straw and starts toward the barn door. And I get up out of the straw and follow. Only last night I took the hammer, and now I beat him in the head until his head comes apart, and all the stink comes out and covers me so bad I know I'll never get it off. He always said he'd fight really hard if he knew he was dying, but his body doesn't fight back hardly at all. Maybe he didn't know.

I hear the noises in the farmhouse and now there are voices and flashlights coming. I scrape my fingers through the straw to find all the pieces of Jesse's head to make him look a little better for these people. I lie down in the straw beside him and close my eyes, leaving just a sliver of milky white under each lid to show them. I drop my mouth open and stop my saliva. I imagine the blue-green colors that will come and paint my body. I imagine the blisters and the insects and the terrible smell my breath has become. But mostly I try to imagine how I'm going to explain to these strangers why I'm enjoying this.

Enduring Art

Robert E. Vardeman

"It's a masterpiece. A goddamn masterpiece, isn't it?"
Marvin Arthurs looked expectantly at his girlfriend.
Anita Kovel stepped back, nervously pushed a vagrant strand of dishwater-blond hair from her eyes
and then licked her lips. Arthurs read her like a book. The
bitch didn't like it. She hated it. And it was good. It was
better than good. She never liked anything he did, not anymore.

"Art, it's . . . so strange," she said. She licked her lips
again and her sea-green eyes darted around. She was looking
for some way to escape confronting his genius. Work of
such magnitude frightened her, and it should, he thought.
This was better than anything the other environmental artists did. Even Jean Verame's painted stones near Amarillo
couldn't compare when he finished. The maquette would
be translated from the bare rock of a mountain in ways not
seen since Gutzon Borglum chiseled away at Mount Rushmore. He would make an even more notable contribution
to environmental art than the current master, James Tur-
rell and the Roden Crater!

"It's the best work I've ever done." Arthurs turned from
the chubby woman and smiled. It *was* good. Damned good.

"It's a piece of shit, Art," Anita said in a quavering voice.

95

"And it's messed up the entire apartment. This place looks more like a pigpen than ever before."

It took him a second to shift from his appreciation of the six-hundred-pound welded iron bar and concrete maquette of a fornicating Cerberus to his surroundings. The welding torch had singed a few of the frilly things Anita had scattered around, and the cement he had used so freely lay like a gray shroud on the furniture. It hardly mattered what he had done to the wood floor. The place was rented. What did she want from him? He had to create. The maquette was his blueprint for the finished piece, an entire mountain carved into the dog's likeness.

"What—" he began.

"Art, I can't go on like this. You rob garbage cans and landfills and hang it all together and call it a . . . masterpiece. You live like a slob. And you haven't paid your share of the rent in six months."

"You've got a grant."

"It's hardly enough for me to live on. I can't keep supporting both of us, Art. I can't!" Anita's voice rose an octave and grated shrilly on Arthurs' ears. He wanted to flip down his welder's mask, turn on the torch and cut out her vocal cords.

"You haven't lost the grant?" His voice was accusing. She was dumb enough to do something like that. They needed that money to keep going. Arthurs wasn't quite sure why the University of Colorado gave her a red cent for studying Pre-Raphaelite poetry, whatever that was, but he needed the money. After finishing with the three-headed Cerberus maquette, he could sell it for thousands and put them on easy street. Who wouldn't buy the miniature of an entire mountain of sculpture known around the world?

"I haven't," she said angrily, "and that's not the point. *You're* the point." Anita turned and pointed in the direction of the bedroom. "*That's* the point, too. And so are *they*." She puffed out her chest and Arthurs knew she was really mad at him. Tears leaked from the corners of her eyes.

"They're my friends. They need a place to stay." Arthurs

faced Jamil and the two men with him. They had returned at a bad time. Why did Anita always have to make a scene in front of his friends?

"Of all the places in Boulder, why do they have to crash here?"

"Please," spoke up Jamil, seeing the problem. "You are upset. My friends do not speak the good English. Art has been kind enough to allow us to reside here. It is not for long." The silent communication passing among the three Iranians was undecipherable. Anita was past caring.

"*You* stay, I'll go. I'll have my things out of here in an hour—if you haven't welded them into some hideous sculpture weighing a million pounds." She jerked free when Arthurs tried to take her arm. Storming into the bedroom, she slammed the door hard enough to send a shock wave through the apartment.

"Mr. Arthurs—" began one of Jamil's friends, but Arthurs wasn't in the mood to listen. He threw off the welder's mask and dropped the torch. He didn't bother checking the tanks to be sure they were tightly valved down. Let the whole place burn—and Anita with it! She deserved it. She couldn't treat him like this. He was an artist. A great one!

Marvin Arthurs stormed into the hallway, saw Jamil's van keys on the table and scooped them up. He heard Jamil and the other two yammering away in Farsi. They were upset. Arthurs thought they had every right to be. Anita could be such a shrew.

He slid into Jamil's battered maroon van parked at the curb. The key was the only thing about the van that worked well. The engine sputtered and sounded as if it were ready to throw a rod. When Arthurs got the van moving, he thought he was driving through molasses. There wasn't any acceleration. He wanted to jam his foot down and roar off. Maybe he could find a pedestrian over by the university. He hunched over the wheel, thoughts of running down someone giving him a moment of savage satisfaction.

Driving aimlessly, he turned onto Baseline Road.

The sheer rock face of the Flatirons rose on his right. He wheeled the protesting van up the road to the Flagstaff

Mountain lookout. He needed to be above the pettiness, the small minds, the people who refused to believe he was a great sculptor. The van gave out before he had gone a quarter of the way up the steep road. Cursing, he pulled over and got out, slamming the door as hard as he could.

Arthurs walked the entire way to the lookout. The cold wind whipping through the Rockies helped take away some of the anger, and he did enjoy looking down on Boulder and the mental midgets there. What the hell did they teach in that red-tile-roofed madhouse they called a university? No one in the art department would talk to him. They had even poisoned Anita against him. They must have told her she'd never get her damned degree if she didn't dump him.

His watery blue eyes lifted from the city, and focused on distant Denver. They were no better out there. Almost two million people and they all conspired to keep him unknown. He'd show them, he'd show them all. His sculpture would bring adoring critics from around the world!

Marvin Arthurs, known to the world as Art. He would *be* art!

Heart beating faster, he started back down the road. He got to Jamil's van and couldn't start it. He pushed it out into the center of the road, then jumped in and let it roll. He got back to Baseline Road before the momentum died. The van refused to turn over. Earlier, this would have infuriated him. Not now. He had a mission. He knew his destiny.

Fame. Greatness. Those were his.

He pushed the car into a deserted lot and left it. Let Jamil fix it. He started walking. It took almost an hour to reach the tree-lined street where he lived.

Arthurs frowned when he neared his apartment. Police cars with lights flashing and military vehicles of all descriptions blocked the street. Arthurs started down the sidewalk but was barred by two soldiers carrying M-16's.

"Secured area. No admittance," one said.

"But I—" Arthurs clamped his mouth shut tightly. He had started to say he lived here and for them to get the hell out of his way. He saw the gurneys coming out of his apartment. Bright orange bags filled with bodies loaded down the wheeled carts. "What's happening?" he asked.

"That's classified information," one said.

The other soldier sneered at the idea of anything being secret and said, "Iranian terrorists. Wasted three of the bastards."

Frightened, Arthurs backed away. He didn't break out in a dead run until he reached the end of the street. Dead. Terrorists. Jamil? Arthurs had known him at Brown University before he had flunked out. He figured Jamil had gone on to graduate. He hadn't seen or heard from him until a week ago when he showed up with his two friends begging for someplace to stay.

He sank down, his back to a tree. He started tracing patterns on the street, using his finger to cast a shadow. Faster and faster he sketched, inspiration on him. The police hadn't thought Jamil was a terrorist. Not really. They wanted *him*. They wanted to stop him from creating his masterwork. Anita might have called them. They'd all moved in unison to keep his genius in check. Poor Jamil and his two yammering friends had only gotten in the way.

He'd have to hurry. Without the Cerberus maquette as a guide, he'd have to create something else that would be too great for a mere police department, even one in league with the federal government, to ignore. Arthurs' mind raced. What could he do? His finger worked harder, building shadow on shadow until a name rose to taunt him.

Christo. The Bulgarian Christ man. The one who always commanded attention with his artistry.

He could do better than the Running Fence or pinkly diapering entire islands in the Bay of Biscayne or the nylon curtain across Rifle Gap. Christo's work was transient, but it was of the proper scale. Big. Magnificent. Arthurs could do better. He *would* do better.

Arthurs walked aimlessly, turning over one scheme after another in his mind. Walking along Pearl Street, he stopped suddenly, grabbed a pencil stub lying on the sidewalk and began scribbling on a wall. He quit only when the owner of the store came out and shouted at him. Arthurs walked on, more excited than ever.

"Art by Art," he muttered. He stopped in front of an appliance store. Fourteen televisions blinked and flashed at him. The opening fragment of the news anchor's lead story caught his attention.

"Three members of the Iranian Freedom Jihad were killed in a shootout at an apartment on Thirty-second Street this afternoon. Authorities refused to reveal details about the shooting, but KVKK news sources have uncovered that the three entered the country illegally two weeks ago, crossing the Canadian border near Banff. Being sought for questioning is the apartment's occupant, Marvin Arthurs."

Arthurs cringed. He hated the name Marvin. He was an artist. Artists didn't have pansy names like Marvin.

"If you have information about this man, contact the Boulder Police immediately or phone the district office of the FBI." Numbers marched across the bottom of the fourteen screens, but Arthurs had moved on.

They wanted him. They wanted him. He had to create! He wouldn't allow the so-called authorities to prevent him from producing the greatest art the world had ever seen. How dare they try to stop him?

He roamed for hours until the streetlights winked on. Arthurs dodged frequent police patrols on the city's main streets. It was as easy to avoid the unmarked cars loaded with men in plain suits and grim expressions. He didn't even have to see the white and blue government plates to know they were federal agents. And they wanted to keep his genius from the world. All of them.

Arthurs returned to Jamil's abandoned van and crawled into it to sleep. He pushed against the curtain separating the front seats from the rear and, to his surprise, found the van filled with a large crate. Squeezing past, he slithered to the back where Jamil had made a small nest.

A rumpled blanket showed how Jamil had curled up and slept. Empty cereal boxes, bags and a few beer bottles marked what his friend had eaten here. Under a pile of potato chip sacks Arthurs saw the edge of a small spiral notebook. He pulled it free. He couldn't understand the curlicue script on most of the pages. It might as well have been written in code, but the parts in English in Jamil's precise hand made him read faster.

A map of Colorado Springs clearly marked NORAD and Cheyenne Mountain. But these had been crossed off with heavy black X's. A smaller section carried the caption "The Second Big Blue Cube." Odd footnotes about a spy satellite control center meant nothing to Arthurs.

Details on detonating the thirty-kiloton nuclear device in the van did, though. Any fool could have followed them because Jamil was a meticulous planner.

Arthurs licked the grease from inside several discarded potato chip bags. His stomach growled but a fire burned in his belly and brain. He knew what to do. He knew how to make all the damned critics—including that bitch Anita!—sit up and notice him. Marvin Arthurs curled up in the tight space on the dirty blanket, his head resting against the bomb crate, thoughts of creating irresistible art fluttering across his tortured dreams.

Arthurs awoke, feverish and afraid. He thrashed around, smashing his hand against the bomb. He recoiled, then calmed. His eyes fixed on the simple wooden crate. Reaching out, he placed a trembling hand on it, caressing it like a lover's hair. Then he pulled back.

"I must work. Work. I cannot make any mistakes." He found Jamil's notebook and went through it page by page. The light shining in the van's dirty back window fell on the pages like a laser. Only one line at a time was illuminated. That was fine with Arthurs. He didn't want to miss a single detail.

As he read, he realized some of the Arabic nake tracks were done to keep prying English-reading eyes rrom secrets. The English parts were intended to keep Jamil's two assistants from discovering that they were to be sacrificed in a funeral of fire, dying for the glory of the Iranian Freedom Jihad. These pages Arthurs hurried past. He lingered on those describing the blast range, the radiation release, the radioactive filth to be kicked up into the atmosphere. Jamil had intended not only for the spy satellite control complex to be destroyed, he wanted fallout to blanket Denver for years to come. With any luck, the entire Rockies might be overlaid with deadly dust, forcing the Air Force to abandon NORAD and Cheyenne Mountain.

Arthurs knew nothing of politics, except as it applied to his art. He had been denied NEA grants repeatedly. The thought crossed his mind that he might have been refused because of Jamil. How had they known he was friends with an Iranian terrorist? He hadn't known that himself.

Arthurs shook off such a notion. They wanted to keep him in the ghetto. They didn't want the world to see the splendor of his work. He let out a deep sigh. It was a pity to lose the Cerberus sculpture, but he dared not go back to his apartment. He might drive by and not see anyone, but they were watching. The authorities were everywhere, all searching for him.

Again he patted the side of the atomic weapon. He had no idea where Jamil had gotten it. He'd mentioned something about touring India. Maybe he had stolen it there—or been given it by the Indians. They never cared for the US, after all, cozying up to the Commies every chance they got. Arthurs felt a rage building. The Indians might have sent the bomb over to prevent his public from viewing his work.

The thirty-kiloton explosion Jamil envisioned in Colorado Springs would take all the attention away from Marvin Arthurs' work, where it belonged.

A stub of a pencil wedged between the van's floor and wall popped free. Arthurs began scribbling on the back of a blank sheet from Jamil's spiral notebook. Radiation. X-rays. Set up a functional, if expendable, sculpture that focused attention on a bigger arena.

He chucked to himself, rubbing his finger across the now clean potato chip bag. Who needed to eat? He had his art to sustain him!

Arthurs went to work in earnest looking for the right

place for the van—and his tour de force, his masterpiece, the sculpture that would bring him the celebrity his genius deserved.

Flagstaff Mountain was less than seven thousand feet high, but the Flatirons were prominent enough for his work. Marvin Arthurs eyed them critically, estimating height and width. They must be a full three thousand feet high. Rock climbers scaled their treachery throughout the year, several dying in the attempt each year. They rose majestically, inclined just slightly away from true perpendicular, flat, bare, barren rock.

Christo's work was forgotten in a few weeks. It was nothing but gaudy nylon and rope and fencing. Arthurs knew how to create permanent sculpture, a work so vital that tourists and art lovers the world over would flock to Boulder to see it.

And it would be his work. No one else's. They'd never be able to forget him after he unveiled it.

He wiped away the sweat on his upper lip and studied his stony easel. Then he set to work accumulating the material he would need.

Arthurs grew increasingly nervous. The police had been hunting him for three days. Jamil's van was too conspicuous. But he had made progress. He had wood struts. He had damned near a square mile of thin sheet aluminum, or so it seemed as he lugged it out of the construction site where he had stolen it.

"Don't need that much," he told himself. "Just enough for Proud Aphrodite." Arthurs glowed when he thought of the sculpture. His name for it sang lyrically in his ears. He wheeled through the steep streets of Boulder in a rental car, going past the university, searching for just the right spot to build.

"She'll be worshiped by millions," he muttered, swerving and cutting off a young woman in a battered blue VW.

She honked. He paid no attention. His eyes were on the Flatirons. He wouldn't need the entire expanse. Just fifteen hundred feet. That would be enough to burn in his artistry.

Arthurs slammed on the brakes when he saw the run-down flophouse. His mouth went dry and his heart clenched like a tight fist in his chest. The brick building dated from the turn of the century; it was sturdily built. And it was the four stories he needed.

He fumbled for Jamil's notebook and his calculations. Proportions and triangles and lines ran everywhere. He found the part about being 320 feet away to give the proper angle for the radiation from the blast.

"Here, here it is," he whispered, as if touching a holy relic. His grimy finger traced across the page, smearing it. He lifted his finger slightly, letting the shadow delineate the angles and heights. "I need to park three hundred and twenty feet feet from a four-story tall building. And then Proud Aphrodite goes onto the roof!"

Arthurs fell forward, facedown over the passenger's bucket seat when he spotted a prowl car cruising down the street. They were everywhere. And if he avoided the police, the FBI and CIA picked up the trail. Having to cut the CIA spy's throat yesterday with the jagged piece of glass had bothered him. She had been so pretty. But she would have kept him from creating his art. She'd had to die.

Cautiously looking up over the dashboard, he saw that the cruiser had moved on. Arthurs jumped from the van and ran to the side of the building. He had thought about this for hours. He knew how to do it right. Finding the Flatirons was easy. They stretched up the mountain five miles behind the hotel. He started pacing, each step a precise one yard.

"One hundred six, one hundred seven," he finished. He swallowed hard and wiped more sweat from his face, in spite of the increasingly brisk, chill wind blowing down off the Rockies. His stomach growled in protest from not having eaten in days, but when he turned and sighted along the line the blast would follow, Marvin Arthurs knew the fast was worth it.

He parked the van as close to the spot he had marked as possible, then went to take a room in the hotel.

"Mister, I don't care jackshit what you're doin' in there, just be quiet, will ya? It's past midnight and people are trying to sleep."

Arthurs hunkered down, his body protecting the frame for Proud Aphrodite. The hotel room was cramped. He had to move to the roof soon now that it was dark, but when he did there would be no turning back. Everything had to be precisely in place.

The irate clerk left, mumbling all the way down the hall. Arthurs heard the elevator clank in protest as it lowered the fat clerk to the lobby where he belonged. Arthurs smiled crookedly. Soon enough the clerk would become part of history. He would die in a fiery blast that both destroyed filth and created marvelous art. Arthurs wished he could tell him of his noble role, but he didn't. Too many cops came and went. And the man across the hall might look like a derelict, but he had to be a spy for the military. There was a glint in his eye that didn't go along with the vast quantities of cheap wine he guzzled.

They were everywhere and they wanted to stop him. But they were too late!

Arthurs peered into the hall. The only sounds he heard were the settling of the building and the soft gusting of night wind off the mountain. Dragging the wooden frame behind him, he got to the emergency door leading to the roof. He cursed at the time it took to file off the padlock. They'd put it here to slow him down. He knew it. It wouldn't do them any good. It wouldn't!

The sweat matting his T-shirt to his body dried as a sudden frigid blast of the ever-present wind tugged at him. Arthurs pulled the frame onto the roof and closed the door.

"That side of the roof. Over there. I can anchor it with wire. There's time. There's plenty of time." He dropped the frame and went back to his room. The sheets of thin aluminum would be perfect for his shadow creation. He didn't remember where he had read it, but radiation would cause neutrons to explode from the aluminum as it vaporized in the onslaught of X-rays. This would darken the shadow left on the Flatirons even more.

Proud Aphrodite would be etched into stone for all time. His conception would endure longer than Mount Rushmore!

Arthurs wrestled the aluminum sheets onto the roof and began working. Over the past two days, he had cut the pieces, preparing them for assembly. His vision would be magnified from the ten feet on the roof of the hotel to fifteen hundred feet on the Flatirons. Fired directly into stone, Proud Aphrodite would combine classical art work with the modern technology of the atomic bomb.

His hammer rose and fell in just the right amounts. Nails held the sheeting to the wooden frame, but only in the exact spots art demanded. Always art. It spoke to him. It commanded him to create. And Marvin Arthurs obeyed.

When he began walking the ten-foot-high sculpture up to the side of the roof, it was perfect. He used thick wire to anchor Proud Aphrodite upright, taking several turns around vent pipes and other convenient protuberances. Arthurs stepped back and stared at it.

"They'll know now. They'll know. Anita laughed. The bitch didn't think I had it in me, but I do."

He looked down from his four-story perch through the faint dawn and saw Jamil's van. Arthurs turned and stared up at the Flatirons five miles away. More than half their expanse would be branded with true art by noon.

High noon. Gunfighters. Daring men living and dying for their convictions. Sun directly overhead. A new sun, a creating sun on the ground. Jamil had figured that this small a device would only kill everyone within a half-mile radius. Arthurs regretted that they had to die for his art, but it was worth it. Most were spies and police trying to stop him, anyway. Let them die for the glory of Proud Aphrodite!

Arthurs hurried to his hotel room, shucked off his sweaty clothing and put on another set he had taken from an un-

106

dercover policeman who had almost caught him the evening before. The plaid shirt was bloodstained and too small, and the pants almost cut him in two, but Arthurs barely noticed such discomfort. To be so close to completion was all that mattered.

He took the clanking elevator to the lobby and ignored the clerk at the desk. The man looked at him curiously, but Arthurs refused to catch his eye. To do so might create alarm. He radiated victory. They must not know until it was too late.

The back of the van seemed even more crowded than it had before. Arthurs gently worked off the side of the wood crate. With Jamil's notes spread on the bomb casing, he began the tedious work of setting the timer. It was entirely electronic, and he wasn't sure he had set it properly. He went over the instructions left by his dead friend and patron of the arts. When Arthurs had finished, he ran through the directions a third time.

All was ready. At noon, the searing nuclear blast would produce art unlike any ever seen in the United States. Why go to Hiroshima when real art work could be viewed at home?

Marvin Arthurs stood next to the van and stretched mightily. It was a lovely day, the first fingers of false dawn stroking the far horizon. This was one thing he liked about Boulder. When the sun rose, it cast its rays across the plains and city and foothills in a panorama unmatched anywhere else in the world.

Tomorrow, the rising sun would shine for the first time on the dark likeness of Aphrodite—*his* masterpiece.

Wind whipped along the street, kicking up dust and debris. Arthurs started walking toward the bus depot. He had almost six hours to get to Denver. That ought to be far enough away for him to view the result of his artistic innovation.

He had gone only half a block when a sudden gust of wind, stronger than the others, blew against his face. A grinding sound startled him. Arthurs' eyes widened in horror when he saw Proud Aphrodite wobbling.

"No! No! You can't! Don't do this to me!" He turned back to the hotel and ran through the lobby.

"Hey, buddy, you stayin' another night? You got to pay in advance. And no more of that bangin' noise."

"Proud Aphrodite," he muttered.

"What's that? You have a broad up there?"

Arthurs ignored the ignorant clerk and punched repeatedly at the elevator button. The cage was stuck on the third floor. Frantic, he turned for the stairs.

"Mister, wait—"

He left the complaining clerk behind. The man might have crept to the roof after he'd left and cut the wires. Just one or two undone guy wires would bring the entire sculpture down. Arthurs cursed himself for not having dealt with all his enemies. The clerk was a guilty party, he knew. And what about the man in the room across the hall? That had to be a spy hunting him down. The clerk and the derelict must be in a partnership of evil to keep him from completing his life's work.

Out of breath, sweating from every pore, Arthurs burst onto the roof. The sheet-aluminum Aphrodite swayed precariously in the high wind coming down the mountainside. He rushed forward, hands trying to steady the ten-foot-high sculpture.

The aluminum bent. Two support wires whipped about from a new gust. Arthurs caught at the sculpture, trying to support it. He failed. The heavy outline of the Greek goddess of love slipped flat onto the roof.

"There's time," he muttered. He set to work with a feverish intensity unlike anything possessing him before. He hammered and strengthened, he pulled and shaped and formed until Proud Aphrodite was whole once more.

The sun crept up in the sky as he struggled to finish his repairs. Everything had to be perfect. Nothing less would do. Hours later, he pushed the heavy sculpture back erect. A period of relative calm allowed Arthurs to cinch down the guy wires. He stepped back and stared up at his noble work.

He went to the edge of the roof and checked the van. He

almost puked when he saw the police car. Relief better than any sex swept through him when the cruiser didn't even slow.

"Proud Aphrodite, my sweet goddess. You'll give loving testimony to the world of my genius."

The wind from the mountain blew the sculpture over the edge of the roof. It broke apart before it hit the ground.

Arthurs stared at the ruined work four stories below him. Then he looked at his watch.

A few seconds before noon.

His eyes darted from the van with the armed nuclear weapon in it to the Flatirons, all pristine and barren of true art. He had to change that. His hands rose.

The forty-seven thousand people who died and were blinded by the blast never saw the product of Marvin Arthurs' genius. Burned into the Flatirons was his seven-hundred-foot silhouette and a one-hundred-foot-high finger-play shadow dog barking forever at the world.

A Determined Woman

Billie Sue Mosiman

Patrol Officer Beatty heard the call come in at 8:05 Saturday night. The streets were alive with crime, just another Saturday night in Fort Lauderdale, Florida, and every other city of any size in America. The crack houses west of Interstate 95 swarmed with roachlike activity. The hookers strolled the palm-lined boulevards picking up fresh young tourist meat. Drunks beat their women and sloe-eyed teenagers skulked outside empty bungalows looking for a way to enter and make off with the retirees' jewelry.

Beatty patrolled her midtown beat with her mind trained on the radio so she was ready when the dispatcher's voice gave the code and address. There had been four child rape-and-mutilation cases in as many weeks. Lauderdale had an epidemic on its hands. If there was anything Officer Beatty would not countenance it was molestation of children. She could understand prostitution. She could see the monkey-grip crack cocaine had on the underprivileged. She could wade through the cesspool of criminal element without getting a taint of the scent on her, without being too warped out of a semioptimistic mental state, but when the slime went after the kids—and when they *mur-*

111

dered them—the night bloomed red. All she wanted to do was bust the guy. When no one was around. Bust him so good he'd never be able to hurt another kid again. This violent attitude didn't bother her. The male officers felt the same way. They wanted every pervert to hang from a crucifix.

She sped down Andrews Avenue toward the tall lighted buildings. There were two cars at the scene before her. She parked with a screech of tires and was out of the patrol car within seconds of slamming the transmission into park. An ambulance roared up behind her.

A tall, freckled rookie by the name of Gene turned and saw her approach. "Hey," he said in greeting. At first glance Beatty was often taken for a male officer. She stood an even six feet in her uniform. Her shoulders were strong and wide. She weighed a hefty one hundred and seventy, all of it muscle she kept firm with regular workout weights at home. Her blond hair was cut to just below her ears, the police cap over it. The single telling evidence that she was a woman was the firm, sturdy breasts that filled the front of her shirt.

Gene finally recognized it was Beatty coming their way and he nudged his partner. Beatty saw how nervous he looked. The men turned and barred her way.

Frowning, Beatty said, "Another kid?"

"You don't wanna see, Beatty."

"Fuck that. I work this district, what're you saying? Now move over." She pressed between them expecting to be let past. The two officers stood their ground, each of them giving her a stern look that said don't push it.

Beatty stepped back. "What's going on? Talk to me."

Gene's older partner, Everett, coughed into a fist. He lowered his head and his voice. "Girl," he said softly. "It's real bad, Beatty."

Beatty leaned in. "Yeah?"

"Little girl. Dead. It's . . . bad . . ."

Beatty felt sour night sweat break out on the back of her neck. They knew she hated it when kids were trashed, but why were they trying to keep her from the scene? What were they up to?

112

"So let me through."

Everett shook his head. "You don't wanna go over there."
He meant the alleyway between a Chinese restaurant and
an office building where the paramedics were scooping up
the child's cold remains.

"Why wouldn't I? I've followed all these cases. What's
wrong with you guys anyway? This is getting fucking ridiculous."

"It's fucking ridiculous all right," Gene said. "It's fucking sick outrageous."

Everett gave him a sidelong look. Gene gazed past Beatty,
his lips held in a prim line.

Everett said, "Beatty, prelim ID on the kid says . . ."

"What?" Now Beatty felt her spine stiffen and her broad
shoulders hitched back. She'd stopped breathing.

". . . kid's someone you know."

Sally. Beatty's vision blurred. The lights swam into a
fuzzy halo. *Couldn't be Sally. Her niece, her sister's girl.
That's the only kid she knew. That's the only kid they'd
be trying to keep her from viewing.*

"You got the wrong ID." That's all she could think to
say. They *must* have the wrong ID. Wrong kid. Sally was
home, safe. No reason Sally would be down here on her
own where the killer could get to her.

"Sally Selkirk. Name was written in ballpoint pen on the
sides of her Reeboks," Everett said.

Beatty glared at him for a full thirty seconds before she
armed him aside and stepped past the two officers. She had
bought the Reeboks for Sally. Birthday present. Two
months ago. She'd watched while Sally wrote her name
along the rubber soles with a departmental pen she borrowed from Beatty's pocket.

She strode over to where the body bag was being zipped
on the gurney. She snatched the zipper and raked it down
the small body. She bent over, squinching her eyes against
what she would see.

*Sally. Eight years old. Yellow T-shirt torn jaggedly across
her chest. A purpling bruise around her neck where she'd
been strangled. From the waist down her clothes gone and
on her thighs dark shadows of blood stains.*

113

Beatty turned away and walked several feet into the shadowed lee of the building. Everett came over and put a hand on her arm. She shook off his touch. He sighed and moved away.

Beatty didn't cry. Beatty was a police officer, a trained veteran who lived by procedure. She was a policewoman before she was a woman. Tears did not belong to police personnel. She hadn't cried since she was fourteen. She would not give in to emotion now.

It was four in the morning before Beatty walked into her inner-city Florida two-bedroom bungalow and took off her hat and gun holster. She had met her sister and brother-in-law at the morgue and from there she accompanied them to the station. Sally, they said, had merely offered to take the trash outside to the curb while her mother finished the dinner dishes. This happened at six-thirty. When Sally didn't return in a couple of minutes, they went to investigate. They'd searched the street, knocked on neighbors' doors, panicking like crazy each second their daughter was missing. Not long after they called the police, the first squad car found the body.

Beatty sank into a kitchen chair and twirled her hat on the Formica tabletop. The clock on the wall ticked loudly. The refrigerator purred to life. A blue beam from a yard light came through the kitchen window and lay like a soft scarf on the tile floor.

Get a life. Her sister, Margo, had said that when they had recently argued. They argued seldom. When they did, it could be ugly. One sister small and feminine and sweet. Like fresh cream and Georgia peaches. University of Miami graduate. Married a med student. Had Sally and taught school at a private academy for the rich and famous who lived in the Greater Fort Lauderdale area. Then there was Beatty. Charlene Beatty, always called Charlie even as a gangly kid. Took after their father. Inherited his bone structure, his linebacker stature. Could have been pretty had she not been so large. She didn't want to go to college. She wanted to go into law enforcement. She was made for it, wasn't she? She'd be as strong and agile as any male officer. She'd be able to hold her own. She'd be *respected* instead of ridiculed. She'd *be* somebody. Then it wouldn't matter she didn't have boyfriends and a love life.

But that wasn't good enough for Margo. "You need to get a life," she'd said. "There's more to living than riding around in a car with bubble lights, a billy stick hanging from your hip. Charlie, you're not old and you're not ugly. There are plenty of big men who—"

"Let it be," Beatty said. "Just let me live the way I want. Not every woman has to have a husband and kids."

That was a mistaken thing to say. They knew how she doted on Sally. She spoiled the child every chance she got. She spent her days off taking Sally to the zoo, to concerts and films and the playhouse. Misdirected maternal instincts? Beatty could accept that. So what was so wrong with it anyway? She didn't have time for romance and roses. She didn't have time for pregnancy and babies. But she *did* have time for Sally.

And now Sally was gone. Brutally taken. Butchered like a piglet, sacrificed to the demon of Lust and Perversion. Dying the way no one should be made to die in a filthy dark alley, her screams going unheard. And for what reason? Where was the logic?

Beatty balled a fist and brought it down slowly on the rim of her hat, crushing it flat. She wiped dampness from her cheeks. Her eyes were leaking from staring from their sockets without blinking. That's all. For she never cried.

Not Officer Beatty.

Beatty caught the first one on a lark. He was soliciting a twelve-year-old runaway on Sunrise Boulevard. He had the girl backed to the edge of the sidewalk, hovering over her like a bird of prey. He was shabby and unshaven. He wore red high-topped tennis shoes. He must have thought the girls would like that.

Beatty pulled to the curb and scared him off. He took to

115

the pavement like a marathon runner. Beatty watched the runaway run away. She wished her luck. Kid was gonna need it.

Couldn't let the perverts ID a cop so she let the guy run while she trailed him from a safe distance. When he entered a side street, she popped from the car like a genie. She had the black cloth stuffed in her right pants pocket. She took off on foot and caught him turning the next corner. Caught him from behind in a chokehold. His feet came off the sidewalk a moment. He was shorter than she, though just as heavy. She jerked out the cloth and wrapped it around his eyes, tied it tight. Then she handcuffed him and led him docilely back to the patrol car. He was bleating all the way, thinking a drug dealer had him for ransom.

"Hey, whatju doin to me?" the pervert whined. "I ain't done nuthin'. I ain't got no blow."

Beatty drove toward the Everglades, out of town. She ignored the whiner's bitching from the backseat. She ignored the calls she'd damped down to a croon on the radio. She ignored the warning voice in her head that said, "Charlie, Charlie, is this any way for an officer of the law to act?"

When the lights dwindled and the palmettos grew to the side of the two-lane, Beatty found a spot and pulled over. She killed the engine. She could hear the slobbering fool banging his head on the window. She let him out and prodded him into the dense cypress and palmetto wilderness lining the road. A wild parrot swore about holy terror beneath a silver moon and flew into the mild night from a stand of weepy fir trees. This was a desolate place, a place for dying. It was a perfect place.

Beatty made him turn around. He smelled of quick, nasty sex acts performed in the back booths of X-rated joints. He was a scroungy bit of humanity that caused Beatty to wrinkle her nose at him. "You're disgusting," she said in a fake, deep voice that camouflaged her own voice.

"Now c'mon, I wasn't doin' nuthin' to that girl back there. Just offering her money to get home on. Honest to

God. And man, I ain't got no stash. Ain't got no money. What you want?"

"Lay down on the ground."

"What're you gonna do?"

"LAY DOWN." She pushed at his chest and he toppled backward and landed with a grunt of expelled air.

"Wait a minute . . ."

"You do that little girl last Saturday night? The one off Andrews?"

He was weeping inconsolably now. "No, no, no, I didn't do nuthin', no, no . . ."

"Well, if you didn't do her, you've done others. That's enough for me."

He kicked while she hauled down his floppy pants around the red high-tops. He screamed blindly at the moon while she wrapped the garbage bag tie wrap around the root of his testicles. He was found moaning in shock fifteen hours later when it was too late to save him from the rather simple, if crude and torturous, castration that had been performed on him.

Beatty knew she couldn't rely on finding the child molesters on the streets. She'd miss three fourths of them that way. She might hurt innocent men too. That wasn't her plan. When in the station, she made it her business to check the computer databank on known local pedophiles when typing in her paperwork each shift. She figured she could castrate two a week when she had their names and addresses and familiar hangouts.

She left some of them in empty warehouses. She put one beneath an overpass and he was discovered by the winos the next morning. After two weeks, another child rape-murder occurred. This meant she hadn't caught the right one yet. But she would. Oh yes, she would. Eventually. If he continued in her territory, she'd get her man.

The thought of it made her laugh. If only she could tell Margo she was seriously after a man now. "I'm a normal woman, after all," she'd tell her. "I'm going after my man tooth and nail, just like every other woman does. Nothing can deter a determined woman."

Beatty laughed and laughed at the idea.

But she was careful not to smile when the guys at the station talked about the castrations. It made them uneasy, these strange crimes. The victims were all pedophiles with rap sheets. All with their balls tied off blue as blazes and dead as snails left to dry in the sun. Served 'em right, of course. Seemed downright Biblical. But still, it was unlawful, wasn't it, to castrate a man without benefit of trial or jury or judge? Made a man feel a little vulnerable and antsy; made him want to check his crotch when no one was looking, make sure everything was intact.

Weeks after Sally's funeral, Beatty's sister came to the house. She wore a black pantsuit and her hair was swept back from her finely furrowed forehead. She sat on the sofa, her legs crossed, eyes downcast. She took the coffee mug Charlie handed her and hugged it with both hands. She looked smaller than ever to Charlie. Drabber. Lost. Death did that to you.

"Charlie, I've come to talk."

"Well, I didn't think you were coming over to borrow a recipe." Charlie sat across from her in a wicker rocker, scrutinizing Margo's bitten fingernails.

"Don't be a smartass, Charlie. It's in the papers all the time."

"What is?"

"About the castrations. The . . . pedophiles."

Beatty permitted herself a cat's smile behind the rim of her coffee mug. "Hmmm."

"Are you doing it?"

Beatty tried not to flinch. She didn't think her sister had the inventiveness to figure out something like that. The men all claimed it was a male who accosted them from behind, blindfolded and handcuffed them, then left them some place where they'd be found hours later. The guy was big, they claimed. And strong. And he had a deep, gravelly

118

voice. Mean-ass son of a bitch. Heartless bastard, maiming them for life.

"What makes you ask something like that?"

"Charlie, I know you. I know how much you loved Sally. And . . ."

"And what?"

"There's been something wrong for a long time, Charlie. You've been . . . obsessed . . . for a long time."

Beatty kept silent. She wouldn't move now. Wouldn't say anything to start an argument, start in on the recriminations. What she was doing was between her and the perverts. The courts couldn't stop them. Let them out on bond, let them out after short sentences. Nothing short of taking their manhood away could stop them. Everyone knew that, but no one had the stomach for it. The liberal governing body thought castration, either physically or chemically, an inhumane act. As if raping a five-month-old baby girl was humane. As if ripping apart the vagina of eight-year-old Sally was humane. *She'd get them all. Eventually.*

Margo was jabbering. ". . . if it's you, Charlie, we have to do something. I've already lost my daughter. I don't want to lose my sister too."

"You're grieving," Charlie said. "Imagining things. It's not me."

"Would you tell me the truth if you were doing it?"

"Sure," Charlie said, going for the coffee pot so her sister wouldn't notice the tightening behind her eyes where the determination sat still and ready on a throne made of pallid bone.

The first murder happened accidentally. Beatty left her victim in an empty rental house near the beach. She figured the real estate people would be showing it within the next day or two. It was a nice house with a big price tag, the rooms done in pastels, the yard sculptured with white shell and tall cacti. She left a bucket of water for the pervert just in case it was a while before he was found. Then she forgot about him.

Four days later the station was full of talk. Castration victim found dead, they said. His bucket of water was overturned. He'd crawled on his belly to the locked door, but no one heard the banging. His ankles were tied. Hands cuffed behind his back. Blindfolded. Tie-wrapped. And dead. His balls, they said, had rotted off. Just like they do when a farmer puts a thick rubber band on a hog's balls. He had swelled up and begun to blow fumes strong enough to reach outdoors before someone called the cops to check it out.

Beatty felt a twinge. Not of guilt, for guilt was beyond the bounds of her reasoning in the matter. Guilt was the reserve of the pedophiles. That and fear. She'd given them the fear. Many of them who had lived in the Lauderdale area had left for cooler climes. She went stalking the addresses and hangouts some nights now and discovered the freaks had moved on. It always made her furious.

No, the twinge, on learning of the pervert's death, was one of minute joy. It tingled way down inside like an itch in her innards where she couldn't get at it. She began to wonder, as she prowled the beat in her squad car at night, if maybe she shouldn't just off the rest of the squirrely bastards. It might take more planning, more cunning, but why not go for it? Castration was fine for a warmup, but wasn't dying the real thing? Sally didn't get any second chances.

Sally liked comedy movies. Sally liked pistachio ice cream. Sally told her once she wanted to grow up and be a cop like her aunt Charlie. Just like her. Be a big, fine, strong cop who kept the city safe for all the decent people.

But then again, murder, that was something much more serious than castrating the deserving. Her victims were formally charged pedophiles. Guys who had been apprehended and were out on appeal or had served a little time. Culprits. Bonafide. So castration was called for. It was just and right and there's no telling how many little children she'd saved from the clutches of sure doom because of her actions. But murder, now that was definite. A real crime against man. She was supposed to uphold the law and keep the peace. Was she also supposed to wipe out the scum single-handedly? Well, why not? If not for her, they'd fill the gutters with dead children. Pedestrians would have to step over them to go to the corner store for a quart of milk. No one wanted that. She was performing a needed civil service. Absolutely.

The memory of Sally in the body bag, the swirling lights flickering over her small dead face, brought Beatty to a firm decision.

Kids died. Bereft of trial by a jury of their peers. Lacking bondsmen and endless appeals.

So let murder begin. Castration wasn't good enough for the worms. Not nearly.

It was another Saturday night. Sultry, the air tasting of salt water. Palms rustling with soft breezes. Jaguars and Mercedes trolling the byways and avenues. The pink and peach and turquoise club buildings bristled with pie-eyed snowbird patrols from Quebec and the Eastern Seaboard.

Beatty scanned the sidewalks for one particular suspicious character. She had a copy of his rap sheet on the seat beside her. She saw a drug deal going down and rolled on past. They scurried into the shadows. She saw a hooker enter a Silver Cloud Rolls-Royce. She whipped around the car, waving at the stunned chauffeur.

Minor infractions, these. Nothing to get bent out of shape over. She was after bigger game. Had been for months now. Although the child murders had ceased, she was not convinced the man who killed Sally had been fixed yet. That's how she thought of it. *Fixed*. Before she'd fixed them the way you fix a tomcat. Now she meant to fix them permanently. She had a knife handy for the job. She kept it beneath the driver's seat when on duty. When off duty, it lay beneath the driver's seat of her Hyundai.

121

She saw a lone man on the sidewalk. He wore tight-fitting jeans and an oversize beach shirt printed with pink palm trees. His face fit the photograph on the rap sheet. He swerved at a corner when he noticed the patrol car pacing him. Beatty felt her antenna wriggle and she reached to feel the knife just to be sure it was there. She stopped the car at the curb and was after him like a bolt of lightning homing in on a metal rooftop rooster.

He was really moving. Beating it down into a lower-class working neighborhood where there were no streetlights. Beatty felt the itch start in her guts and work its way up to her lungs as she ran after him, wind singing past her ears. Dogs barked from fenced yards. The sickle moon peeked through coconut trees as she passed beneath them. He had taken to the middle of the street now, arms and legs pumping. He sounded like a locomotive.

Beatty decided to try it. "Halt! Police!"

He glanced back, slowing down. He turned, windmilling his arms for balance, then finally came to a stop. He was out of breath when she reached him. "Jesus! I didn't know it was a cop."

"That's why you flew when you saw my squad car."

He laughed a little guiltily. "What's the problem here, Officer?"

"Turn around, present your back to me." Beatty had the cuffs off her belt loop.

"Now what'd I want to do that for?"

Beatty grabbed his arm and whipped him around. She cuffed him and led him back to the car. He complained all the way, but Beatty had tuned him out. She was thinking about the palmetto fields west of town and the knife beneath the car seat.

"You kill the little girl off Andrews Avenue?" she asked. She asked them all that without expecting a confession. It just had to be asked, that's all, part of the procedure.

"I never killed no one!"

She pushed him into the backseat. "Yeah," she said. "I bet you're lily-white innocent. I bet you never touched a kid before in all your lousy, slimy life."

The road was dark and empty, the lights of Lauderdale left far behind to leave a peach candy smear on the eastern horizon. The pervert had long since stopped talking. When Beatty shut the engine, the only sound was an irregular ticking from beneath the hood.

This was Beatty's favorite dumping ground. She figured two castrations and one murder would make it forever off limits, but it would still remain her favorite place. The low, spiky palmettos covered acres. To the right of the field stood a line of tall pine and fir and palms, soldiers to witness justice done.

Beatty jerked him from the car. "Your name is Jose Calendero, is that correct?" She had the knife in her hand. He seemed fascinated by the moonlight glinting from the stainless steel blade. She prodded him with the tip. "Your name is . . . ?"

"Yeah, yeah, I'm Calendero. So what? Whatju wanna do about it?"

"Cocky bastard, aren't you? C'mon, move it."

She moved him, stumbling and cursing, along a zigzag path through the palmettos. Once far enough from the road, she had him face her.

"Calendero, you do kids. You're a leech and a sicko. You spent four years for assault on a minor, beat two more rape charges, and you spend your waking hours figuring out how to entrap children for your own perverse pleasure. For that, you die, Jose. If you killed the little girl near Andrews, you killed the thing I loved most. If you didn't kill her, you might as well have. It's your kind who are responsible for it."

During this speech, Calendero kept glancing nervously toward the treeline. Beatty looked over, too, when she saw him give a crooked little smile. She was astonished to see a ragged line of men coming toward them in the center of the palmetto field. They carried flashlights and shotguns cradled in their arms. A voice called: "Officer Beatty, this is Sargeant Delmar. Lay down your weapon. I repeat, lay down your weapon!"

Calendero was grinning like a drunken baboon. "We set

you up, Beatty. They got your ass now. They been watching you like coon dogs ever since we left the street."

Beatty stepped close to Calendero as if to embrace him. He automatically jerked away, but he was too late. The knife handle protruded from his belly. He grunted in soft surprise, his dark eyes inches from her own. "You crazy mutherfucker . . ."

"Maybe, Jose. But you're one dead mutherfucker. And that suits me just fine."

Beatty tried twice, but they saved her each time. It was months before they let her out of solitary. Margo was allowed to visit once a week. Beatty wanted to say goodbye, but that would clue everyone in and she couldn't have that. She talked about Sally instead.

"I guess you were right, Margo. The shrinks have convinced me. I was over the edge even before we lost Sally. They think I used Sally to make up for everything that was missing in my life. Just like you tried to tell me."

"Losing . . . Sally, put us all over the edge, Charlie. It wasn't your fault."

"I see you're going to have another baby." This pleased Beatty immensely, her chief regret the fact she'd never live to be an aunt again.

Margo shrugged. "I don't know how I feel about it. Nothing can replace. . . . nothing can make . . ."

Beatty brought a finger to her lips. "Don't say it. Life goes on. It's not safe, it's not secure, and it's not even fair, but it goes on."

When Margo left, Beatty stood at the separation window with her fingertips pressed against the glass until a guard took her away. That night she carefully scooped out the metal shavings she'd taken bit by bit from where the workmen were putting in new plumbing in the women's showers. She swallowed a few shavings at a time, chased by tap water. She curled up on the mattress when it was done, and thought about her empty life and Sally's useless, empty

124

death. When her stomach lining was eaten out and the hemorrhaging began, she smiled silently into the dark. This time they wouldn't save her. No more interference. She'd get her way finally. She'd chew her fist off before she'd utter a sound.

A determined woman could always get what she wanted. Eventually. Officer Charlene Beatty would make book on it.

Kessel's Party

Michael Berry

With so many adult pleasures at hand, the guests were at first reluctant to play a children's game. But when the nineteen-year-old actress let herself be blindfolded with the bra of her bikini, people began to get into the spirit of things.

Kessel watched with satisfaction and amusement. He sipped at his Scotch, one arm around Catherine. Someone behind him said, "Happy birthday, Dennis. Great party!"

Kessel only nodded in reply. He didn't want to miss anything.

A laughing fat man took the actress by her bare, tanned shoulders and spun her around several times. He let go, and she stumbled twice before finally catching her balance. Giggling, she patted her stomach and said, "Don't make me toss my cookies, Harry!"

Brian Levesque, Kessel's friend and bodyguard, handed the girl a sawed-off length of broom handle. "Good luck," he said, then got out of the way as the actress began swinging the stick wildly.

The guests laughed and clapped. The actress lashed out, missing her unseen target by a good two feet.

"Where is it?" she squealed.

Kessel looked at Catherine and saw his enjoyment of the scene reflected in her pale grey eyes. He smiled broadly, something he rarely did.

"Warm! Warmer! Cooler! Cold!" The group chanted hints at the girl, wanting the game to go on, but also wanting her to end the suspense.

It had been thirty years since Kessel had last had a piñata at his birthday party. When he was ten, his family's cook, Gloria, gave him his first, a beautiful papier-mâché donkey filled with treats and trinkets. It had seemed a shame to break such a beautiful thing, but he loved it when his friends from school scrambled for the treasures it held, shrieking with glee and greed. It had been a genuine hit, and his popularity on the playground skyrocketed afterward. Gloria brought him a piñata every year until his thirteenth birthday. After that his parents were dead, and there were no more family parties.

The bare-chested girl homed in on her target, grazing it with the broom handle, but not with enough force to shatter the piñata. "Dammit!" She laughed, as those around her groaned with disappointment.

This piñata, too, was a donkey, but made from hand-fired clay, instead of paper. Señor Gutierrez, ninety-five if he was a day, had made it himself in his small, cluttered studio in the barrio. He did it as a personal favor to Kessel. Painted in brilliant reds, blues and greens, the piñata was truly a work of art, worthy of a spot in a museum.

"Mr. Kessel? Can I talk to you?"

Kessel kept his eyes fixed on the girl, the stick and the piñata. "Not now."

"It's kind of important—"

"Not *now*, Michael!"

The actress, sure now where the piñata hung, leaned back and smacked it a good one. The pottery broke, and all the goodies spilled out onto the carpet.

The crowd fell on the prizes, as raucous and avaricious as his grade school playmates. Today, however, the stakes were higher, and the partygoers had to scramble to snatch the choicest items. For among the Tootsie Rolls, lollipops and plastic party favors lay other, more significant surprises: Godiva chocolates, Cartier wristwatches, wads of rolled-up currency, bindles of white crystal.

Kessel watched his guests trampling each other and laughed. He pulled Catherine to him and kissed her deeply. The guests crowded around to express their gratitude. The actress, able to see now but still half-naked, giggled thanks for her watch. The mirthful fat man held up his dust-filled baggie and winked. While other guests patted him on the back and chattered about the lovely surprise, Kessel reveled in their pleasure. The party was a success.

"Mr. Kessel, I really must talk to you."

Kessel sighed, knowing it useless to resist. Michael Wheaton would not go away.

Excusing himself from the party, Kessel draped an arm around the kid's thin shoulders and steered him into the den, shutting the door behind them. "Okay, Michael," he said, "what is so important that it can't wait, that I have to hear about it on my birthday?"

Wheaton slumped onto the sofa, a tall, sandy-haired farm boy with bad posture and big feet. He looked as if he belonged on the third string of a second-rate Minnesota basketball team. Instead, he was a Ph.D. candidate in chemistry at one of the nation's most prestigious universities.

Pulling at the cuffs of a sport jacket too small for him, Wheaton said, without looking at Kessel, "I'm having problems with analog D-9."

Kessel poured himself another drink, offering nothing to Wheaton. "What sort of problems?"

"It's very unpredictable. It may not produce the effects we want."

"We still have time before Christmas."

Wheaton seemed to consult a mental calendar, then shook his head. "It probably won't be ready."

"That will disappoint a lot of people, Michael. Myself included."

Analog D-9 was to be a new designer drug, something different for Kessel's clients. It would be chemically similar to the compound in the little bindles from the piñata, D-8, or Lazer, as it was commonly known. The energy and euphoria it produced, however, would theoretically last ten times as long as the momentary rush induced by Lazer. Even though Wheaton had not yet found the formula, D-9 was already in demand.

Wheaton brushed an unruly hank of hair from his blue eyes. "I'm sorry, Mr. Kessel. But these analogs are tricky."

Kessel, whose knowledge of chemistry was limited to mixing a passable martini, said, "I thought all it took was a few extra molecules here, a couple there. No big deal."

Wheaton grimaced at this oversimplification. "Analogs of a given compound *are* simple to create. But it's impossible to predict the exact effect a new analog will have on the human body. D-9 may produce undesirable effects."

Laughter and music from the party filtered through the closed den door. Kessel wanted to get back to his guests, back to Catherine. "Look, you're a genius, right, Michael? You'll come up with something. I've got plenty of faith in you."

"I appreciate your confidence in me, Mr. Kessel, but I can't promise anything by Christmas. There's another problem, as well."

"And what's that?"

Wheaton swallowed nervously, setting his lumpy Adam's apple abob. "I'm getting married in three months."

Kessel laughed. "Kid, that's great! That's not a problem."

"She works for the district attorney's office."

Kessel shrugged. "So what? You're not doing anything illegal. That stuff you whip up in your lab has never existed before, so there are no laws against it. You're perfectly clean."

"Excuse me for saying this, Mr. Kessel, but I can't associate with you once I'm married. It could ruin Angie's career."

Kessel kept his temper in check. "Michael, you can't let a woman run your life like that. Now, if she wants to play Mrs. Perry Mason, that's all right. But you can't give up a very lucrative venture, like these analogs, because of her."

130

"Mr. Kessel, you don't understand—"

Kessel grabbed the kid by one bony shoulder and squeezed. Very quietly, he said, "Yes I do, Michael. I understand that I'm not going to let a fortune slip through my hands because my main chemist is pussy-whipped."

The kid had nothing to say to that. After a moment, Kessel said, "So, does she know anything now about our business dealings?"

"I haven't said anything. I was afraid—"

"Good. So all you have to do is keep your mouth shut. That should be easy enough."

Wheaton stood, his skinny body trembling and his face red. "Mr. Kessel, please! Don't make me do this anymore. I've almost paid off my debt to you. The D-series analogs have made you millions. Please, let me just get on with my life."

Kessel opened the den door. Party noise roared into the room. Kessel said, "I'm telling you, Michael, it's in your best interest to keep working on D-9. Trust me." Without looking back, he returned to the birthday festivities.

Kessel opened the oversized envelope Michael Wheaton had handed him. It contained one hundred hundred-dollar bills.

It was a month after the birthday party. Kessel had been home, waiting for a phone call from Catherine. Then Wheaton showed up with the stack of cash.

Kessel smirked. "Very nice. Where'd you get it?"

Wheaton wouldn't look him in the eye. "What does it matter? It's what I owe you, isn't it?"

"It matters if you're holding out on me, Michael. It matters if you're peddling the new analog to my competitors."

The kid looked up, and Kessel read the bright fear in his eyes. Wheaton shook his head vigorously. "Oh, no. No, Mr. Kessel. I wouldn't do that. I got the money from a relative."

"A relative?"

"My grandfather."

"I see."

The telephone rang, and Kessel snatched it up. "Hello?"

"Hi, lover," said Catherine, and the sound of her honey-toned voice sent an exquisite jolt through Kessel's groin. Thousands of miles away, she could still do it to him.

"Catherine! I've been waiting for you to call. How's the shoot going?"

"It's okay, even though Trinidad is something of a bore. I'll be glad to get home tomorrow."

Kessel said, "Any word about New York in December?"

"Uh-huh. Gregor wants to do the *Vogue* cover at his studio the Friday before Christmas."

"Damn. That's the day before our party."

"I'll catch a noon flight on Saturday and be home by four or five. Please, Dennis. That assignment means a lot."

"Okay. As long as you're home in time."

"I will be, I promise." She paused, and Kessel could almost hear her licking her gorgeous lips. "Dennis," she said, "do you miss me?"

What he wanted to do was launch into an explicit discussion of how much he missed her and what he would do with her when she returned. But Michael Wheaton was fidgeting in the chair across the room, staring at him with a big, dopey farm-boy expression, so Kessel said merely, "Yes. Yes, I do."

"See you tomorrow," said Catherine. "I love you."

"Love you too."

They hung up. Kessel said to Wheaton, "So, your grandfather gave you ten grand."

Wheaton started, as if not expecting to be spoken to so soon. "Uh, yes."

"How come he didn't help you out before?"

"He spends a lot of time out of the country. He just got back a couple weeks ago."

Kessel stood up and walked to the wall safe. His back to the kid, he dialed the combination, opened the door, deposited the money-filled envelope and shut the door.

"Okay, Michael," he said as he turned around. "You've paid off the principal. But there's still some interest to be reckoned with."

The chemist sighed. "How much more?"

"Not much. Deliver D-9 by the first of the week, and we'll call everything square."

Wheaton swallowed and chewed his lip. "I—I don't know, Mr. Kessel. D-9 is proving to be the trickiest analog of them all. There are some very serious side effects. I don't want to rush it."

"Suit yourself," said Kessel. "But remember, Michael, I own you until you deliver." He punched the intercom button. "Brian, would you please show Michael out?"

Kessel looked at the bedewed bottle of Dom Pérignon and said to the waiter, "I'm sorry, André, but I didn't order that."

With a flourish, André uncorked the champagne, saying, "It is a gift from the gentleman at table eleven, Mr. Kessel."

Kessel looked across the restaurant and located his benefactor, a bald man in a wheelchair, dining with two blond gentlemen in European suits.

Catherine, following his gaze, held out her glass in a silent toast. The old man nodded. His companions did not move a muscle.

"Do you know him?" whispered Catherine.

"Not yet," said Kessel.

After a suitable interval, the old man wheeled himself over to their table, leaving his dinner guests behind.

"You enjoyed the champagne, I trust, Mr. Kessel?" he said, with just a trace of a German accent.

"Very much. And I thank you," said Kessel. "But I don't believe we've ever met, sir."

"We have not. My name is Konrad Fleischer. I am Michael's grandfather."

"Michael Wheaton?"

"Exactly."

Catherine said, "Do his genius genes come from your side of the family, Mr. Fleischer?"

The old man smiled proudly, displaying strong, white teeth. "I do not know, Miss Weathers. The mysteries of genetics are beyond me."

Kessel caught André's eye and signaled that it was time

for the check. He said to Fleischer, "You gave him the ten grand, didn't you?"

Fleischer dropped his smile. "Yes. I had hoped that it would end his indebtedness to you."

"I am afraid not. Michael still owes me something money can't buy."

"He has told me." The old man rolled his wheelchair closer to the table. "Mr. Kessel, I am asking you, as a gentleman, to please end your relationship with Michael. He is the only son of my only daughter, and he means a great deal to me. I do not wish to see him hurt."

"And neither do I, Mr. Fleischer. But we have a business deal, and Michael has not yet lived up to his part of the bargain."

Fleischer waggled a thin finger at him. "That is not true, Mr. Kessel. The simple fact is that you are a greedy pig."

Catherine gasped, but Kessel merely laughed. "Am I? Well, your little Mikey is no saint himself, Fleischer. His greed got the better of him when he thought he could write a computer program that would beat the roulette wheel. That's what got him into this whole mess."

"Young people can be so foolish. But his real mistake was in borrowing from you. He could have asked me to advance him the money. It would have been no problem at all."

"Then why didn't he?"

Fleischer shrugged. "I am hard to track down sometimes. But also, I think Michael is just a little bit ashamed of his grampa Fleischer."

Catherine, sipping her glass of champagne, obviously intrigued by this conversation, said, "What business are you in, Mr. Fleischer?"

"Cutlery," said the old man. "My company makes some of the finest knives in the world. No doubt the prime rib you had this evening was carved with one of my blades."

Taking Catherine's arm, Kessel stood. "This has all been very interesting, Mr. Fleischer, but nothing you say will change anything. Thanks again for the champagne."

As they made their way out of the restaurant, old, crippled Fleischer called after them, unmindful of the other patrons, "Do not hurt him, Kessel! Hurt him, and you will regret it for the rest of your life!"

Kessel lay on his back, basking in the afterglow. He patted Catherine on the rear and sighed contentedly.

The bedside phone rang. Kessel answered it.

"You bastard!" screamed a voice.

"Who is this?"

"You idiot! Didn't you know what might happen?"

"Michael? Is that you?"

"You couldn't wait, could you?"

Kessel figured out what the kid was raving about. "How the hell did you get this number?"

"I'm not a complete moron, Kessel! I know more about you than you think I do."

Kessel took a deep breath and expelled it. "Okay, calm down, Michael. What happened?"

"Don't you watch the news? Eight junkies dead in an abandoned building downtown!"

"So?"

"You took some D-9, didn't you? Stole my samples before they were ready! Sold them to human guinea pigs!"

Kessel tried to sound reasonable. "How do you know I had anything to do with it?"

"Don't give me that! I checked the lab, and I'm missing twenty grams. Witnesses said six people died in convulsions. The other two turned psychotic and were shot to death by the police. Christ, I hadn't even tested the new batch on *rats*!"

Kessel said, "Michael, I am going back to bed right now, and I am going to forget all about this. You should do the same."

"Oh, no, you asshole! You're not getting away with this!"

Kessel hung up.

On the other end of the line, calling from his car phone, Brian Levesque said, "They're in the lab."

"Both?" said Kessel.

"Uh-huh. He's spilling his guts to her. Wonder if she's having second thoughts about marrying him now."

"She might not have long to worry about it. Did you get all his notebooks?"

"Yes."

"And his library of floppy disks?"

"Everything."

"Then do it," said Kessel.

"Will do," said Levesque.

Kessel hung up. He shook his head. Such a shame. With Wheaton's notes, one of Kessel's back-up chemists might be able to come up with the correct formula for D-9. But it looked as if there would be no wonderful surprises under this year's Christmas tree.

At the beginning, he hadn't wanted to have another piñata; didn't want to play the same game twice. But the first had made such an impression on his friends and colleagues. "Gonna have another one at your Christmas bash?" they all asked, eager for a second chance at nabbing some choice goodies. Ultimately, Kessel couldn't say no.

Still, he had one trick up his sleeve, something that would make this party especially memorable. Kessel opened the velvet box and stared at the ring inside. Its diamonds and gold glittered seductively, and Kessel knew that Catherine would not be able to refuse his gift. She would gladly become Mrs. Dennis Kessel.

He had spoken with her the night before, just as she was ordering a late, light snack from room service, ready to sleep in an empty bed three thousand miles away. The shoot had gone especially well, she said. Kessel would be proud when he saw the magazine cover.

Now Catherine was somewhere in the air, jetting home from New York. If all went well, Brian would pick her up at the airport at five, and she'd be ready for the party at eight.

Kessel couldn't wait to see her, to touch her, to run his fingers through her golden hair.

The doorbell rang, and Kessel answered it himself. A deliveryman stood on the stoop, an enormous ceramic Santa Claus beside him.

Kessel looked at the piñata and beamed. "It's magnificent. My compliments to Señor Gutierrez."

The deliveryman lowered his eyes. "I'm sorry to tell you, Mr. Kessel, but Señor Gutierrez died in his sleep last night. Your piñata was the last piece he completed."

Kessel did not allow himself much sentimentality, but he genuinely felt bad about the passing of Señor Gutierrez. The old man had been a true artist, a true friend. Kessel muttered his thanks to the deliveryman and hauled the Santa piñata inside.

Señor Gutierrez had packed it with presents and sealed the bottom tight. Kessel grunted as he carried it out to the patio. He signaled one of the workmen setting up for the party and instructed him to hang the piñata securely from a pole by the swimming pool.

Around five-thirty, Brian Levesque called from the airport. Catherine's plane had been delayed at O'Hare for five hours because of a snowstorm. She wouldn't be getting in until around eleven.

Kessel cursed. He had been afraid something like that would happen. "Okay," he said, "c'mon back to the house and pick her up later. I can use a hand getting ready for the party."

"Be there in about an hour. Traffic's kind of thick."

"Fine."

Guests began arriving at quarter to eight. Kessel greeted them with customary cordiality, steering them toward the bar and the sumptuous buffet. A number of people commented on the piñata, exclaiming over its craftsmanship.

Looking at Señor Gutierrez's final gift, Kessel regretted that Michael Wheaton's notes had proved worthless, that there was no D-9 tucked away inside the clay Santa. No one had been able to find the secret formula. If only Wheaton had kept his cool.

In the past two months, there had been surprisingly little fallout from the bombing of Wheaton's lab. A couple of Homicide dicks had stopped by to see Kessel one day, but

they hadn't been able to prove anything at all. In fact, Kessel could tell they weren't all that sure Michael Wheaton hadn't blown up himself and his fiancée in an experiment gone awry.

Nor had Kessel heard from Herr Fleischer. After the encounter in the restaurant, Kessel made some discreet inquiries about the cutlery magnate and learned that Fleischer was well connected in Europe, although he reportedly had little influence within American circles. He also heard that there was more than just a hint of unsavoriness surrounding the old gentleman, perhaps lingering as far back as the Second World War.

A couple of things still bothered Kessel. Like, how had the old man known Kessel would be dining at that particular restaurant that night? And what had Michael Wheaton meant by, "I know more about you than you think I do" when he called Kessel's unlisted number?

But as the weeks went by and nothing happened, Kessel decided that the Wheaton business was finished after all.

As the evening wore on, Kessel could see that this party was not destined to be as big a success as its predecessor. Although they scarfed down the free food and drinks, the guests seemed bored and restless. Perhaps they were taking cues from Kessel himself, who kept brooding about absent Catherine and the engagement ring in the velvet box.

At quarter past ten, Kessel dispatched Brian Levesque to the airport. And after making chitchat for the next half-hour, he decided it was time for the piñata, before the party died completely. Catherine would be disappointed to have missed it, but it served her right, Kessel figured. He would make it up to her with the ring.

The cute little actress from the last party wasn't present, so Kessel found another fetching volunteer, a busty brunette model. Since the night air was brisk, Kessel blindfolded her with a scarf, rather than with one of her undergarments. The other guests clapped and hooted as he gave her the broomstick and spun her around.

A servant approached Kessel with a cordless phone. "It's Mr. Levesque," he said. "Says it's very important."

138

Sticking a finger in one ear to muffle the party noise, Kessel took the phone. "What's up?"

"She wasn't on the plane." He sounded scared, and it took a hell of a lot to throw a fright into Brian Levesque.

Kessel felt his stomach twist and his nuts contract. "What do you mean?"

"Someone used her ticket, but she didn't get off the plane."

Christ . . . oh, Christ. "You check with New York?"

"Yeah. Never checked out of the hotel. She ordered room service last night but somehow split before it arrived."

All around him, partygoers laughed, stamped their feet, called out directions and hints. Kessel felt as if it were he who was blindfolded and spinning around.

"Warm!" the guests shouted. "Warmer! Hot!"

"Dennis?" said Levesque. "What do you want me to do?"

"Shit. I don't know. I don't know."

Kessel hung up.

The phone rang in his hand.

"Hello?"

"Happy holidays," said a voice with a trace of a German accent.

Kessel's tongue felt three sizes too big for his mouth. "Fleischer? Is that you?"

"I warned you, didn't I?" said the voice.

Kessel twirled around, scanning the darkened hillsides that surrounded his patio. Nothing. No lights, no sign of anything.

"What have you done?" Kessel said.

"Do you know what my name means?" said the voice.

"Huh?"

The whisper of a broom handle cutting through the air.

"It means 'butcher,' Mr. Kessel. In German, the word means 'butcher.' "

The sound of shattering pottery.

"Too bad all of her wouldn't fit," said Fleischer.

A dial tone in Kessel's ear.

The night filled with screams.

139

Him, Her, Them

William F. Nolan

▲ Him ▲

He walked in darkness.

He was quite tall, with startling blue eyes and a sleek, strong body that he was proud of, that he worked on constantly, the way a mechanic works on the engine of a fine automobile. All the stomach muscles were sharply defined, and the biceps were terrific. (That's what one of his women had told him: "You have terrific biceps.")

He liked women, enjoyed the thrill he got out of them, but he didn't respect them. Women were, by nature, cheats and liars, and you could never dare to trust one. They never say what they really mean. Men are usually more honest and direct. *Real* men, that is. It disgusted him to think of Rock Hudson. The rugged actor had been one of his top favorites, especially in Westerns. He liked Westerns. Lots of shooting but very little blood.

He hated blood.

Blood made him sick, the sight of it. You want to kill a chicken, you wring its neck. Hands are extremely effective instruments. Strong, muscled hands.

He had become very angry at Hudson when he found out that the Rock (the way he used to refer to him) was actually a homosexual. Doing it with other men! A real shock, finding out a thing like that about the Rock. Well, at least Hudson was dead now. God's vengeance. The fruits of perdition. Ha! Double meaning there.

He didn't actually believe in any *particular* God, just God in general. He could envision a kind of white-bearded old gentleman in a flowing robe seated on a golden throne with lightning bolts coming out of each extended hand, out of the fingertips. Blue and silver lightning that kills. Without blood. You don't screw around with the Old Man.

He liked to walk at night. Darkness soothed him; it was soft and inviting. Really exciting things happen in the dark. Daylight was harsh and unforgiving; the sun stabbed at his pale blue eyes. ("You have eyes just like Paul Newman," a woman told him at a motel in Detroit. She was really attractive, but quite stupid. And she'd doused herself with cheap perfume that made him want to throw up. But he got the thrill out of her, so it was okay. Getting the thrill was all that counted.)

He always wore his shades in daylight to protect his delicate eyes—but at night he was like a hunting cat; he could see extraordinarily well in the dark. One of his gifts. From the Old Man. From God. Ha!

He had weights in the back of his van and he worked out with them for at least an hour each morning. This way he was able to build muscle mass and maintain the basic strength of body necessary to survive. He needed strength in his arms to handle the big, cross-country rigs he'd driven. And in his shoulders and back for construction jobs. And in his legs for warehouse work. And in his hands . . .

Men are strong. Women are weak. His mother used to tell him that. She was an invalid. Stayed in bed most of the time. He'd go into her room that smelled of medicine and dead flowers and she'd read to him from the Bible every day when he was a kid. Now he couldn't remember a single word from the Good Book. She'd never held him or kissed him or told him she loved him; she read all those Bible words to him instead. Her way of expressing love. God's love, through the Good Book. That's when he began thinking of God as the Old Man. When she was gone the Old Man would be looking out for him.

142

His own father had never looked out for him. His father was a cold bastard. Never spoke to his mother, once she got sick. Blamed her for it. His parents were like two strangers living in the same house. And they died in that house without ever saying goodbye. To each other, or to him. No goodbyes.

He was thirty-six and had never been married. Never in love, so why get married? Women had always been attracted to him, to his smile and intense blue eyes and muscled body. And he was good at telling jokes. Could make a woman laugh like a loon. ("Guy couldn't afford to buy any cheese for his mouse trap, so he cut out a *picture* of some cheese and used that in the trap. Guess what he caught? He caught a *picture* of a mouse!") Trouble was, they were ugly when they laughed, their red mouths too wide. You could see their repaired teeth and their fat tongues all coated with saliva. He'd never liked to tongue-kiss. Exchanging saliva. Ugh!

But he liked them for the thrill. They gave him that, each of them—in hotel rooms across the country, in their bedrooms, in motels and the backs of vans and sometimes in their cars. The place didn't much matter, so long as it was at night. In the dark, always, with the lights out and his hands on them . . .

Then he saw her, crossing at the far corner and heading for an all-night drugstore. He knew right away that *she* was the one. It was an instinct he had, a kind of gut reaction that he always trusted. Never doubt your instincts. His mother had told him that.

His pale eyes studied her as she entered the drugstore.

She was young, maybe twenty or so. With a good, firm body and a lovely soft fall of blond hair along her back—like burning gold.

He went in after her.

She was standing near the front counter, her back to him. The overhead lights shone on her hair. "Do you have *Cosmo?*" she asked the clerk. He hardly glanced at her. Probably a homosexual.

"We're all sold out," he told her, fiddling with something behind the counter. "New issue comes in next week."

143

"Then I'll just take a pack of Camels," she said, handing him a five-dollar bill.

He was over by the candy display, watching as she got her cigarettes and change. Smoking was really bad for her; she was a fool to smoke. But then, he thought, with a faint smile, most women are fools. This one was a lovely young fool with burnt-gold hair and all he wanted from her was the thrill. So it didn't matter if she smoked Camels. He disliked those billboards with a camel all dressed up like James Bond in a tux, smoking and trying to look super-cool. A camel was ugly; it could never look like James Bond.

The suave secret agent was a passion of his. The way 007 handled women excited him. Bond was rough with them. Just took what he wanted and left them flat. He had never read the books, but he'd seen all the movies. His favorite was *Goldfinger*, had seen it four times. He liked the way the girl died, all covered in gold paint. That was very exciting.

Now she glanced in his direction as she moved toward the door with her cigarettes. He could tell she was instantly attracted to him. There was sudden electricity in the air between them, sparked by his Newman-blue eyes. Hers were brown, like the eyes of a fawn.

He followed her outside. She looked back at him as he approached her.

"Pardon me, but I know where you can get a copy of *Cosmopolitan*," he said.

She looked amused, standing by the door of her orange Honda Civic. "You heard me ask for it?"

He nodded, smiling. (He had a terrific smile.)

"It's got an article on Meryl Streep," she told him.

"Probably the best actress in films today," he said.

The young woman shrugged. "Well, *do* you?"

"Do I what?"

"Know where I can get the latest issue?"

"Oh, sure. Sure I do." He moved closer to her, close enough to detect the subtle fragrance of her hair. The scent excited him. "All-night newsstand. On Jonathan at Fifth."

"I've just moved here," she said. "Afraid I don't know where—"

144

"I can show you. It's really not far."

She hesitated, then unlocked the passenger door. "Climb in. After I buy the issue I'll drive you back here again. Will that be all right?"

"Fine," he said. "That'll be fine."

As they drove away into the darkness, he was thinking how simple it was for him to deal with women, once that initial attraction was established. It was always so easy, picking them up. He'd read in the papers about how careful women were being these days, with all the rapes and murders happening in the big cities, and maybe *some* women were like that, very careful about meeting strange men. But he'd never had any problems along this line. Maybe it was his smile.

"You live here in town?" she asked, flicking her soft brown eyes at him.

"No, I'm just passing through," he told her. "I like to keep on the move. Natural traveling man."

"A salesman?"

"I've sold things. But not often. Mostly I just work at whatever comes along. Guess you could say I've done a little of everything."

What he'd said made her suspicious. "If you're just passing through town, how do you know where the all-night newsstand is?"

"I read a lot of newspapers—from different cities," he said. "So I check the phonebook. I always look up the biggest newsstand when I come to a new place."

"Why do you read so many papers?"

"I just like to keep up with things," he said. "Habit I got into."

"Don't you watch the news on TV?"

He shook his head. "No. It's too thin and superficial. Newspapers cover things in depth. Television goes for surface sensationalism."

They were moving along Jonathan when he pointed ahead. "There's Fifth Street, at the next corner."

She pulled the Honda to a stop in front of Al's All-Night Newsstand, cut the engine. She smiled at him. "This is real nice of you. I'll only be a minute."

145

"Take your time. I got nowhere to go."

He watched the way she walked, watched her buying the magazine, watched the way her body moved under the tight blue dress, smooth and silky-sexy. The dress was snug across her buttocks and he watched the play of muscle. Tight and fine. Her legs were firm, long thighed, the way he liked.

This one would give him a real thrill, all right. All he had to do was play it cool. Guess the Old Man was still looking out for him.

When they were driving down Jonathan again he said, "Where you from? Before you came here."

"Indianapolis. Native Hoosier. Love basketball, but I hate Indiana winters."

"Yeah, I know what you mean," he said. "Cold cuts right through you like a knife. Chicago's even worse."

"That where you're from . . . Chicago?"

"I grew up in Waukegan. Guess you could say it's part of Greater Chicago."

"I've heard of it. Wasn't Hemingway born there?"

He laughed. "No, that's Oak Park. But you're close. They're both part of the same general area. And the winters are murder."

"So we're both summer people," she said, smiling. Her teeth were white and perfect in the faint reflected light from the dash. He liked perfect teeth.

"What do *you* do?" he asked.

"I'm a legal secretary. Just started this new job, but it looks like it's going to be a good one. Kind of a challenge. I like challenges."

So do I, he thought. What he said was, "You're not married then? I mean, you don't *sound* married."

"Nope. Mr. Wonderful hasn't stopped by to tap on my door yet. Someday, maybe." She flashed her brown eyes at him. "You?"

"The same. I never met a woman I wanted to marry."

"Maybe we're both too particular," she said.

"Listen," he said, leaning across the seat as she drove, close enough to catch the scent of her brushed-gold hair. "I've got a challenge for you."

146

"What's that?" she said.

"I challenge you to have a drink with me. You're fun to talk to."

"So are you," she said, turning her head to look into his eyes. "Where?"

"There's bound to be a bar along here if we keep driving."

"I hate bars," she told him. "They're always too noisy and I wind up with a headache. Why not have a drink at my place?"

"Great," he said. And his lips curved in a faint smile of triumph. This was working out just the way he hoped it would. Her place. Perfect.

Just perfect.

She stopped the Honda on a side street next to a tall pink stucco two-story building with a clipped hedge. Town house. Classy.

They got out, walked up a short flight of outside steps, and she keyed open a side door, waving him inside. A light was on in the kitchen and it made her skin seem phosphorescent.

Once the door was closed, she turned to him, pushing back her hair. Her forest eyes were shining. She raised her hand, gently touched his cheek.

He leaned forward to meet her, took her confidently into his arms. The kiss was deep, intense. He could feel her body tremble.

She was his.

He felt the soft pressure of her full breasts pressing into his chest. Heat seemed to shimmer from her skin. She wants it, he thought. She can't wait for it.

Like most women, she didn't turn on the light in the bedroom. They undressed in darkness. Not total darkness; he could see the white of her curved body as she turned to him.

"Wow," she said softly, her voice a deep cat-purr. "You must work out." She traced a slow finger along his muscled shoulder. "You must work out a *lot*."

"I do," he said. "My body is my temple."

He picked her up, walked to the bed, lowered her onto the soft flowered sheets. She was ready.

Vulnerable.

Open.

Ready.

He entered in a single, deep, hard-thrusting movement, igniting the sensual thrill that only a willing woman could provide.

A deep guttural sound issued from her throat, exciting him. "Wait . . . before . . ." She thrust up against him, her hips seeking, greedy. "I have something . . . be good for us both . . ." Her right hand was fumbling in the drawer of the night table next to the bed.

Drugs, he thought. She has something to give us an extra jolt.

"Try this," she said—and plunged the slim silver ice pick solidly into his back, skillfully penetrating his central heart muscle.

He heard three more words from her before he died.

"You were easy," she said.

▲ Her ▲

The next afternoon, a Saturday, she went to a horror movie. Got in for the matinee price. She had a genuine passion for horror on the screen, an addiction that began when she was ten and her mom had taken her to see Vincent Price in a movie about a wax museum where really frightening things happened. There was a fire and all the people melted, their skin boiling and blistering and rippling away, glass eyes sliding down their cheeks, hands and feet shriveling and curling . . . That film had given her nightmares for a month, and she had felt her own skin melting from her bones in the darkness of her bed. She'd wake up screaming, heart pounding.

Daddy was furious with her mom for taking her to see such a scary movie. They had a terrible, shouting fight over it, one of the many fights they had. Daddy always won because he could shout louder—and once he pointed a loaded gun at her mom. It was that one time, with the gun, that made Mom divorce him.

That afternoon she was scanning the local news in a coffee shop downtown when she saw the announcement. In
the entertainment section:

She was suddenly flushed and shaking. What a marvelous
opportunity—the chance to meet a genius whose mind
spawned epics of terror, who understood the true power of
darkness and death. Besides, she'd have a brand-new Carter
book to read. She'd heard he was working on a new one,
and here it was. What an opportunity!

She checked her watch: 3 P.M. Still plenty of time. The
Magic Mall was just two blocks away, opposite the Federal
Building. Easy walking distance. Should she go home first
and shower? Put on fresh makeup, change her clothes?

By the time she was in high school, Daddy had moved to
Kansas City and she saw him only on vacations. He looked
worse each time, drinking the way he did. His face began
to look melted, like the figures in the museum.

Mom enjoyed being single again; she dated a new man

every weekend, and most of them spent the night. Her mom told her she felt "free."

Now, as a grown woman, she didn't see her mom anymore. Didn't care to. Didn't love her. Didn't love her daddy, either. As a child, she'd been just one more thing for them to argue over, an object more than a person. So there wasn't any love among the three of them. She knew her parents never really gave a damn about her, and the feeling was mutual.

She had a pretty face and a sexy body (terrific boobs at thirteen!) and guys liked her. She never dated boys her own age. At fifteen, she was sleeping with a thirty-five-year-old man. Young boys were boring, and they never had enough money to give her a good time.

She was hit on constantly—at the movies, in stores, at the shopping mall, and often at the gym where she worked out to maintain her figure. She was obsessive when it came to her figure; if she gained a pound or two she'd live on water and grapefruit until the extra weight had vanished.

She was puzzled about why she could never seem to fall in love. Maybe it was because there had never been any love in her childhood and she didn't know *how* to love someone. She felt desire, sexual excitement, but that wasn't the same.

She began to see men as predatory animals, on the hunt for physical delights, using her to obtain these delights. Just an object—as she'd always been from childhood.

She hated being used.

The great thing about horror movies was that death solved all the problems. The monster came along and chopped everybody up and got away neat to come back in the next picture and do it all over again. As she watched, she always cheered the monster on. Oh, yeah! *Do* it to them! Go, big Daddy! Slice 'n' dice!

Love was an ax, or a knife, or an ice pick.

She especially enjoyed watching Freddy in that *Nightmare on Elm Street* series, with his razor-gloved hand and his glittery pig eyes and fire-ravaged skin. Freddy was great! He liked to make little jokes before he slashed up his victims. He was a riot! Great sense of humor. He was always able to crack her up, the things he said. She'd laugh so hard sometimes the tears would come to her eyes—and then quite suddenly she'd be crying. She didn't know why she did that, why she cried after laughing. But both things would happen at once. Weird.

She liked to read horror books almost as much as seeing horror movies. Had a complete collection of Stephen King paperbacks. He was her favorite. In fact, his book *The Shining* was a whole lot scarier than the movie. In the movie you didn't get to see those animals made out of bushes, didn't get to see them come to life the way they did in the book. Now every time she walked by the high, trimmed hedge outside her building she imagined it was moving, growing teeth and eyes, getting ready to attack her. It was a scary feeling, but it was also kind of *delicious*.

Of course, she knew it couldn't really happen, that a hedge creature could never slash her flesh, so the fear was never tangible, never truly real.

Still, it was a lot of fun to think about stuff like that.

Beyond Stephen King, her second-favorite horror writer was Terry Carter. What a warm, happy name for the man called the Master of Mayhem. That's how his publishers described him in the ads for his books: "Another Tour into Terror from the Master of Mayhem!"

She'd read every one of his four best-sellers (devoured was more the word for it): *Slash by Night, Slaughter Sisters, Bloodaxe,* and *The Nightstabbers.* The last one was really frightening, about this gang of kids who started out human and gradually turned into alien things who slashed up everybody they met, then ate them, even their bones. There would just be this little pile of clothing left on the street for the cops to find. Certainly, it was Carter's best novel, no doubt about that. When she read about gangs in the papers she always thought about the Nightstabbers.

No. She couldn't wait that long to meet him; even the short walk to the mall would be torture. Knowing that Terry Carter was waiting for her was enough to set her pulse racing.

151

Questions burned in her mind. Could she lure him to her bed as she had lured so many others? Would he be attracted to her? Would her body serve to draw him to her as the fly is drawn to the web? It wouldn't be enough, just meeting Terry Carter.

Not nearly enough.

B. Dalton was crowded as usual on a Saturday, and a line had formed at the rear of the store. Mostly women. Giggling nervously. Clutching their newly purchased copies of *Death Devils*. Waiting to get a personal autograph from the Master of Mayhem.

The procedure was to pay for the book, then line up for an autograph. She couldn't see what Terry Carter looked like; the line forked around a corner where he was seated at a desk. But that was all right. First she wanted to examine his latest book. She picked up a copy from the tall stack on the display table.

The dust jacket pictured a blazing-eyed Hell Creature crouched over a screaming young woman who was spread-eagled on a lab table. The demon was in the process of clawing the clothes from her body. His fingernails were long daggers (like Freddy's glove!) and he had already ripped away most of her blouse.

She noted that the illustration was in good taste since a swirl of hellish steam obscured the victim's naked breasts (you couldn't see the nipples). The colors were bright and garish, emphasizing the red veins in the terrified girl's popping eyes.

Obviously, another Carter classic.

When she rounded the fork in the line and got her first sight of Terry Carter she was shocked. And amused. Now she could understand why no photo of him had ever been used on the jackets of any of his books—because he was *not* what his readers would have expected. Terry Carter was anything but sinister. He was, in fact, a mild, gentle-faced man. Perhaps thirty-five. With a full head of dark hair and tranquil gray eyes. An easy-smiling man in a dark blue, neatly pressed suit and cream-colored button-down shirt, wearing a classic red striped tie. Could have been dressed for a Yale college reunion. No monster. Just a pleasant fellow who spoke softly and acknowledged each compliment with a warm smile.

In the line, she'd been framing the words she would say to him; it was important that she make a strong initial impression.

"Every one of your books is a masterwork, and your characters are totally alive on the page. I think you write better than Edgar Allan Poe."

He looked up at her with a degree of amazement, taking the copy of *Death Devils* from her slim-fingered hand. "That's wonderful to hear," he said, his voice smooth and deep-toned. "No one has ever told me I write better than Mr. Poe. I'd like to believe you!"

And he gave her one of his warmest smiles.

"Could you personalize the inscription?" she asked.

"Of course." His black felt-tip was poised above the title page. "I'll need your name."

"Judy," she said. "Just make it Judy."

And he wrote, in a flowing scrawl across the page: "Happy Nightmares to Judy, from Terry Carter."

At first, she hadn't been certain she could pull it off, seducing this quiet man in his conservative suit—but as he handed the book to her their eyes locked and held. And she knew he was hers. Her prize. All hers.

To do with as she desired.

It was in his eyes. His surrender was implicit—and total.

She was waiting for him just after five outside B. Dalton, watching him shake hands with the store manager. The middle-aged woman was nervous and flustered; her smile was strained and her hand shook. Genius and fame can intimidate.

He left the store carrying a scuffed leather briefcase, and she walked up to him just as he reached the elevators.

"Remember me?" she said brightly. "Judy?"

The warm smile. The flash of eyes. "Of course. How could I ever forget you?" he said. "The perceptive lady who tells me I write better than Poe."

"You're on a book tour, right? One town to the next?"

"That's right. I'm due in Des Moines tomorrow afternoon."

"And you're traveling alone?"

"Unhappily, yes."

"And you have nowhere in particular to go? Tonight, I mean?"

"Right again." He smiled.

"I think you deserve some company. I'm volunteering." She canted her head, pushing a strand of hair away from her face. "I hate to see a man like you eating all alone."

He nodded, smiling again. "That's very sweet of you, to care about a stranger."

"You're no stranger to me," she told him. "I've read all your books at least three times. I feel as if we're old friends."

"I know what you mean. I've always felt there's a special bond between writer and reader. A bond of . . . intimacy, perhaps."

"Then you'll let me take you to dinner?"

"So long as you allow *me* to pay for it. My publisher is footing the bills for this tour."

"Okay, Mr. Carter, we've got a deal." And she put out her hand.

He took it gently, turning the handshake into a kiss. His lips pressed her fingers. "Terry. After all, as you point out, we're really old friends."

She drove him to one of the town's best seafood restaurants. (A friend at work had mentioned the place, giving it high marks.) They both admitted to a passion for sand dabs with hollandaise sauce.

The food was superb.

Over wine, at the end of the meal, she leaned toward him: "There's something I've always wanted to know about you."

"Ah." He tipped back his head. "Which is?"

"Well . . . I've read all the bios on the dust jackets of your books, and I read that article on you in *Writer's Digest* last year . . ."

"I'm afraid I sounded a bit pompous in that one."

"Not at all," she said. "It was a wonderful interview. I just wondered why you've never married. I know it's none of my business, and very personal, but—"

"Oh, I don't mind talking about it. The truth is, I was, in fact, married once. To a girl I met in college. We fell in love and married right after graduation. But it didn't last long." His voice dropped. "She died in an accident. I've just found it too painful to discuss with interviewers, so I leave out that part of my life. At least for public consumption. Understand?"

"Absolutely," she said, pressing his hand across the table. "And I'm so glad you were willing to confide in me."

It was easy, getting him to stop at her place for a nightcap before he returned to his hotel. And it was easy to get him into bed.

She was about to add the Master of Mayhem to her list of conquests.

"I have something here in my purse for you," she said. "I think it will be a surprise."

"Wonderful," he said, reaching into his briefcase by the side of the bed. "But I have something I think will surprise *you*."

And he removed the hunting knife his father had given him on his sixteenth birthday and plunged it into her throat.

Judy's purse tipped sideways and the small vial of cocaine rolled to the floor.

She bled a lot, but he didn't mind. His wife had been like that, after he'd done her. A bleeder. And there were so many others along the way. A lot of blood.

He was smiling when she died.

▲ Them ▲

They met in Des Moines where his tour took him next. She had driven there in the Honda after quitting her job with the law firm.

She'd delivered her last victim to a garbage dump at the outskirts of town before she headed for Iowa. The police would eventually find the corpse, but there was no possible way to connect her to the murder. She was always careful about details. (She ascribed this to her astrological chart: out of ten major natal positions, she had seven in Virgo.)

He had chopped up Judy's body for easier transport and had buried her in a lime pit. The lime would take care of the body parts. As he boarded the plane for Des Moines he dismissed Judy from his thoughts. Well, not entirely, since he planned to use the entire incident in his next novel.

Hemingway had expressed it beautifully: "Live it up, write it down." Splendid advice for any professional writer. Maybe Terry Carter's books were not great literature (he knew Judy was bullshitting him about Poe), but at least he wrote out of personal experience. His books were, at the very least, *authentic*. He'd dispatched more than a dozen women. Each one snuffed out in a different way. And with none of the murders connected to the mild, self-effacing author of best-selling novels.

"Tell us, Mr. Carter, where on earth do you get all those weird, murderous ideas of yours?"

"Oh, that's an easy one to answer." And he would smile warmly at the questioner. "I just go around killing people and then write it all down."

That answer always got a big laugh. A real crowd-pleaser. Then he'd follow it with a broad wink at his interviewer. A horror writer with a wry sense of humor; his fans loved him.

The first thing he'd noticed about her, when they met in a downtown seafood restaurant (both of them waiting for a table), was the lovely burned-gold hair which reminded him of a lion's mane. It occasioned his first words to her.

"You have beautiful hair. I hope you don't mind my saying so."

"Not at all." Her smile was radiant. "And you, sir, have wonderfully soft gray eyes."

"So long as you drop the 'sir,' and call me Terry, I think we're off to a great start."

"Terry." Her voice was husky. "A name to match your eyes."

And she stood very close to him, pressing her thigh against his.

It was going to be an interesting evening for them both.

▼▼▼▼▼▼▼

Clutter

Brad Linaweaver
▲▲▲▲▲▲▲▲

After his parents died on the interstate, Paul Kraft, a small, freckle-faced boy going on fourteen, was moved into Aunt Rose's house over in Culver City. It was an old two-story house surrounded by tall trees and he fell in love with it on first sight. Then, with the opening of a door, he came face to face with Aunt Rose, who until that meeting had only been a vague childhood memory, a shadow guest at his seventh birthday party: She stood thin in the doorway, a fifty-two-year-old librarian who had lived most of her years alone.

She invited Paul inside, showed him to an upstairs room and waited quietly as the people from the moving van moved his possessions into the house—some clothes, a monster mask and a lot of books. With the boy settled in, the cousin who had overseen the transfer said his goodbyes and departed from Jefferson Lane, leaving behind two people to get acquainted who had in common blue eyes and virginity.

The first thing Paul learned was that Aunt Rose cleaned house twice a week. The whole house. It was a strategy she had worked out against her arch-enemy, dust. Days when she didn't clean were lulls between battles, a time for planning. When she was engaged in the grand effort, all brooms and dustpans, she had no time for so trifling a concern as a nephew's privacy. His door was without a lock and he soon learned that Aunt Rose didn't knock. No closed door could withstand her determination to get into a room at precisely the moment she desired entry. There was never any telling when she would decide a certain rug or bureau required her immediate attention. After a month of diplomatic entreaties, Paul succeeded in being granted the privilege of cleaning his own room. As he had expected, inspections were twice a week.

Occasionally, Aunt Rose would call him downstairs for the announcement of a shopping expedition. Then would ensue an hour of methodical preparation, Rose dressing herself in an outdated, high-collared dress smelling of mothballs, and having Paul dress in a suit purchased on an earlier outing, starched little-young-man clothes with the look of a mail-order catalogue about them. On the first trip, he had criticized his guardian's selection of clothes when in a department store she asked what he thought of a shirt she was buying for him. He hadn't liked it. She didn't ask his opinion again. Instead, she frequently told him that it was a great sacrifice on her part to take him shopping and he obviously lacked gratitude for her generosity. She didn't let him go in bookstores when they were out.

When summer came, Aunt Rose opened the door to his room one evening, poked her head inside and asked, "Paul, dear, are you busy?"

"No," he answered, "not really. Just reading."

"I wanted to ask if you know what today is?"

"Wednesday, the eighteenth."

"Yes, dear. It has been over three months since the death of your parents, one season in fact." She peered intently at Paul's eyes; he looked at her indifferently.

"What is it, Aunt Rose?"

She gave a little shrug. "Well, I thought you should know. You should think about it."

"Are we going to the cemetery?" he asked.

"Would you like that?" she asked back. He said nothing.

He was confused by the pleasant tone in her usually neutral voice. "Yes, Paul," she continued, "we are going after we've finished the den." He understood his cue and got up to help her with the vacuum cleaner.

They only spent a few minutes at the cemetery because a strong wind disturbed Aunt Rose's hair. On the way back she said she was glad their visit with his parents had been taken care of, as though a duty had been discharged. He wondered how many more anniversaries of the accident would be observed by his aunt . . . and then, feeling anxiety and impatience, concluded he must be depraved for thinking such a thing. Not able to understand his uneasy emotions, he put them out of his mind as best he could. He spent the rest of the day on Mars, courtesy of Edgar Rice Burroughs.

It was a predictable Saturday. He didn't get out to a movie, but when the cleaning was done, and he'd settled himself in his room to read, a knock came on his door—a knock!—he steeled himself for the worst. What could have inspired a formal visit from Aunt Rose?

She entered, sat in a dark chair next to the window. She surveyed his bookshelf and its double row of books, and she studied the contents of a box at the foot of his bed— there like a footlocker, packed with books—and then she looked at Paul and said, "You have too many books."

His mouth hung open for a moment before he said, "I don't understand, Aunt Rose."

"For one thing, you don't have enough shelf space."

"They fit, don't they? So there's room, isn't there?"

"It doesn't look very nice. When your door is open you can see the box from the hallway."

"I can move the box."

"But that's not the point." She looked down at the thin, white hands in her lap, clasped them, and then glanced up at Paul—but she didn't look in his eyes; she was staring at the top of his head. "Paul, dear," she said, "surely you don't read them all. You couldn't possibly have read them *all*."

"I've read over seventy-five percent of them."

"You see?"

"But Aunt Rose. . . ."

"Your hair is uncombed."

"I'll comb it." He pulled out a comb.

"Even if you did read them all, that wouldn't be good for you. It would take up too much of your time. It wouldn't be healthy for a young boy to spend so much time reading. It would be bad for his eyes."

"Aunt Rose," he said, his voice growing louder, "I like to read!"

She raised her eyebrows in surprise. "Why, Paul, there's no need to shout. You notice that I never shout. People will listen to you if you are quiet and polite."

"I'm trying to be polite."

"Don't you realize if you had fewer books it would be easier to clean your room?"

"I collect books."

"That's much better, dear. You may put your comb away." He put his comb away. Aunt Rose sighed and said, "It's not good to spend so much time cooped up in a room. You should get out more often."

Paul replied much too swiftly, "But you don't like me to go to the playground or to the lot where they have the football games. You don't like me to come home dirty."

She grinned in triumph. "You could go to parties. You could get out and still stay relatively clean. You really ought to."

"I don't like parties."

She stood. "Think about it, dear. I'm really trying to do my best to raise you, although I never expected there would be a child in the house. Still, I'll do my best." At the door she paused, turned back and said, "Don't forget what I said about the books." His white stare met her gray one and she hurried out the door.

That encounter got him to thinking about how his aunt used her spare time. He hardly ever saw her read. She didn't even enjoy the newspaper. This struck him as peculiar because of her job. As the town librarian, she was entombed daily among a thousand volumes. But reading for recreation was not part of her life. In the house there was a small bookcase chock-a-block full of fiction and essays and poetry left over from Grandma and Grandpa. Aunt Rose didn't use it. Paul remembered that his mother, Rose's younger sister, had liked to read.

The only time Paul saw Rose opening the books was when she was cleaning the house and moving things about. She muttered over them like a sorceress, vainly attempting to exorcise the dust that clung to the leather covers. She handled them roughly, reserving delicacy for dusting objects of fine china—a zoo of small porcelain animals and a cherished teacup that dated way back.

Not long after Aunt Rose's complaint about his personal library, he was vacuuming and she was dusting and talking to the books. He resolved to find out what made her tick. He turned off the machine, came into the study and asked, "Why don't you like books?"

She started, laughed without pleasure. "Why, whatever made you say something like that?"

"I was only asking a question."

"It's so foolish!"

"Do you like books, then?"

"Books are important tools. That's why we have libraries."

"Thank you," said Paul, still unsatisfied, returning to his vacuum cleaner.

Later that day, at dinner, Aunt Rose said, "If you went to the library more often, you wouldn't have to waste your money buying all those paperbacks."

"I earn that money mowing lawns."

"Is that good reason to spend it on things that just lie around getting dusty? Libraries exist so you won't have to buy books."

He got to wondering if Aunt Rose was happy. He felt a profound discontent in the air when she was present. Although she smiled often, it was always perfunctory when talking to him. He had the idea she was about to suddenly look over her shoulder, as though she were being stalked

. . . but it was only Paul who was there. She complained if he made too much noise, which soon became almost any noise he authored, and worried out loud that he did too much walking in the house; that the old house wasn't used to it and he might wear it out if he didn't exercise more care. He hid in his room but that afforded only temporary sanctuary. He did a lot of thinking there.

It seemed like a thousand years ago that his mother told him about her elder sister. She described the family history, complete with particulars, tactfully stated, of Rose's self-imposed loneliness. The old-maid sister had a knack for antagonizing virtually everyone except Paul's mother and her employer.

The story went that Aunt Rose suffered through a bad childhood inflicted on her by an older brother, Joda, who reached some kind of distorted pinnacle when, brandishing a baseball bat, he chased and terrified her. Joda was like that. The father doted on the boy because he was the only son—through him the family name was supposed to live on. Joda never married, however. If the patriarch had had his way, the son would have inherited everything except whatever stray cash was left for the girls to divide. The mother, who had half the estate in her name, intervened on behalf of her daughters and Rose inherited, among other dispensations, the house. Paul's mother inherited some stocks and bonds and money. Joda inherited the other stocks and bonds, the rest of the money and the family business, which he managed to bankrupt within a few years. No one was surprised that Rose elected to spend the rest of her life in the very house that had been the site of so many childhood traumas, rather than sell it as her sister advised.

Paul remembered his mother's words about Aunt Rose in a special way, as if they had just been whispered in his ear—her soft, calm voice telling him about the house of her parents, now haunted by the autumn-leaf woman blown from room to room by vagrant breezes, and sometimes blown out the door and down the street to the library. And always, the house waiting to suck her back inside.

One Sunday evening, Paul came downstairs excited over

something he'd read, intending to share it. Aunt Rose stopped him cold in mid-enthusiasm and snapped, "What do your books teach you?"

He faltered, then said, "Well, they teach me about adventure, about fun, about good and evil . . ."

"There!" said Aunt Rose. "Morality. What do you know about it? What does that"—she gestured disdainfully—"sordid book of science fiction teach you about morality?" He said nothing. She continued. "Does it teach you consideration for others?"

He said, "There's a story in here about a hero. It shows how a man can win if he's honest with himself, if he's smart."

"Does it show that we have duties to others, that society comes first?"

"What are you talking about?" he asked coldly.

She smiled a mirthless smile and translated: "Don't be selfish."

"Oh," he replied.

She approached him and brushed a lock of hair from his eyes. "We must bear in mind the importance of balance," she said in a disinterested monotone. "We must avoid extremes. That's why I worry that you have an obsession with books."

There was a malicious glint in his eyes as he said, "But don't you go to extremes in cleaning the house?"

"Don't be precocious," she admonished him. He bit his lip. "Now run along," said Aunt Rose. Paul ran along.

Back in his room, he considered an evening stroll but knew she wouldn't grant permission. Out there was darkness and she didn't like the idea of darkness. But then, he observed, she wasn't very fond of light either. The drapes were kept drawn twenty-four hours a day except for the faded yellow ones that hung at the kitchen window. They would be under the same roof for another evening, as usual.

Precocious! *There* was a word, much as he loved words, to hate. It had dogged him all his life. In first grade, while his peers were struggling through Big Golden Books, he was reading mystery comics and deducing the solutions to admittedly transparent plots. In fourth grade he was bored by the basic reader and discovered science fiction. Jules Verne was the launchpad, and H. G. Wells the rocket that shot him up high where waited the prose of Ray Bradbury; where people with real human passions dreamed robot dreams— he was drunk on thoughts of the future. Seventh grade: while his class was one year away from being assigned Bradbury, he was well along in Dostoevsky. At first it surprised Paul that other students resented him for his speedy comprehension in English class but at length he became used to it. What he was never able to accept were the teachers who criticized him for his ability and called him precocious whenever he tried to express a thought.

It had finally seemed unimportant what opinions were expressed by the people at school. He was comfortable at home. He overheard his parents talking of how it was a good possibility that Paul would earn himself a scholarship to a university when the time came. Naturally they encouraged his voracious reading. But they soon found their ministrations to be unnecessary. He was on a nonstop roller coaster of words. His father proudly suggested that nothing human could derail him.

But then, with the screaming of metal on concrete, and an ambulance vainly seeking to cry out for the side of life with as much conviction as death's grinding of bones, Mr. and Mrs. Kraft were borne away. It had seemed so out of place, so wrong. With one hammer blow on his chest, Paul had felt his world diminished. They were gone. He was alone. Standing in a private limbo, peeking at a world awry, he'd seen his life packed away, all bundled up, and moved in big boxes via a handle-with-care van to Aunt Rose's mausoleum.

The first night, lying awake in a feather bed, listening to crickets outside his window, he decided he was disembodied and his spirit was wandering up and down the stairs, listening for the creaking sounds that are the very pulse of an old house. He imagined the house was carrying on a conversation with the night creatures and there was a general agreement that Paul Kraft wasn't really there; that it was just a grim joke being played; that he'd wake up the next day to find his existence intact once again. But he never got to sleep that night. Within a week he accepted the existence of Aunt Rose, and then the gray days began to creep by, leaving him with the knowledge that he was waiting, but he didn't know for what. He began to think that perhaps he had been in the car with his parents and accompanied them into the grave.

He thought that he had arrived, terribly alone, in a special kind of Hell where not even Charon or Cerberus would set foot—a place reserved for Paul and his tormentor. He got to thinking of it a lot. He even got to dreaming about it and one night he screamed about it, the night he dreamed he was locked in the bathroom, sitting in a pool of dirty water in the bathtub, sweating black dirt while Rose banged on the door from the other side. He could hear the vacuum cleaner roaring. And he heard her saying that he was every bit as dirty as his books. As he woke up, heart pounding, head dizzy with fear, he had heard his aunt's voice at the door asking in a low voice, "Why did you scream?"

"I had a nightmare," he'd answered abruptly, then added, "it won't happen again."

"Good night, then," had come the voice through the door. A pause. "Dear."

When his fourteenth birthday came around, he spent the day away from the house at a double-feature movie and in every bookstore within walking distance of the theatre. There was enough money left over from the pictures to purchase a few paperback anthologies, but he lamented the lost period of his life when there had been a regular flow of stories. Now he spent some of his time at the library as his aunt advised, but always on her day off. He read fiction when what he was after wasn't checked out. Paying his money for the books, he smiled inwardly, knowing that soon he'd have more money because of three recent additions to his lawn-mowing list. It was a fine present.

At five o'clock she picked him up in front of a drugstore. He was still cheerful. He stayed that way for almost an hour until she reminded him that any money he would be earning should go toward important things, such as savings for a college education; and of course there was the matter of his clothes.

He gave his aunt her due, however. When she had asked him if he wanted a birthday party, he appreciated the reticence with which she asked the question. At least they shared a mutual dislike of such events, or so he thought until she surprised him in subsequent weeks by insisting more and more frequently that he attend parties. The announcement came over a meal of lamb chops: "You," she said, "are going to Barbara Struthers's party." Well, when her voice had that tone, that was that. He cursed the bad luck that allowed Aunt Rose to make the acquaintance of Emma Struthers, a schoolteacher of all things, and now it was naturally assumed that the daughter of a teacher and the nephew of a librarian would get together and enjoy some kind of intuitive camaraderie. He savagely attacked the remains on his plate.

When the day arrived, he dressed reluctantly while she stood outside his door talking all the time about how much he'd enjoy the party. She finally inspired compliance with her edict when he saw the party as a means of escape. But before he got out the front door, she spied his bulging coat pocket and made him leave his book behind. With present in hand, he was off.

"Don't forget to be back before dark," she called halfheartedly.

Now that Paul was gone, Aunt Rose tried to forget about nephews and other troubles. It was time to relax. She sat in a rocking chair and contemplated a corner of the room. She thought about dust. She observed it, floating, swirling in the light shaft that slid between two almost-drawn curtains. There were so many motes of dust, a world of flickering particles made visible in one ray of light coming through the window, stopping on an empty corner. It bothered her.

She even dreamed about it. She had swept, mopped and vacuumed her way through so many nightmares; and still there was the dust, the infinity of little white specks. They

were outside her and inside her—under-the-fingernail specks, inhaled specks, captured-in-the-ridges-of-fingerprints specks, everywhere specks. Sitting in her rocker, rocking, stirring up whirlpools of the stuff, Aunt Rose sighed, and from her left nostril there exited a particle of matter that once had been the flesh of an Egyptian pharoah. The rocking woman felt time pressing against her eyelids.

Dust, if not bad enough in itself, conjured up images of even worse things, like dirt, like the filthy earth she was rolled in when brother Joda roughhoused her, like the dirty hands of her father patting her when he came in from working in the yard, like the grime that nested in her mother's pores (even though her mother was a fastidious woman, Rose could see pollution in the flesh when she was close up). She took baths twice, sometimes three times a day. She had done so for a long time, until her skin was almost the pallor of soap, and she got rashes on her oversensitive, flaking skin. She never felt clean. Each night she dreaded the prospect of working the next day because the big, dirty world was waiting to sully her. The library was so damnably full of dust. But if she didn't venture out to earn money to buy her protection, then one day that world might be able to touch her so hard she couldn't stand it.

Why, she agonized, couldn't Paul understand? He was grown up for his age. Surely he could see that she braved the outdoors for him. The busy, bustling department stores were bad enough . . . but when she went to the cemetery it was truly terrible—just the thought of all that dirt around so many bodies. When she'd offered to make the supreme sacrifice (to let him have a party at the house even though such an event would mean a flow of dirt from outside), she thanked God he hadn't taken her up on it. The relief she felt didn't keep her from criticizing him for his stubbornness. "You'll never get ahead, dear, unless you're more social," she had warned him with all the conviction born of bitter experience. Paul didn't argue the issue that time. Which pleased her. He ignored it. Which frustrated her. He was so hard to reach. So hard to understand.

At least she was alone, now. She liked that. Not that

Paul was an exceptionally bothersome child—in fact he was quieter than many adults she knew. The problem was that he was there. She couldn't sleep at night when he was reading because his room was next door. Although it was a big house, all the bedrooms were together. The light from his lamp would creep under her door and its soft radiance would warm her face. She'd open her eyes, see dust in the light. Then she'd hear Paul turn the pages. It seemed that he was constantly reading. How books accumulated dust and how swiftly a few of them grew into an enormous inconvenience. In the twilight state preceding sleep, she would hear pages turn and she'd just have to stay awake, waiting for the next one. It was like the dripping of a faucet, only not as regular. Paul was a fast reader, getting to the next page before she could doze off. *Crinkle* would go the page in his fingers, as he turned it slowly, lovingly. *Crinkle.* Sometimes in the middle of late-night reading, he would take a break and move around. He even closed doors. Sometimes she could hear the creaking of bedsprings. Sometimes she didn't dream about dust.

She was growing to resent Paul. All he wanted to do was talk about his books—usually he'd get the most excited over a book she'd never heard of—and he liked to push tomes into her hands, proposing in a most insistent voice that she read them. She knew that if she complied, he would want to talk about them, which meant a discussion afterward. She so hated argumentative people. Paul was very aggressive, a prime example of the type. She blamed her sister for the boy's poor manners. Worst of all, she had discovered that he was smuggling new books into the house as if he didn't have enough already. Some of them were those dreadful horror stories.

She got up and entered the kitchen to fix herself a cup of tea. There a moment of courage gripped her. She selected the prize teacup, poured in the hot brew and went back to a rocking chair that protested, squeaking a little, when she sat down—but that was all right because it was her sound. She sipped her tea with a hearty *sssssut!* Outside, a car passed by and the shifting of the gears grated on her nerves.

A dog barked. How noisy, how messy the world. At least she had her house, her sanctuary, and the world was on the other side of her door.

Except for Paul.

Shortly before dusk, a grinning Paul Kraft left the home of Barbara Struthers, and berated himself for having supposed the party would be a bore. He had to face it. He could not deny that he'd had a great time. Barbara proved to be quite a hostess. He hadn't even known that she liked him before this. But now he could hardly believe the proof of her fondness. In his hands he carried the fruit of that pleasant encounter—a book. Ah, such a book, an old and valuable one. If Barbara Struthers were a bit crazy to give gifts on her birthday, as well as receive them, it was a sweet madness. He would remember and do his best to pay her back. She was like no other girl he knew—most seemed annoying pests to him—and he found her exciting.

He felt very much alive as he walked, ran, skipped his way home over bone-white sidewalks. To his left, the daytime moon peered over an elm tree. It was a friendly orb, good company for his elated mood. The sky was a curious mixture of pink and dark blue. And then . . . 3700 Jefferson Lane: the haunted house, so full of mystery, that was his residence. The kitchen drapes were open, allowing twilight into an otherwise gray cave. There was a dying carnation in a vase in the window. He looked at it and thought about how Aunt Rose was fond of telling him to pay attention to worldly things, to come down from his fantasies and acquire some common sense as compensation for the journey. Well, he would make her happy tonight. He'd surprise her by bursting in with the good news.

"Aunt Rose," he shouted as the door slammed shut. From inside the house came the fragile sound of breaking porcelain. He stopped, pondered. *Not her favorite teacup*, he prayed.

"Paul." Her voice was quiet, almost a whisper. He shivered. "Please come into the parlor."

171

He came. Sitting still in her Boston rocker, she appraised him. The shards of broken china, white like midget icebergs, were scattered in a sea of purple carpet. "Please clean up *your* mess," she said.

"How did it break?" he asked, too bluntly he realized as soon as the words were out of his mouth. One wasn't blunt with Aunt Rose. "I mean the carpet . . . how?"

She didn't answer. She was looking away from him, looking at a corner of the room. He tried to follow her gaze, to see the object of her interest, but immediately her eyes darted back, held his gaze in a cobwebby stare. She said, "It broke on the arm of the rocker. You see that the arm is made of wood. Wood is hard. Porcelain is delicate and must be protected from hard things. You startled me." It was like listening to a list being read by an executioner, a calm, dry tone enumerating your heinous offenses one last time, before the axe descends. Paul looked down at his feet.

"What's that in your hand?" she asked suddenly. He had forgotten about the book. In his haste, he had neglected to leave it on the living room table or to put it in the bookcase. A fool, he thought, I bring it into the lion's den. "What are you hiding?" she snapped.

"I'm not hiding anything!"

"Then let me have it."

"I brought it in for you to see," he said as he released it to her white hands, which held the book delicately, as if holding old papyrus. She started to look through it. "It's *Dark Carnival!*" he said. "By Ray Bradbury!"

"I can read," she replied.

"It's something I've wanted for a long time. It's a fine book, his rarest, his first, and the hardest to find."

She finished thumbing the pages and held the book up to the lamp next to her chair, examining it as if it were a fine crystal, slowly turning it, letting the light play around the brown, worn edges.

"It's worth a lot of money," Paul said in a cracking voice, wondering why he was afraid. He was suffocating. "A lot of money," he repeated, trying to recapture the intensity of his point. One word was shouting in his brain: *No!*

172

"Paul, dear, what if I were to damage your book?" she asked. He said nothing as the world collapsed around him. "What if I were to bend it, crease it?" He said nothing. "But no, it wouldn't really be broken then. What if I were to light a match?" He closed his eyes. "I shouldn't want to burn it completely. Just partially. We'd put out the fire before it was all gone." He wanted to cry. But he didn't cry. Silence was heavy in the room, for at least an eternity.

Finally he asked, "Why do you hate me, Aunt Rose?"

She shrugged and laid his book on the table. "I don't hate you, child. I love you. But you have to learn a very important lesson or else you'll be self-centered for the rest of your life. You never think about other people. You never consider other people's feelings."

"Are you talking about yourself? No one else has ever told me—"

"I'm talking about how selfish you are. Oh, I don't blame you. How could you be otherwise after the way you were raised. But now you must learn to be considerate of others."

"I was coming home to tell you how much I enjoyed the party, to share with you how—"

"Very well. Tell me about the party. We should change the subject. I hate people who argue."

He took a deep breath. "It was the best party I've ever been to. When Barbara gave me the book—" His throat contracted as Aunt Rose picked up his book, a limited edition, and hurled it against the wall. The binding snapped instantly. The thing was dead before it hit the floor—its neck broken, two halves of a book swinging drunkenly, held together by the slimmest hopes of glue and thread. As it fell to the floor, heretofore undamaged pages crumpled. He was thinking through a haze of panic: the pages can be salvaged, they can be rebound, and it doesn't really matter what's happened, not really. But he had heard the book scream.

"I have kept my patience with you," said Aunt Rose. "I've made allowances for your age and haven't forgotten the tragedy you've recently suffered. But now you're my responsibility and rank insolence I will not abide. You can

173

forget to observe the memory of your parents if you want to, and you can keep me awake all night long with your noise and pages and doors and creeping in and out, if you want to, but you will not deliberately provoke me!"

He was thinking: *In time it can be repaired. I'll have the money as soon as I get a real job, and I'll fix the book and rent a place to keep the rest of my things in, and I'll move there. Except it's so hard to find work. I wish I was older. Surely I can find something.*

"Paul! Have you heard what I've been saying?"

. . . *Who is this woman? Oh yes, Aunt Rose.* Yes, he had heard every word although he didn't understand a thing she had said. "I think so," he answered, tasting blood in his mouth. It occurred to him that he'd been biting his tongue for over a minute.

"You will not provoke me again," she went on. "After we had agreed to change the topic, you deliberately mentioned that dirty old book, that silly book. I read a few sentences in it, Paul. Do you know what I found? Fanciful sentences, that's what. A waste of time, a dust magnet . . . You were going to tell me what happened at the party; instead you mention that book. Now, what do you have to say for yourself?"

He repeated a sentence several times in his mind and then, sure of the words, said, "Barbara Struthers gave it to me. That's why I liked the party."

She rose. She slapped him. She said, "You will not lie!"

He was far away. It took him a moment to notice that his face was hurting. He was still thinking about the blood in his mouth. "What?" he asked quietly, confused.

"I tried to stop you from taking that book along," said Aunt Rose. "You took it anyway. You had to be punished."

"But no, no," he said, starting to laugh. "I had to be punished for breaking the cup. Remember the cup?" He pointed to the pieces on the floor. "It was a paperback book I tried to take with me, much smaller than what I brought back. You've mixed them up!" He laughed louder.

"Don't you dare laugh at me!" she shrieked. "You clean up my teacup! I buy you your clothes and this is how you

174

treat me." *Had she screamed?* he marveled. *But she never raises her voice.* There were things he wanted to say. Arguments, logic, reasons, crowded his brain. Somewhere a mistake had been made. All he had to do was run it back to the beginning, find the error, bring it out. But when he opened his mouth, all that came out was laughter. "I'll show you!" she screamed again. "You selfish monster!" This time there was no doubt. She had most definitely raised her voice.

He asked himself why she was running upstairs, heading for his bedroom, then he remembered the one important thing about that room—his collection. He stopped laughing and began to throw up on the carpet. She rushed back down with an armful of books. Then she saw what he was doing. "Paul!" she cried out. Three times? But she doesn't raise her voice ... "My carpet!" He noticed a yellow stain spreading on what before had been consistent purple. The remains of the teacup were being surrounded by the splotch. She threw down her load, ran back upstairs to get more.

He thought: I really ought to do something. Maybe I can gather the pages of *Dark Carnival* and leave with that much. I'll have to do it quickly.

THUMP! She was back and the pile of his books doubled. She tossed his monster mask on top for good measure.

"Shall I tell you what I'm going to do?" she hissed, suddenly standing over him, swaying ominously like a scarecrow about to topple. He looked up, wiped the tears from his eyes and found that he could breathe again. Standing, he faced her.

"What is it, Aunt Rose?"

"Go to the kitchen," she commanded, "and bring back the matches."

Something happened inside Paul—the rage and fire and terror were gone. There was nothing left but a quiet, hollow center. "No," he said.

"I've had enough of your defiance."

"You're mad," he answered softly.

With an incredulous expression, she turned from her nephew and hurried away from him. In a moment the

175

sounds of a frantic search came rattling and clanging to Paul's ear. She was always misplacing those matches. Even as he remembered he had last seen them in the cabinet above the refrigerator, a triumphant cackle stung him as though she had reached out a long, bony arm holding a needle with which to pierce him.

She returned, the box of matches held high in her right hand. "Now!" she gasped.

Looking around him, Paul realized that the picture was ludicrous: it was made up of a carpet fastidiously clean but for the stain Paul had left behind, the lamps that had been dusted so often that the shades seemed to be made of tightly pulled, translucent human skin and the flowery wallpaper that smelled not of gardens but of the crushed, dead flowers you find in old *books*. He could not believe for a moment that she was going to play with fire in this museum.

Her eyes were staring, first at the pile of books, then at her nephew. He could swear she hadn't blinked in the past few minutes.

At length she spoke of her plan: "We will take the books to the porch. There is a barbecue grill there." Paul tried to remember a single time they had cooked dinner outside. The grill was as spotless as if it had just come from the department store. A Christmas gift left over from years past, waiting for one unholy fire, an innocuous device that was to be transformed into a sacrificial altar for Paul's library.

He still held *Dark Carnival*. Outside was the sidewalk, winding away into the safety of the night. Paul knew that he could run, hide, escape . . . and never have to come back.

"Damn you," he muttered in the direction of the wraith-like being bearing matches, dressed in a turquoise dress. She was carrying the books outside, five and six at a time. Her face had the quality of wounded pride—she wouldn't even grant him the role of victim.

Paul decided he wasn't leaving, not just yet. "Let me help you," he called out, his voice a bit shrill, as he headed for the utility room where she kept the one unused can of lighter fluid. By the time he returned, all the books and the mask were in a pile on the grill. She had a match in her hand that she was trying futilely to ignite. Paul waited as the liquid sloshed back and forth in the can.

She heard the sound and asked him, "What are you doing?"

"Helping." He stepped out onto the porch. There was no turning away from what he would learn now. A small hope wouldn't let go of his mind: it seemed to promise that she was all bluster and fear, not a monster really.

Screwing off the cap, he held the can above the books. And waited. Aunt Rose said nothing. Slowly, carefully, he placed the can on the floor. They could hear each other's breathing.

"Well?" she said.

"You do it," he answered.

She did. The fluid splashed on the floor and the thick odor was suddenly everywhere. She started striking the match, standing right over the pyre. "Christ," whispered Paul. *Shik, shik,* went the match. The fumes reached up, encircled the clawlike hand. Paul began trembling. He grabbed the can and shook it in her face. "Do you want to die?" he yelled. She didn't seem to see him. *Shik, shik, shik.* . . .

Paul dropped the can, grabbed *Dark Carnival* and ran. He was halfway through the living room when he heard the sound, like the rush of air when a match is put over a pilot light that has gone out in a gas oven. Turning around, he saw Aunt Rose caressed by a long tongue of flame. She raised her hand, dropping the box of matches that flared and fell from her like a lonely comet. The suddenly-old woman's head was crowned in fire and her hand pointed at him in a last gesture of disapproval. The dried flesh was eaten up with a snapping and popping. The body collapsed as flame tentatively reached out for the rest of the house . . . then spread in triumphantly.

With a slam, Paul was out the front door. Lights were on in nearby houses—neighbors opening their eyes to accuse. He could feel the heat of the inferno on the back of his neck. And so he walked faster. Then started running. By the time he heard the sirens, he couldn't see, smell or hear the fire anymore.

Hurrying on into the enveloping arms of night: in its darkness he did not imagine the myriad monsters of his books, the fiends his aunt had insisted populated his deepest dreams. The real monster was gone, behind him in a blaze of light. Ahead in the shadows waited the freedom of a quiet privacy, where light was used for reading instead of burning.

Dreaming in Black and White

Susan Shwartz

Crossing Water Street, downtown flows like a great brown river choked with battered cars that wash up on Confucius Place. Traffic lights flicker red and green, but no one obeys them. Dodging a stripped-down car, Stephanie thrust past a side road and into the main street just as the light turned. Brakes and car horns shrieked, followed by gabble she heard only as oaths. A Hyundai lunged forward, and she leapt like a bullfighter for the sanctuary of the curb.

"Damned fool! You want to be road kill?" she scolded herself, and leaned against the fast-food turned family dentist (advertising in English and Chinese). *You'd do anything to miss this lunch, right, Steff?* Sheldon's carefully modulated, reasonable tones whispered in her mind. *But I wouldn't like that at all.*

She glanced into the streaked windows where a miniature TV's coarse screen flickered with the image of a gray-haired woman in a violet sweater. The woman had the face of a boxer—puffed lips, drawn down a little, a flattened nose, and ancient, empty eyes. She dabbed them with a wad of tissue, but never stopped dripping tears.

The Joel and Hedda show was on again. What had started

179

as his trial for killing his illegally adopted child and beating Hedda had become hers—days of testimony that exposed her life and her weakness. Day after day, professionally compassionate people drove her in from that Westchester psychiatric hospital with the name Stephanie liked—Four Winds—to witness against the man who had killed . . . Stephanie's eyes filled. She could never watch such things for long; the pictures of the little girl, now dead, had driven her from Sheldon's living room in tears.

I could have done a better job, she told herself. *Why couldn't they have given her to* me?

You can barely take care of yourself, Sheldon had declared when Stephanie had protested that Hedda Nussbaum had been so badgered and battered that she had no will or self-respect left. *She asked for it. Too bad it cost the child's life, too.* Sheldon was big on free choice, bigger on using a soft reasoned tone for questions that all started with "isn't it true that." Stephanie's tears and bewilderment never stood up well against that kind of cross-examination.

You could get worn down, she'd tried to say. You could get scared. You could even escape, yet be too scared to keep on running. *There but for the grace of God . . .* Sheldon had sworn that he never wanted to hurt her. She had believed him. If that was true, why did she feel so bad?

Her hands shook, then stilled. Two years of Sheldon's not wanting to hurt her were enough. Clever as she was sure he was, she was better off making her own mistakes—and enjoying her own successes—than following the intricate plans he was so proud of devising. Frankly, they always seemed to her like more bother than they were worth.

She had cleared a long lunch hour with her supervisor, and she would break with Sheldon today. At lunch at the Pongsri Thai on Bayard. It was crowded, and they made you eat fast. It would be safe to tell him there.

It would be safer to play in traffic. Her hands shook again.

As she dodged down Mulberry Street, her attention flickered, and the world turned black and white. Just like her dreams. She had always liked Chinatown for its color; had always reveled in color; had always dreamed in it. Recently, though, she had begun to dream in black and white. And now the dreams were finally manifesting themselves in her life. From now on, she would have to move in a colorless world. She glanced back to test it. Sure enough, Hedda's violet sweater, the padded blue jackets that the most recent immigrants wore, her own tidy, inexpensive suit, even the flowers for sale and the sky and the children's clothing, had all turned black and white.

Oh, I understand you better than you do yourself. Your problem is that you only see in black and white. She didn't even need to have Sheldon around for her to hear him coaxing, insinuating, controlling. She dodged a couple with linked arms who looked like they'd walk straight through her. *You're so spineless you let people just crowd you off the sidewalk into the street, Steff?* She clapped hands to her ears with such force that they rang.

A little sheepishly—what if Sheldon had been walking down Carmine and saw her acting crazy?—she removed her hands. Then she heard the music.

Four men in shabby uniforms and beaked caps formed a huddle outside one of the Chinese funeral homes that lined the street. They looked like Salvation Army, though their uniforms lacked braid trim, and their faces lacked the ruddy cheer of Army men. Oddly enough, they were Westerners, not Asians. They beat their feet in time as their dented instruments plodded through Chopin's Funeral March. Ludicrous from a thousand Saturday-morning cartoons, trumpet, baritone, trombone, and tuba honked and blatted, voice to the mourning dragon that wound up the street: car after car, each bearing its little Chinese banner, following a flatbed hearse. The huge coffin was heaped with flowers, surmounted by a picture of the deceased, encircled by more Chinese characters.

And pictures, flowers, hearse, even the musicians themselves, were all black and white, like the 1950s cartoons that turned the Funeral March into gallows humor. Following that cortege, as if dragon followed dragon like circus elephants, came another. Noontime was for funerals in Chinatown.

Stephanie wanted to comment to anyone nearby, but some invisible membrane seemed to block her speech. She could feel air vibrating against it as she opened her mouth. Recently, she'd felt as if she'd swallowed a piece of plastic bag and it had gotten lodged in her throat.

She hurried down Bayard toward the Pongsri Thai. You had to get there by 12:15 or the lines of jurors, court officials, lawyers, and *Wall Street Journal* staffers intent on a cheap, tasty lunch could stretch round the block. She was lucky. The sweatered owner steered her by the picture of this year's Miss Thailand and the table of indigestible pistachio sweets and the fierce, winking masks on the walls to an empty side table, neatly ensconced beneath tiny indoor pagodas. Sheldon wasn't there yet, but they'd have privacy for what she wanted to say.

Stephanie knew that the sweets were bilious green, the walls golden wood, well polished, the masks glaring with every color of rhinestone and sequin, just as she knew that the fraying Leatherette menu cover was maroon. Today, though, all of it was as black and white as Miss Thailand's photo. Even the yellowed newsprint looked bleached out.

I must tell Sheldon about the funerals. He was big on wanting her to notice things that he thought were downtown and sharp. That *he* thought. He had enjoyed guiding her taste in the nightmare months right after she'd moved to New York, when her hair was too long, her clothes too fussy, her speech not crisp enough. Now she dressed appropriately—another favorite word—but now she dreamed only in black and white.

Sheldon would say he was entitled to someone who dreamed in color. He was always entitled: to sex when *he* wanted it, even if that meant waking her; to his choice of movies; to a woman who had a good job and a private-college education, maybe even inherited money (he always told Stephanie the net worth of the women in his

182

office), yet who always agreed with him. Steff was such a disappointment, he let her know; it was a wonder he bothered.

Well, Stephanie was tired of being a traffic jam on the fast track. Now he could go claim one of those superior women, and she wished them both luck. Her watch showed 12:30; the waiter's face, impatience. Sheldon still hadn't arrived. The sick feeling, like catching a bad mistake at work, or her supervisor's notes, *come see me*, began to chill her stomach. She ordered a Coke and drank it. When it was gone, she placated the waiter with a nervous smile and ordered a beer. Sheldon disapproved of alcohol at lunch. The tables were filling up, and still no Sheldon. She would have to get up soon, or order.

Around her people were sitting, chatting and laughing. Some had been here as long as she; they hadn't ordered either, but the waiters did not scowl at them. Those were entitled people, just like Sheldon. They had a right to attention and patience. No one watched and judged them every moment. How could people tell which was which? Steff was as well dressed, as well made-up . . . but the waiters knew. Maybe it was because they dressed in, dreamed in color, and she didn't. She was vulnerable, Sheldon always said. The Big V stands for victim. She could feel a letter, which normal people would see as scarlet, pulsate on her forehead.

Like Hedda. Sheldon must have spotted it right away. Most people could. Steff had learned that in her year of the Bad Bosses, arrayed like wicked Caesars. There'd been the one she privately called Little Caesar, the society matron who spent mornings on the phone with her maid, yet blamed her if the work wasn't done, the workaholic with a subpoena in his past, the Long Island ad man who went broke and laid her off with a day's notice. *Why'd you pick those jobs?* Sheldon had asked. *If you cared about your career, you'd learn to choose better.* He wouldn't listen when she told him: when it was between a bad job and no job, you took; you didn't choose. But now she was tired of trying to convince him. A "relationship" (his term; too sentimental by half, Steff would have called it a love affair) shouldn't turn into an endurance test.

Well, she had a good job now. And office friends. They'd told her to come here for lunch because it was fast and public, to take what time she needed, not to worry. *You listen to them, not me? After all I've done for you?*

She summoned the hovering waiter and ordered chicken in some sort of cornstarch sauce that would probably reek of garlic, then yielded her menu.

How else could I keep the table? She could hear the placating coward's whine even in her mental voice. *And why should I care if he's pleased or not?*

If she said that, Sheldon would start on the "you shoulds." *You should be more assertive. You should trust me more. You should understand how very busy I am, how I can't always be there for you when you think you need me.* She could hear the finicky precision of his consonants in her head, and she was glad that today would be the last day she'd have to hear them.

Sometimes she wondered if he watched her from outside, watched to see if she behaved appropriately. Sheldon had a whole litany of appropriates—appropriate dinner-party food, appropriate napkins, appropriate flowers, books by someone named Martha Stewart who boasted of the difference in color between a quiche made with eggs from her own hens and the inferior product, made with paler, commercially bought eggs. Sheldon claimed to enjoy what he called "the fun of working in the kitchennnn," his voice tuning up for a whine that Stephanie didn't leap at the chance. "The fun of working in the kitchennnn" usually meant that she cooked and he groped her, apologized for the distraction, then went off to nap while she cleaned up.

When *The New York Post* published Hedda's lists of what she must remember about Joel's hair, Joel's shoes, Joel's penthouse-to-be, Sheldon had smirked.

Don't even think of it, she had warned. That evening he'd made a joke of telling their guests how often he'd had to help her job hunt.

That was it. *He's lucky that I don't get up and leave. After all, I have to eat, too.*

184

She thought of working on her notes. Like her life, like the life of damned near every overeducated, underemployed person in Manhattan, she Wrote. The capital letter was a talisman to distinguish Writing from unglamorous letters and memos.

Sheldon claimed to Write too when they'd met at a bookstore signing. *I'm as good as Cheever,* he'd told her, and his confidence had won her. But he'd never let her read a word he wrote.

Had he ever written a word besides ad proposals? Steff thought suddenly. She practiced asking the question in her throat, and the membrane buzzed. He was always working on Something. Even on Sunday mornings, he was so serious about his work that she'd have to get out of bed and go home early, just about the time that other couples were getting dressed for brunch.

He could kiss that shit good-bye.

Her food arrived just as Sheldon did. An apology trembled in her throat, but the membrane kept her from blurting it out. She swallowed hard, hungry despite her wretched nerves. At least, unlike Joel Steinberg, he'd never asked her to freebase. (Surely, he wouldn't. After all, he was still—at age thirty-eight—talking of heading for medical school on Grenada because American medical schools were too restrictive. Would she quit her job and come, too?) Would she have done drugs if he'd wanted? No, she promised herself. That she would not have done. Could she be *sure?*

She swallowed and nodded, and the balloon slid down to her belly. Even if she ate, the food would fill the balloon, not her, and she'd starve.

At least, though, the balloon—she thought it was a red one—had saved her from apologizing again. Sheldon hated apologies, though he always made sure she made them.

He glanced at her, his eyes narrowing in the in-trouble-again look. He was a short man, with scant dark hair and a beard that he and a senior stylist from Sassoon tended with fanatical precision. As always, he was painstakingly dressed in a dark jacket—he had three all alike—and a Calvin Klein shirt, maybe the one he had tried to teach her to

185

iron. (She'd felt like burning it, but she'd felt it was a crime to scorch a poor, innocent designer shirt.)

"Dearest," he said, and leaned over her lunch to kiss her in front of everyone. The perfect lover. His lips were cold against her face. With an upraised finger, he summoned the waiter, made great play of opening the menu, *discussing* the food, improving his pronunciation of the various dishes, and instructing her that Thai was a tonal language, before, finally, he ordered. The waiter smiled at the charming, civilized man. *Look what you've forfeited this time*, this display of urbanity told her.

Well, blurt it out. Say, "Sheldon, I want out," pay your tab, and get up and leave. She hated herself, but she sat; one didn't make a scene.

"You go ahead and eat. You already ordered, so you must be hungry, though it wouldn't hurt you to lose weight. You could have waited for me. You knew I'd be along. I had some very important phone calls to return." His soft voice took on the whine that meant he wanted to punish her.

"Calls could have waited," she murmured. She picked up chopsticks and forced down the cornstarch and limp vegetables. The ginger caught in her throat and burned. The food looked like shredded newsprint on her plate. She swallowed.

"You know I'm doing it all for us," he said.

She glanced up and found him watching her. She glanced away, too quickly, lest he see what was in her mind: Joel Steinberg, leaning over his shoulder to stare at the woman he had beaten. To instruct, to hint, to control, even from Rikers Island and the defendant's bench.

Stephanie flinched. That too was irrational. Sheldon prided himself on his sensitivity. He would never hit her. He didn't even raise his voice. The whole idea was paranoid, lower-class. After all, who else would have loved her during the crazy year of the Four Bosses, or when the Unemployment people jeered at her—college degree and all, and she couldn't even hold a job. Sheldon had been her strength then. When she'd tried to temp and come home exhausted, he'd taken off her shoes and massaged her feet.

186

Too stubborn to retreat to the Midwest, too hopeful to give up, she had mastered the tricks of the job-hunting trade, then of the job itself. Gradually, she was growing into a woman she thought she might like, one of these days . . . except when Sheldon told her how far short of expectations she fell.

Stand up to him, her office friends, many flashing diamond solitaires, had told her. He'll respect you more. Or if you decide you want out, make a clean break. *You* decide.

Hedda had tried to leave. Once she'd gotten as far as the airport, then called him and asked him to bring her back. As if the effort of getting that far had drained her of all further power. Steff was not Hedda.

The masks on the polished walls grimaced, scolding her in the instant before Sheldon opened his mouth. "You know, if you order before other people at a business lunch, they'll think you're badly socialized and you won't get anywhere," he advised. "And you shouldn't drink. It's so important to you to do well, since you say you're serious this time about your career. Does your supervisor still think you're unstable?"

She smiled. This was obvious, shake-your-confidence stuff. Stephanie had stopped beseeching even file clerks for reassurance months ago. And her six-months' review had been outstanding.

"She's fine," Stephanie said. "But Sheldon, I want to tell you what I saw on the way over here. I heard this band playing Chopin's—"

Though Stephanie had minored in French, Sheldon held up a forefinger and corrected her pronunciation. She plunged on.

"And I saw this Chinese funeral. Christian Chinese. It looked like a mourning dragon. Do you think—"

"I think it's charming of you to tell me about it. Like the child in the poem about what he saw on Mulberry Street, when he really didn't see anything." His meticulous imitation of a child's sing-song made her flush. "If you really cared about pleasing me, though, you'd have waited to order lunch." The whine was back.

She shrugged. "Then," she said, on a deep breath (the balloon in her stomach, half full from the food that she had so inconsiderately ordered, pulsed and began to fill a little more), "I must not care about pleasing you."

As he began his next reproof, the balloon began to swell, as if the air pressure inside the restaurant had changed. And it was going to get bigger as things got stuffed into it, things like tasty food, and colored dreams, and even the anger that she felt scorching her eyes and throat, as if she'd eaten the tiny, devastating Far Eastern chilies she never dared to order. She imagined that the balloon looked like the threat display of that lizard she'd seen the last time she was in Florida. She had alarmed it, and it had inflated its red throat sac to warn her off.

She had told Sheldon about it, and he had claimed to have studied herpetology or whatever you called it when you studied lizards. She had been in Florida to give a paper; she had asked him to please come, but he had been too busy. Just as he'd been too busy when she'd asked him to be her date at her best friend's wedding, where she was the bridesmaid. Steff always went to his family things and was "Sheldon's girl . . . isn't she sweet?" But Sheldon hated being someone's sidekick, and he never went with her.

Injustice inflated the balloon further and smothered her hunger. Her plate only half-emptied, she laid down her chopsticks with the elegance of the woman at the next table, whose fiancé smiled at her without a hint of condemnation in his eyes. Oh, she was going to be so glad to get this over with! She'd go home tonight—her own apartment, not his, even though his was so much nicer—and sleep, maybe even dream in color . . .

What if I don't? Lately, as she'd started to stay late at the office, to question what he was entitled to, he'd been hinting that she'd lost ground and was losing her grip. "You try too hard to be sane," he'd whisper to her, just before she fell asleep. "It isn't normal for you to care so much about your career, about what your office thinks of you. You're pushing yourself to where you're burning out."

Well, maybe she was crazy. Maybe she'd have a breakdown and go on disability. Maybe she could check into that Four Winds place that Hedda was at. She *knew* she'd get her colors back there. She clenched her fingers before they could shake. The balloon quivered and swelled.

Across the tiny table, Sheldon's voice droned on. A good thing she wasn't listening. His eyes flashed suddenly, and he reached out with chopsticks to snatch a bite of chicken from her plate. Usually, he hated to share food.

"Why'd you do that?" she asked.

"To get your attention. Because I'm hungry too and you didn't offer to share."

She looked down at her watch. "I have to get back soon." That was a lie, but suddenly she didn't want to spend any longer than she had to with him. But she was pinned behind this table.

"You used to *want* me to pay you attention. You clung to me. But now you've got this job. Now you don't need me. You *used* me to get this job, and now you're going to discard me just like all these bitches in my office who think they're on the fast track . . . Do you think you'll ever be able to handle a career and a relationship?"

"That's not fair!" she was stung into replying against her better judgment. "You know how long I waited saying that it was all right for you to introduce me to your headhunter friend. You asked; I didn't. I didn't *want* to use you; you were special to me."

"Were special?"

She shook her head, and her eyes filled. She didn't see rainbows through her tears, just black and white. He had been special. So she had hung on, hoping that something that she could do would restore how wonderful things had been when they'd started out together. Bring back the pink tulips and the red roses and the truffles they'd fed the waitress at the Rainbow Room, where he'd taken her the night they'd seen *Phantom*. Her tears were nostalgia only for the dreams, not for Sheldon. And now her dreams were only black and white.

"It's not working, Sheldon," Stephanie said softly. "I want out. I have to get out." She waited for him to say

189

something. He didn't, so her abject demon possessed her and she said, "I'm sorry."

"You should be!" Sheldon's food arrived. He gestured the waiter curtly away. "I hope you realize I won't be able to eat a bite. Just you remember. I helped you get started. I *bothered* with you when no one else would, when you were so crazy it was a wonder you didn't wind up on the street."

He thrust vicious chopsticks into his curry.

"I did my best," Stephanie offered. "I'm sorry."

Why apologize, dammit? Hedda had probably apologized each time Joel slammed her into the wall. Sorry for being bad. Sorry for being.

"Sorry isn't good enough!" Sheldon exploded in a whisper. "You're not sorry. You're crazy and hateful. What if I let people know just how crazy and hateful you are?"

The one time before she had tried to break up with him, he had called her every five minutes until she'd been so worn down, she'd let him come over in a taxi.

"I'd rather do this with dignity," Stephanie said. "But if you cause trouble, this time I'll tell people, 'I'm trying to break up with my boyfriend, and he's harassing me.' Don't try to reach me. I'll give the phone company your name and address. The post office, too. And my friends . . . already know . . ."

I'll call the cops, she thought. *I'll throw your stuff out for beggars. I'll call a priest to exorcise my place.*

"You *told* them about us?" He took an outraged bite of curry, then gulped water. His discomfort would be her fault, too. He glared at her, and she remembered: he wore one contact lens, a red one, to correct a mild case of color blindness. Maybe he didn't see colors, either; maybe he struck out at her because he too was afraid that he didn't measure up, couldn't see colors, couldn't be what he dreamed of being—the writer, or the doctor, or the man.

Stephanie looked at him. Black and white. Flat. History. Her hands trembled beneath the table as she fumbled for the sidewalk Vuitton handbag he'd ridiculed her for buying, though all his clothes had designer labels. She groped for her wallet, and drew out the first bill she came to. A ten.

"This should cover lunch," she said.

She drew a breath. The balloon in her belly groaned, it was so full. If he stopped her, she'd scream and the balloon would break, spitting violent colors all over the room.

She rose and shut her eyes, imagining Four Winds. Where, she imagined, buttery sunlight came in through sparkling windows, and where breakfast came arrayed prettily on trays; where even the arrangement of the lunchtime carrots and celery and apples was soothing. Where walks were prescribed and people spoke softly, helping you heal.

More savagely hurt than she, Hedda had Four Winds to help her. Stephanie, with only her own strength, had to envy her. God, what dirt she was, envying Hedda.

Carefully, she edged past Sheldon, flinching as if she expected him to grab at her, gesturing at the waiter that the money was on the table. A clatter behind her. An overturned chair. Her eyes filled, black and white blurring to gray, and she felt her way outside, down Bayard, back onto Mulberry.

Halfway down the street, she found herself stopped by a TV in a laundry window. Hedda again, covering her face with tissue, Joel flicking a basilisk stare at her. She wore her violet sweater. At Four Winds, they'd probably chosen it, helped her dress, combed her gray curls to hide the bald patches, and told her she looked nice, their Niobe with cauliflower ears.

A hand caressed the nape of her neck, then closed on it. She stiffened, ready to whirl and scream.

"Poor darling," came Sheldon's voice. "You're so melodramatic. You make it sound like you're fighting for your life. As if everything's black and white."

The happy couple. She'd seen men playfully convey struggling women by the scruffs of their necks, and she'd wondered why in the world anyone would think that was cute. She used to love it when Sheldon called her darling. Now she knew that "darling" meant punishment—and no

191

one would ever know, because he called her darling and enforced his wishes by a grasp at the scruff of her neck, like a kitten he wanted to drown.

"We need to talk about this. About us," he crooned.

She jerked her head free, her attention on Hedda. Her stomach felt bloated.

"Why are you watching that shit?" His voice went momentarily sharp. "I can't believe it. That's what's bothering you? Stupid bitch. She asked for it. She should have trusted him. Maybe then he wouldn't have had to . . ."

He could make black seem white and white, black. And if he went on talking, she might even believe him. She had to get away, but his fingers were groping beneath her hair for her neck and that hateful, mock-loving pinch.

"I don't want to talk about it," she said. "I don't want to talk to you."

"Why?" That was another trick. Get her to do what he called "discuss," which meant that she stammered and he got to interrupt with "isn't it true."

"Have I ever laid a hand on you?"

She freed herself from the neck vise. "You *push*!" Stephanie felt herself goaded into replying, as the balloon in her stomach throbbed. "We're walking down the street, and you push me away."

"Only because I see further than you, and I've seen someone I don't want to get near you. You're so trusting, darling, so vulnerable. What if I weren't there to protect you and a bum or a mugger hurt you? You know you can't take care of yourself. Come on. I'll walk back to your office with you and you can explain that you need to take the rest of the day off. Maybe more. Isn't it true you're not in good shape, Stephanie . . ."

Let him get her alone, "taking care" of her, and she'd be his prisoner. She might not wind up with a face like Hedda's, but the eyes, the damned, lost look in the eyes would be the same. He might never hit her, but she knew what her life would be like: a life of soft-voiced, cloistered terror, worrying if Sheldon had the right brand of tuna for the sandwich he'd expect her to fix him at midnight, if she wore the appropriate dress for an important dinner, as he said, with the ballbreaker (pardon my French, darling) he was stuck with as a boss, if she spoke one word too many, or too few. She would have to fear him as she had feared her first supervisors, and he would never let her go. He would devour her and her fear.

"Just leave me alone," she said, low-voiced.

"Steff, darling," he began, stalking her. "Isn't it true I have a right to care for you? Don't I deserve the best? That's you, babe."

"Then why do you make me feel like shit?"

"You make *you* feel like shit!"

Sensing potential craziness, Asian and Western passersby began to ignore them. The sky and ground began to whirl, the garbage and the dog crap and the people. Whirling with it came the crunch of heavy vehicles on broken glass and the lugubrious, inept Chopin.

"Get away!"

With two long steps he was at her side, had grabbed her arm in a grip that pinched and bruised. "This has gone on long enough!" he said. "Now you're coming with me, and I'll teach you how to behave to a man who only wants to keep you from hurting yourself."

And so she would go with him. She could see it clearly. He would probably make her quit her job, too. And when her surrender was finally abject enough, maybe he would marry her. Maybe they would have children: two children. She had been absurdly pleased when he'd praised her for wanting just the same number of children that he did. Assuming that she could have them. For the past six months, he had begun to lecture her how her biological clock was running out. Because the fault would have to be in *her* genes, wouldn't it? Sheldon was entitled to undamaged genes . . .

Though he was color-blind, if they had a child who was flawed, he'd blame it on her. Why would she want to have kids with his problems? Hedda couldn't have kids; maybe she couldn't, either. Would he *steal* kids for them, too?

Either way, once kids came, she could never escape.

She'd never be smart enough to sneak the kids away, and she'd be afraid of how he'd bring them up alone: little Sheldons, precise, cold, and hateful. Monsters. Her kids as monsters.

"No," she said. "No." Of all the torments in Hedda's hell, the worst surely had to be that she'd let her kids be used, let one be killed, even, and stood by because she trusted the man who did it. Where was mother tiger when they needed her?

"You go to hell!" She dodged out into the narrow street and he followed her.

If he touched her, the red balloon would burst, and all her rage, all her hurt, all her hatred would spew out on the street, leaving her limp, like the damp, flaccid scrap that's all you have left when balloons burst.

The Funeral March grew louder, and voices buzzed in the background, rose in alarm, as the crunching neared and the rumble of powerful engines grew louder.

"You're so bad! Stop fighting me!" Sheldon grabbed her arm again, sinking in well-manicured fingers just where he'd bruised her before. She yelped and turned at bay.

"They should never have let you loose. You ought to be locked up to pick the wings off flies. They should never turn you loose on people!"

He backhanded her face, and she whirled, breaking free in her fury. Blood spurted from her nose onto the dirty street.

She was facing yet another mourning dragon of a funeral procession, all black and white, from the hood of the hearse to the opulent coffin to the black, open mouth of the driver. All black and white, even the flowers, except for the flowers above the dead man's photo: a heart worked of carnations as red as a throbbing heart—or a red balloon.

She screamed and the balloon inside her went thin and stretched. If there'd been letters on it like there were on the balloons she'd gotten at county fairs in her childhood, they'd have gone all pale, then vanished.

Then the balloon burst. Fragments of color and sound

exploded from her mouth and eyes and transfixed Sheldon where he stood, his own mouth open. For an instant, they saw each other in each other's eyes, surrounded by violent flame. Then the balloon released everything it held. Blame, hatred, and fear splattered at their feet.

This was the time he had abandoned her at a party; that was the time he had turned away from her in bed after she had corrected him in public; *that* was the time he had ridiculed a report she'd slaved over, scribbling on the final copy; and this one was for the embarrassment of submitting to public fondling that she'd hated as he made her demonstrate the soft-voiced and charming docility he liked, while his men friends grinned and their dates' nostrils flared with fear and contempt.

He caught the vision of himself in her eyes and tried to speak, but her sheer audacity in fighting and the image of Sheldon as monster stunned him. All the months and years of "darling," of abuse, trapped him as if fury had melted the asphalt at his feet.

The explosion stabbed at him from her eyes and mouth, and he flinched from it, flinched, for the first time, from his victim.

Propelled by its force, impossibly lithe with rage and terror, Stephanie jumped for the curb. "He's going to kill me!" she screamed, and heard answering shouts in English, Spanish, and Mandarin.

"Whatsa matter, lady?"

"Hey, gotta crazy!"

"He gotta knife?"

"Get a cop! Someone call 911!"

Her screams and the shouts of the crowd cut off the Funeral March, which flatted and honked, not into silence, but into the shriek of brakes and horror as the hearse, unable to stop in time, rolled into Sheldon, then over him, crunching, followed by the rest of the cortege, a dragon trampling its prey into a damp and tiny red rag.

Not even three hardhats could keep her from seeing what lay beneath the hearse when it finally ground to a stop. The mourners swarmed out, screaming, and Stephanie sank to her knees, vomiting a thin red stream into the gutter.

She was shaking, but her hands felt warm, and the balloon in her belly was gone.

"Jesus, Mary, and Joseph!" The voice was Brooklyn, with Irish overtones. "All right, youse all, move 'em on out, gedda move on here. Lady, you move too, you don't wanna see that."

She felt a large, official presence take up its stance over her as another, equally official voice sent people about their business, then sank into a routine buzz of names- and number-taking.

"Here's another one!" came the first cop's voice. "Jeez, they say she was running away from this dude, like he was trying to kill her, and she'd run out into the street, screaming. *Who* says he had a knife? Hey, Joe, you finda knife, some kinda edged weapon there?"

A shout came from beyond him.

The man standing over her muttered. "Another damned crazy. Like that fucking Steinberg." He bent, and used gentle force to pry Stephanie's hands away from her face.

"Say, lady, are you all right? Did he hurt you?" A long pause. "Touch you . . . you know?"

The sympathy in his voice lured her back, and she opened her eyes to meet his. When Irish eyes were frowning—blue, in a ruddy face, with black hair, going a little salt and pepper—she'd got her colors back! He released her wrists, and light glinted off the wedding ring he wore as he wiped the blood from her nose with a tissue.

She shook her head. "He hit me today. That's the only time," she said. "I'll be fine."

"Was he your husband, or maybe your fyan-say?"

"Just my boyfriend, thank God." She held out her bruised arm. "I'd been trying to break up, and he said I was crazy, had been going crazy for months now . . . and I had to get away, and he grabbed me . . ."

Her voice rose up into a thin wail, and she knew how feeble her protestations that she'd be fine, she should be let go, let alone, must sound.

"Another one," said the policeman. "Get an ambulance. We gotta get this one to Bellevue. Women! Why do nice women link up with these creeps? Oughta plug these guys in the electric chair. Somebody get me a blanket, or she's gonna go into shock! Awright, lady, don' worry."

The first blanket that the laundryman brought out was maroon, like the blood clotting in the gutter, and Stephanie shuddered away from it. The second, a blackish-green, she let the nice officer wrap around her, and she just shook as he patted her head, waiting for the ambulances to arrive.

She woke in sunlight. She had pleaded that she was fine now, but they had not believed her, had they? Now she remembered needles in her arm, murmurs, being dressed while half-awake, and a ride past miles of buildings, past them to a place of hedges and clean walls.

A tray of toast and juice rested on a table near the bed. She looked around for a knife. The toast was already buttered. When she finished eating, she sat, waiting like a child.

Gradually, the fact that the room contained a closet occurred to her, and she explored it, found clothes, and dressed. Shortly afterward, a nurse came in, praised her, and took her for a walk in the sun. But people came, with cameras, and they had to hurry away.

She sat in a place where other people did crafts. She looked for Hedda, who wasn't there. A big man came and led her to an office, interrupting her thoughts and halting words. She was upset, he told her. She had a right to be upset. She'd been subjected to sadism and psychological abuse, followed by a terrible accident. But she was not to worry. There would be no indictment.

Indictment?

He shook his head and his authoritative face grew grave. Her fiancé's parents were wealthy, influential. They had pressed for an indictment against her. They blamed her for the death of their only son. But enough people had seen

197

him hit her, had heard her scream. And Officer O'Shea had made a deposition: she had been abused. So she was not to worry. She was only to get well.

"Did they want to squash me like a bug with torn-off wings? Like their son."

"You didn't let him," said the doctor.

"It was self-defense," she said, almost parroting the words from *New York Post* headlines. She folded her hands across her stomach as if it held something: a red balloon, maybe, or her unborn self. She was fine; she knew it, but they didn't. Or maybe they did, and this place was a gift of gentle treatment, her prize for the months of suffering. She would look at it that way. After all, it wasn't all black and white.

"You should be very proud of how you fought."

Now she actually had a right. She never had a right before. Her new self leapt beneath her hands, moving toward birth.

There were hazel flecks in the doctor's eyes, the color of the wood of his desk. She felt like she could drown in this restored world of colors. After a while, he called a nurse. Lunch was ready, nicely laid out, with a sandwich and a red apple. All food you could eat with your fingers.

This place had sun and trees and walls. She didn't know if it was really Four Winds or not. Did it matter? It was health; it was help; it became the world. The people in it were kind. For a while, they were all that was.

A little later, the people from work sent fruit and flowers and a card saying not to worry about her job. The nurses let her share the fruit, and everyone smiled at her. Nice Stephanie. Generous Stephanie. That was a good day. The next days were good, too. The feeling of being stuffed with anger she couldn't get out never returned.

The good days drew out. One morning, it occurred to her that even walls had a gate. Tomorrow, perhaps, she might go and look at it. She might even step outside.

She sat and crooned a lullaby to her unborn self, which crooned back silently. When the nurse turned the lights out, she slept without a pill, and her dreams, when they came, were all in color.

The Secret Blade

Edward D. Hoch

t was Pierre Frayer's job, that warm April morning in 1792, to bring forth the corpses that would be used in testing the machine. Two days earlier, on the fifteenth, several live sheep had been sacrificed in the initial experiments. Pierre had helped with those too, trussing the poor creatures and positioning them for the blade. Now, in the courtyard of the hospital at Paris's Bicêtre prison, where the final test was to be held, Pierre wheeled out the fresh cadavers of two men and one woman.

The others were close at hand, of course. Dr. Joseph Guillotin, who had campaigned for a quick and painless method of capital punishment, stood to one side with Antoine Louis and others from the French Constituent Assembly. The chief surgeon of the prison hospital and delegates from other Paris hospitals were there as well. It was Granston from the Ministry of Justice who ordered Pierre about, barking commands with his loud voice for all to hear.

Pierre secured the first of the male cadavers to the movable plank or *bascule* upon which the condemned person was laid full-length. Then he fitted two semicircular pieces of wood around the head to hold it in place. In the background he could hear Dr. Guillotin expounding to the others about the device. "A mechanical machine somewhat like this was used for executions in Ireland nearly five hundred years ago," he told them. "Even in France there have been decapitations by mechanical methods. This particular design was developed by Antoine Louis."

At his side Louis started to protest, but already someone in the group murmured that the device should be christened "La louisette." Pierre saw and heard all this as he went about the preliminary tasks, stepping back finally so that Charles-Henri Sanson, the city's official executioner, could take over. Sanson's son and two brothers made certain the cadaver was positioned properly, and then the executioner took a deep breath.

The rope was cut, the heavy blade released, and almost before Pierre realized what was happening the head of the dead man was severed from his body and dropped into a basket that had been placed to catch it. Though no one cheered, there was obvious satisfaction among the spectators. The next two bodies followed in rapid succession, the woman first and then the second man. Each time the falling blade did its job, almost faster than the eye could follow.

One of the men standing near Pierre grunted and turned away after the last one. "A blade so swift can do naught but harm," he said. "Heads will roll in the gutter."

The first one came eight days later in the Place de Grève at three in the afternoon. His name was Jacques Pelletier and he had been a thief. Pierre Frayer was in the front row among the spectators.

During the weeks that followed, Pierre never missed an execution. They quickly became more frequent during that long spring and summer of '92. Gradually the word got around that it was not Antoine Louis but Joseph Guillotin himself who had played the major role in designing the machine. Paris started calling it by his name, and soon the city seemed in the grip of a mania for guillotines. Women wore miniature replicas for earrings, and children played

202

with toy versions. Tiny dolls filled with sweet liqueur were decapitated with dessert at the dinner table.

It was during the heat of summer that Pierre bought one of the miniature mahogany guillotines and used it to cut the head off a chicken. He watched intently as the little blade fell, as the blood spurted. It was good, but the sheep had been better.

He decided to build himself a small guillotine in the dank basement of the old house he shared with his sister. Her name was Rosette and she earned a living by selling flowers at various locations around the city. Lately she had been selling them at the executions, because that was where the crowds gathered. He had spotted her two or three times, but they never spoke of it.

"What are you doing with the wood?" she asked him one afternoon when he'd begun assembling the raw materials for his basement project. When she asked him questions like that she sounded exactly like their mother, who'd died in an influenza outbreak when they were both children.

"Building a cabinet for my room," he answered. "I need space for storage."

"What storage? You don't own anything but your clothes and that little guillotine you wasted money on."

He continued down to the basement, ignoring her. It was a small area beneath the house, with a dirt floor and rough stone walls dating from the early years of the century. Pierre could reach the ceiling easily without standing on tiptoe, and he judged it to be no more than seven feet high. That would be a problem, ruling out the construction of a full-size machine. But if he scaled down the height of the uprights, he wondered if the blade would have enough distance for its deadly plunge.

After studying the question for some time he decided that two possibilities presented themselves. He could dig up part of the earthen floor to allow for a greater height, or he could weight the blade to give it more force when it hit. Finally he decided upon a combination of these two techniques.

The next day he purchased the remainder of the supplies

he would need, everything but the heavy triangular blade itself, and he thought he knew where he could get one of those. In the earliest designs the blade was crescent-shaped, and it was said to be the King himself who had suggested it be triangular. Pierre knew that the carpenter named Guidon who'd built the machine had made a couple of false starts on the ironwork. One blade proved to be too small to fit neatly into the copper-lined grooves of the uprights, and had to be discarded. If he could locate it in the junkyard in back of the carpenter's shop, it might be just what he needed.

That night, after Rosette was asleep, he went to the junkyard and prowled around among the old timbers and bits of metal behind the carpenter's shop. Before long he found what he sought—a triangular piece of unsharpened iron, obviously meant for the guillotine but cut to the wrong size. Though it was heavy to carry, Pierre managed to get it back to his own dwelling. Knowing now the necessary width between his uprights, he set to work the next day on the actual construction. Rosette had gone out to sell her flowers, believing him to be doing some sort of manual labor for the Ministry of Justice.

By nightfall when she returned he had completed the basic framework for the machine. He covered it over with a paint-stained sheet and went up to greet her. "What have you been doing?" she asked. "Working on your cabinet?"

"That's right." He poured water from the pitcher into the basin and washed the grime from his hands. "How was business today?"

"I made a little. It's always better when there's an execution. They draw the biggest crowds."

"There's one tomorrow," he told her, almost casually. "An execution."

"Are you going?"

"I might."

The crowd that day was unusually restless, with rumors everywhere that the monarchy would soon be overthrown.

Pierre listened to a cheer go up as the cart carrying the condemned man, a convicted forger, came into view. Most executions these days were performed on the Place du Carrousel, under a hot August sky that showed no mercy. Some of the spectators were fanning themselves. He looked around for some glimpse of Rosette and her flowers, but he could see her nowhere.

Sometimes as he watched the executions, Pierre's gaze stayed fixed on the blade, other times he kept his eyes on their faces. He was unable to decide which was the more exciting. In the case of the forger, his eyes were on the blade. He watched it fall, as if it had been slowed just for him, and he could almost feel its sharpness at the moment of impact.

That night he went home and worked on his own machine with renewed vigor. The blade fit well into its grooves and when at last he was finished he stood back to admire his workmanship. He'd been able to dig out nearly two feet of dirt from the cellar floor, and though the uprights still weren't as tall as the real guillotine, its overall height approached nine feet. He'd never measured the machine in the Place du Carrousel, but he estimated it to be about twelve feet tall. His blade would have three feet less to drop. Would it be heavy enough to make a clean cut?

He spent all the following day sharpening his blade, knowing how important that was. He barely heard when Rosette returned that night with word that the monarchy had at last been overthrown and Louis XVI had been imprisoned, along with the Queen, his sister and his two children. There was talk that if Louis went to the guillotine, that particular blade would never be used again. This last bit of rumor did manage to penetrate the walls of Pierre's preoccupation, and for a time he considered the possibilities. If he could manage to steal the very blade with which the King had been decapitated—

But he put it out of his mind. The execution, if there ever was one, might be months away. His machine was complete and waiting only to be tested. The following morning he went in search of a sheep. He finally located one in the big open-air farmers' market, but as soon as he saw it he rejected the idea. A sheep was too large and too expensive for him to handle, and its smell would be quickly detected by his sister.

He remembered the scrawny stray dogs he sometimes saw going through garbage behind a café near his house. One of those would serve his purpose as well as a sheep, and it would be easier all around. But today, as luck would have it, he saw none of the stray dogs. There was only a boy playing by himself in the mud of a dried-up puddle.

"Where are the dogs?" Pierre asked the youth.

"Away. The owner of the café beat them and drove them away."

"Old Arnoux? I can't believe he'd do such a thing."

The boy shrugged, uncaring. "Believe what you want."

"What is your name?"

"Gustave Hune."

"Could you find one of the dogs for me, Gustave, and bring it to me? I live near here, and I will give you a coin."

After a bit of bickering a price was agreed upon and Gustave went off in search of a stray dog. He returned in less than an hour with a sickly-looking mongrel in tow. "This is the best I could do," he told Pierre.

"Fine, that will be fine!" He gave the lad two coins and took the dog in tow. Getting it to the basement proved a bit more difficult. Finally he clubbed it with a piece of timber and dragged it down the steps.

He tied it to the board in the event it regained consciousness, though he was beginning to suspect the dog was dead. Then he positioned the head into the *lunette* and took a deep breath before releasing the blade.

It fell with a swiftness that delighted him, and though there was not as much blood as there'd been with the sheep, he was satisfied. It had been only a test, and it had worked well. The next one would be the real thing.

Through that August the revolutionary fervor grew. There was talk of all sorts of changes—even renaming the days and months—and almost every official of government was marked for the guillotine at one time or another. The executions became so frequent that some spoke of a Reign of Terror, and Pierre was giddy with delight on those frequent days when the horse-drawn tumbrel would come into view carrying five or six victims bound for the guillotine. Most were thieves, forgers and arsonists, though the vague phrase "crimes against the state" was being heard with increasing regularity.

The guillotine was moved frequently now, from one city square to another. For five days it might be placed before the ruins of the Bastille, then for a month it might do its work at the Barrière du Trône Renversé. Whenever he could, Pierre accompanied it. Occasionally he was in the work party that transported it. More frequently he stayed away from his job and went on his own to view the executions. Once when the executioner's wicker basket fell from the cart almost at his feet, he managed to dip his hand into the blood before it was taken away.

One day Pierre saw the boy Gustave playing on the road. "I need another dog," he said. "Bring it to my house."

"It will cost you three coins this time."

"Very well. Make it quick."

An hour later the boy arrived on his doorstep with a mangy black cat. "I could not find a dog today. Will this cat do?"

Pierre hesitated only an instant. "All right. Come in and I will pay you."

The boy followed him inside. He was still looking at the cat when Pierre brought the wooden club down across his right temple. As he fell the cat jumped from his arms and ran out the door. No matter, Pierre thought. It is the boy I want anyhow.

He dragged the limp body down the steps to the basement, avoiding the hole he'd dug earlier. He'd reached a decision with the dog that it was too great a risk to remove the bodies, even after dark. The dirt floor seemed a natural burial ground. Rosette had not set foot in the basement in months, and he could find excuses to keep her out of there.

207

Sometimes he wondered if the crowd was part of the ecstasy he felt, if that helped explain why the dog had not been quite so good as the others. But as he released the blade now he knew differently. He had never felt anything like this tingling that ran through his entire body, right down to his toes. It was better than the sheep, better than all those forgers and thieves.

Better because he'd done it himself.

The following day he went out to work as usual, with only a few words to Rosette over breakfast. As it happened he was assigned to a work detail at the home of Jacques Granston from the Ministry of Justice. The overbearing Granston came out of the house himself to supervise as they began to clean out a carriage house adjacent to the main living quarters.

"Move that trash out of there!" he shouted in his familiar loud voice. "We need the space for a new carriage."

He was about to depart when his sharp eyes settled on Pierre. "You there! Weren't you at Bicêtre the day we tested the guillotine, back in the spring?"

"I was," Pierre admitted, wondering if he was marked somehow for life.

"I thought I recognized you," he said with a nod of his head, as if pleased with this confirmation of his excellent memory. "We have been busy since then. Madame Guillotine has been busy."

"Yes, sir," Pierre murmured and moved away.

Granston stared after him for just a moment and then moved on.

Two days later Rosette returned home earlier than expected, while Pierre was still in the basement. She called out to him from the doorway and when he made his way upstairs, she asked, "What is it you do so much down there? What is that foul odor I smell sometimes?"

"I smell no odor."

"No, you wouldn't." She went about the task of preparing supper for them both.

208

Pierre brooded all through the meal, wondering just how much she knew or suspected. When she went off to work the following day he rigged a simple trap, running a thin piece of string loosely across the top step leading to the basement. It would not trip anyone, but if it was disturbed, he'd know Rosette was spying on his activities.

It had taken him a long time to clean the blood from the blade and the mechanism. He hadn't realized this would be such a problem, and he wondered if the revolutionary government was having the same trouble with its full-sized machine. Finally it was clean again, the blade sparkling, the grooved track free of impediments. He was ready.

There was no work that day, but he didn't care. An execution was scheduled for the Place de Grève at noon, and he wanted to be there. He stepped carefully over his telltale string as he left the basement and let himself out the front door.

At the Place de Grève a crowd had already gathered well before the scheduled execution. Some of the faces were familiar from other days, and one he recognized was old Arnoux, owner of the café down the street from his house. "Is that you, Pierre Frayer? Come to watch another head roll?"

Pierre moistened his lips and managed a nod.

"It's said we may get a bonus today. Three heads instead of one. Multiple executions are becoming commonplace."

He had barely spoken when the red tumbrel came into view, pulled by two horses. One prisoner was sobbing, another had his eyes closed, his lips moving in silent prayer. The third stood stoically. They were quickly unloaded from the cart and lined up with their backs to the guillotine. Another red cart stood waiting nearby to remove the bodies after execution. Someone in the crowd hurled a head of cabbage at the condemned men, and the spectators laughed.

The crowd was so large today that getting a good view of the scaffold was difficult. Some had climbed onto ladders, others stood on carriages and carts. Pierre had to move away from Arnoux to find a spot for himself that commanded a better view.

The first man shouted something as he was laid on the wooden plank and had his neck imprisoned by the collar. But the roar of the crowd drowned him out, swelling to almost deafening proportions as the heavy blade fell.

It was good. The second and third were even better. But they still did not match the moment of ecstasy he felt when he'd done it himself.

Watching them load the bodies into the red cart, he suddenly became aware that a pair of eyes were upon him. He turned and saw Jacques Granston from the Ministry of Justice, watching from about fifty feet away. Granston's expression was indecipherable, but there was no doubt he had recognized Pierre.

Time to leave, he decided, heading quickly in the opposite direction. The crowd was dispersing and before he knew it he found himself in step with old Arnoux. "I couldn't really see it when the blade fell," the café owner told him. "The crowd was too big today."

"Big," Pierre agreed.

"How is your sister? I haven't seen her lately."

"Rosette is well."

Arnoux spoke of their neighbors and of the effect the revolutionary activity was having on his business. "More people come for a bottle of wine or a brandy in the evenings," he said. "They come to celebrate the changes, but they are worried, too. Some fear the revolution is getting out of hand. What do you think?"

"Perhaps it is," Pierre mumbled.

"All these decapitations in the city squares—"

As they neared the café Arnoux's one-sided conversation shifted to the condition of the streets. "Look at this rubbish everywhere! There was a boy named Gustave who cleaned up around my place and kept the dogs away, but now he's gone off somewhere. I haven't seen him lately."

"I saw him," Pierre said, wetting his lips.

"What? You?"

"He left a note for me when he went away."

"I didn't even know he could read and write!"

"Come to my house and I will show you."

Arnoux followed a bit uncertainly. "All right, just for a moment. I have never been to your place, although your sister pointed it out to me once."

The old man had trouble with steps, and Pierre knew he could never be persuaded to visit the basement. He got him as far as the kitchen and invited him to have a sip of wine while he located the letter. He got out the wooden club he'd used on the boy and walked around behind Arnoux. The old man never suspected a thing.

He weighed very little and it was not a difficult task to open the basement door and then drag him across the floor and down the steps. Pierre strapped him to the board in case he should awaken and then positioned the wooden collar about his neck.

This was the first adult he'd done, and he was surprised that there was so much blood to be cleaned up afterward.

It was while he was finishing his cleaning chores that he remembered the string. It was no longer across the top step, and he was certain it had been missing when he first dragged old Arnoux down the stairs.

Rosette told him the news the following morning. "That café owner down the street, Monsieur Arnoux, has disappeared. They say he never came to work last night and hasn't been home since."

Pierre grunted and went on with his breakfast.

"Did you see him yesterday?"

"No."

"The Ministry of Justice is looking into it. They suspect someone may have killed him for his money."

"Oh, no!" Pierre protested. He had visions of Granston on the prowl.

"That's what they think."

There was something strange in her voice, and he raised his eyes, almost afraid to meet hers. She turned away and went back to frying her breakfast eggs.

211

He found excuses to remain in the house until after she'd left for work, then once again placed the loose piece of string on the top step of the basement stairs. The dirt floor was smooth again, but he knew there would be traces of his digging. And of course there was the machine itself, standing there quite openly though covered by the paint-spattered sheet.

He went out, but could not go to work. Instead he circled the block, actually walking by the café, and climbed in a back window of his house. For a long time he merely stood in the kitchen, listening for the slightest sound.

After a bit Pierre went down to the basement, and there too he simply waited and listened. His eyes scanned the earthen floor, seeking anything that might be out of place.

Suddenly the door at the top of the stairs was thrown open.

He saw the figure outlined against the light, descending toward him. It was Granston, it had to be Granston, come to seal his doom. He moved backward until he came against the basement's rough stone wall, but still the figure advanced. Now it was reaching out a hand to him.

"Pierre, what are you doing down here?"

It was his mother, catching him again on one of his sinful basement visits. It was Granston, come to avenge those he had killed without the revolution's approval.

"Pierre, it's Rosette! What's the matter with you?"

His vision cleared and he saw that it was indeed his sister. She was gripping his shoulders and shaking him. "I—I—"

"Pierre, listen to me! What is this thing you're hiding down here? I found it yesterday when I was looking for some dust rags. Did you build this yourself?"

"Yes," he murmured.

"It's just like the real one. The blade is even sharp. What will you use it for?"

Perhaps she didn't know. Perhaps he could still fool her.

"I built it for the revolutionary government. They will

transport it around the provinces as a model for the building of more full-sized guillotines."

"They are paying you for it?" she asked dubiously.

"Yes, yes!"

"Pierre, you've never been able to lie to me, any more than you could lie to Mother."

"Look," he said, hurrying to pull the paint-spattered sheet from the machine. "I will show you how well it works."

"Pierre—"

But he was on her in a flash, forcing her to the floor, reaching out for any weapon he could grab. They fought silently, as they had so many times in their youth, when the older and stronger Rosette usually won.

This time was different.

When she was too weak to fight any more he lifted her onto the board. She opened her eyes once and looked at him, muttering, "What are you doing to me?" That was all.

The blade seemed to sing as it dropped, something he'd never noticed before.

The house was quieter without Rosette, and neighbors immediately wondered what had happened to her. Pierre had a story for everyone who asked, but it was not always the same story. To one woman he said she was ill, being treated at a hospital outside Paris. To another he said she'd run off, possibly with a blacksmith from Versailles. He did not repeat the latter story, realizing himself how unbelievable it sounded.

A man who sometimes employed Pierre to do carpentry work was the first to comment on the almost simultaneous disappearance of old Arnoux and Rosette. "I'm sure they'll both return," Pierre said, trying to make light of it. "When I visit my sister in hospital I will see if Arnoux is hiding under the bed."

For a full week he stayed away from the executions, fearful that he might run into Granston again. Finally, though, he could deprive himself no longer. On a day when four were scheduled to die, he walked down to the Place de Grève, where the guillotine was still located. Jacques Granston recognized him and came over to where he stood.

"You are Pierre Frayer. I have seen you often at the beheadings."

"This is my first in more than a week," Pierre answered defensively. "Others come more often than that."

Granston agreed. "I myself am here every day now. There is rarely a day when Madame Guillotine is not in use."

The man from the Ministry of Justice slipped his hand around Pierre's shoulder. "Come—I will get us a good view up front."

True to his word, he guided Pierre up to the very front ranks, only a few feet from the platform itself. He could study the wicker basket clearly, resting there to receive its offering.

There was the usual roar as the tumbrel entered the square, this time bearing four victims for the guillotine. They were unloaded virtually in front of Pierre, and as the first one climbed the steps the other three stood with their backs to the machine, facing the crowd. One stood directly in front of Pierre, so close they could have touched if the man's hands had not been tied behind him. He looked so young, Pierre thought, barely older than the boy Gustave.

The first roar went up from the crowd, and the young man shuddered. It was quickly apparent that he would be the last to climb the steps, and all color had drained from his face. *Come with me,* Pierre wanted to cry out. *I will hold you as the blade falls. I will comfort you to the last.*

The second roar went up.

"You see how efficient we are," Granston commented. "One day recently we had six. That is all the tumbrel can carry, and we will soon be forced to press a second cart into service."

Pierre moistened his lips. "What are their crimes?"

"These four? Murder, high treason, rape and theft. We have abolished torture, you know. This is much more humane."

The third victim was quickly disposed of, and it was the turn of the young man who stood facing them. The executioner's assistants came for him, turning him toward the steps.

I will comfort you, Pierre repeated silently.

The young man was strapped into position and the wooden collar fitted around his neck. The blade was released as Pierre watched, his breath coming in short, quick gasps.

He had never seen the blood spurt so far. But the executioner had miscalculated the exact placement of the wicker basket. The head hit the edge of it, bounded off the platform and onto the cobblestone pavement.

"Disgusting!" Jacques Granston growled. "Must we be subjected to such incompetence?"

Pierre had hoped that the conclusion of the executions would mean his parting from the Justice Ministry man. But as the crowd in the square broke up, Granston remained close by his side.

"I saw you walking with Arnoux after the executions one day," he said. "It might have been the day the old man disappeared."

"No, no!" Pierre insisted.

"Yes, it might have been. Where do you live? Near Arnoux's café?"

"Not far from it," he admitted reluctantly.

Pierre was silent for the remainder of their walk, although the large man at his side continued chatting. "The revolution will soon touch the lives of everyone in France. Already there are plans for more guillotines to be used in the provinces."

"I have something to show you at my house," Pierre heard himself saying. "It is a model which you may be able to use."

215

"What? What's that? Speak up, man!"

"Come into my house. I will show you."

Granston looked puzzled but followed him inside. "This kitchen is filthy. Don't you have a sister who looks after you?"

"She's away," Pierre mumbled. "How did you know about her?"

"Rosette? I have seen her some nights at the café, selling flowers. Now I wonder what has become of her."

"Down here." Pierre motioned. "The basement."

"These are steep stairs. You should be careful of accidents. What is this you have for me here?"

Pierre reached the bottom and pulled the sheet from his masterpiece. "It is a working model. A fully working model."

Granston's eyes widened. "I had no idea—"

Pierre smiled as he picked up his wooden club. "Here, let me show you."

In the last instant Granston's hamlike fist came up to smash against his jaw.

Pierre was smiling as he stepped from the red tumbrel. The roar of the crowd seemed deafening, louder than he'd ever heard before. He was first this day, and he mounted the steps without the help of the executioner's assistants. He could see Granston standing in the front row, watching him, and perhaps the others were there too—the boy Gustave, and old Arnoux, and even Rosette.

He stretched out on the wooden plank as they bound him in place, and then felt his neck imprisoned by the wooden collar. His eyes were cast down toward the wicker basket. "A bit to the left with the basket," he cautioned the executioner. "I saw a head bounce out recently."

The executioner moved it an inch to the left, gazing at him in silence.

Then Pierre was able to relax, to savor this moment he had anticipated for so long. This was the greatest ecstasy

216

of all, greater than watching it done or even doing it himself. This—

He heard the blade begin to fall as the crowd roared.

Yes, this!

Now now now no—

Kin

Charles L. Grant

The thing is, the thing that I do, it's the kind of thing you can't plan, you know what I mean? It's like spontaneous. It happens. Sometimes you don't even know it until it's almost over. You think too much about it, it takes all the fun out of it. I remember the time when I was in college and this junior, his name was Gary, he wanted to take some little freshman girl, Esther something, to dinner. So he spends the whole week doing all the conversations in his head, everything from the first phone call asking her out to what he's gonna say over dessert, to the line he's gonna use when he gets her back to the dorm. What a joke. By the time the night was over, he was so wrecked from steering things to the way he'd planned it, I think she was ready to kill him.

Planning is what kills, man, planning.

What you gotta do is, you gotta let things flow. Like you're on a river or something, you know what I mean? You keep your eye on the banks, look out for crap popping up outta the water, stuff like that; but as long as you're going the same way the water is, you're gonna get where you're going sooner or later, so why waste sweat?

Like the woman in St. Louis. Out at the Arch place, that

thing they built by the river. We'd sort of met at the park there, and got in line about the same time to take the ride up inside that Arch. No special reason. We just rode up so we could see all to hell and back, she was sighing and hanging on, laughing like a dope. Over at the horizon there was a bunch of clouds, black and gray, if you took a quick look you'd think they were mountains or something. She pointed them out, said she prayed that storm wasn't coming in our direction, and wondered what would happen if a hurricane came along. Stuff like that. She got herself so spooked, it was easy, you know, to get her to stick close. I played the Big Man.

"Hey, don't worry," I said. "No sweat. A hurricane comes, I'll just blow it back the other way."

She laughed and kissed the back of my hand. No kidding. And I laughed back and said, "So you free for dinner?"

She gave me the kind of look, you know what it is, it makes you feel like you got your fly open, something like that, and then, seeing that I wasn't no ax murderer, anything like that, she says, "Sure."

"And if a hurricane comes," I told her on the way back down, "we can hide under the table and eat olives until the Red Cross comes and saves us."

Dumb; but she laughed.

That's the important thing—she laughed.

So we found this place on the river, some kind of fish and steak place, and we had a pretty good time. I told her I was a computer guy, the one that makes the machines do fancy pictures and stuff, and she thought that was the greatest thing since sliced bread. Very impressed, if you know what I mean. She didn't know much about them, the computers, but they had them at her office and she was a little scared of them. So we talked about that for a while, and by the time dessert came, we was pretty good friends.

She didn't ask me back to her place.

I didn't even hint that I wanted to go.

Planning, see?

If I'd planned to go back with her, all them signals she wasn't sending would've blown me right out of the water.

I'd've had to put on the pressure. And pressure's no good. They get all bent outta shape, you put the pressure on.

So I didn't.

She relaxed.

I said I was heading west in a couple of days, Colorado, would it be all right if I called her once before I went, maybe have lunch or something. See, no dinner. That's at night. Night's spooky too. Daylight, everyone can see everyone else, no pressure, no problem.

She said sure.

She died.

Hell, if I'd planned it that way, it wouldn't have happened. The poor thing'd still be in St. Louis, married, couple of kids, wondering whatever happened to the nerd that took her out to dinner that time. Sad. Really sad.

Like Lillie, down in New Orleans. What a case. I was down by the riverfront hotels and that convention center, riding the ferry back and forth across the Mississippi, only a ten-minute trip, something like that, nothing fancy on the boat, but it was warm. Hell, it was hot, and the breeze from that boat was the only good thing going that day. She was at the railing on the top passenger deck, just staring at the water and smoking up a storm. I saw her, knew right away she was going to jump soon as she got the nerve.

"Got a light?" I asked, not too close, but close enough for her to hear over the engines. Woman damn near fell over the side right then, but when she saw this guy, a not-old probably tourist type but without all the cameras and stuff, she kind of shrugged and handed over her lighter. I lit up, handed it back, watched the river and smoked, watched the hotels on the bank get big, and small, and big again, until she turned to me, I swear to God, and she said, "If you jump, you'll die."

"Ain't gonna jump," I said without looking at her. "Just watching the water go along, that's all."

"Boring."

"Peaceful." I glanced over, then looked back at the river. "It knows where it's going, isn't in no hurry to get there, it's going to get there anyway, no matter all the damn boats and ships and stuff gets in its way."

"Yeah," she grumbled, "but they keep putting up dams and locks."

I pointed at a deep curve in the bank. "They can put up mountains, sooner or later it gets around them. Once in a while, it even knocks them down."

She turned and stared at me, kind of with one eye partly closed. "Are you a preacher or something?"

"No. I work with computers. Not the most exciting job in the world, not like hunting sharks or anything, but they do teach you there's always a way around if you're patient enough." I nodded at the water. "The river's patient." I grinned. "And it always gets around."

"Are you hungry?"

I almost said no.

I didn't.

We got off the ferry on the Canal Street side and walked up to the Quarter. I'd been there a few times in the past, and despite all the changes, it never changes. We found this open-air restaurant and had a late lunch. We didn't talk much, but I knew she was looking at me all the time, trying to figure me out.

I already had her figured out.

I could almost see the suckers on her fingers, the scars they'd leave on my arms when they clung there for a while. But she was pleasant enough, we had a few laughs, had a few drinks, joked about the tourists gawking at us as if we were natives.

They were in too much a hurry, see, to go from one place to another. Time, in New Orleans, ain't a hurrying thing.

The river, though, is a lot stronger than it looks.

And deeper.

Like the forests outside Minneapolis.

The mountains outside Taos.

I met a woman, one of them that doesn't have an age even though she doesn't do nothing very special, in Georgia. She wanted me, after a couple of hours dancing around and sizing me up, to see the swamps.

222

I hadn't thought of that.

Planning never figured.

A guy in some newspaper, I don't remember which one there's been so damn many, he says I'm obviously filled with hatred for my mother. What the hell? He don't know much, and read all that in books, I bet. Says women are attracted to me because I'm secretly afraid of them, they know this, they think they can dominate me or some shit like that. God. I mean, did Lillie sound like she wanted to dominate me? Hell, all I did there was give her just what she wanted when I met her.

Dumb jerk writer, looking to make a buck, I don't blame him, but it's too bad he's where I already was too short a time ago. I'd like to take him out to lunch sometime, show him where his book ends and his life begins.

Tell him about the faces.

You read this stuff, you know, you think it's so until some guy, like this writer, they tell you it's all made up. You can't tell nothing from anybody's eyes, for example, lest they want you to, secretly or not. Right. And most people, whether they know it or not, can keep a secret with their eyes. Right. And only in the movies do people look deep into someone's eyes and come up with a whole damn life history, stuff like that. Right.

Not true.

Not really.

Eyes tell you where things are, where people want to go, where people wish they were, things like that. You work at it long enough, you can say you're the King of England, for God's sake, and people who think they can read your eyes will believe it if the eyes tell them it's true.

Right.

All the time, though, you're the one checking them out, and you don't gotta stare either. A look is all it takes. A check of the eyes. And the corners of the mouth. The cheeks. The forehead. The chin. A look.

It takes it all in, all the face, and I looked at Suzanne and saw that she didn't much care for what she saw. A lost case, I thought; nothing here to worry about. Standing in the check-out line, some two-bit convenience store in Boston, I ask her anyway if she wants to put her stuff on the counter, I got only a pack of cigarettes, she's got a whole load of stuff. She nodded, ignored the polite smile, dumped her stuff and fussed with her purse, she's already got the total in her head.

I pay and leave.

Lots of time, I'm never in any hurry.

Don't have any plans.

She comes out, sees me walking up the street, calls after me. I turned around, couldn't believe my ears, and she wants to know would I help her, the damn bag's breaking already.

"Do you have a car?"

She's tall, a little heavy but certainly not fat, reddish kind of hair. She could walk to New Hampshire, I figure, and break only a little sweat.

"Sorry." I pointed over my shoulder. "My hotel's just a couple of blocks away. I'm only in town for a few days." A shrug. "Computer stuff over in Cambridge."

"Oh." She shrugs, and points the other way. "My place is a couple blocks down there."

It's dark. Cold. Breath in the air like we was panting horses, snow piled on the curbs, the streetlights sharp. Most of the buildings have no lights in their windows, trash scattered around, papers blowing.

I don't like it, what she said. Not that I don't mind getting picked up now and then, makes for a full life and is better than watching TV, but this ain't sitting right with me, you know what I mean? All parts of her face are telling me different stuff, and its confuses the hell out of me.

"You need some help?"

I couldn't believe I said that. I mean, I was so surprised I stuttered until she started to laugh. Not a particularly nice laugh, but damn, it made me feel weird.

"I'm not going to bite," she said. "You live up that way, I live down that way, and it's late. You can see what the neighborhood's like. I'd appreciate the company to the stoop."

224

Confusion. I could learn something here, I figured suddenly, even if nothing came of it, so I played the good guy, took one of the bags and walked with her. Damn, it was cold! But I didn't say nothing because I kept trying to catch her out, make her face talk to me whenever we passed under a streetlight or a car came along and nailed her with the headlamps.

All it did was grin.

All the way to her apartment house in a section of town I didn't blame her that she wanted company.

She took the bag and said, "So look, you gonna be free anytime?"

Take it where you can get it, I told myself.

"Yeah. Tomorrow afternoon, in fact."

"You know Boston?"

Her breath, like her face, was smoke.

"Nope. First time." No lie. I'm never in one place more than once, except New Orleans where I fit in better than most, though Lillie was the only time I did something about it. Some guys, more of them writer types, they got me spending years in the same state, for God's sake. Like I'm an idiot or something. "Last time I was in Massachusetts, about ten years ago, I think, I never got the chance to come here." No lie, either.

"Well, tell you what," she said, starting up the steps, talking at me without looking around, "if you want, you can meet me at the store around one, I'll show you some of the sights."

"Well . . . hey, thanks."

"No problem." At the door she looked over her shoulder. "Could be fun."

I guess.

I never thought of it as fun.

It was just something to do, traveling and meeting people and traveling on. Interesting, always; once in a while a little exciting; every so often dull, but not so often that I'm tempted to settle down. But fun? Strange. I really never thought of it that way.

So what the hell, no plans, right?, and the next day we

225

do the subway thing, with cars like trolleys, which I thought was kind of fascinating and a hell of a lot better than New York's mole, checked out a couple of places what had plaques on them and all, and walked along the Charles River, which was damn cold what with all the wind and all, and we didn't say much. Talked a lot. Didn't say much. It was . . . unsettling, I guess. Couldn't get that handle, couldn't read that face, and couldn't find a place where I could get things done and be done with it.

By the time we got back to my hotel, were in the lobby bar having a drink, I realized for the first time that day what the hell was wrong with me, and I laughed. Very loud. People stared, I didn't care, because for just one second there I was scared.

Never been that before.

Really scared.

For my life.

But I was. Then. Glass of beer touching my lips, looking at her trying to figure out what the hell had gone wrong, why I was still with her.

In that second, that one there with the glass and the look, I got scared.

Suzanne saw it.

And I read her face.

And I laughed.

"You're drunk," she said in mild disgust.

"Not me," I answered, laughed again, though this time a little quieter because all them people they were looking at me too long, some out-of-town idiot they wish would take the next flight back to the sticks. "I'm sorry, Suzanne, but I just had what you might call a revelation."

An eyebrow lifted.

The scare was gone.

She took a bill out of her purse, made like she was gonna pay for the drinks, and I couldn't help it—I reached over the table and took her wrist.

"You been in Boston long?" I said.

She blinked.

"You haven't been," I told her. Frowned a little. "Not all

that long." I tapped her arm to tell her not to lie, and let her go.

And stared at her until she was forced to look at me. I mean, really look at me. Not sneaking looks, not phony looks—a real look.

Then she laughed.

I nodded.

She stood up and shook her head. "Damn," she said, "I thought I was the only one, you know?"

"Me too," I said. I was gonna lie, but she would've known it. "Nice to meet you."

"You leaving town?"

"In the morning, I guess."

"Have any fun?" She giggled.

"Nope. Thought I was, though." I laughed.

She laughed back, and damn if she didn't lean over then and kiss me on the cheek. First damn real kiss I've had in years. She looked at me again, kissed me again, and waved like we was old friends as she headed for the door.

I didn't go after her.

But I felt so good I stayed in my chair most of the night, sipping, watching, making a couple of brief contacts that I didn't feel like picking up on even though they were pleasant enough. Didn't matter, though. There would be more. There are always more. Always would be until I got too old.

But this was special.

This was the most special night of my life.

Hell, I had just met my first kin, the first person like me I'd ever met.

Should've known, though, there was more.

Stands to reason.

All them prisons, all them trials, all them stories in the newspapers, all the movies with all that blood and spilling brains and arms cut off, heads cut off, eyes poked out, trials and manhunts and headlines and cops—stands to reason there had to be some like me, right?

Had to be.

We're the ones you see in your dreams.
We're the ones who don't have any faces.
Why?
Hell, that's easy too.
We're the ones that never get caught.

Call
Home

Dennis Etchison

▲▲▲▲▲▲▲

When he walked in, the red light on the answering machine was blinking.

He dropped the mail on the coffee table and sat down. He ran a hand through his hair and leaned into the sofa, his ears still ringing from the rush-hour traffic.

He was in no hurry to replay his messages. It was easy to guess what they wanted: time, money, answers. He had none to spare. He reached out and stirred the pile of letters.

More of the same.

He got up, went to the bedroom and changed his clothes. Then he came back and sank deeper into the cushions. He propped his feet up and closed his eyes.

When the phone rang again, he let the machine take over.

"I'm not home right now," he heard his own recorded voice say, *"but if you care to leave a message, please begin speaking when you hear the tone. Thank you for calling. . . ."*

Beep.

A pause, and the incoming tape started rolling.

He waited to monitor the call.

Static. A rush of white noise. Like traffic.

No one there. Or someone who did not like talking to a machine.

A few more seconds and it would hang up automatically.

"Daddy? Is t-that you?"

He opened his eyes.

"Please, c-can you come get me? I don't know how to get home . . . and I'm scared!"

What?

"It's getting cold . . . and dark . . . ."

He sat forward.

"There's a man here . . . and he's bothering me! I think he's crazy! And it's going to rain and . . . and . . . Daddy, tell me what to do!"

He got to his feet.

"I don't like this place! There's a rooster . . . it's burning . . . and a gas station . . . and a sign. It says, um, it starts with a p. P-I-C-O . . . ."

He crossed the living room.

"Daddy, please come quick . . . !"

He snatched up the receiver.

"Hello?" he said.

The child's voice began to sing brokenly.

"Ladybird, ladybird, fly away home . . . your house is on fire . . . and your children will burn. . . ."

Her voice trailed off as she started to cry.

"Hello? Hello?"

Click.

He stood there holding the phone, wondering what to do.

He was sure of only one thing.

He had no daughter.

So what if it was a wrong number? She was in trouble. A child, a little girl. What if something happened to her?

He couldn't let it go.

She had spelled out a word. P-I-C-O. The sign. A rooster, a gas station . . . yes, it sounded familiar.

The chicken restaurant. Next to the 76 station. On Pico Boulevard.

230

It wasn't far.

The traffic was still gridlocked. He crossed Wilshire in low gear, then Santa Monica, and turned west. A stream of cars growled past him, ragged music and demanding voices leaking from beneath shimmering hoods. He made a left on Westwood and kept to the right as he passed Olympic, slowing to a crawl as he came to the next corner.

She was huddled in the doorway of El Pollo Muerto, a school book bag at her feet. Her legs were dirty and her hair was in her eyes. A few yards away, at the gas station, was the phone booth. She did not look up as he braked by a loading zone.

He leaned over and rolled down the window.

"Hey!"

The people at the bus stop glanced his way blankly, then stared past him down the street.

She lowered her head, resting her forehead on her arms.

He cleared his throat and shouted above the din. "Hey, little girl!"

She raised her head.

A woman eyed him suspiciously.

"Hi!" he called. "Hello, there! Do you need any help?"

The woman glared at him.

He ignored her and spoke to the girl.

"Are you the one who—?" Suddenly he felt foolish. "Did you call me?"

The little girl's face brightened.

"Daddy?"

The crowd moved closer. Then there was a rumbling and a pumping of brakes. He saw in his rearview mirror that an RTD bus had pulled up behind him.

"Come on," he said. "And your books—"

He opened the door for her as the bus sounded its horn.

"Daddy, it *is* you!"

The crowd surged past. The woman took notice of his license plate. The bus tapped his bumper.

"Get in."

He slipped into gear and got away from the curb. The pressure of traffic carried him across the intersection.

"Where do you want to go?" he asked. He passed another corner before it was possible to turn. "What's the address?"

"I don't know," said the little girl.

"You don't remember?"

She did not answer.

"Well, you'll have to tell me. Which way?"

"Want to go home," she said. She was now sitting straight in her seat, watching the lights with wide eyes.

"Are you all right?"

"I guess so."

At least it hasn't started to rain, he thought. "Did anyone hurt you?"

"I'm kind of hungry," she said.

He idled at a red light and got a good look at her. Seven, maybe eight years old and skinny as a rail. The bones in her wrists showed like white knuckles through the thin skin.

"When was the last time you had anything to eat?"

"I don't know."

She crossed her legs, angling a bruised ankle on a knobby knee, and he saw that her legs were streaked and smudged all the way up. My God, he thought, how long since she's had a bath? Has she been living on the streets?

"Well then," he said, "the first thing we'll do is get you some food." And then he would figure out what to do with her. "Okay?"

He took her to a deli. She gulped down a hot dog, leaving the bun on the plate, and watched him as he chewed his sandwich. He started to order her another, and realized something. He touched his hip pocket. Empty. He had forgotten his wallet when he changed his clothes.

"Take half of mine," he told her, trying to think.

"I don't like that kind."

She continued to watch him.

Finally he said, "Do you want another hot dog?"

"Yes, please!"

He ordered one more and saw to it that she drank her milk.

232

Afterward, while the waitress was in another part of the restaurant, he said abruptly, "Let's go."

They drove away as the waitress came out onto the sidewalk.

"That was good," said the little girl.

"Glad you liked it. Now—"

"The way you did that. You didn't even leave a tip. You did it for me, didn't you?"

"Yes." *What was I supposed to do?* he thought. *I'll come back tomorrow and take care of it.* "Now where are we going?"

"Home," she said. "Oh, Daddy, you're so silly! Where did you think?"

"You've got to tell me," he said in the driveway.

"Tell you what?"

She got out and skipped to the front door, dragging her book bag. She waited for him on the porch.

He shook his head.

"Well," he said once they were inside, "are you going to tell me?"

"Um, where's the bathroom?"

"In there." He went to the phone. "But first—"

He heard water running.

He stood outside the bathroom door and listened. The shower was hissing, and presently she began to sing a song.

In the living room, the phone rang.

"I'm not home right now—"

"Jack, would you pick it up, please? I know you're there. . . ."

"Hello, Chrissie. Sorry. I just got in."

"So late? Poor baby . . ."

"Listen, Chrissie, can I call you back? There's something I have to—"

"Are Ruth and Will there yet?"

"What?"

"Don't tell me you forgot! Well, I guess I can pick up something on the way over. You know, maybe we can get rid of them early. Would you like that?"

233

"Yeah, sure. But—"

"*See you in a few minutes, love. And Jack? I've missed you . . . !*"

Click.

"Daddy," called the little girl, "can you come here?"

He entered the darkened bedroom.

The bathroom door was open and steaming. She wrapped herself in a big towel and jumped up on the bed. She opened the towel.

"Dry me?"

"Listen," he said, "who told you to do this? I don't think it's such a good idea to—"

" 'S okay. I can do it myself." She made a few swipes with the towel and dropped it on the bed. Even in the faint light he could see how pink, how clean she was. And how small, and how vulnerable. She lay down and wriggled under the sheet.

"Sleepy," she said.

He sat next to her, on the edge of the mattress.

"Kiss me good-night," she said. Her pale arms stretched out. He started to push her away, but she clung to him with all her might. He felt her tears as sobs wracked her body.

"There," he told her, patting her between sharp shoulder blades. "Shh, now . . ."

"Don't go," she said.

"I'm not going anywhere."

"Promise?"

"I promise."

He lay down next to her till her breathing became slow and regular. After a while he covered her with the blanket, and planted a kiss on her cool forehead before he left the room.

Ruth and Will parked behind Chrissie. He watched from the porch as they helped her carry the take-out food into the house.

He cleared his throat. "There's something I have to tell you."

"We already know," said Ruth.

"How?"

"They didn't hear it from me, I swear," said Chrissie.

"A little bird told me," Ruth said. "And all I can say is, it's about time."

Will plopped down on the sofa. "Well, I think it's great. No point in paying rent on two places."

"*This* place sure isn't big enough," said Ruth. She stopped on the way to the kitchen and scanned the dining room. "Even if you got rid of these bookcases, it wouldn't work. You need more space."

"You know, Jack," said Will, "I have a friend in the real estate business. If you need any advice. Where's the Scotch?"

"Hold on . . ."

Chrissie winked at him as she passed. "They want to know if we've set the date. What do you think? Should we tell them everything?"

"Yes," he said.

"Wait a minute," said Will, rising and navigating for the bedroom door. "I want to hear this."

His stomach clenched. "Where are you going?"

Will grinned. "To take a leak. That all right with you?"

"Uh, would you mind using the other bathroom? This one's—stopped up."

Chrissie said, "It is? You didn't tell me that."

"I was going to. I was going to tell you all."

"Tell us what?" asked Ruth, coming out of the kitchen.

They looked at him expectantly. There was a long pause. His hands were shaking.

"I don't know where to start," he said. He tried a laugh but it came out wrong.

"Take your time," said Ruth. "We've got all evening."

Chrissie squeezed his arm. "Who needs a drink?" she said.

"Yes," he said. "Maybe we could have a drink first."

"What's this?" said Chrissie. She kicked the book bag on the floor, where the little girl had left it.

"Nothing," he said. "Here. Let me give you a hand."

He walked her to the kitchen.

"I can explain," he said.

"Explain what? You look tired, Jack. Was it an awful week?"

He took a deep breath. "Just this. I know it sounds crazy, but—"

On his way out of the small bathroom, Will stuck his head in the kitchen.

"Am I interrupting anything?"

"Of course not," said Chrissie.

"If this is a bad night for you two—"

There was a piercing scream from another part of the house.

He knew what it was before he got there.

The little girl was in the bedroom doorway, rubbing her eyes. She had on one of his shirts.

"Daddy?"

Ruth and Will looked at her. So did Chrissie. Then they looked at him.

"Oh, Daddy, there you are! I had a nightmare. There were people. Are they going now?"

"Daddy?" Chrissie stared at him as though she had never seen him before.

He focused on the little girl as his stomach clenched tighter.

"Tell them," he said.

"What?"

"Everything."

"I don't know what you mean, Daddy."

"All right," he said, "that's it. You're leaving—right now. I'll tell them the whole story myself. Come on. Let's go."

"No! I'll tell. How you picked me up at the bus stop and got me in the car in front of all those people? Or how you cheated and stole for me? Or the part where you gave me a bath and dried me and kissed me and we took a nap together?"

"I think we'd better be leaving," Ruth said.

"Yes," said Chrissie. "That might be a good idea. A very, very good idea."

236

"Wait." He followed her out. "Chris, I—"

"Don't," she said. "I have to think. And don't call me."

He watched numbly as the cars drove off. It started to rain softly, a misting drizzle in the trees above the mercury-vapor lamps. He watched until their red taillights turned the corner, like the reflection of a fire passing and moving on, leaving the street darker than ever.

"No," he said, hunching his shoulders. "No. No. No . . ."

He went back into the house.

"Where are you?" he shouted.

She was in the kitchen, helping herself to the food.

"Hi, Daddy," she said. "You got dinner for us. Just you and me. Thank you!"

"Who the hell do you think you are?"

He shook her violently.

"Daddy, you're hurting me!"

"I'm not your daddy and you know it, you little wretch."

"You're scaring me!"

"Don't bother to turn on the tears this time," he said. "It won't work."

She broke free and ran.

He braced himself against the table to stop shaking while he reached for the bottle of scotch and poured a double shot.

Then he walked slowly, deliberately to the living room.

"Out," he said. "I don't care if it's raining. You've done enough. Get your things and—"

She had the phone in her hand.

"Daddy?" she said into the mouthpiece. "C-can you come get me? I don't know how to get home . . . and I'm scared!"

He tried to take the phone away, but she dodged him and kept on talking.

"It's cold . . . and dark . . . and there's a man here . . . I think he's crazy! Daddy, tell me what to do! I don't like this place!"

She gave a description of his street.

"Daddy, please come quick!"

Then she began to sing sweetly, a high, plaintive keening

like the wind outside, and the rain that blew with it, settling so coldly over the house.

"Ladybird, ladybird, fly away home . . . your house is on fire . . . and your children will burn. . . ."

Her voice trailed off as she started to cry.

She hung up. She stopped crying. Then she went about her business, collecting her clothing and her book bag as though he no longer existed.

He stood there, wondering what it was that was supposed to happen next.

▼▼▼▼▼▼

Waste

Kathleen Buckley
▲▲▲▲▲▲▲

T he sweet-sour smell of corruption filled Mildred's nostrils, overwhelming the scent of damp earth and rotting vegetation. Her first thought was that some animal had crept into the brush-ringed hollow to die. But by the gray light she saw that the accumulation of fallen leaves no longer lay as smooth here as it had on her last inspection of the ravine.

Oh, drat, she thought, overcoming an impulse to back away. She really could not let squeamishness interfere with her schedule. Her morning jog had another half hour to go, which did not allow time to find another place. So she edged closer and began to nudge the mold aside.

There was a foot—about size six and a half—in a turquoise leather pump. Working northward, Mildred made out a length of slim leg, a skirt shorter than strictly necessary even for a young girl. Then a silky-looking blouse stained, torn, and plastered to the slimy flesh. At the sight of the mangled face, Mildred's stomach roiled and tried to surge toward open air. She fought it down. Thank goodness she never ate before her morning exercise.

No point in uncovering more. She scraped the toe of her running shoe on clean leaves before starting back to her car. The back road was still deserted, she found with satisfaction. Some of the other teachers advised her to stay on the main roads where there was traffic. "But I don't want to have to dodge around joggers and people walking their dogs and waiting for the bus and bicycling," she always answered. "I like to be able to commune with nature." And they shook their heads and talked about crime in general and all those missing girls and children in particular. "Those girls weren't exercising," Mildred pointed out. "They all vanished from bars. Besides, I'm too old to fit the pattern." "The third one was thirty-eight," the vice principal said. "She was a swinger," Mildred said dismissively. "In any case, I am not the stuff of which victims are made."

So she continued to take her exercise in the lonely places, and really, it was difficult to know how she could have done anything else, under the circumstances. She glanced automatically in both directions before opening the trunk. She heaved the plastic-wrapped bundle out, slammed the trunk and half slid, half trotted down the slope into the trees. If she had not taken up aerobics after her nearly disastrous second project, it would have been hard for her to carry so much dead weight over rough ground.

It fitted neatly into the hollow beside the other. Mildred carefully spread over it the leaves she had shifted earlier. Then she kicked around the rest of the tiny clearing so that the disturbance in the depression was less noticeable. Good! It looked as if children had scuffled up the newly fallen leaves.

Back on the road, she still had time for a quick run before going home to shower, dress, and eat a light breakfast. She limited herself to grapefruit juice and half a cup of granola. So much better than a heavy meal first thing in the morning. Naturally, she recommended that the children eat more—well, they needed it to build up their little bones and muscles, didn't they? She looked forward to going to work each day. Teaching was so much fun: especially when you could help the children learn and change. Turning the difficult ones around was her life.

Tanya Roberts played tag with several of the other girls at recess; Jason raised his hand in arithmetic—and his answer was correct. Peter wet his pants, but it had been a whole three weeks since the last incident, so Mildred did not consider it a major setback. With one thing and another, it was not until the end of the day that she had time to consider her discovery.

It was not until she left school that she began to think it through. She felt quite indignant that someone else was using her ravine. She had only employed it once before and had expected it to serve her for some time. Her first several deposits had been made inconveniently far from home. And now she would have to look for a new disposal site. It hardly seemed fair.

Over a cup of herbal tea she wondered whether the interloper posed a danger to her. The disappearance of half a dozen young women had upset everyone; the discovery of one of the supposed victims, her face hacked beyond recognition, raised a storm of demands for police action. As long as he was at work, people would be watching for any suspicious circumstance. She should have thought of it sooner. Why, someone might even have noticed her taking the dead kitten away from the unspeakable Riccoletti boy.

Besides, he must be a psychopath, Mildred reasoned, shuddering, to pick up all those women and chop their faces up with a hatchet. How could anyone do such a thing? She was reminded of Joshua Stern, who had used his mother's Chinese cleaver to chop off his baby brother's ears. And Joshua had seemed a nice, well-mannered little boy. It was only afterward that she realized his eyes were as empty as an erased chalkboard. She knew then, although some people believed Joshua's story about a masked intruder. Perhaps no one ever believes that a friend or family member would rape or murder or torture animals or set fires. Mildred could not understand it, but she knew it was true: ninety-nine of a hundred students were basically good. The hundredth was bad to the core. It was unfortunate no one had recognized the pattern in the serial killer when he was in school. Now women were dead because of him, and it was every good citizen's duty to stop him. Mildred prided herself on teaching her classes to do their civic duty.

What if he came when she wasn't here to watch? Mildred asked herself, pulling her knitted cap down over her ears. Of if he never used the ravine to dump another victim? She wriggled her toes inside her hiking boots and wondered if it was cold enough for frostbite. There was too much traffic on the road for him to risk stopping during the day, as she knew from her own experience. And no other approach to the ravine was practical, not for someone carrying a large, heavy load. So he must come at night or around dawn. He would not abandon such a convenient location: it was too hard to find a place.

She had read all the newspaper articles about the disappearances. The police refused to speculate about his modus operandi—if that was what it was called—but Mildred thought she could make a pretty good guess. For the last three weeks she had spent every Friday and Saturday evening from after dark to shortly after dawn crouched in a bush near the entrance to the ravine. Her bicycle was stowed away in the weeds nearby.

Mildred peeled off her gloves and fumbled with her thermos of hot chocolate. An hour ago she had already been able to see her breath; it was going to get colder still. Maybe she should give up and go home now. She drained the plastic cup; the dregs were cold. Stealthily she returned the thermos to her pack and felt for her flashlight. She was preparing to ease out of the bush when she heard the car. She froze: a passerby might think it was odd to see someone crawling out of the shrubbery on a deserted road.

The automobile slowed and pulled off the road onto the rutted track, stopping at the barrier with its NO DUMPING sign. The driver switched off the lights. In the darkness, the car would be almost invisible from the road. Mildred waited, peeking cautiously from her screen of blackberry bushes. Was it a couple looking for a lovers' lane? To her dark-adapted eyes, the car looked expensive: knife-sleek and low-slung.

The driver's door opened and a tall figure swung himself out and ran lightly around to the other side to open that door.

"Here we are." The pleasant baritone carried clearly in the chill air.

"It's dark as a cow's inside," a woman's voice remarked. She sounded common as dirt to Mildred. "I'm not really dressed for this, Barry."

"There's a good path. You won't have any trouble. Anyway, it's worth it to see the stars the way you're going to see them. You can't appreciate them from a city street, because the lights drown them out. You can lie on your back looking up at them and be part of the cosmos."

"But it's cold and the ground will be damp and hard and full of bugs."

"No problem!" Barry, whoever he was, had opened the trunk. "See this bag? There's a down sleeping bag in here, a flask of brandy and a ground cloth. Also a battery-powered cassette player with a tape of Ravel's 'Bolero.' Perfect music for a little bump-bump, if you know what I mean."

"All in that little bag? Really?"

"The best down bags pack small. The recorder is the kind NASA uses in space. Microchips and miniature cassette tapes. Nothing but the best for me, Karen, baby."

The boasting annoyed Mildred. He wasn't the one whose back was going to come into contact with the ground, after all. His bubble-headed little friend should have held out for a nice warm apartment or at least a seedy motel room, if she must be immoral.

Mildred listened to their voices recede, Karen squealing every time a springy branch swatted her. Once she uttered "Oh, shit!" Probably she had twisted her ankle. The way down to the ravine was treacherous enough even for someone wearing hiking boots or running shoes.

Presently a breathless voice asked, "Are we there?"

"Yes," the man said. "This is the end of the line." There

243

was a pause. Deploying the tools of seduction, Mildred supposed.

"I hope I haven't snagged my pantyhose ... Barry? Bar ... !"

The meaty *swak! swak!* was perfectly audible and seemed to go on for a long time.

Very carefully Mildred crept out of the brush and scuttled over to the car. Stepping softly, she pointed the flashlight at the rear license plate and snapped it on. "EZX-666, EZX-666," she whispered, then played the beam over the trunk. The car was canary yellow, and the make was foreign and not too common. Then she returned to her hiding place—the chances were he would leave soon. She could hardly follow him on her bicycle, while if she left first, he might overtake her and be startled to see a bicyclist out so late, on such a road.

Before Mildred's heartbeat had returned to normal, he went back the way he had come. That was no clue: the town was in that direction, and so were a shopping mall and several apartment complexes which housed overflow from the city twenty miles away. She emptied the vacuum flask, screwed the cap on tightly and retrieved her bicycle. Tomorrow was going to be a busy day.

". . . so since you're the only dealership in town, I was wondering if he's ever brought it in here for service. It's just the model and color I want, but of course it is second-hand and I wouldn't want it if it's going to need a lot of work. I didn't catch his last name; we only talked for a few minutes at the laundromat, but his first name is Barry. You don't happen to remember working on it?"

"Yeah, sure. It's been in here a time or two. That's Barry Lind. I've never done any major work on it; fixed some scratches on the door once and gave it a tune-up. He's real careful how that car looks. Nice guy; he wouldn't cheat you, but I'll be glad to check it out for you before you buy it."

"Oh, I'm so glad," Mildred said. "Perhaps I'll make him

an offer next time I see him. You won't mention I talked to you about it, will you? I wouldn't want him to think I didn't trust him."

"Nahhh—not if you promise to bring it in regular." The mechanic grinned.

"If I buy it, I will."

It was easy to find Barry Lind in the phone book. Later that afternoon, Mildred drove past the address. The building, a hundred one- and two-bedroom units meant for singles, was quite similar to her own. The tenants never got acquainted, never noticed who came or went, which was, she thought, rather sad. She spotted the yellow car in the parking area and smiled. In a week or two her plan would be ripe.

In the teachers' lounge, Pat said, "Brian stole that Black Forest carving from the international display."

"Oh, dear."

"I found out when he tried to slip it out of his desk and into his lunch bag." The third-grade teacher began to peel her orange, easing the rind off in a long spiral. "He said it wasn't the same figure, that it was a similar one his uncle had brought him from Germany. He gave me a confused story about how he had brought it with him to use as a decoy to catch the real thief. I'm condensing, of course; it took ten minutes to tell, with numerous asides about his uncle the fighter pilot and how Brian always keeps the gnome on his bedside table and how he saw this cop show on TV where the detective used some powdered soap in place of cocaine to catch a drug dealer."

"Yes, I can hear him telling it," Mildred said. She had had encounters with Brian while on playground duty. "I don't suppose his uncle actually had . . . ?"

Pat looked at her pityingly. "I called Brian's mother and asked. One of his uncles repairs appliances. The other is a Baptist preacher. Neither one has ever been out of the country. Mrs. Hajny says Brian doesn't have anything remotely like that figure. Furthermore, I asked Janie for a detailed description of her gnome, and it tallied—right down to a bit that had broken off and been glued back on."

"Then what happened?" Mildred asked, although she could guess.

"Brian claimed Janie had given it to him and was now lying because she was afraid her parents would be angry. Brian's mother says he has a wonderful imagination. She says the other kids are always telling lies about him," Pat added flatly.

"Oh, dear."

"At second recess yesterday he set a fire in his locker."

"I hadn't heard that." But it wasn't at all surprising.

"It didn't do much harm: someone noticed the smell. His rain boots were sort of melted and I guess his locker is going to be pretty stinky for a while, but that's about all. His mother is complaining about crime in the school, although three reliable witnesses saw Brian at his locker at recess. I don't know what's wrong with that boy."

He's simply evil, Mildred thought, but she knew better than to say it. So many people preferred to ignore the truth. She sighed. Someone was going to have to do something about Brian.

Mildred nervously eyed her reflection in the glass door (pearl earrings, lace-collared pink dress—the one she wore to weddings) before she pushed into the cocktail lounge. She felt a bit embarrassed about going to such a place by herself, although she had occasionally gone out with friends. This place, all polished oak and brass and planters of ficuses and hanging baskets of ferns, seemed quite nice, if rather dim. What if she couldn't recognize him? she wondered. She had waited down the street from his building every evening for days, inconspicuous in her little blue sedan.

One night he'd come out and she had followed him at a discreet distance, but he had only gone to a convenience store before returning home. Twice he had not come home after work at all—or at least, not until after Mildred had given up for the evening. But this was Friday, and as she had hoped, he had stopped at his apartment only long enough to eat dinner and change his clothes. She herself had eaten a tuna-fish sandwich and strips of raw vegetable during her vigil.

With an assumed air of calm, she glanced around, searching for a face or back she knew. There seemed to be no large groups, only couples and singles. Deliberately—the only way she could move in her high heels—she strolled into the room.

There, in the corner! She remembered that sleek hair. He was sitting at a table for two, scanning the crowd. Mildred made her way between occupied tables, carefully disregarding an empty one and several tall stools at the counter.

"Do you mind if I sit here?" she asked, with a shy smile. *I cannot believe I am doing this.*

The blue eyes scanned her, dispassionate as camera lenses.

"Sorry, I'm expecting someone."

"I knew you must be," Mildred explained. "So am I, but I'm afraid to wait alone until he comes. Perhaps it's silly, but all this talk about women disappearing makes me nervous. I assure you I am not in the habit of . . . of making overtures to strange men."

The straight, rather wide mouth curled up in a smile. "I can see you aren't. And I'm not a *strange* man, anyway. Scout's honor. I guess we're both looking for company." The man's eyes were flat as blue glass.

"What are you drinking?" he asked when the waitress came up.

"Oh—a pink squirrel, please," she said. "It will match my dress," she added with a little laugh.

"I'll have a scotch and soda. Is this your first time at the Green Macaw, Miss . . . ?"

"You may call me Millicent. Yes, I'm new to the, er, singles scene."

"I'm not exactly a regular myself. My name is Barry. Tell me all about yourself. I'll bet you're a Gemini. If I'm not being too inquisitive." He flashed another smile.

"That's very perceptive: my birthday is in June." Although she did not believe in astrology, she found herself impressed—until she remembered she was wearing her moonstone ring. So, if he knew the birthstones and astrological signs, he stood a good chance of deducing correctly. If he were mistaken, it was still a conversational opening. But she did not want to waste time on meaningless chatter; she wanted more information about him. She volunteered, "I work for the school district. And I suddenly decided it was time to sow some wild oats," she confided—artlessly, she hoped. "What about you?"

"I'm in the R and D department at Cook-Corry. You may have heard we're developing a new tungsten alloy for shuttlecraft wings."

Their drinks came and they toasted the future. According to Barry, his parents were wealthy and split their time between Connecticut and the Florida Keys. He had been transferred to the local plant several months ago—a promotion, he admitted modestly—and since he had been working twelve-hour days, he had not yet made many friends. He excused himself and went off toward the restrooms.

No one at the adjoining tables was paying any attention. Casually, she slipped the plastic envelope out of her purse and tipped its contents into the scotch and soda left-handed, while pretending to fiddle with the card that listed the house specialties. She twirled the swizzle stick to disperse the powder and hoped it dissolved quickly. The scotch ought to mask the acrid taste of the barbiturates.

Then for distraction she concentrated on the conversations at neighboring tables.

". . . and I said, 'This is your two-week warning' . . ."

". . . awful. Now this kid Brian Hine—Hodge?—is missing. I don't know what the world's coming to."

". . . we could, you know, maybe go to my place . . ."

". . . really like to jog but my doctor says . . ."

"I don't care what they say, Beta's better."

She jumped when he came up behind her and joked, "A nickel for your thoughts."

What would he say if she told him? What should she be thinking about? "It's sad that no one has any roots anymore. Look at all these people—like you and me—trying to find friends or . . . or . . ."

"Significant others," Barry suggested.

"Whatever," Mildred agreed. "Where were you located before?"

"Philadelphia," he replied, staring at a blond girl in tight pants.

"I didn't know Cook-Corry had a facility there," Mildred remarked. Actually, she knew almost nothing about the firm: she only wished to see how he would respond.

He was momentarily at a loss. "I didn't work for them then. I was employed by . . . Harrison Aerospace. A corporate headhunter lured me here."

"Oh, I see. Something you said made me think you'd been working for Cook-Corry all along."

"No, I never said anything like that. Say, has anyone ever told you that you look just like Katharine Hepburn?" He sipped his drink, made a face and said anyone could tell he didn't drink much of the hard stuff. He drank the rest of it at one gulp.

They ordered another round; he switched to beer. Mildred thought she could tolerate another pink squirrel. Barry glanced at his wristwatch several times; Mildred noticed because it was the kind that did half a dozen other things besides providing the day, minute, second and date. At 8:02, something beeped.

"Uh-oh, that's my pager. Excuse me while I call in? In case the drinks come while I'm gone—" He put a ten down.

She watched as he strode out to find a telephone. The phones were apparently in the same direction as the restrooms, she noted. Could he have called someone on his previous trip, and requested to be paged at eight?

The drinks came, the waitress made change and left. Mildred glanced toward the door. No sign of Barry Lind yet. How long would the drug take to work? She had given him the stiffest dose it seemed possible to incorporate in a cocktail. Would it come on slowly—or was he stretched unconscious on the floor? No, apparently not: he was striding through the entrance, distinctive in his open-necked cream shirt and a tweed jacket. Mildred recognized the need to be the center of attention.

"Someone at the lab has a problem," he explained when he returned. "I'm afraid I'm going to have to cut our evening short."

"But you must at least finish your drink," she said. "All work and no play, you know." Did barbiturates lose strength? They'd only been a couple of years old.

"Can't let good beer go to waste." He finished it and mumbled, "I'll be glad to get out—it's getting stuffy in here."

"I'd better be going, too—if you wouldn't mind walking me out to my car? There's so much crime now."

"My pleasure," he muttered.

He stumbled as they went out. His eyes looked even glassier than before, Mildred noted: they were now fixed as well as flat.

"Don't you feel well, Barry?" she asked as they crossed the parking lot.

He peered at her as if trying to remember who she was. He shook his head in a puzzled way. "Uh-uh."

"I don't think you should drive. Please give me your keys."

Leaning against the fender, he fished in his pocket, swaying.

"Here," she disentangled his hand from his pocket and pulled out the keychain. She got him into the passenger seat, and none too soon. She had to fasten his seat belt for him.

The car handled quite differently from her own, but she drove sedately through town to Riverside Park. At the intersection of Sixteenth and Rose she found herself stopped at a light beside a police car. The officer gave her a sharp look and was evidently reassured by her obvious sobriety: at least he nodded approvingly. Mildred smiled back. It was nice to know the police were on the alert for drunk drivers. The slaughter on the roads was truly shocking.

The park ran along the river bluff, a long narrow strip, with parking spaces facing the river. The lot tilted toward the water, with only a low rail to separate it from an abrupt drop. When the roads were icy, drivers avoided the outlook. Not, Mildred thought reasonably, that anyone would want to sit looking at the river when it was that cold. The PTA had been campaigning for a chainlink fence: children would slide on the parking lot when there was ice or snow and skateboard there the rest of the year. It was a miracle some adventurous boy had not gone over the edge already.

By accident, Mildred added to herself—Lee Jones did not count. Although he had brought it on himself, the way he terrorized the smaller children. She had found him tightrope-walking on that rail during one of her early morning jogs. It had seemed an opportunity to speak to him away from school, off the record. He wasn't one of her students, being a sixth-grader—but hers had suffered from his bullying. Mildred knew, of course, that some children were simply bad, but Lee was not stupid so he must be redeemable.

He had stayed on the rail while she was talking to him, ignoring her warning that it was dangerous. When she finished, he jeered, "I don't have to do what you say—all you can do is order little kids around. And you have to do that because you're so dumb and bossy, no one wants to screw you!"

The foul language did not shock her, since even her second-graders occasionally surprised her with the terms they picked up from older siblings. It was the unfairness of the accusation that made her strike out. She only meant to grab him by his jacket and pull him off his perch, to make him see he was not as big or as impervious as he thought. Her sudden movement made him flinch back. He hung there, overbalanced, for what seemed like eternity, but not so long she had time to catch his arm or jacket. Then he fell, plummeting in dull blue denim and bright blue ripstop nylon. Mildred watched the body hit the rocky slope, bounce and roll. It ended up facedown in the water.

It never occurred to her that he could be alive. Even if he were, by the time someone got down to him, he would have drowned. Her first thought was, thank goodness it wasn't a nice boy. No one was in the park so early, and the buildings on the street side were all businesses that opened later. Why shouldn't everyone think Lee had simply tumbled over? It would be better that way. And she had promptly continued her exercise. It was later, after she had recovered from the shock, that Mildred realized that what had happened by accident might as easily be done intentionally. She imagined the effect on classes and on the world in general if the rotten apples were removed from the barrel before they spread their contamination.

However, she had avoided Riverside Park ever since. Now she was glad, because it would be the perfect place for this project. She stopped the yellow sports car in the deeper shadow of a willow tree near the entrance, its sleek hood pointed downhill, toward the river.

She sat for a moment, trying to think whether she had forgotten anything. This was quite different from culling the one from the ninety and nine. In procedure, at least; the principle was the same. She shifted to neutral and switched off the ignition, keeping her foot on the brake pedal. There was no traffic on the street behind them: the bank, clothing stores, omelette house and antique shop fronting the river were closed and it was too early for anyone to be thinking of the park as a lovers' lane.

Mildred disengaged her seat belt, opened the car door and awkwardly got her left foot out—she was less than agile in high heels, and preferred not to risk the car beginning its roll to judgment prematurely. Then she took her right foot off the brake, twisted out and backed away to see if the darn thing would move. If it didn't, she would have to wake Barry up enough to get him out of the car, help him over to the edge and let nature take its course.

The car did roll, almost to her surprise. You could always count on people to act certain ways, but mechanical things were not so consistent. It was not moving very fast, but she had aimed it at the middle of the rail, between two of the squat, square posts. The wooden rail burst outward under the car's weight and the yellow import surged over the

252

brink, falling tail over nose. When it was found, it would appear that Barry's companion had escaped the car then been swept away by the river. It happened: Lee's body never came to shore. He was thought to have run away. It would seem like a straightforward accident.

Now that it was finished, she wished she were at home with a good book and a mug of hot chocolate. The two pink squirrels stirred restlessly, and her pumps were proving not to be as comfortable as she had remembered. Mildred sighed. Should she walk over two blocks and catch the Center Street bus as planned? Or should she splurge and call a taxi? There was a pay phone across the street. It would be safer not to be seen anywhere near here; on the other hand, how safe was it for a woman to wait for a bus downtown at night? She might be mugged—or worse. With some relief (since it was not mere self-indulgence), Mildred opted for commonsense over economy.

"I suppose it seems strange for a woman to be down here at night," she ventured.

The driver glanced at his rearview mirror. "Your car break down?"

If she said yes, would he offer to call a tow truck? Besides, she had told the dispatcher she wanted to go to the Green Macaw. Oh, what a tangled web we weave, when first we practice to deceive! Mildred reflected. Honesty is infinitely the best policy. "No, I had a difference of opinion with my, my date as to his driving, so I got out. Please take me to the Green Macaw."

The driver twisted his head around to look at her— fortunately, they were sitting at a red light. He was an attractive young man. "That's where the action is on a Friday night," he commented.

"That's where my car is," Mildred retorted, so he would not think she was the kind of person who went out looking for "action," then blushed. Even she had heard that if there were a hundred cars parked in the Green Macaw's lot at the height of the evening, there would still be fifty cars left

253

when all the customers were gone. To cover her embarrassment, she said, "You must know all the . . . well, places where the action is."

He laughed a little. "Only by taking people to them."

Mildred was pleased. She had always suspected that cab drivers might be lowlifes who spent their spare time in pool halls or bars. "What do you do in your spare time?" He really ought to be making something of himself. She would suggest that he apply at the community college . . .

"I'm working on my master's degree in sociology at the university," he said. "With this job, I can gather material for a study and get paid for it at the same time."

After that, they had a very interesting chat. Gilbert told her some of his adventures as a cabbie and she related some amusing classroom incidents. It turned out that Gilbert's nephew had been in her class last year. He had been a delightful child.

What a pleasant way to end a difficult evening, Mildred thought when she paid her fare. She added a generous tip; as a student, Gilbert no doubt needed it. She noted with approval that he waited until she was in her car, had locked the door, started the ignition and switched on the headlights before he pulled away with a wave of farewell.

The PTA was going to use the accident to press the city council to put a chain-link fence around Riverside Park. Five days later, Mildred was peeling the adhesive strips off her blisters and deciding it wouldn't be necessary to replace them, when her doorbell rang. They looked like a nice professional couple—now, whose parents were they? She thought she'd met at least one of all her students' parents.

"Ms. Mildred Thorson? Police." They displayed their badges in unison.

"Won't you come in? I don't have any coffee, but I could make some herbal tea," she offered. "Or there's orange juice."

"Thank you," the woman said, "but please don't bother."

"We'd like to ask you some questions about an accident," the man added.

254

"I'll do anything I can to help."

"Ms. Thorson, were you at the Green Macaw Lounge last Friday evening?"

Mildred smiled. "I teach second grade, you know. It really wouldn't be suitable for me to frequent such a place."

"Ms. Thorson, do you own a pale pink dress with a round neck trimmed with lace?" the woman officer asked. "We do have a search warrant." She pulled a document out of an inside pocket of her jacket.

"Yes, I have a dress like that."

"Can I ask where you were last Friday evening?" the man inquired.

She smiled archly at him. "Of course you *can* ask. You also *may* ask. 'Can' has to do with the physical ability to perform an action, while 'may' requests permission to do it."

The plainclothes officers exchanged glances. The man rolled his eyes in a manner Mildred found quite unprofessional. After several moments, the woman spoke again.

"May we . . . that is, we'd like you to come to the police station with us, Ms. Thorson."

"Why, of course. My students will be fascinated to hear about this. I wonder if it would be possible to arrange a tour? I think it would give them a real feeling for what the police actually do, don't you?"

As they were going out the door, she thought she heard the man mutter, "A second-grade teacher, for Chrissake. What the hell's the world coming to?"

Mildred wondered, too. Imagine an officer of the law using such language!

255

Red Devils

Hugh B. Cave

S ee Colin.

See Sheldon admiring Colin.

See three other boys, making five altogether, lounging in a nearly new Continental in the parking lot of a Burger Mac on Florida's east coast.

They are five young sons of Florida east coast wealth, and bored tonight, as usual.

"I read about it in a newspaper clipping my dad's sister sent from Los Angeles."

The speaker is the driver, Colin Casserly. He is seventeen, blond, and handsome. He wears chinos with a name on them. He wears a striped sport shirt that cost his parents forty-odd dollars. That is more money than Colin has ever in his life earned by working.

"About these gangs out there," he concludes, aiming the words at the rearview mirror in which he can see the three youths in the rear.

"But the paper said they're not gangs of street punks like the ones in New York." This speaker is Sheldon Smikle, seated at Colin's side in front. He is Colin's best friend and most eager ally. He too is seventeen. "What they do—and just for kicks, see, because they don't need money any more'n we do—what they do is swipe expensive cars and sell 'em. Or break into rich people's homes for stuff to steal. Or mug people for money and jewelry."

Colin Casserly now turns on the front seat, hamburger in hand, to grin at the three in the rear. "They have real cool names. We could have one, too."

"Like, say, the Red Devils," echoes Sheldon Smikle. "And when we're on a job, we'd wear red sweats and red ski masks."

A backseat boy with pimples vaguely protests. "Gee, I dunno, guys. If my folks ever found out I was into a thing like that—"

"What's to worry about?" Colin sneers. "You think bank presidents know what goes on in the real world?"

"Well, doctors do." This backseater wags his head in slow motion. "You'd be surprised how much my dad knows."

"Are you chicken, too?" Colin demands of the third boy in back.

"Well, no!"

"Tell you what." Colin stuffs the last of his burger into his mouth and swallows it. Wipes mustard off his lips with the back of his hand. Clears his throat. "Tell you what, then. Shel and I will show you tomorrow night."

The rear-seat three say "Huh?" by letting their mouths silently drop open.

"My folks are throwing a party," Colin continues. "Their twentieth anniversary. We promised to help out."

"Help out doing what?" a doubter wants to know.

"I dunno. Serve drinks, most likely. Keep the buffet stocked; my mom's big for buffets. Anyway, we'll pick out some guy who don't know us and wait for him in the condo parking lot."

"And *mug* him, Colin?"

"Oh, for Pete's sake, we won't *hurt* him. Just shove a gun in his belly button and take his billfold, to show you guys how easy it is. I got that twenty-two automatic I bought in the hock shop a while back, for kicks."

Sheldon Smikle frowns at this. "We really *don't* wanna hurt anybody, Colin."

258

"I *said* that. We're just gonna scare him."

"What if he don't scare?"

"He will. I got an idea." Colin directs his grin at the three in back again. "Well, you guys? If we show you how it's done, will you be ready to join up? Are we gonna be the Five Red Devils?"

It is only natural for them to nod their heads in acquiescence, mumbling. "Well, all right, Colin," "Okay, Colin," "Whatever you say, Colin." After all, he is the one they look to for new ways to make life exciting. He is their Crown Prince of Cool.

"All ri-i-ght, then!" With a grin of triumph he swings around to grab the wheel. The Continental leaves rubber on the Burger Mac blacktop as it roars out to A1A.

See a man and a woman, later that evening, dining in a posh restaurant overlooking the ocean. The woman is beautiful, blond, blue-eyed, slim and happy. The man is neither handsome nor otherwise, taller than she, a few pounds overweight. Not obese, by any means—just enough over the norm to look easygoing and nonviolent. He too is happy.

They are Manon Rowe and Roger Randall. They have known each other two months and feel good about each other.

"Would you, Rog?" Manon reaches across the table to touch the back of his hand. A big hand. This man is a Vietnam vet. "I hate to go without you."

"You could go with someone they know." His smile has an imp in it, and talking to people is easy for him because he owns and runs a respected private detective agency.

"Uh-uh." She shakes her lovely head. "If we don't go together, I go alone."

"What's their names? Maybe I know them."

"Bradford and Eileen Casserly. Twenty years married tomorrow, and they're nice, really. He owns Casserly Jewelers."

"And they live in your condo?"

"Two floors below me." Manon's is a two-bedroom penthouse apartment on the fifteenth floor. "You won't have to do anything much, Rog. Just be yourself while the women look you over and envy me. What do you think?"

Roger's brown eyes focus on her face, and he smiles now without the imp. He has known many women in his forty-odd years of living, but never until now one with whom he felt so inclined to try for a permanent relationship. Until a year ago she shared her condo apartment with her mother, whose money had bought it. Mother was dead now of a heart attack.

Manon works as a hygienist with Roger's dentist. They met when she cleaned his teeth her first day on the job. He can still shut his eyes and see her lovely face hovering over his while he told himself he had to know her better.

"What time shall I pick you up?" he asks her now.

"You mean you'll go?"

"Of course I'll go. Whither thou goest . . ." He turns his hand over to clasp hers, and leans toward her. "You'd better get used to having me around, lady."

They agree that he will call for her the following evening about seven. Still holding hands, they then look out the restaurant window beside them and see a ship passing, so bright with lights it can only be a cruise ship.

"That's an idea," Roger Randall says.

"What's an idea?"

"For a honeymoon. Would you consider me for a husband, to have and frequently hold, if I dangle that as bait?"

"You don't need to dangle any bait," she says without hesitation.

"You will, then? You'll marry me?"

"How about next week, on my day off?"

To push back the panic, Roger squeezed his eyes shut and told himself that it must have happened to hundreds of others before him and could happen to anyone at any time. He'd got drunk, was all. He'd had too much to drink at the Casserlys' party. Now he was stretched out on his own bed in his own apartment, fully dressed even to shoes, and didn't know how he had got there.

Try to remember, he ordered himself. You know you picked Manon up at her place in that same building around seven. You know what she looked like: ravishing in a backless white linen dress that showed off her golden tan so much it had you drooling. You know you walked her down two floors to the anniversary celebration where she introduced you to Eileen and Brad Casserly and their guests.

Everything was okay at that point. More than okay, because Manon was so obviously pleased to have you for her escort. You even got to thinking about that talk you had with her in the restaurant, when you looked out the window and saw the cruise ship passing.

God, he felt awful. His head when he moved it felt as though it were full of steel balls that banged against one another, careening off to thud against the inside of his skull. His eyes when he opened them refused to focus on the ceiling and saw everything through a swirl of colors. His whole body ached, and his right hand felt full of pain.

He lifted that arm and looked at the hand, or tried to, and, yes, it seemed to be swollen. The skin was off the knuckles, leaving them red and raw, with blood caked in the hollows between. Must have fallen, he thought. On something solid and rough, like concrete. But where? When?

You were at the party, Randall. With Manon in that stunning dress without a back. Lots of people there. Two kids serving drinks. Eileen Casserly's famous buffet overflowing a table that filled one whole end of the living room. Music from an expensive stereo. Twenty, thirty people present. Lots of talk. You drank your usual Scotch and water and no more than your usual two or three before it hit you. So why did it hit you so hard?

With the ball bearings clunking inside his skull and the rest of his body hurting like a bad tooth, he shut his eyes and struggled to recall details. When had he first felt he was losing control?

About ten-thirty, he decided. Yes. He could be pretty sure because Manon and he had been talking to some woman and her husband at the buffet table, and the woman had asked the time and he'd said it was about ten-thirty, and

261

she'd said to her husband, "We'll have to go soon, darling."
And to Manon and himself by way of explanation she had
added, "We came up from Miami and Harry just hates I-95
at night, they drive so *fast*."

Ten-thirty, then. Yes. Manon and he were talking to the
couple from Miami, and he had just finished a drink handed
to him about fifteen minutes before by one of the kid bar-
tenders, and was standing there clutching the glass because
he felt it was going to explode. Or *he* was going to explode.

So what happened then, Randall?

You put the glass down on the buffet table, remember.
And you shook your head like a dog coming out of the
ocean, because the room was spinning and you had to make
it stop. The room was changing colors, too. Instead of the
expensively furnished apartment you had walked into a
while before, it was now like one of those disco joints with
psychedelic lights twisting and weaving over the walls. It
and the people in it had gone crazy, and you kept shaking
your head in a struggle to get things back to normal. And
the couple from Miami backed away, staring at you as
though they were scared. And Manon put a hand on your
arm and said, "What is it, Rog? What's wrong?"

"I don't know," you said.

"Is it the liquor? Have you had too much?"

You looked at the empty glass on the table, the glass that
had threatened to explode in your hand, and you said, "I've
only had three. I don't get this way on three."

"Let's leave, anyway," she said. "Let's go up to my place
where you can lie down."

Had they said good night to their host and hostess? Yes,
he seemed to remember doing that. And he definitely remembered Manon putting an arm around him and steering
him down the interior hall to the elevator because, of
course, he was in no condition to climb any stairs. They
rode a car up to her floor and went along that to her door,
and she opened the door with her key and led him inside
and insisted he lie on the sofa in the living room.

"I'm going to make you some coffee," she said. "Maybe
it was only three drinks you had, but those kids could have

262

made them stronger than you're used to. You know how kids are."

Funny, but even in her apartment the lights were disco-crazy. You lay there with your eyes shut and tried to blot them out, he thought, but could see them as clearly through your eyelids as when your eyes were wide open. All the time she was making coffee that's what you thought about, remember? How could you see the lights just the same when you had your eyes squeezed *shut*?

The coffee did help, though. You sat up and gulped it down, desperately wanting relief from the churning colors and the vertigo and the even worse feeling that your mind was coming apart. Manon sat beside you, holding your hand and stroking it and saying things like "You ought to see a doctor tomorrow, Rog" and "There may be more to this than just a drink too many" and, finally, "Would you like to stay here tonight, darling, instead of trying to go home?"

You said no, home wasn't that far and you were feeling better already, thanks to the coffee. So she poured you a second coffee and you drank that, and then you left, mumbling apologies for causing so much trouble and being urged by her to see a doctor if you still felt below par in the morning.

"Remember," she said at the door when she kissed you, "I'm counting on that honeymoon cruise you promised me."

So you walked to the elevators and pushed a button, and a car came up and you stepped into it. And then . . . what?

The lights had been fading since he drank the coffee, he recalled. Now as the elevator door hummed shut they went out altogether and so did the dome light in the roof of the car. Whatever had hit him after that third drink at the party was happening again. Not in the same way, though. Now instead of being crazy with colors, his world was all dark.

You ought to go back to Manon, he thought. You're in no shape to drive home. But it was too late. He had already pushed the lobby button, and the elevator was on its way down.

As he lay on the bed remembering it now, he mostly

remembered how the darkness had affected his mind. Remember what you decided? You convinced yourself that that wasn't any ordinary elevator in a beachfront condo. It was a cage they put you in after you died, and its destination was hell. That's why the blackness. Oh God, how black it was! As though some slimy, living monstrosity had oozed from the cage walls and wrapped itself around you, to suck the juices out of you while the cage carried you down.

Down . . . down . . . to hell.

Remember what you did, Randall? You threw yourself against the elevator door and tried to open it. While that damned cage was still descending you tried to force the door open and get out. Of course, you couldn't. It wasn't designed to be opened from the inside by the clawing hands of a freaked-out madman. That must be how you skinned these knuckles, though.

Lifting his hands, he stared wide-eyed at his knuckles again. At the hardened blood in the hollows between them. And remembered more.

You could have stopped the elevator by pushing the STOP button, he thought. Why, for God's sake, didn't you do it? Stopping it at a floor, you could have escaped by pushing another button to open the door. But you didn't. All you could think of was that you were dead and headed for hell, going down to the fiery furnace for a living cremation. You'd stepped into that elevator on the fifteenth floor, and you acted like a madman the whole way down.

Not to hell but to the lobby. Yes. The car stopped at the lobby. The door opened and you stumbled out.

Then what?

A phone was ringing beside the bed. As he turned on his side to reach for it with his left hand, he saw the watch on his wrist. Its hands stood at seven-twenty. Seven-twenty what? Morning or evening?

"Hello?" he managed, though it came out so feebly he had to lick his lips and repeat it.

"Roger? How are you?"

He wet his lips again. "Hi, hon. All right, I guess."

"I worried about you going home the way you were. I couldn't sleep. Are you sure you're all right?"

"I am now."

"Good, because I've got something terrible to tell you. You remember young Colin Casserly, who served drinks at the party?"

"Yes, of course."

"He's in the hospital, Roger. In a coma."

"What?"

"Florence Ives just called me. You met her at the party. He and his friend Sheldon Smikle left just after we did, she said. Then when Colin didn't return, his father became anxious and went looking for him. That was about two o'clock. Brad found him in the condo's parking area—the section reserved for guests—beaten up and unconscious."

"My God," Randall said. "Do they have any idea who did it?"

"No. Do you suppose *you* could help, Rog? I mean, you run a detective agency. Perhaps if you got some of your people—"

"They've reported this to the police, of course."

"Yes, but—"

"If there's any way I can help, I will. Look, I'll be over. We'll talk to the boy's parents together." Unless he was completely disoriented, this was Sunday morning and Manon would not have to go to work. Or *was* it Sunday morning? He turned his head to scowl at a window.

Daylight. But there would be light at this hour both morning and evening.

Manon took him off the hook. "All right. I'll fix some breakfast for us."

Of course. She never would have waited until evening to call and ask how he was. Get with it, Randall, he told himself angrily. If you're going to be a detective, you'd better get off that damned elevator and shake the ball bearings out of your head.

He wormed off the bed, got out of his clothes and headed for the bathroom. Not until he had showered hot and cold, then shaved and slapped aftershave on his face, did he feel anything like himself again.

At Manon's condo, as he walked into the lobby, more of last night's nightmare suddenly came back to him.

The lobby. You *do* remember getting off the elevator, he told himself as he stood there reaching for details to fill in the gaps.

The residents of this particular condo had a standing joke about their lobby—excluding, of course, the members of the board, who had run up a whopping special assessment to make it look like this. "The fanciest funeral parlor on the beach," they called it, referring to its clutter of urns, stone benches, artificial ferns, and phony palm trees.

An anteroom, he thought. That's what you believed it was, Randall—an anteroom. Definition: an outer chamber forming an entrance to something bigger, and sometimes used as a waiting room. You thought you were in hell's waiting room. Yes.

But you didn't wait long, did you? You got impatient and started walking.

He remembered walking across the lobby here, past the urns and benches and ferns and palms. Walking to where? To what? To his car, most likely, though at the time he had thought himself in hell, he was sure.

No time to worry about that now, though. Later, when he was over the effects of it all and able to think straight again, he would sit down and try to put the rest of the puzzle pieces in place. Right now he had to see Manon.

He rode the elevator to the top floor and went along the carpeted hall to her door. Rang the bell. Heard hurrying footsteps. The door opened and her hands found his arms as she peered anxiously up at his face.

"It's all right," he said. "I'm okay."

"I was so worried, Rog." She had on a simple flowered dress this morning, appropriate to the look of deep concern on her solemn face.

"I drank too much, is all," he said.

"Rog, I don't believe it. The boys brought me a drink every time they brought you one."

"Something else must have floored me, then. Something I had before I got there."

She led him to her dining table and sat him down to scrambled eggs, toast, and coffee. "Thought I'd better keep it simple," she said. "Rog, I called the Casserlys and told

266

them we'd be down. They're grateful to you for wanting to help."

"Let's hope I can."

She frowned at him again the way she had at the door. "You're *not* all right, are you? Your eyes . . ."

"What about my eyes?" he said when she hesitated.

"They look—what's the word?—haunted, I think."

Should he tell her what had happened to him after he left her last night? The elevator's descent into the abyss? His flight from hell's antechamber into a blackout from which he awoke in his own place with ball bearings in his head? No, he decided. Because it made no sense to him yet, and how could you talk rationally about a thing that made no sense.

Wait.

Breakfast finished, they walked down to the Casserlys' apartment, where the door was opened by Bradford Casserly. The man appeared to have aged ten years since last evening. His hand, going through the motions of shaking Randall's, was clammy and limp.

"Eileen is at the hospital," he said. "Excuse the looks of things, please." He meant the apartment, which looked as though the last guest had only just departed.

Randall walked over to the buffet table. It resembled a battlefield after hostilities, and he saw nothing suspicious. Stepping to the bar, he scanned the many bottles. Then, turning, he said, "Your boy left here with his buddy last night, Mr. Casserly?"

"With Sheldon. Yes."

"They left just after we did, Manon tells me."

"About ten-thirty, I think. I'm not really sure."

"Have you talked to the Smikle boy?"

With a heavy sigh the older man sat and shook his head. "I've been with Eileen at the hospital. The police talked to him, I understand."

"But you don't know what he told them."

"No. I'm sorry."

"Are you up to telling me how you found your son, Mr. Casserly?"

In a voice that was just barely audible, Casserly said he

267

had gone looking for the boy about two A.M. "First I went down along the beach. Colin has always been fond of walking there at night. Then I wondered if he'd taken the car, and I started through the guest parking to the owners' side to see if my car was gone. And I found him."

"In the guest lot."

"Yes." Casserly put his hands to his face and said the rest through his fingers. "Beaten—so badly—I hardly—recognized him. Who could have done such a thing? Who?"

"Maybe he'll be able to tell us when he comes out of it," Randall said. "Can you tell me where the Smikle boy lives?"

"I know," Manon said. "I'll drive you there."

But before leaving, Randall had a few more questions. Turning to Bradford Casserly again, he said, "You say the two boys left here together last night. You're sure of that, sir?"

"Yes, yes, I'm sure. We talked to them—Eileen and I and Sheldon's parents—just before they left."

"Did they say where they were going?"

"I don't think so. No, they didn't. It wasn't late; they wouldn't have to."

"All right, Mr. Casserly. I'll do my best to find out what happened." With a last glance at the buffet table and the bar, Randall nodded to Manon.

They rode an elevator to the basement where her car was parked, and she drove him to a home half a mile or so distant on the Intracoastal Waterway. A home with spacious grounds that required professional maintenance, a pool as large as most condo pools, and a uniformed maid, young and pretty, who opened the door to them.

Mr. and Mrs. Smikle were not at home, the maid informed them. "They are at the hospital. Only Sheldon is here."

Colin's friend, it seemed, had not yet left his room this morning. Nor had he touched the breakfast she took to him. "He is terribly upset about what happened. The police talked to him in his room."

"It might be better if he came out of there," Randall said.

268

"And who shall I say is here to see him, please?"

Manon answered that. "Miss Rowe and Mr. Randall. He knows us."

"Yes." The maid motioned them toward an elegantly furnished living room and went away. When she returned, Randall stared at the young man beside her and wondered if it could possibly be the same young man he had met last evening.

That Sheldon Smikle had been ruddy-cheeked, bright-eyed, almost a bit obnoxious as he strutted around the Casserlys' apartment serving drinks. As if he'd been trying to imitate some teenage hotshot in a movie. This Sheldon Smikle's eyes were red and swollen from crying, his face seemed molded of offwhite cheese, his mouth quivered as he nodded to them and stuttered, "H-h-hi."

Manon said, "Sheldon, this is Roger Randall. You met him last night. He's head of a detective agency."

The boy looked at Randall and took a faltering step backward, almost losing his balance.

"Like to hear from you what happened after you two boys left the party last night," Randall said. "Can we sit down?"

Sheldon Smikle sank into an overstuffed chair. Randall and Manon sat facing him on a sectional sofa half as long as a Pullman. The maid looked undecided, then departed.

"I already told the police everything I know," Sheldon said.

"I'm sure you have," Manon said. "But please tell Mr. Randall, too. He wants to help as a friend."

The youth looked at Randall and waited.

"What time did you leave the party?" Randall asked.

"Ten-thirty, sir. About."

"Where'd you go?"

"Well, we walked along the beach a ways, like we do a lot. Then we went over to the Burger Mac for hamburgers."

"You were *hungry*? After that buffet at the party?"

"We didn't eat much at the party. We were too busy tendin' bar and servin' drinks."

"All right." Randall leaned toward him, hands on knees,

269

frowning at him now. "You went to the Burger Mac for hamburgers. What then?"

"We took them to a booth and started eatin'. Then we saw these two big guys eyein' us from one of the tables."

"Two big guys." Randall repeated the words slowly. "Eyeing you. And?"

"Well, jeez, they scared us the way they were lookin' at us! I mean, they were guys in their thirties maybe, like pro football players, and they kept starin'."

"Did you tell the police this?"

"Yeah. Sure."

"And did you give them a description?"

"Uh-huh. Like—you know—they were in their thirties and real big, like I said, and—"

"Black or white?"

"White."

"Dressed how?"

"Well, like I told the cops, one had on jeans and a gray sweatshirt, and the other was wearin' dark pants and a black leather jacket."

"And they looked at you."

"Like—you know—they were gettin' ready to jump us."

"For what? Your money, you think?"

"Maybe. Or maybe somethin' else. If you been readin' the papers, you know what happens to young guys on the beach sometimes. There's a motorcycle gang hangs around the pier there."

"So what did you do?"

"We split. Never even finished the burgers."

"And?"

"When we got to the corner, the two guys were just comin' out of the Burger Mac, headin' in our direction. So Colin said we ought to break up and confuse them. 'Go on home,' he said. 'Beat it!' So I did."

Randall looked sideways at Manon, then back at the scared face in front of him. "You think it was those two who beat up Colin? Followed him to the condo and attacked him?"

"Well, I can't be sure. But they came out of the Burger Mac *after* us and didn't follow *me*."

270

"Wait," Manon said, and both Randall and the boy looked at her expectantly. "Colin was attacked in the guest parking area," she said. "If he'd been coming from the Burger Mac, he wouldn't have gone through there."

She and Randall looked at Sheldon Smikle.

It seemed to Randall that the youth's face grew even paler and his eyes became those of a cornered animal. "He could've been tryin' to throw them off," was the best the youth could do.

"All right." Randall stood up. "I've got something to start on, at least. Thanks for your help, Sheldon." He turned to Manon. "You ready, hon?" His look said, Let's get out of here.

They departed, nodding to the maid as she appeared at the door to let them out. Back in the car Manon said with a frown, "He didn't tell us everything, did he?"

"I doubt it. Do you know the fast-food place he talked about?"

"I go there often."

"The people there. The workers. Do you know them?"

"Some of them."

"Let's drop in."

It was typical of such establishments. Apparently the breakfast rush was over; only a few tables and booths were in use, and only two customers waited at the serving counter. Manon led Randall to an employee who was stacking coffee cups with her back to them. At Manon's "Hi, Aggie" she turned. About thirty, she was a plump, freckled redhead.

"Well, hi, Manon."

"Can we talk a minute? It's important."

"Of course."

"We want to know if two of the neighborhood kids were in here last night. Were you here about ten-thirty?"

"Uh-huh, I was. I worked late last night."

"Do you know a couple of teenage boys named Colin Casserly and Sheldon Smikle?"

"Sure. They come in all the time. Those and three, four other kids from around here. But I don't remember them being in last night."

Randall said, "Think hard, will you, Aggie? We have to be sure."

The woman pressed a hand to her chin and half shut her eyes, then wagged her head. "No, I'd remember if they were here."

Manon said, "Maybe you were busy. Is anyone else here who was working last night?"

The redhead looked along the counter. "Edgar was. I'll ask him."

She went away. She came back shaking her head. "Uh-uh. He doesn't remember seeing them. And *I* don't. So it's pretty certain they weren't here."

"Something else," Randall said. "Do you remember two big fellows sitting at a table last night about that time—ten-thirty or so? The Smikle boy described them. Tough-looking characters, he said. White. One was wearing jeans and a gray sweatshirt, the other dark pants and a black leather jacket."

Aggie shook her head again. "No way."

"They weren't here?"

"*Sheldon* said they were?"

Manon said, "Yes, he did."

"When he wasn't even here himself? What's going on?"

"We're trying to find out," Randall said. "Thanks for your help." He caught Manon's hand. "We'd better talk to Sheldon again, don't you think?"

"You go. Take my car," she said, and handed him the keys. "I'll walk back to the condo and see what I can do for the Casserlys."

"Right."

From the sidewalk in front of the Burger Mac he watched her cross the street and head for the fifteen-story building in which she and the Casserlys lived. Lovely woman, he thought. You've got the right one this time, Randall; hang on to her for dear life. Then in her car he drove back to the handsome house on the Intracoastal.

The same maid opened the door. "Sheldon?" she said. "He's in his room, sir. He'd been on the bed there, crying, since you and the lady left."

"No need to call him out. I'll talk to him there."

She led him through the house to the bedroom, and it was the kind of room only a son of wealthy parents could have. Big as two ordinary bedrooms, it had a picture window overlooking the Intracoastal where the family's cabin cruiser gleamed like a forty-foot jewel at its private dock. Having a boat of his own—a modest one—Randall could not resist staring through the glass at this one as he stepped past an expensive stereo rig, a home computer, and an over-sized TV set to the bed.

The maid, having entered the room before him to speak to its occupant, now placed a chair beside the bed for his convenience and departed.

Randall sat and looked at the boy. Said nothing.

Sheldon Smikle had indeed been crying. His eyes were even more inflamed and swollen than before. His expression was one of abject fright.

"Why did you come back?" The question was barely audible.

"Because you lied to me."

"No . . ."

"You said you and Colin Casserly went to the Burger Mac. You said two big guys followed you out of there. But you weren't there, Sheldon, and no such goons were there, either."

If the boy could have crawled into a hiding place, he might have done so. His hands began to shake, his mouth to quiver; his eyes seemed big enough to burst until suddenly the lids shuddered shut to hide them. Or was it to shield them from Randall's accusing gaze?

"Where *did* you go when you left the party?"

No answer.

"All right, I'll wait." Randall looked out the picture window at the boat again, and around the room at the stereo, the TV, the computer. And then—for no particular reason—his gaze strayed to a closet, the sliding door of which was open.

The closet contained clothes. All the high-style slacks and jackets and shirts a youth like Sheldon Smikle would be expected to own, and a rack of expensive shoes on the floor, and ... what *was* the red thing hanging at the very end, all but hidden by a transparent raincoat?

Randall walked to the closet and slid the raincoat aside. And found himself gazing at a red sweatshirt on a hanger, with a red ski mask hanging limply, like a Salvador Dali watch, over the edge of the shelf above.

He stood there and began remembering again.

The lobby, Randall. You rode the elevator down to hell and got off in an anteroom where you were supposed to wait for someone to come and get you. Get out of there, you told yourself. You were a Vietnam vet, God damn it; you've been a hand-to-hand combat instructor. Nobody with your training should stand around helpless, waiting to be dragged to a fiery furnace.

Walk, Randall! Walk, man! There must be a way out of here somewhere! That's what you told yourself.

So you walked. Remember? You walked and walked and it was dark, dark, dark and you didn't know where in hell you were going, and all at once these two hell-dwellers in red loomed up in front of you, telling you to halt.

Remember, Randall? "Hold it right there, mister," the one with the gun said. Not loud. Just loud enough for you to make out the words. "Hold it right *there!*" If you hadn't been in hell and recognized demons sent to escort you to the fires, you might have thought it was just two dressed-up punks with a gun, wanting money for drugs or something.

But no demons in red or any other color, with a gun or without one, were going to drag you to the fires. Not the Sergeant Roger Randall who had taught GIs how to handle themselves in such situations. Remember what you did? You chopped that weapon out of the gunman's hand and put a knee in his groin and went to work on his face with your fists. The second demon turned and ran like a scared rabbit, but you had the head one on the floor of that tunnel where they'd waylaid you. That tunnel to the innermost part of hell, down which you'd have been led like a lamb to the burning.

Remember it, Randall? How you worked the red one over so he'd never be able to carry out Satan's commands again? How you left him there and walked on, knowing you had to get away before any more of them came for you, but your foot kicked the gun you'd knocked out of his hand and you bent down and picked it up and took it with you in your pocket?

He remembered. And knew that the two demons he had encountered in that passageway to the fires of hell had been only a pair of wild teenagers named Colin Casserly and Sheldon Smikle.

He turned from the closet and looked at the boy on the bed. Sheldon's gaze was fixed on the closet now. His mouth made wet bubbling sounds as though he were drowning. His hands clutched the bedspread so fiercely that pulling the spread away would have been impossible without breaking some fingers.

My God, Randall thought. Oh, my God. No wonder he's scared. He knows I was the one.

In another part of the house a phone was ringing. He heard the voice of the maid answering it. Then he heard footsteps approaching, and the maid appeared in the bedroom doorway.

"Mr. Randall—"

"Yes?"

"Miss Rowe just called. Colin Casserly died a few minutes ago, at the hospital."

She waited for him to say something. When he did not, she directed an odd frown at him, glanced at the boy on the bed, turned herself around and went away.

Randall went, too. Out of the room. Out of the house. Out to Manon's car at the curb.

He drove to his own apartment building and left the car in a guest parking slot with the keys in it. She would know where to look for it. His unsteady steps carried him to the elevator, and while it rose to his floor he was a figure carved in stone, staring at nothing. From the elevator he walked like

275

a zombie along the fourth-floor hall to his door, then through his apartment to the chest of drawers in his bedroom.

You killed him, Randall. You and your hand-to-hand-combat training. You were drunk.

The weapon was in the top drawer, where he now remembered having dropped it last night. He stood there looking at it through burning dry eyes that wanted so much to find relief in tears but couldn't. A Smith and Wesson Model 46 .22 automatic. It had to be the boy's gun. His own, on a shelf in the closet, was a .38.

Again like a zombie he went down the hall to the living room and sat by a window, looking out at the ocean. He hadn't noticed, but the morning must be hot; the beach was crowded, and many in the crowd were high school kids like Casserly and Smikle. He sat there watching them without really seeing them. All that registered was a blur of color and motion against the sea's restless backdrop.

He must have been sitting there an hour or more when the phone rang. He let it ring until it stopped. What could he say to anyone?

You did it, Randall. You were drunk. You killed a kid whose only crime was being stupid.

Ten minutes later the phone rang again. Again he ignored it, continuing to look at the young people cavorting on the beach and in the surf. There was only one thing he could do now.

He went into the second bedroom, which he used for a study. Sat at the desk there. Took paper from a drawer and began to write a letter.

Dear Manon.

No. With a fresh sheet of paper he began again.

My dearest Manon

I know now what happened last night to the Casserly boy. He and his pal confronted me when I was walking through the guest parking lot to my car. They pretended it was a stickup, though of course it was just some crazy

276

kind of gag. But I was drunk and thought they meant it. You know what I was in Vietnam—the kind of training I had. They didn't have a chance, even with a gun. The Smikle boy ran. Casserly wasn't so lucky.

I can't live with this, darling. The longer I sit here thinking about it, the more I realize there is only one decent way out.

I'm so very sorry. A life with you would have been the greatest—and you're the only woman I've ever felt that way about. But I killed him, love. I was drunk and I killed him.

Forgive me. If I use his gun, there'll at least be a certain twisted kind of justice.

Rog

With the letter in an envelope addressed to her, he walked back to the living room and placed it on a table there. Eventually she would get it. He went to sit in the chair by the window again. But the longer he looked at the gun, the more he knew he would not use it.

He placed it on the floor, returned to the table, and added a paragraph to his letter.

Hon, I've decided against the gun. It would have been poetic justice, but I just couldn't. I must do this a cleaner, better way, with nothing like that for you to remember. Am going to take my boat out. Way out. Not to come back. So long, darling. I love you.

It was not far to the marina where he kept his boat; he often walked it. He walked it now, only dimly aware of the people he passed, the tall buildings towering above him, the sights and sounds of life in a beachside community. At the marina he nodded to people who spoke to him, but kept walking until he reached his boat. Taking it out alone was no problem. He went alone more often than not.

Just head out to sea, Randall. Just keep going until the fuel's gone. You've a debt to pay.

The beach colors slowly receded and became just a blur of beige. The condos behind it faded into pale cubist shapes in a watercolor wash. Then there was only the gently heaving water on all sides of him and the brilliant blue sky above, and he thought of Hemingway's *The Old Man and the Sea*.

Only he'd had a fish on the line and a chance to win. Something to hang on to life for.

It took the boat a long time to run out of fuel. Such a long time. When it did, and silence enfolded him, he simply let go of the wheel and sat down, staring eastward toward the invisible Bahamas. He must be about halfway between the coast of Florida and Northwest Providence Channel, he thought. When he started swimming, it would be toward the channel. He wouldn't get there, of course. He was no long-distance swimmer.

At the stern he pulled off his shirt and slacks, knelt to take off his shoes. Because even though it was hopeless he meant to swim, not just to sink. To swim on—and on— and on—until he just couldn't make his arms move any more.

When he straightened for the plunge, he heard a sound in the stillness. The pulsing throb of a helicopter approaching from the land he had left such a measureless time ago.

The Coast Guard? They had copters, of course. But this was not one of theirs. It came banking toward him, glittering in the sunlight, and he saw something white fluttering from a hand thrust out of it. A handkerchief? Being waved at him?

Being *frantically* waved at him?

Shoeless, in only his shorts, he stood scowling up at the machine while it maneuvered to a position directly above him and a rope ladder was lowered from it to touch the boat's deck.

A slender, surefooted figure in white slacks and a bright orange shirt descended the ladder and dropped to the deck beside him. Turned swiftly to face him. Cried "Thank God!" and lunged at him and wrapped both arms around him.

The copter banked and headed back to Florida, its pilot waving.

"He'll send someone to tow us in," Manon said. "You *are* out of gas, aren't you?"

"Yes, but—"

"We figured that's what you'd do. Listen. When you didn't come back with my car, I borrowed a neighbor's and drove to the Smikles', thinking I'd find you there. You'd left. Young Sheldon went to pieces when he heard of Colin's death. He broke down and told me what happened. Sit down, Rog. Please."

Standing before him, her gaze unblinkingly fixed on his face, she said, "You weren't drunk, Roger. What happened was not your fault."

"I—"

"No. I knew you weren't drunk because I had as much to drink as you did, and I didn't even feel it. Sheldon said they spiked your drinks. That is, Colin did. They were—"

"With what?"

"Red Devils."

"*What?*"

"Colin was forming a gang of kids out for kicks. This was their first caper. You were chosen because you didn't know them. Spiking your drink was supposed to make it easier."

"What did they use on me?"

"He wasn't sure. Colin called it a Red Devils cocktail, he said—LSD, angel dust, MDMA. It could have been a mix."

"Hallucinogens, all of them. No wonder I thought I was in hell." Randall got hold of her hands and pulled her down to him. "After he told you this, you went to my place and found my note?"

"And called the Coast Guard to look for you."

"That wasn't a Coast Guard copter."

"No. One of our patients flies it. I called him, too."

"I owe you, love. Lord, how I owe you."

She smiled against his lips. "When you're able to forget all this, can we have that cruise?"

"And anything else I can give you, partner. Anything in this crazy, mixed-up world." Randall spoke the words against her lips and hung on to her, telling himself she might change herself into a gull and fly away.

Just off the bow of the boat a dolphin leaped from the sea in a glittering arc, creating a rainbow of spray before it disappeared with a soft splash.

Pick Me Up

David J. Schow

feel the way an executioner must feel, a heartbeat before he does the thing that kills. Every time I stick out my thumb, I feel.

I think of the SURGE button on the panel that feeds the electric chair. That special button with the hinged metal lid to prevent anyone from depressing it accidentally. I think of the DROP switch that prompts the intermix of cyanide in the gas chamber. My thumb. I see it cocking the hammer of a Smith and Wesson Model 39, my favorite automatic. They haven't manufactured that one for nearly a decade, now.

I stick my thumb into the rainfall and feel the usual good feelings. A flash of headlights passes me by. My thumb's dripping. Rain does funny things to people. Some, it makes benevolent: *Oh that poor man, stuck out there in the elements.* Others wonder what brand of lunatic would be hitchhiking in the rain in the first place.

Those latter are alive today, generally.

I begrudge the discomfort, but not the coming of the rain. I get more rides in the rain. It's those former people, running their little logic chains about me, and why they should pick me up just this once.

281

Once is enough.
Keep on rationalizin', sez me.

KABOOM!

Lightning scritched across the night sky and I swear I can feel fork tines raking acrost the back of my skull from the inside. Shot past afore I could slam my eyeballs shut. Light strobed the wipers acrost the windshield of my Truck.

What a show; all for free.

The best things in life are low-cost and high-maintenance. That's a joke.

Excepting my Truck. Tuck and roll *costs*, lifters and glass-packs *cost*. You think riders ever pitch in uncoached? It all comes out of my wallet, which is a Lord Buxton and weren't no cheap billfold, neither. I got it for free when I bought two pair boots—one fancy lizard skin, the other regular black cowboy, which I'm wearing right now. My wallet is safe in my hip pocket.

All props. My Truck is the stage. The show usually goes on.

Ever try to clean blood off Mexican leather? I mean, even that thin hide they use for them one-day, in-and-out, south-of-the-border upholstery jobs? Sweet Jesus! I finally had to dye the stiching black with boot creme to make everything uniform. I used Meltonian. That ain't cheap. But nothing but the best for my Truck.

Sometimes the only thing that makes any earthly sense to me is gobbling highway stripes as fast as my Truck can feed 'em to me and farting them out rearways. Zip in. Zip out. I'm on the high-speed high wire; stay outta my way because I don't slow down until I feel what Grampaw used to call *the grumble of honest appetite*.

Shoot. Road's picked clean. I eased down the footstomper and listened to my tires sing in the rain.

Even before the high beams slow and pull left I know this is a single guy, doing the white-line trance routine in the middle of the night. It's never a woman, not on a night like this. If there is a woman, she is always accompanied by a husband of recent vintage, and she always vocally disapproves of giving a lift to a stranger. Domestic disagreements have been the foundation of some of my more exhilarating kills. I get picked up because the woman in the car says *don't pick that guy up, John* in the wrong tone for her man's mood.

Bang, bang, double zero, nobody gets laid. Sorry.

In girl/guy combos the man usually has to be killed first. Easy, because at this time of night the man is usually the driver. He makes his honey snooze across the backseat so the hitchhiker won't get any ideas . . . just in case he's a pervert or recently escaped mental case.

Okay by me. Girl or guy, alone or together, once those headlights slow down and pull over I know I'm going to reap some action. The ingredients don't matter.

I try not to carry weapons. If the hypos roust me and rummage my pack (and they have, hundreds of times, never mind *my* rights, thanks), they'll find my kit, my clothes, and whatever ID I care to flash them. I know sleight of hand. I can make a deck of playing cards do gymnastics in the palm of my right while juggling three golf balls with my left. I went to dealer's school in Reno and once did a six-month gig on a cruise ship as the onboard magician. I was the guy who did tricks while chefs cooked at your tableside.

I can pluck out your larynx and show it to you before you realize I've twitched.

The killing part I learned from the army and jail. Fort Benning and Folsom. That's some nasty business you don't really need to hear about.

Anyhow, my clothes are always clean. And the ID cards—I have twenty, all for different states. I prestidigitate them and don't spend too much vagrant time in the slam unless the local badgemen are hardcases who don't like my hair or my looks.

I move on and they forget about me. Usually.

So the first thing I check on an incoming car are the

lights. No flashbar. Then I check to see if it's an unmarked cruiser. You can tell by the tires or the rear deck. If I can't spot a bubble light, I can read the codex of municipal license plates.

Not cops. Not this time.

I lean out and shield my eyes from the rain and glare as the cabin light pops on to reveal a single guy. I win again. Late twenties or early thirties. Longish hair. Well-built. Good clothes, clean. Careful smile.

I smile right back. Showtime.

This dude looked like trouble waiting to happen, so at the first moment I cranked hard right, floored the footstomper and mashed him good. My Truck's ram bumper ate his face and he pinked one of the headlights. Rain rinsed in clear in no time at all.

His stuff was soaked through. His backpack was cheap. He had twenty-seven bucks and some chicken change. Took nearly all of it just to gas up.

Rainspots hobble my Truck's finish, but raintime means better hunting. When the elements sour, folks will hitch with fewer qualms. When they're wet and shivering in the grip of a stormy night, they're not so particular about the character of whomever pulls over to help them along. Storms make it simpler for me to help them along.

So to speak.

Along near eleven I hit the Stop 'N Go to get me a couple of them microwave burritos. A hypo growler was up front, parked acrost three spaces. Turns out the place had just been robbed.

Damn, but I do hate that. Them little joints is the only outlets open for night owls anymore. Guy works a dead-dog shift selling smokes and beer to unemployed groundpounders, and for his trouble he gets a Smith and Wesson stuck up his nose by some pimply faggot with Underalls on his head.

The robber had shot the place up. No kills, though.

Guy working the counter had a name tag that said ROCKO.

But nobody works a detail like this using his or her real name. He seemed to take the robbery in stride, like it was all no strain. But I was mad and told him so. Cop glared at me. What good are the cops if they couldn't respond while a robbery-in-progress was still in progress?

I've always had much more use for convenience stores than I've ever had for law enforcers.

Guy working the counter drove a big-block Camaro. Looked like he took care of it okay, and so it took care of him. Course, if it ever broke down and stranded him on the roadside, at night, in this kind of rain . . . well, things would be different.

I hit the driver in the throat, a good hard chop. The car is going forty; my hand, about seventy.

He gets this expression as though he is terribly disappointed in bad clichés, like the ones about picking up hitchers. Then he tries to kill me. At least, he thinks he does.

The essence of victory is total commitment.

Normal people never expect you to reach over and strike them while the car is moving. My advantage. What the hell do they think seat belts are *for*, anyway? Five seconds past that thought, things are usually academic.

And here I am.

But this chap wants the old struggle-for-life bit. Bared teeth in the face of imminent demise. The protohuman shucking his facade of civilization. Last-ditch time.

His car jumps the abutment and wraps its grille around a boulder. The storm has caused rockfalls and washouts. He is still trussed up in his seat belt as we hit. I get a few scratches from his flailing around.

One sharp rap to his upper row of teeth, one more to the bridge of his nose, and he's done. I rifle his junk while blood purples his eye sockets. By the time I find his gun, he looks kind of like the Lone Ranger. Then he stops twitching like a spazz.

The revolver is not my favorite firearm. I prefer automatics, remember? But it was a Smith and Wesson. Now, say that name a few times: Smith and Wesson. Sounds like power, doesn't it? Power. Right there in your hand.

He has some credit cards and a hundred bucks in cash. I strip the car of documents the way I strip him of his very identity. In seconds he is nothing more than a lump of protein. Nobody. He no longer has an identity. I've taken it.

I ditch the corpse and burn the registration. Mr. Gun takes a siesta in my pack, which is waterproof. I don't find a box of shells. Six rounds only, snug and dry.

Since I've won the piece I decide to bag a Stop 'N Go that turns up. It takes two shots: one for the camera and one for the surveillance mirror, to make sure there isn't a rent-a-cop snoozing back there. Sometimes they give rent-a-cops rubber guns. Or real guns with no bullets.

Bang, bang, and Mister Counterman damn near pops his spine making me wealthier. Half the time those floor safes sit open anyway. The rest of the time, the employee knows the combination, and no one faults him for spilling it under the sort of duress a Smith and Wesson in the ear can provide.

Say it: Smith and Wesson.

And remember that always: The safes are there for you to empty.

I take the cash and coin rolls and ignore the money-order blanks. Into a small bag goes a six of imported beer and some of those thick-sliced potato chips with the skins still on. Beef jerky and chocolate-chip cookies and a quart of low-fat milk. A flashlight and some fresh batteries. They're dated now so you can tell how new they are. A locked counter spinner holds pocket knives, imitation Swiss army issue. I take the one that does the most things.

Never would I have killed the counterman. He is just logging his hours and understands, as I do, that insurance companies conquer all. On the road I would have taken him, his Camaro, everything. But there in his workplace he is safe from the likes of me and will probably never appreciate this or even realize it.

I pay cash for the motel cabin. I take a very hot shower. There are sex movies on the cable TV. I sleep like a babe until past noon the next day.

* * *

Tiresome. Folks in general can be so tiresome.

My favorite part of acceleration is the shifting: 1-2-3-4, watch that needle climb. The game is to make it not stutter, like not jiggling the bottle when you're decanting some fine wine, which I've heard you ought not to do. I learned that from a guy I picked up.

Not this guy today. This guy was a talker. Talked from beat one, like he was trying too hard to form some kind of bond with me. The fellowship of the road. Bum pals for life. I killed him and sort of made the second part true right away. My eyes were the last thing he ever saw with his.

He had rattled on, very academician, about what he called the psychology of hitchhiking. How in the sixties there had been so much trust, and how an entire generation of happy rebels had Yupped out to the point where they wouldn't even give each other rides home because car pools were a status dip. He talked too fast, trying to reassure himself that *I* was okay in terms of *his* manifesto. Dumb shit. Dumb overeducated shit. What he never found time to understand is that hitching a ride is a gamble. A risk consciously taken. Life is a risk. And I am the law of averages. Nothing personal. He died well.

I used this hank of piano wire with wooden grips. I made it myself and hadn't used it in a while. Variety's the spice.

Then I hit the road, 1-2-3-4, no further interrupts, and it was good.

His chatter, though, got me to thinking about small towns. You know, those desert suburbs full of retirees. And trust. Living there, you always saw folks like him in the crosswalks. Usually while you were warming a booth in some sleepy coffee shop. And you thought to yourself *transient*. Cops should come sweep him up. Hustle that sucker along smartly to the next town. Don't let him linger and keep him on the move.

Like school. Like the military. Keep moving. I keep moving, but on my own terms. Nobody tells me when to sit or git.

Long as the transients keep moving, the flabasses dent-

287

ing their recliners don't have to bleat about some dude coming through their doggie door to liberate the flatware. If transients were organized, if they communicated, why hell, they could wipe Suburbia USA clean. Dumb people already have too much leisure time. Give a dude nothing to do and pretty soon he invents alcoholism and lynching. And before you know it he's sniping from a freeway overpass or wrapping gerbils in duct tape to jam up his butthole.

I'm passionate about self-sufficiency and using my time wisely. Had to sit jury duty once. One of the questions they ask you, in criminal cases, is, "Have you ever been the victim of a crime?" And my answer was, "Yeah, every April fifteenth the U.S. government rapes me."

Bye-bye jury duty, and my time is mine once again.

The rain let up enough to make mud everywhere. Bad for my Truck's finish. Can you believe it, even mud is corrosive now? I pull to the shoulder in that kind of mud, it'd better be worth it.

I actually passed one of two hitchers up. Boring. Too much like the one I just did. Variety, right?

I was in the mood for love. I could've made a whole day of a woman.

Jesus, I hope I'm not getting a cold.

The good old boys piloting pickups always want to talk classic Man Stuff. Forged iron, true grit, honest labor in the heartland. Conquering the weaker sex. All in the crudest detail. They wear baseball caps with stupid patches. They have no taste in cologne.

Not this guy.

Ever notice jeeps? Real ones, not those bogus tin-can rice rockets. If a woman is driving one, she's always attractive. If it's a man, nine times out of ten it's the sort who should be driving a pickup truck instead. Rattling loudly on about bar fights and beer and pussy and which team kicked butt. They're ugly and hostile. They slap dumb bumper stickers over good clean chrome.

ASS GRASS OR GAS—NOBODY RIDES FOR FREE
THIS VEHICLE PROTECTED BY SMITH & WESSON
IF YOU'RE RICH I'M SINGLE

Proof that in America there's too much spare time available to people who haven't the dimmest notion of how to utilize it. No potential Magrittes or Nietzsches there.

I can spare them some of their pain.

So I spot the outline in the rain and think, *damn, another truck*, because of my experience of longbed rednecks. The kind that still joke are-you-a-boy-or-a-girl if you sport anything lengthier than a jarhead buzzcut with pink sidewalls.

Noise and light from behind the oncoming truck, sudden and jolting. A speeding ambulance cuts a wide berth around the truck and blazes past me. I get splashed in the name of their mission of mercy. On their way to some accident.

The truck is still poking up the hill long after the ambulance fades. It is kept up well. No bumper stickers.

I decide to put out my thumb as it nears. I feel that killing power once again.

Spotted flashbars and for a sec thought it was them hypos from the Stop 'N Go last night. Instead it was a van-type ambulance. The paramedics rode level with me. I blinked them around in plenty of time, hi-lo with the lights, and nuzzled the shoulder as best I could in the rain.

They cut their siren, out of respect or courtesy it don't matter. Good of 'em. They blew past close enough to rake water acrost my windows. I felt my Truck sway. What a joke: Their mission to save lives costs me mine as I tumble ass over teapot down the cliff. Next story.

There's sure something hypnotic, though, about them red and blue flashing lights as they cut the storm. The colors of civilization.

Those boys were on their way to an accident. A real one. I haven't seen any action tonight, and what I do can't rightly be called accidental.

289

Road's snaky. Makes the flashbar prettier as it loops and dwindles and finally hits the top of the hump and drops out of sight. Still no siren.

Even in this piss-poor visibility I can see the dude they just passed. Up ahead, two hundred yards, give or take. Dunked and drenched, thumb out and dripping. Hitchhiking in the rain and thinking to himself: *Just my rat luck, an ambulance. Where're they going that they can't give me a quick lift at 90 per? Wherever they're going, it's closer to civilization. No riders. Damn my rat luck.*

Selfish for folks to think that way. Dudes who think that way never needed first aid before. Till now.

I'm still not going too fast because of the ambulance and it's pretty much already decided that I'm gonna pull over.

"Hey, thanks for stopping," the rider said, shucking loose water like a hound dog.

"Climb on in afore you have to *swim* in," said the driver.

"Sorry about your seat."

"Don't mind that. I waterproofed it."

"Had it waterproofed, huh?"

"No. Did the job myself with that tri-chloroethane spray stuff." He pronounced the word carefully. He would not be expected to know such big words. "Saturated it."

"You did it up right, then. I don't feel so bad." The rider patted himself down and tried to scare up a dry cigarette.

"No smokin' in my truck," said the driver. "If you don't mind."

"Bad habit anyway." The rider shrugged and chuckled. "Like smoking will make you dry on the inside when you're soaked on the outside, or something."

"What's that?"

The driver didn't get it. The rider let it die. As they hit the grade he watched the driver shift gears. He was pretty good at it.

"Where you bound?"

"What's that?" Now the rider felt foolish. When the

driver had said *bound* he'd thought he'd meant tied up. There was water in his left ear.

The driver enunciated. "Where do you need to get to?"

"Oh. Well, where are *you* going?"

It was another game of the road. Don't say where you're headed and swat the question back. Then feign delighted surprise when the answer turns out to be *right near* the destination you'd intended all along!

"Up toward Lansdale. Got a friend I haul loads for, back and forth."

"That'll cut a chunk off my travel time," said the rider. "Mind if I stick with you that far?"

"Long as you talk and help keep me awake. Radio reception sucks out here."

"It's the ozone. The storm."

"That's what I said."

The rider sneezed explosively, once, twice. Then came that third hanger-on sneeze you can never quite coax out in rhythm.

"You need a Kleenex?"

The rider nodded and automatically pushed the glove-box button. It was locked.

The driver reached behind his head and produced a tissue from the dark clutter rearward, seemingly out of nowhere. The rider watched the driver's hands with interest. Then he blew his nose.

"Not gonna see town lights for twenty minutes even at dry-road speed," said the driver. "Nobody out here but us. Animals are all hiding. I heard there's this one kind of snake that waits till it rains to hunt. Knows all the other animals are in their burrows hiding from the rain. Doesn't have to forage."

"Wow." It wasn't yet time to ask the driver what time he thought it was.

They passed another mile in silence.

"How 'bout that ambulance?"

"Hope they made it okay," said the rider. "That must be a crap detail and a half. Rescue in the rain. Think you could spot me another Kleenex?"

"Sure."

When the rider sneezed again the driver grabbed a fistful of the kid's hair and rammed his forehead into the glovebox button, which did not budge.

Except that the rider really hadn't sneezed. It was a fake that neatly covered the lateral chop aimed at the driver's windpipe.

Which the driver inadvertently deflected with his hair grab.

The truck slowed and wandered into the oncoming lane. It lurched as its accelerator got pinned, then picked up speed like it had a purpose.

The two men inside were all over each other. The pilot window starred to a crushed-ice pattern. The rearview mirror snapped off. The truck executed a question mark trajectory up the far side of the road, then crossed to drop over the edge. It rolled, picked up speed and began to throw off broken and twisted parts.

It was a long time falling.

Take this one down by hand. Something about the hitch-hiker's eyes made me want this kill to be from the gut. Immediate. Knuckle-skinning.

Problem is, I'm a touch too cocky and sometimes I get what I ask for. Shoulda just jammed my buck knife into his gobblebox and clicked him off, first thing. What do I think I am, some artist, like a fag chef on TV?

Dammit.

I knew he was going to hit me. Knew it the second he did it, which made me half a second too slow. Figured I'd turn his head cold to my advantage and nail him while he was busy sneezing. You get in the first two hits, you can generally call yourself the winner. But he faked me out and the next thing I saw clearly was headlights acrost dirt and I thought, *we're bailing.*

Thought I was dreaming about rocking in a bed. Earthquake. Woke up and saw hoses and canvas straps and aluminum tubework. I saw a dude flicking his fingernail against a hypodermic needle, and even though I could see his orange hazard jersey it took me a long while to figure out that I was in the ambulance, horizontal and hurting good. Like having a word right on the tip of your tongue that drives you nuts until you can pin it.

The siren was off. Maybe that helped confuse me.

Felt like my shoulder was dislocated. Could feel it grind and pulse even though I was strapped in firm. I knew that when the paramedic saw my eyes open he'd say *there he is* and ask *how do you feel, captain* and tell me *now don't try to move*. He did all that while I was wondering where the blood on his shirtfront came from.

Then he spoke mystic words like *concussion* and *greenstick fracture* and *compound broken this or that* and I finally swooned. Fainted dead out, wondering how much damage was prevented by my seat belt versus how much had been caused by it.

The rider had never buckled his. Hitchers almost never do. They don't want their getaway hindered in case their ride turns out to be a psycho or a groper.

When I opened up my eyes again the paramedic said *take it easy* and mentioned how lucky I was.

I knew I got in a lick or two. Good solid ones. Wasn't as if I never took one down while driving. I know the risks. But like I said, something about this particular rider made me want to cancel him out even before we hit my planned excuse to stop.

Maybe it was the sense that with *this* dude, I'd never get the opportunity to pull over, stop, and do it neat. Not have to mop his brains off the tuck and roll.

Maybe it was because I'd seen his eyes, plenty of times, already looking back at me from my own rearview mirror. Thought that in a flash as I was using the mirror to knock his teeth through his brain pan.

Part of me died with the realization that my Truck was probably a goner from the moment that guy put his hand on the door handle.

Then another part of me tried to die. I felt something snap slack inside, like a water balloon busting and making my lungs all hot.

When the paramedic moved I saw the rider. He was lay-

293

ing in the rack acrost from me and there was blood all over his face and he had been watching me the whole time.

And while that paramedic's back was turned, the rider's eyes said to me:

There's a helluva lot two guys like us could do with an ambulance.

A miscalculation, that's what it was. For this man, driving this pickup, I should have saved the Smith and Wesson. On the other hand, it is probably good that the paramedics have not caught me packing. Questions. After that sort of questioning always comes cell time.

I swear the son of a bitch *knew* I was going to snag him while we were still moving. Damn, but he reacted fast. I'm right-handed. The advantage was his.

No, not Mister Country Pud in his pickup, not at all.

Funny: Only two vehicles on this road all night, and I get to ride in both of them.

I recall thinking the driver is no problem because I can see his class ring hanging on a thong from the rearview. As though he has peaked out in high school, given up on making anything of himself, and so stops wearing the ring because it reminds him of that failure, yet doesn't have the heart to toss it, so it winds up on the mirror.

My teeth are folded back and my whole mouth is numb. I recall meeting the dashboard head-on before falling base over apex down the hillside. I don't think I sustained any broken bones. Score one for no seat belts.

When the driver regains consciousness I catch him looking at me and think, okay. Now the masks are off. He'd handled me like he's used to it. My gag with the tissue didn't detour him nearly enough.

Call me the Kleenex Killer, I think. Hah. What shall we call you, my truck-driving comrade?

He spasms. Some kind of convulsion, subtle. As the paramedic turns I spot a hemostat on the van's rubberized floor. I reach down to retrieve it, feeling my muscles work. Some kind of painkiller is amping me.

The ambulance driver says something and the paramedic steps forward. That's when I catch the pickup driver's eye again. His expression tells me that, if I want him to, he can arrange another little seizure as a perfect distraction.

I can put out the paramedic's eye with the hemostat. Jam it into his brain. A hard enough swing will bury it in his carotid. It doesn't have to be sharp. 1-2-3-4.

The paramedic comes back to check on me. Taps up a vein to give me an injection. More jungle juice. It'll help me and the pickup driver get our thing done.

"We're doing you a big favor," says the paramedic.

As the plunger goes down I see the orange bubbles in the syringe. I smell the gasoline. The pickup driver, tied securely down, begins to make noises.

But the needle empties and I know I'll never get my fist up in time.